Sickle Through The Sand

Ste Newell

Copyright © 2018 Ste Newell

All rights reserved.

ISBN: 9781717710680

Hope you enjoy
Thanks for the support
S. N—

For Harry

ACKNOWLEDGMENTS

Thanks to Billy Cox for reading the first draft
Maria Newell for cover design and all things digital.
And friends and family for your continual support.

CHAPTER 1

Jess stood in the tree line she put her hand up to signal to the rest of the gang to hold position while she focused on the clearing ahead. She wore a long sand blown leather duster and a beaten old western style hat with her long dark hair tied in a ponytail bound with a bit of green twine. Brae clearly ignored her request to stay put and edged up to her left flank. Jess sighed and shook her head slightly.

"Are they there Jess?" He whispered. When she crouched Brae dropped down into the ferns beside her.

"Can't see shit at the moment, unless they are holed up in that shack." She said gesturing to get lower. They scanned the large clearing to the two story wooden shack in the centre, no smoke rose from the chimney so they feared they had already missed out on the bounty.

"Darn it! I bet Milo tipped them off, they could have headed north and crossed the river already!" Brae said with contempt in his tone.
"Well you did start asking around Red Town, word was bound to get back to Milo. If you had just listened to me and let me ask my contact then they wouldn't have been tipped off." She bared her teeth showing her signature front missing tooth, her piercing green eyes

were like daggers which made Brae turn away from her glare. She was just about to signal the rest of the gang to move up to their position when the door of the shack opened. Brae started to un-shoulder his rifle, she snatched his wrist tightly, his face winced under the strength of her grip.

"By the bright are you stupid? It could be Brady's whore!" She hissed. He shrugged an apology as they saw one of Brady's gang members staggering out of the shack, a demijohn of cloudy cider in his hand.

"That's Big Eddie, where there is Eddie then Henry Brady is never too far away." She said quietly. Brae agreed with a nod and un-slung his rifle, this time Jess didn't stop him and she did the same and pulled out both of her nickel plated 1911's. They watched as Big Eddie drunk walked to a low tree stump and started to piss while he whistled a camp town song. The one about the whore who joined the Desert Rangers, she tried to remember the words of the song but she couldn't remember, even if it had a catchy tune. Brae signalled to Yolanda and Grit to flank out, they nodded and went in opposite directions curving up the low hill like bull horns. Jess had worked with this group before, they were a little sloppy but for some reason they had also been very lucky on jobs.

When the others were in position Jess signalled for them all to cover her while she crawled forwards toward the drunk, who had finished pissing and now was swaying around looking up to the sun, for some stupid reason?

"Henry get your ass out here, have you seen this!" Eddie yelled and nearly fell over under the effort of his buckling knees.

"Fuck off Eddie, you drunken bastard, you already showed me that you can see the moon during the day, it's not like its fucking hiding!" Henry's muffled voice issued from the shack, clearly angry. Eddie swayed around a little and started to wander back mumbling something under his breath that the bounty hunters couldn't hear from the tree line. Jess got to her feet quickly and raced up behind Big Eddie, bowie knife in hand, she put her boot against the back of Eddies right leg dropping him to his knees and then pushed his head forwards before running her knife cleanly across his neck. Contra to popular belief it is a lot easier to open up a victim's neck when the neck muscles are flaccid. Eddie gurgled and slumped forwards as Jess put her knee to his spine and used all her strength to pull his head back. Poor Eddie couldn't yell an alarm because his lungs were no longer connected to his voice box. She waited a few seconds while he bled out onto the grass. She signalled to the rest of the gang to move in. She wiped her knife, holstered it and pulled out her pistols as the gang rushed to the shack.

Low moans, gasps and rocking bed sounds came from inside the shack along with intoxicated snoring. Jess edged into the dimly illuminated shack followed by Brae, Yolanda and Grit taking up the rear. She could make out two men sleeping near the fire hearth and slow sex going on behind a blanket covered section to the back of the shack. She signalled to the wooden stairs to the next floor and Grit nodded and cautiously ascended with his shotgun ready.

"Oh...Oh...Oh Yeah!" The orgasm came from behind the blanket obscured section and the bed rocking ended, as the two snoring men started to stir near the fire hearth. Yolanda and Brae were on them quickly with knives and fucked it up badly, the rude awakening with knives made the drunks yell out. Jess had to move quickly, she barged her way through the blanket and saw a woman dismounting and Henry reaching for a double barrelled shotgun at the side of the bed. She was damned if she was going to risk her life taking the bastard in alive so she aimed both pistols and blasted away. Henry took three to the chest and one to the face, all the while the whore screamed and scrambled away from the gunfire.

"Stay your ground whore!" She said aiming her pistols at her, that's when a gunshot ringed out from the second floor followed by more gunshots. Grit came bounding down the stairs covered in blood, his shot gun clattering to the floor at the foot of the stairs. Yolanda and Brae left their knives in the dead drunks and got their rifles ready, however this was clearly not going down the way they planned. Gunshots started coming through the ceiling randomly, Jess quickly calculated two assailants and whipped up the double barrelled shot gun from the side of the bed. Seconds later Yolanda had now taken in the situation and it hit home that Grit was dead. She dropped her rifle and rushed to

Grits body wailing, the proper grief wailing when a loved one was no more. Brae was busy dodging bullets coming through the ceiling yelling things that made no sense in these circumstances. A floor board buckled and Jess took up the advantage, she put both barrels of the shotgun through the ceiling, she heard a heavy slump from above and blood dribbled down through the holes and cracks. Meanwhile Yolanda was in a fit of tears and high pitched wailing as she cradled Grits head in her lap.

"Let me go you fucks! I have no bounty on my head, I only joined the gang last week!" A desperate voice came from the second floor, barely audible due to Yolanda making so much fucking noise. However Jess recognised the voice to be Cutter Joe, one of Brady's thugs. Brae fired a single shot up the stairs and grabbed hold of Yolanda's hand and dragged her away from the body, she was limp and easy to manhandle.

"We will let you go... We have wounded down here. If you weren't part of the gang then we have no beef with you." Jess lied.

"I have your word?" Joe questioned. Jess shifted to the stairs.

"By the Bright you have my word! You can go and be free!" She said trying not to grin and tried to sound convincing.

"Okay then, I'm coming down... I swear to the Bright no tricks!" Joe sounded relived. The floor boards creaked and bowed towards the stairs, as soon as the first footfall stepped down, Jess emptied both her pistols. Cutter Joe bounced down the stairs breaking a few of the stairs as he cascaded down. He landed in a heap on top of Grits body. As Jess reloaded, Brae put his rifle to Joes head and pulled the trigger, it was messy.

While Brae comforted Yolanda, Jess started to decapitate those who had a bounty on their heads, she made two bags, one bag held Henry Brady's head and the other bag held the rest of the mother fuckers. She wandered back into the shack to see Yolanda passed out in Brae's arms. She tossed a bag of heads towards him and began to peer around the shack. She stalked towards the blanketed area and pulled a leather satchel from under the bed. Having rifled through the satchel she found about a thousand coins. She took a good bunch of coins for herself and split what was left with into two piles. With that done she grabbed up the bag with Henry's head in, which happened to be a three hundred coin bounty. When she went into the main room of the shack she noticed Yolanda was now awake.

"This is your share." She handed the two bags of coins. "You should get a two hundred for the heads. I'm taking Henry's bounty, I was the one who shot him." She grinned holding the blood stained sack. Brae and Yolanda looked at each other and looked mortified.

"Hang on I thought this was going to be an equal share among us all?"

"Situations change and I put down the leader, so I have the lions share, no hard feelings."

"What of Grit's share?" Yolanda said finding her voice all of a sudden. Jess shrugged.

"He got himself killed, so four now becomes three." Yolanda said angrily and started to stand up but Brae grabbed hold of her having seen Jess's unforgiving green eyes.

"Yolanda, you fucked up, in that situation you compromised the entire team, if it wasn't for Brae dragging you away from the gun fire, me and Brae would be sharing out the wealth!" Jess barked. Brae appeared confused and looked to Yolanda for support.

"I still don't understand why this isn't an equal split like we agreed?" He moaned. Jessica grinned and shrugged.

"Brae, you fucked it up blabbing your mouth in Red town, the way I see it, you put my life at risk and risked the bounty escaping." Brae looked to the floor knowing the truth.

"You're right! Take your lions share, just take it! Me and Yolanda will hole up here and bury Grit in a proper burial, fuck you for not staying!" He said, emotions running high in his voice. Jessica started to chuckle, she shouldered the bag with Brady's head in and winked at Brae.

"Happy trails, I have a bounty to collect!" And with that she walked out of the shack, heading back the way they came.

Jess wandered away from the shack with paranoia ever present in her mind, they could be a rifle trained on the back of her head. However she didn't care very much, she was quite happy with the thought of being put down in the grass and trees and she knew Brae wasn't the kind of guy to shoot a person in the back. She wandered down the main track towards Red Town and squinted up to the sun, she estimated she would be back to the gates of Red Town by nightfall, at a push. She stopped for a small while and drank a slug of corn spirit from a hip-flask, she felt the acrid spirit burning away the memories of the last twenty four hours.

"Fuck them, they are weak!" She whispered into the forest, but she still felt a tang of guilt. She looked to the sun again and grimaced knowing she would have to camp up in a few hours, she had underestimated the time to get back, especially through thick forest. Maybe she should have stayed with the others and holed up with them, she had holed up thousands of times outdoors but it was always handy having someone on watch.

It started to rain, small drops at first then large, the kind of rain drops that bend the branches of trees. She changed direction and headed for the rocky sections to the west, on the way she grabbed up some fire wood. She quickly found an overhang of rock which would keep most of the shitty weather off her back and started to make a small camp fire. The wood spat and crackled for a few minutes but it started to catch fire.

"Should have holed up with them!" Jess whispered, angrily poking the fire with a stick. Luckily it was just a down pour and very little wind, so she stayed moderately dry. She pulled out a silver pocket watch, the watch was ancient she knew it was old from before the bombs fell due to the date on the etched back plate.

"1910", she giggled. There were several theories to the exact date nowadays, but going off the U.S Rangers postal service they believe it was around 2110ad. Apparently they had worked it out or something but Jess suspected there were too many variables to be anywhere near the proper date. She once met this loony who had a more believable theory who reckoned it was more like 2080ad. He seemed convinced and showed her some of his workings out in a notebook he carried with him. Apparently he had worked it out from the half-lives of debris found in the ruined cities, or some such shit.

"Crazy bastard!" She grinned fondly remembering Mr Venice. One thing was certain though and everybody knew the date. May 20th the year 2020... The day the bombs fell, the day that pushed mankind back to the brink, a fucked up day at best! Jess tried to imagine the terror, the wail of frightened folks and then the boom. She assumed it went boom, most explosives did, then again it could have made a real weird noise, she just thanked the heavens that she wasn't there to witness the fucker. She finally settled on 'boom', it seemed logical. She pulled out one of her 1911's and started to strip and clean it, she knew she wouldn't be sleeping sound tonight being alone out in the wild.

The rains had died down to a back ground pitter-patter ambience, the fire had also died back to embers and she began to unroll her bed roll. The skies had cleared and the moon was out and mostly full. Before she bedded down she cocked her ear to the night and held her breath as long as she could. The forest was silent apart from the occasional drip of water cascading from the high canopy above. The wet forest smell drifted on the breeze bringing a chill to her face as she bedded down, pistol ever ready in her right hand.

"They are dead Jess and it's your fault, you could have stopped them but you ran away!" An old man barked and sobbed on his knees surrounded by dead friends. Jess looked to a number of corpses all shot up and bled out on the floor of a rough tap room. She recognised some folks that she had considered to be friends from different times in her life. However she didn't recognise the man who was laying the blame at her feet.

"I didn't run!" she hissed peering at his wrinkled face, tears rolling down his prune like cheeks.

"Don't lie! You ran and saved yourself and your friends perished!" He said through wails and body shaking sobs. She tried to remember the scene but couldn't nail down the exact time, it was so unlike her to run, she feared very little. Confused she walked from corpse to corpse and shook her head. "I didn't cause this damn you!" But the man carried on weeping shaking his head and pointing at her.

"Look at the blood, look at your sister!" Jess knelt

at the side of a female corpse, she lifted the girl off the floor and jumped because she stared at her own face...

Sunlight shone on her brow, she kicked herself out of the bedroll aiming her pistol around the woodland, looking for a target to shoot. Sweat had dribbled into her eyes, half blinding her. When she found no movement or target she sat down near the burnt out camp fire. It was a bad dream that's all, the dream made no sense but it had fired up her blood. Anxiety faded as she looked to the rising sun and laughed.

"Pull yourself together Jess, it was just a stupid fucking dream!" She grinned nervously and felt a little embarrassed even though there was nobody around to see her foolish actions. Her heart beat relaxed back to a normal drum beat as she started to break camp. When she had packed away her gear she pulled out a leather wrap of jerky and had a chewy breakfast of preserved meat. She couldn't wait to get back to Red town, have a bath at Roody's whore house and drink a few fingers of whiskey. After all she wouldn't need to work for a while having earned enough money to live a few months of relaxation. With the thought of a nice bath and a whiskey high she smiled and headed down the forest towards Red town with a brisk step in her walk.

From the high vantage point Jess could see the wooden walled township down below, smoke rose from the many chimneys and even from here she could hear the welcoming metal working sounds on the wind. The sun was high in the blue cloudless sky and civilisation was a welcoming sight. She picked up the main trail and headed towards the high heavy wooden double doors of Red town. A couple of the rifle armed sentries spotted her progress, at first they aimed rifles until they recognised the confident walk of Jessica the gunslinger.

"Howdy Jess, back so soon, I thought it might have been weeks until we saw you again." The sentry said with a smile.

"Get this gate open Karl, I could drink out of a drifter boot at the moment!" She said jokingly. Karl grinned and signalled to the gate keeper to open the gate. The gate creaked open on heavy metal hinges bringing the stench of human settlements with it on the breeze.

"You take care Jess, hey later on do you fancy a drink?" Karl asked. She grinned back at him and shook her head.

"Not after last time Karl, you know by now you are not my type!" She said giggling and feigning a gun slingers narrow eye gaze. Karl started to laugh.

"No choice Jess, I will be buying you some drinks. I want to know what you have been upto lately. Besides which I have nothing else to spend my hard earned silver on, even though I ain't paid shit!"

"Okay Karl later on, let me get my shit together and then yes I suppose we can go for a few drinks."

Jess cautiously wandered down the main street of Red town dodging the animal shit and trying not to engage in conversation with folks she knew. She headed straight for Roody's whore house and entered. She had smelt the place about thirty yards before she saw the three story building. The tap room was empty at this time of day, most of the farmers, smiths and hunters were all busy doing their jobs. She spotted Roody, a grizzled, wide shouldered man drinking from a bottle of whiskey. He wore a stained fancy shirt and leather faded pants, a bullet pistol belt hanging loosely on his left side, holding a pearl handled high calibre revolver. He was quick with the pistol for a lefty. Lots of folk had perished assuming he wouldn't be quick being left handed. He eyed Jess as she wandered in and scowled slightly.

"By the Bright Jess, you alone?" He grumbled and took another swig from the yellowish bottle. Jess nodded and put her hands on her hips.

"I wouldn't have it any other way Roody, you know that by now."

"Sorry Jess, but Melinda... Well Melinda is busy at the moment. Got herself a man, she be courting, got some time off now, fully paid by her new feller." Jess's heart sank as she approached the bar to order a double whiskey.

"She moved on then?" She asked trying not to shake her voice. Roody sighed and nodded.

"It's been a while Jess... She wouldn't wait forever, not for a hired gun like you. I'm sorry Jess, I should have told you when you passed through two days back but I didn't have the heart to tell you. After all you have been working up north for so long... Sorry Jess." Roody made a face of sadness then took another swig from the whiskey bottle. She tried her best to not appear upset.

"I need a bath my friend, the trail has been hard but let's say I have enough for a good number of relaxing weeks." She grinned and Roody mirrored showing yellow broken teeth. He stretched and composed himself. "I've procured a new whore, fresh from Silver town, she is clean and new to the game, I'm pretty sure she will distract you from Melinda?" He shrugged, not knowing which way Jess would choose. She reached into her sling bag and gave a hefty number of coins to Roody which he greedily snatched.

"Get yourself upstairs my friend!" He quickly counted the coins and his eyes grew wide.

"I see you're staying a while, drink as much as you wish and you have enough scratch for a bath, a whore and a week's stay."

"What's her name?" She asked while Roody recounted the silver dollars.

"I will let you get settled in, room four, best room as always Jess, I will send her up soon, her name is Phoebe." He said distracted by the amount of silver dollars in his gnarly mitts.

Jess entered the room, she knew this room well, she pulled a side table next to the old tin bath and placed her twin 1911's in hands reach and her magazine belt and holsters she put under the table. She waited with butterflies in her stomach.

"Stop this nonsense!" She said and took a few deep breaths to calm herself, all the while she was thinking how she should appear to the new girl, she didn't want to show any nervousness in front of the new working girl. The door to the room opened and a number of male porters came in carrying heavy buckets of hot water. One by one they begin to fill the bath and one of them emptied a bucket of apple blossoms into the hot water, along with some powdered soap. The water started to foam under a few hand waves by one of the porters who did not look at her while she worked.

"Phoebe will join you shortly." The male porter said with his head down and then he left shutting the door behind him. Jess took another deep breath and waited patiently. After what seemed an age there was a knock at the door. Jess raced to the door and opened it to see a petite blonde haired girl, no more than eighteen years old. The girl feigns a smile and entered.

"Do you want me to undress you?" She asked innocently. Jess nodded and shrugged. The girl first takes off Jess's long leather duster placing it down on a nearby chair. She then un-buckled Jess's chain-mail vest, dropping it on to the floor, due to the weight of the armoured vest. She then pulled off the leather jerkin that Jess wore under the armoured vest. Jess could already smell her own unwashed body due to being on the trail so long, she felt a tad embarrassed. Phoebe noticed the change and attempted to relax Jess.

"You don't smell half as bad as some of the farmhands, just relax and let me undress you" The blonde haired girl said with a reassuring smile. She continues to undress her until Jess stood naked like the day she was born. Phoebe then unclasped her gown letting it fall to the floor revealing her nakedness. Jess took a deep breath seeing her wonderful body and tried not to squeeze her thighs together. Phoebe guided Jess to the bath and climbed in with her. The hot water lapped up against her breasts as she sank into the soapy bath.

"You are my first woman" Phoebe admitted with a pretend smile which made Jessica very nervous.

"Are you sure about this, I don't want..." Phoebe reached forward and put her finger to Jess's mouth and shushed her.

"It maybe my first time but I don't have to pretend with you being a female." Jess relaxed slightly as Phoebe moves along the length of her body kissing here and there. Her breasts touching her, as her tongue met Jess's tongue, she can feel Phoebe's hand on her, caressing her in the most intimate way. Jess started to gasp...

Sunlight started to filter through the wooden shutters, Jess stretched and yawned which accidentally wakes the blonde haired girl spooning her. She smiled remembering the lack of sleep and the night of sex. Phoebe shifted the covers over her eyes and groaned, as Jess scrambled out of bed and started to dress. She wandered over to her belongings and reached into her satchel and pulled out a number of silver dollars and placed them on the bed room table as a tip. She stopped to admire the beautiful blonde in bed and then came to her senses. She loaded her 1911's and put them in the holsters before swigging a good mouthful of whiskey from the courtesy bottle that had been sent up. The warm fiery liquid gave her a wakeup call for her slender body. Having dressed she sneaked out of the room and went down to the tap room where three very sleepy looking folks were still playing cards, with a sizable amount in the pot. Having walked through the tap room she exited and headed towards the Temple bank. The stench of animal shit ever present in her nose as she headed to the place where she could deposit her hard earned cash.

The Temple bank was one of those pre-war buildings, made of concrete and rebar. Three guards wielding old assault rifles manned the door, they gave her a sneer as she entered. The main room in the silver Temple bank had more guards inside holding pre-war assault rifles. There was nobody waiting to deposit or relinquish coin so she went to the only booth that was open. An old woman wearing a grey cowl and nearby there was a double barrelled sawn off-shotgun on the counter behind the iron bars.

"Deposit or draw out?" The old woman said with fatigue in her voice.

"Deposit, under the name Jessica Ryding!" Jess said confidently. The old woman curled her lip.

"You're the gun-slinger, hired gun, yes?"

"Here to deposit!" Jess said with confidence in her tone. The old woman made a gesture to receive cash. Jess piled up a serious amount of silver dollars on the counter behind the iron bars. The bank woman counted out ever single coin and then nodded before counting out a number of trade chits, which could be transferred at any Silver dollar bank in the known country. Jess snatched the trade chits and put them in her satchel next to her coin pouch. While she was safe in the bank, Jess placed her Trade chits with the rest of her own personal chits in her bullet belt, she only had six more chit slots left empty in the belt. She quickly counted up the trade chits in her hidden belt and it came to an eye popping amount. *By the bright you have been busy old girl*. She thought. As Jess left the bank she knew she could live a good life on her savings but she was itching for more... She would be damned if she would finish up and retire, hell she was only thirty winters old, give or take.

Jess left the bank and headed back to Roody's whore house, she was going to live it up for a while and she didn't want to take any more contracts on, if they be guarding shipments, assassination, or bounty hunting... Especially now that her favourite whore Melinda has now got a husband and now there is a new squeeze in the form of Phoebe. Jess was taking a holiday...

CHAPTER 2

Joshua Du'Laurantus stood in the safe room scanning the massive piles of books, he curled his lip seeing the piles of filth.

"I should burn you and that would make it right in the eyes of the Bright!" He raged kicking down a pile of leather bound tomes. The books cascaded to the floor and Joshua grinned with a broken toothy grin. He composed himself, straight backed and tall dressed in his black robe covering his lean six foot stature.

"You try to corrupt my faithful flock, how dare you!" He yelled as he clenched his fists. A knock at the sanctum door brought him out of his bravado. He looked to the door over his shoulder.

"Deacon Smith, prepare my sermon this day!" He could hear a sigh behind the door and then the Deacons footsteps padding away towards the main church. Joshua eyed the books for a few more minutes while he calmed himself down. He turned his back on the room full of books and tomes.

"That's right old gods, you will have no more tribute in my lands!" With that he brushed down his black robes and grabbed up his sermon papers that he had written for today's gathering.

Joshua, climbed the stairs to overlook his flock that

had gathered for today's sermon dedicated to the bright. He caught his breath having climbed the overlook and looked to the many farm hands, smiths and merchant families. He looked over his gathered flock and took a deep breath.

"This morning the Bright has told me the error is our ways, we need to stop this debauchery in the taverns and whore houses that has infected out township of Red Town!" About half the gathered folk yelled 'Praise the Bright' (Mostly female and a few god fearing males), the others just mumbled 'Amen'. Joshua sighed and appeared to be angry. He took another deep breath and eyed the gathered folk.

"I will read an extract from the tome of the Bright! Chapter twelve!" All who had gathered seemed to bend forward to listen to the words of the priest?

"The Bright was angry with the old world and as the old world concentrated on all that would be evil, hand held devices that could reveal every person in the world! Communicating filth and lies" Joshua waved his arms in the air.

"We must repel the instinct to go down the dark path, the path of darkness!" He yelled and noticed a third of his flock were on their knees praying to the power of the bright. Joshua rose up his arms and made a gesture of cascading fire down on his patrons. The folk that hadn't knelt already fell to their knees. Joshua knew he had them now.

"Praise the Bright, because he will guide you through the darkness and banish the evil to the four corners of this wonderful America!" Some of the patrons started to thrash around yelling praise be to the bright etc. Joshua had been practicing his speech all morning and it was all going as planned, but he needed to stir them up, to distract and confuse them so he could weed out the sinners. He put his hands on his hips and started to shake his head in disgust.

"But we still have sinners among the flock, folks who read from the old ways, the ways of ancient times that bore lies into the minds of children and adults alike." He spotted a number of folk avert their eyes from his glare. *Bingo*! He chose his target, he could always get the other sinners in the weeks to come, but today would be Franny Tilder. He had heard a rumour that she had been caught reading a small black leather bound book with a gold cross on the front. He feigned another scan of his flock.

"Franny Tilder!" He pointed as the patrons gasped and shifted away from the poor young women. She paled and looked like she was going to throw up. "Franny you have not been true to the Bright, you have concealed a book of lies!" Her husband rounded on her and was just about to chastise her but Joshua quickly took control of the situation. "Is this true my little gem, is this true that you haven't handed in this tome of lies?" His voice fell to a quiet and disappointed tone. Franny fell to her the floor prostrate and started to sob. Joshua gestured to the Deacon to take Franny home. The Deacon pushed his way through the crowd and gently picked her up in his arms and carried her out of the church with her angry husband apologising in tow. When the heavy church doors shut with a loud thump Joshua stretched and silently claimed this event as a victory for the sun god. He continued his practiced sermon eyeing the others that averted their eyes.

Later that day while a number of church patrons swept the pews and polished the shiny holy alter. Joshua performed a number of small blessings using a mirror and the sun beams shining through the church windows. The day's sermons had gone exceptionally well, especially due to the weeding out of a sinner. The Bright loved sinners more, he knew Franny would be back next Sunday and full of new energy and vigour for the holy Bright. He knew which book she was reading, it was still unfortunately common in the townships due to the scavengers who frequented Red town, finding the old books in pre-war ruins and selling the lies of the old world to the highest bidder. He had a deal with most of the merchants in Red town who would warn him of books of lies entering his holy town. However, of late there seemed to be some kind of underground movement peddling the filthy books, which he hadn't pinned down yet. He wandered to his private quarters where Natasha was grinding beans and making hot coffee. She bowed when he entered and he shone his mirror on her blessing her.

"Praise be the Bright." She put her hands together and whispered his blessing. He purchased Natasha a year or so ago, she was destined for Roody's whore house but he had seen the innocence in her eyes and brought her under his wing as a personal assistant. He had sinned with her a number of times before Deacon Smith caught her jerking him off in his private quarters. He had told the Deacon that it was for research purposes but he knew it was a sin and spent a number of weeks at prayer with the Deacon confessing his sins. He would be damned if he had to endure that shit again so Joshua refrained from the pleasures that Natasha provided. In his mind he saw Natasha as a test from the Bright and the more he refrained the more pure he was in the eyes of god. *I was weak and that shouldn't have happened!* She poured him a stout flagon of coffee as he sat down at his study desk. He took a sip and as always the coffee was perfectly blended a testament of her alchemical skill.

"What would I do without you Natasha." He said relaxing in his cushioned chair. "And I Joshua, you saved me from a life of sin and I will be forever grateful, praise be the Bright!" She said like a true believer. A knock at the door made them both jump which they laughed at for a few seconds.

"Joshua, I have the book." The Deacon Murmured from behind the door.

"You are always welcome Deacon come on in!" Joshua said knowing the Deacon had come up trumps. The Deacon opened the door and popped his head round. "I hope I am not disturbing?" He was obviously hoping he could catch them sinning again.

"Don't be silly Deacon, did you find the offending

tome?" The Deacon nodded and passed the small leather bound book to Natasha. The Deacon was flushed as Natasha grabbed the book, his head down trying not to look at the young woman dressed in the unflattering brown robe she wore. Joshua could see the Deacon was smitten with Natasha after all they were of similar age. Joshua grimaced.

"Is that all Deacon?" The Deacon nodded and quickly retreated closing the door behind him.

"You are a temptation to him my Natasha, but fear not he will repent in prayer." *As do we all!* She didn't seem bothered by the young mans affections on her. She passed the offending book to Joshua who looked with hatred to the book, the gold embossed cross on the book caught the light and he very nearly dropped it.

"You know what this is!" He said as anger boiled in his blood. She nodded and averted her eyes from the item he held.

"This is a relic of the old world, a testament of myths, legends and un-truths preached to a barbaric world... There is one but place for this." He said shaking the book in his hand as though it was a spent match.

"Fire! My holy one!" He could see the hatred that matched his in her eyes.

"No! We must not destroy, but we must lock this away, we gather and keep the lies as testament to the old gods." He barked as he tried to calm his anger. She rushed to him and started to massage his shoulders, he could feel her touch calming his nerves and the betrayal of words contained in the book. He could feel the rough cloth on his penis stirring. He stood up quickly nearly knocking her to the floor in his haste. "I must lock this filth up!" He yelled and rushed to the door in a frenzy.

He locked the door behind him and lit an oil lantern, when the room illuminated he felt sick to the bone. Piles and piles of religious books lie scattered or on wooden shelves. He placed the small book on top of one of the many Jenga piles of religious books that he had collected over the years. The shiny gold cross caught the light again and he averted his vision from it.

"I will not fall... The Bright is the true god!" He was about to lash out again but he saw the many scattered piles of books on the floor so refrained. He fell to his knees and prayed. "Oh Bright one, shine a path for my body to follow and I will follow your path, the path you lay in front of me." He started to sob and quickly wiped his tears when he heard a floorboard creak outside the door. He looked to the door and assumed it was the Deacon listening at the door. *Fucking Deacon trying to find my weaknesses!* He stood up and rushed to the door and opened it hoping to find the Deacon listening against the door. When he opened the door Natasha was stood there her blue eyes wide and tearful. She brushed back her wispy shoulder length blonde hair with her slender hand and tried to wipe her tears from her eyes.

"You are strong my Joshua, fear not I am here to aid you in your darkest hour." She whispered. Joshua felt a little bit embarrassed she had heard his plight from behind the thick wooden door. The blood rushed to his head, he had been so pure. He grabbed her hand and pulled her into the room, kicking the door shut as she started to kiss him. Passion raced inside them both as they embraced each other, it had been nearly a year since they had sinned, but it also felt so pure. They spent a few moments between kissing and pulling off each other's garments. She felt his warm flesh against hers as he kissed her breasts, then her belly and then between her legs. She pushed the back of his head against her and felt her body go taught. She put her hands against her face as she felt his tongue lapping on her then inside her body. She rolled him over and then slid on top of him. The shame, the sin was all gone in a matter of seconds. They both agreed 'Fuck the Bright' this felt too pure and if God made this then go with it. *The bright will understand and forgive!*

    Joshua wandered into Red town, he had pledged to visit Franny due to the hic-up with the contraband and confiscated book she had been reading. Franny's husband owned a small farm holding that bred cattle at the edge of town. Due to this farmstead being out of the fortifications of the main town he assumed they were open to scavenger sales. He was dressed in his long dark robes but he was armed with a double barrelled shotgun which he kept on a shoulder sling, under his right arm. The cloak he wore concealed the shotgun. Even though a priest of the Bright was revered you still armed yourself to be careful. As always the populous of Red Town gave him a wide birth due to religious reasons. Even the scumbag drifters respected a priest of the Bright. Nobody wanted a dead priest on their conscience. He got to the foot of the farmstead and scanned over the lush fields of grass with cattle mooching around. The farm stead was a simple place, a main building and a barn for winter holding and an upper floor for storing hay. He knocked twice on the rough wooden door that had leather straps as hinges and then waited. He expected the man of the house but he was in the fields, instead Franny answered the door.

"Ooohh, Joshua I didn't expect you." She says pulling up her grown to cover her milky white shoulders. *Curse the female kind*. He thought as he tried to repel thoughts of touching her.

"I've come to present a pamphlet for Sundays sermons." He frowned and continued "I hope to see you in church on Sunday I apologise for singling you out but you know I have the Lord god the Bright as my witness." Franny nodded and bowed.

"I'm so sorry, I didn't know what I was doing? I worship the bright as do you, but I got lost when I read that book, but it has passed..." Joshua reached forward and patted her on the shoulder.

"But you have found the true calling now and the Bright forgives you." He smiled.

"I have indeed!" Franny bowed and closed the door... Joshua took that as gospel and wandered back to town passing all the establishments which he deemed terrible for the church of the Bright. He passed a number of bars where the patrons nodded to him and looked a little bit embarrassed. Then he passed a number of whore houses where drifters tipped their hats, but obviously didn't give a shit! *You will be punished in the eyes of our lord!* He thought that but then remembered the sins he performed with Natasha the night before. *We are all sinners and we all need punishment!*

Joshua headed back to the church and all the while he felt he was one of the folks that he has seen in the streets today. A wiry woman staggered out of Roody's whore house, she has a bottle of whiskey in her hand and she stopped in front of him to take a good glug from the bottle. She winked at him and laughed.

"You laugh Harlot?" Joshua hissed. The woman stopped and narrowed her eyes as she swayed back and forth. She stood tall in an inane attempt to look sober and opened her leather duster revealing a holstered pistol.

"Laughing at you!" She said as her right foot crept backwards bracing her body and her right hand ever-present hovering above her holstered pistol. Her hand shook like a shitting dog but Joshua has seen gun fighters before and he would be fucked if he was going to die this day.

"Wait one second, aren't you Jessica the gun fighter?" He was no longer trying to un-sling his shotgun, he knew he had met his match.

"I've been called many names but gun fighter will do!" She said sobering to the event unfolding. She grabbed hold of one of her 1911's and cocked her head to one side eying him.

"Is this how you wanna go down?" She warned. Joshua put his hands up and states "No, I am a holy priest..."

"I don't give a shit, just keep walking mother fucker!" Her fingers flexed over the pistol. Joshua put his head down and bypassed this terrible event. As he walked away he remembered the tales about Jessica the gun fighter. Apparently Jessica used to run with bandits and but before she used to run with the rangers and peace keepers. He could only assume that she is now a freelance bounty hunter? *Even for a gun fighter she is very good looking!* He thought.

The church was quite as Joshua entered, he took a sigh of relief and padded into the large worshipping area. It was all quiet apart from Natasha polishing the main alter which looked like a large brass sun.

"Seems like Franny is going to be the star of next weeks sermon!" Natasha dropped her polishing rag and made a bee line to Joshua.

"Did she repent? Has she seen the light?" She said excitedly.

"She is back in favour of our lord and next week she will read out a handpicked segment of the book of bright!" He raised his hand and pointed in the air above.

"The flock will see her repent and those who delve

in to witchcraft and lies will think twice hence forward!" He hadn't realised that he was now shouting and Natasha was cowering away from the thunder of his voice. The doors to the church slammed open and a man dressed like a filthy drifter wandered in checking out the large area with eagle eyes. Joshua craned his neck and squinted.

"Gregor? Is that you?" Joshua asked with surprise. The man nodded and stalked further in.

"Yep, and it's been a hard fucking road Joshua." He grinned. "But I come baring gifts."

"You have never given anything for free, what have you found?" Joshua said with annoyance and curiosity in his tone.

"I've found a big one, even has a lock on it, but it's a big bad cross book!"

"Well don't just stand there like a horse in the rain, bring it to me." He barked showing off a little bit in front of Natasha. The man rearranged the strap of his rifle slung on his shoulder and peered up from the shadow of his sand blown wide brim hat.

"Gona cost you big time for this one preacher." He reached into a sling bag and pulled out a leather bound book as big as Britannica encyclopaedia and as thick as a mans arm. Even from where Joshua stood he could see the faded gold cross on the front and the locking mechanism on the side. He greedily held his hands open as Gregor placed the heavy book. Joshua rotated the book as he rushed to the church alter, the others followed. He placed the book down and quickly unfastened the simple lock, much to Gregors disgust.

"Fuck! Is that how you open that thing, I spent hours trying to work out how to open the fucker!"

"Hush your bad language in the church of the bright!" Natasha chastised.

"Shut it whore!" Gregor spat as Joshua opened the book.

"What the fuck is this?" Joshua said looking down at the open book. The middle section of the pages had been cut into a recess and only held a collection of hand written notes and trinkets. Natasha softly punched his shoulder.

"Language Joshua!" He apologised and rounded on Gregor who looked stunned.

"Shit I've humped that bastard for miles!" The pile of coins he thought he would receive for such a find diminished in his minds eye.

"I'm not paying for this Gregor, you understand don't you?" Gregor shook his head and nodded, but tried to salvage something from the find.

"Maybe those hand written notes are still religious?" But he knew he wasn't going to be paid. He reached forward and grabbed the book, thinking he could some how sell the trinkets for a few coins, but Joshua grabbed his wrist.

"I am a fair man am I not Gregor? I will pay you ten dollars for what you have found, after all we have a long history together and I would hate to think you might give up looking for such things in the future."

"Make it twelve and it's yours preacher!" Joshua

sighed and agreed especially having seen some of the trinkets in the recess of the book.

"Twelve it is!" He said as he opened his callused palm. Joshua reached into his robe and counted out thirteen silver dollars, he gave him an extra coin to keep the pact.

"Just out of interest, where did you find this item?" He couldn't even bring himself to say Bible.

"I found it in the back of an old truck on the outskirts of the city ruins far to the north east. I suppose who ever left it there must have left in some kind of hurry because I found an old army issue M16 rifle still in good nick and a rotting old sleeping bag. You know the kind the pre-war water proof ones. Well it must have been there for many years because it was thick with dust?"

"Keep hunting Gregor and good luck in the future, I'm assuming you sold the army issue rifle already?"

"Yeah sold that mother when I hit Red town along with some other stuff I found, got quite a haul." The grizzled man said grinning. "I prefer my M21, more penetration than that 5.56mm shit!" Joshua watched Gregor leave before he started to rustle through the hand written notes and trinkets.

"This stuff is strange, I'm guessing it was written a very long time ago, by some person proclaiming to be the Utopian?" Joshua was sat in his private quarters as Natasha brewed up a large pot of freshly ground coffee.

"Strange how?" Natasha said while she poured a

strong looking coffee into his favourite mug, which happened to have a CND motif on the side. He took a sip and nearly burnt his lips.

"It's quite fascinating... This Utopian seems to have travelled down from the north and seems to be either autistic or completely focussed on some kind of quest?"

"Was he following the path of the bright?" She asked while she tried to read some of the documents over his shoulder, she picked out some words she recognised but her reading wasn't too good but she had been practicing reading to please Joshua.

"I'm not sure... In fact I'm not sure why he would hide these documents in this trashy tome, so far I haven't seen any religious doctrine in his notes." He said as he palmed a gold pendant in the form of a 'Star of David', which was one of the trinkets found in the recess of the tome. He felt his mind racing the more he read the hand written notes which described sections of some kind of pilgrimage or mission. Just proof reading some of the documents he recognised some of the locations this upstart described. He had drained his mug of coffee, he looked up and Natasha was preparing a light meal of ham, honey and soda bread. He read on and the more he read the more he wanted to know more about this man called 'Utopian'. Hours passed, he had half eaten the meal that Natasha had made for him, she looked bored now and was darning socks, but she had lit more candles around his desk. *Odd I didn't see her light those?* He read more and he focused on the words, 'I travelled south and found Red town.'

"By the Bright! He came here!" He yelled which startled Natasha. She rushed to his side and started to massage his shoulders.

"Who came?" She whispered. He nearly knocked over a candle in his haste to stand up. "He describes Red Town as a meagre trading hub, a small camp town, nothing like the township it is now! I grew up in these parts, so it must be over fifty years ago because I only remember the bustling township of Red town!" Sweat had beaded on his brow. Natasha was clearly worried now.

"You need to take a break, you are feverish!" She dabbed his forehead with her robes revealing her pale legs. In normal circumstances he would have been aroused by such a glimpse, instead he was distracted by the written notes.

"Bring me the map, not the clean map, the scavengers survey map, the one with the pencil marks all over it!" He was in a fit of bravado. She rushed to the book shelves and pulled out a number of moth eaten maps and spread them out on the desk, some of the maps were so large they dangled over the sides of the desk. He grabbed up his magnifying glass and started to frantically search locations on the old pre-war maps. His eyes searched the locations quickly until his eye fell upon a map location fifty miles to the north-west. He grabbed up a HB pencil and circled an area on the map.

"I need to go there!" He said stabbing the map with his index finger. Natasha narrowed her eyes and peered at the map location.

"But why? Has the Bright opened a path for you?" She whispered as her bright blue eyes opened wide with innocence

"I think so, maybe this is a sign from the Bright?" Natasha saw doubt in his eyes but he gained more vigour.

"It must be, it must be a sign from the Bright, these notes I have read, this Utopian man must be a sign from our creator, for us to follow!"

"Us?" Natasha smiled.

"Of course, we must follow the call! We are the chosen people by our lord, the sun will guide our way." He said in a feverish state.

"But I'm no warrior in this land of hate?" She said with a worried brow.

"We need not be warriors! We can hire a group of hired guns who will protect us in our quest to find Utopia!" He said as he calculated the amount of coin he would have to take from the church coffers. Natasha had her doubts.

"Can we take the churches coin to pursue a mission such as this?"

"Yes we can and I'm sure the good Deacon will keep Red Town pure and good in my absence!" He paused. "Deacon Smith has been taught very well and he will protect Red Town with the sermons of our lord."

"Tomorrow we will hit Red Town, gather up equipment and rustle up some hired guns." That night Natasha shared his bed and they sinned twice.

The next morning Joshua helped himself to a stash of coins cultivated by the church of the bright. *I will pay this back.* Natasha was wearing her Sunday best which was a tattered and stained. The same dress she arrived at Red town to become a whore before Joshua purchased her.

"You look lovely Natasha." Joshua said while he adjusted his shotgun sling under his robes. They wandered to the market square and began to browse the wares on offer. He purchased some standard equipment such as a Giga-counter, medicinal alcohol, preserved foods like meat jerky and a bag of limes to stave of scurvy, some perishable food stuffs and a couple of bed rolls which they tethered to their back packs which they already owned. Joshua purchased a .357 revolver, speed loaders and enough ammo for a sojourn. He gave the snub nose revolver to Natasha and purchased a box of 12 gauge ammo for his double barrelled shotgun. He purchased some more miscellaneous equipment before they headed off to the bars to enlist some gun fighters.

"Its stinks in here!" Natasha said as they enter the tap room. Joshua ignores the stink of beer, body odour and blood and started to scan the tap room for potential mercenaries.

"That is the stink of infidels... But we need to hire some real lowlife scum!" He whispered into Natasha's ear. His eyes fell on a gun fighter type woman who he recognises from the day before. Natasha followed his gaze.

"Are you sure?"

"Yes! I'm pretty sure." He wandered over as the gun fighter tried to drink another shot and got most of the potent liquid down the front of her leather duster.

"We might need to sober her up first!" He grinned as he made sure she wasn't going to pull one of her pistols on him.

"Jessica?" He said softly, so his words didn't alarm the mean gun fighter. She peered at him with bloodshot eyes.

"Yeah?" even though she was clearly pissed she seemed to be able to focus on a conversation.

"I am on a mission to the north and wish to hire folk like you to keep myself and my acolyte safe. He unfolded a map" The gun fighter started to laugh a lot. To the point, where Joshua was about to find another gun fighter in the bar.

"I know where you want to go…" She paused. "Even the bandits don't go up there! But I have travelled past there and know it is very dangerous. Why in the fuck would you want to go up there?" Jessica chuckled as Joshua frowned.

"Look I will pay good coin to escort a small group to that location, are you in or out?" Joshua asked, his patience levels nearly depleted. Jessica gritted her teeth and took another swig of rot gut whiskey.

"Okay, I'm in but you pay for my team also!"

"How many?" He sneered thinking along the lines of being ripped off.

"Two more rifles to cover our backs!"

"Agreed, two more, a hundred silver dollars each!" Jessica laughed.

"Two hundred silver dollars each and a further twenty up front for me!"

"Deal but you only get ten up front! Now get your team together!" Jessica nodded begrudgingly. She pulled out a silver time piece and peered at the face, trying her best to focus on the little hands, which seemed to take quite some time.

"Meet outside Roody's whore house tomorrow at 10am. We will be there!" As Joshua and Natasha began to walk away, Jess thought she would have a hard time enlisting Brae and Yolanda. *They will do it for me!*

CHAPTER 3

"It's just a clear and cut mission, we take the insane preacher up there..." She paused for a few seconds and continued. "Hell we could roll the fucker once we are there, find out where he stashes his silver, double back..." Yolanda had put her hand on Jessica's shoulder.

"We ain't rolling a preacher, Jess, that's not who we are." She said softly as Jessica started to laugh and double up..

"I was joking Yolanda, by the Bright you should have seen how pale your face went." She giggled lots more as Brae and Yolanda shook their heads wondering if she had actually wanted to fuck the holy man over? Brae had his doubts, Jess fucked them over on bounty shares the last time they trod the sand.

"This time you need to be straight down the line and if I even suspect your
gona fuck us over I will drop you myself." Brae shifted his muscular body so the lamp light cast a shadow over Jessica's face. Jess shrugged and nodded and noticed Yolanda's hand hovering over her Bowie knife.

"Guys, stop being so fucking serious, you have my word, I'm straight up." She narrowed her eyes as she felt her blood boiling, lubricating her gun hands.

Yolanda slammed the table nearly knocking over the flagons of ale on the table.

"Quit fucking around, it ain't high noon!" She barked, the tension dissipated as they all started to laugh. Yolanda started to tie her long blonde hair back in a ponytail as Brae chugged his pint of ale.

"You mentioned you had been up there before and it is a dangerous area, what kind of danger can we expect?" Brae asked suddenly serious. Jess put her head down.

"I've never actually been up there, just heard rumours that's all." She took a sip of ale. "I heard a group of rangers got fucked over up there a few years back, no details really but the rumours say there is some old pre-war tech, maybe security bots..." Brae spluttered some of his ale, some of the droplets hit Jessica's face..

"Bots... You mean fucking robots." He looked to Yolanda who was wide eyed in shock.

"Camp fire stories that's all Brae!" Jess wiped her face on her sleeve. "It's been too darned long for robots to be still on line." But Brae remembered years ago coming up against some pre-war tech in the form of sentry guns that took out half a squad of rangers before they put it down. Jessica could almost read his thoughts.

"If you remember Brae, I was there when we took out that sentry gun with those rangers."

"Yeah and we lost five rangers!" He growled.

"Yes and it was an ambush, we had no idea that

something pre-war would still be on line and I seem to remember that I was up front and you cowered in the dirt when it let rip with that machine gun." Jessica countered as Brae tried his best to alter the story that he had previously told Yolanda. Yolanda looked to Brae and appeared slightly hurt due to the fantastic lie he had told her.

"Cheers Jess, I told Yolanda a different tale..."

"Yolanda my friend, your feller is brave and a damned good rifleman, but he..." Before Jess had time to reveal the actual tale Brae grabbed Yolanda's hand.

"Honey, I lied to you..." He sighed. "It was Jess who took out the sentry gun, while I hid in cover. When it opened up killing some of the rangers, Jessica here, flanked the robot and kicked the ammo belt from its housing." He shrugged and smiled. "The bitch saved the day." He chuckled as Yolanda seemed to see Jessica in a whole new light. She grabbed his hand in hers and kissed his cheek.

"Too be honest your story sounded a bit farfetched, I know you Brae my lover, you always did extend the truth when you tell a tale." She cocked her head to one side and kissed his lips. Brae's face was flustered but he accepted the kiss, which started to get a little bit too passionate for Jessica's liking.

"By the Bright get a fucking room you guys!" Jess sneered. She then pulled out her old time piece and noticed it was nearly 10am.

"Shit we have to go, we need to be outside the whore house now!"

The group arrived outside Roody's whore house where the priest and some girl waited patiently. Jess put her hands up and apologised for being slightly late.

"Took your time, I thought you was a professional?" Joshua chastised. Jess looked to the girl.

"Who's the girl?"

"This is Natasha my acolyte she will chronicle our sojourn." Joshua said with pride. Jessica could already see some kind of loving bond they had with one another. *I feel like a gooseberry.* She thought having no recollection of the girl she met yesterday in the throws of a good whiskey haze.

"You didn't mention anything about looking after a squeeze?"

"She comes with me and be damned sure she is protected along with me, or I will hire some other sons-of-bitch's, hell there are plenty of them in Red town." Joshua stated like he was doing a sermon on Sunday. Jess was about to say something but Brae grabbed her shoulder and tightened his grip to shut Jess up.

"The girl and yourself will be protected by our gun hands, fear not." Brae said in the most Nobel way. Jessica dragged the priest off to one side un-folding a map as Yolanda introduced herself to Natasha.

"Stick with me, I will keep you protected." She looped her arm in her strong arm and started to chat among themselves. Brae quickly scanned the group's heavy packs of equipment and trappings. The gun fighters had already done their shopping and had heavy loads themselves. After a brief argument between Joshua and Jessica the group marched out towards the gates of Red town.

By noon the group had mounted the large bluff overlooking the north, the map was out again and already the leaders were in a furious argument again.

"You may wish to get there in one piece, but we need to take the snake trail through the rockies, the river is far too dangerous and it will put a day at least on our journey." It seemed the priest had backed down and begrudgingly agreed to the trail that Jessica had plotted.

"You guys have travelled together before?" Natasha asked innocently.

"Yeah we have travelled many times with Jess, good leader really even though she can go a little crazy every now and then." Yolanda reassured her.

"Don't worry we will keep her in check, even if she is nuts!" She laughed. Yolanda could see that Natasha had a girl crush on her, but it wasn't surprising for a young girl to be smitten with an older and more experienced woman that had already travelled in such a harsh landscape. However she didn't like the way the young girl eyed up her lover Brae.

"He is so rugged and..." Natasha tried to find the words. Yolanda refrained the urge to snap Natasha's her pretty little neck.

"Brae is my lover!" She tried her best not to sound angry but it did.

"I'm, so sorry, I never meant to..."

"Think nothing of it." Yolanda interrupted as she eyed Brae to see if he had noticed the pretty young girls affections. Natasha felt a little bit embarrassed and tried her best to change the subject.

"I have only ever had one man..." She looked to Yolanda's armoured vest. "Joshua bought me when I arrived in Red town, otherwise I would have had been forced into sex with many other men." Her eyes started to fill with tears.

"No tears lass, it is a sign of weakness out here in the Ashland." Yolanda mopped her cheeks with the cuff of her leather duster and hugged her.

"When we camp up I will show you how to use that revolver you have." The weeping had stopped but the young girl still shuddered in her arms. Yolanda narrowed her eyes at the priest. *So the priest preys on pretty young girls!* She swallowed the bile that ascended her throat and tried her best to delete the thought of shooting the priest in the face from her mind. Jessica packed away the map they had been brooding over as Joshua kicked a cactus plant nearby.

"Fine, we go through the Rockies!" Joshua sounded very angry as Jessica started to explain to the group why they shouldn't follow the river.

"We need to avoid the water scourge!" Referring to the strange, half-man-fish creatures, that dwell in the large river. "We only have so much ammo and the last thing we need is a battle against the scourge. Brae I'm right yes?" Brae nodded remembering the fish folk.

"Jessica is right, the scourge have many numbers and it's always a fighting retreat when we encounter the fish folk. Besides which we know many watering holes on the way through the Rockies. Fresh springs so we don't have to drink filthy river water."

"Well I suppose you know more about the Ashland than I, so it's your call." Joshua agreed but in the back of his mind he thought the gun slingers were trying to extend the mission for more coins.

It had been a hard day's travel; they had made good head way through the rocky landscape stopping now and then to fill canteens with fresh spring water. Even Joshua had succumbed to the wisdom and truth of his fellow travellers. They made camp under a jut of rock, just before the heavens opened and cascaded with torrential rain. The sun long gone and dark clouds covered the moon, lighting started to strike random places in the Rockies. Natasha was hugging Joshua tightly while he reassured her that it was the god of Bright purging the land clean, of sinners. Jessica thought his doctrine was full of shit and that nature was just running its course. Every time a lightning bolt hit the ground far way Joshua and Natasha cooed at the might of the electrical storm. Jessica sat by the fire and heard the priest telling the young girl that every lightning strike was brought forth by the Bright and a sinner was vanquished. She also heard the soft moans and sobs of the other couple fucking in their bedroll. When the two couples had fallen asleep and started to purr, she thought back to the whore in the bath in Roody's whore house and felt her loins grow warm and wet.

"Stop it, focus on the mission!" She whispered into the night as the electrical storm subsided. She started to worry about the place where they were headed, she was young and brave the last time she went up against a pre-war robot.

"Young and stupid, I won't make that mistake again! We scout the place out before we head in. Not going to die in the Ashland from a stray bullet." She whispered as she tended the low burning cam p fire. She stretched her legs and looked to her time piece. She then crawled over to Brae and Yolanda and tapped Brae on his forehead. He woke with a start and reached for his rifle but she calmed him.

"Your watch mate." Brae rubbed the sleep from his eyes and nodded as Jessica crawled into Yolanda's bed roll, hugged round her then fell into a deep sleep feeling the warmth of Yolanda, her hair smelt nice and she assumed Yolanda had bathed in a scented bath in Red town.

The sun started to rise, it was red and coloured the rocky land in an orange hue. Yolanda yawned and stretched which woke Jessica from her sleep. They both kicked out of the bed roll and sniffed the air bringing the scent of fresh coffee, eggs and dried meat being fried on the low burning camp fire. Brae manning the pan and cracked open another egg and gestured to wake the others up. Yolanda tried to lift Jessica up but she thrashed around a little in defiance to the point she gave up. She strapped on her armour and then joined Brae by the camp fire. Brae started to dish out meat and eggs to her waiting tin plate.

"Eggs!" Jessica yelled before she clipped on her chain mail vest under her leather duster. Brae chuckled as he broke a few more eggs into the pan.

"You always loved eggs Jess, come on bring your plate!" Jessica riffled through her backpack and found a tin plate, she rushed to the camp fire shoulder bumped Yolanda and then offered the tin plate to Brae. The priest and the girl were late arrivals to the camp fire, but to be fair they had never done this before. The party ate a good breakfast and started to chat among themselves, the mission in hand seemed so far away from their minds. The sun had stopped being red and now cast a bright yellow unforgiving heat to the camp. Brae busied himself making sure that everybody had packed up their belongings properly it was a throw back to when he used to be a ranger. Jessica had seen this so many times before and had to bite her lip when Brae checked some of her belt straps. He meant well but it was very annoying especially to an Ashlander like herself.

"Ready to go?" He said still eyeing the smouldering camp fire. He couldn't help himself when he kicked sand over the fire pit to douse the charcoal, even though the chance of wild fires were extremely low being in a desert.

Jess knew they would have another day's hard travel over the Rockies before they neared their destination. By evening she witnessed Brae looking for a good place to camp. The sun was going down while they foraged around for bracken and shit to burn. Luckily they had done the right thing and filled their canteens at the water springs that Jess and Brae had agreed upon on the map. If you didn't know the secret springs then you would be in a world of hurt and dehydration. *The priest would be fucked without us!* Brae had found a small spring out in the sandy Rockies, they had made a mark on the map using an old brass nautical compass, which had been given to Jessica when she ran with the desert rangers. She knew Brae had one too.

"We camp here!" Brae said with an undertone of command. Everyone looked around to the sandy desert and couldn't see any geographical point apart from the large standing rock where he had decided to camp. A small spring of water trickled out of the collection of rocks. Jessica explained through experience that this was a ranger stop off point. However, there were wheel prints in the sands, obviously made previously from a merchant caravan which the wind hadn't hidden.

"I can't see anything but dunes of sand?" Joshua said obviously alarmed and suspecting the gun fighters have took them out here to perish.

"See this compass, then we camp here and tomorrow we head north east, by noon we will leave the desert and head back into woodland." Jessica stated as Brae agreed.

"Jess has bypassed the dodgy areas deemed dangerous for such a small party, trust her, by evening tomorrow we will arrive at the location you wish to get too."

Joshua stared at the endless sands and started to doubt there words, he looked to Natasha who was chatting with the blonde haired female.

"Are you trying to fuck us?" He grimaced. "It's on you tall one, get us to the place we seek!" He had singled out the muscular warrior Brae.

"We head from here north east tomorrow, but we need to camp now before the sun goes down!"

"Just camp down priest, unless you want to wander around in the dark?" Jess said throwing her rucksack to the ground. She watched the turmoil shifting on Joshua's face, he clearly didn't like taking orders, especially from a woman. *Yeah I bet that pisses you right off don't it!* Joshua sneered and threw off his back pack.

"Fine, we camp here but I'm keeping an eye on you lot!" He warned. Brae could see the tension in Joshua, it was very unsurprising really, the priest didn't really know any of the hired guns. He was wise to be wary. He reached into his backpack and after several minutes he located an old deck of cards, he knew some of the cards were missing but they could still play.

"Anyone fancy a game of poker?" At first nobody seemed to want to play until Natasha beamed and sat down next to Brae. He noticed Yolanda eyeing the pretty girl but he ignored her.

"I've played poker before but didn't do very well I'm sure the girls I played with were making up rules just to take my coin." Natasha said as she picked up her deal. Jessica shrugged and then joined the group to play cards.

"Everyone chip in a coin." She said as she started to gather up small stones to use as chips.

"I won't gamble like the moon!" He said referring to the moon in the Bright religion similar to Satan in the Christian bible. "Shame on you Natasha, I didn't put you under my wing just to see you gamble like a whore!" The young girl was about to put her cards down until Jessica grabbed her wrist.

"It's just a game, ignore that religious freak, play and have some fun." The young woman nodded but her cheeks were flushed with embarrassment. Joshua stood up and then wandered away from the camp, he sat down with his back to the rest of the party obviously sulking.

The game of cards went on for an hour or so before they decided on who takes the first watch. Joshua was already snoring in his bed roll and Jessica had won the pot, it had been a very easy win but at the end of the day she had more experience in bar games. Yolanda and Brae were making out in the bed roll about ten foot from camp, which left Jessica alone with Natasha. Jess had thrown her bed roll around herself and Natasha and began to teach her how to speed load the girl's revolver.

"Then quickly grab the speed loader and place it in like this." She said twisting the speed loader allowing the bullets to fall into the barrel of the pistol. Natasha watched as the gun fighter deftly loaded the weapon and cocked the revolver.

"Too be honest you would be better with an automatic, it's much quicker to load a magazine than fucking around with a revolver speed loader." She pulled out one of her 1911's and showed the lass how quick it is to load an automatic. Natasha agreed and looked to the bed roll where the priest snored loudly.

"I hope I don't need to use this..." She paused as the moonlight augmented her blue eyes. "I don't think I could take a life!" She said grimly. Jess laughed.

"You're in the Ashland now and knowing how to use that piece of shit could save your life." Jess sighed. "Look, tomorrow we will do some target practice..." A noise out on the sands alerted Jess, she leaped out of the bed roll startling Natasha.

"Wake them up!" She hissed as she cocked both of her forty fives and cautiously ventured away from the camp fire. The young girl rushed to Joshua and shook him awake.

"By all that is Bright, what is up Natasha!" He barked as gunshot retorts alerted the camp. Somewhere past the illumination of the camp fire the priest could see Jessica firing into the darkness and then Jessica falling to the ground with something large on top of her. Yolanda and Brae had kicked off the bed roll and were already reaching for firearms. Natasha raised up her revolver and noticed her hand was shaking terribly.

"Jessica!" Brae yelled as he rushed out into the dark, rifle first to see a large coyote savaging his friend. Jess was kicking and screaming trying to get the wild dog off her. Brae witnessed more shadows rushing in followed by feral barking. He rushed to Jessica and kicked the dog in its snout which tumbled in the air. Jess had her knife out and dived onto the dog stabbing and grappling. Brae dropped to one knee and traced a shadow moving quickly towards the camp. He aimed and squeezed the trigger dropping one of the shadows. Jess was still stabbing the beast as another wild dog pounced on her back. The dog fell to one side, bloody and wet as Yolanda's bullet hit its flank. Jess scrambled to her feet, she abandoned the knife which was still stuck in the dog and combat rolled to the pistols that were knocked out of her hands.

"Get behind me Jess!" She grabbed her pistols and rushed to Brae and Yolanda who were firing into the shadows. Bullet casings fell from the ejector ports as the rifles rang out into the night, hitting fast moving shadows.

"There retreating!" Brae announced as though the wild dogs had some kind of strategy. Jess looked to her arm where the wild dog had ragged her, luckily the metal brace she wore had taken the savage attack, although it was buckled and had some canine like holes in it now. However the leather sleeve had seen better days, it was torn to shreds.

"Look at that, look at it!" Jess yelled in a fury. "I'm gona need to buy another leather duster, the bastard destroyed it!" She showed the rag torn sleeve to Yolanda.

"You're lucky to be alive, Jess, by the Bright you would have been dead if you had travelled alone!" Jess could see Yolanda was breathing quickly, burning off the adrenalin. Joshua was hugging Natasha while she wept against his chest. Brae had wandered off into the night making sure the wild dogs had fled.

"Wild dogs! Is this how I would have checked out!" Jess said angrily as she retrieved her bowie knife. She stabbed the dog a distasteful amount of times before she wandered back to the warmth of the low burning camp fire.

"It's dead Jess, it ain't coming back, calm down." Yolanda tried to hug Jessica but she dodged Yolanda's affections. Brae wandered back into camp.

"They're gone, everyone get some sleep I will stay on watch." He looked over at Jess who was sat near the camp fire tying some twine around her sleeve to keep it in tact.

"You okay Jess, you need bandaging?"

"Do I look okay? I've just been savaged by wild fucking dogs, yeah I'm okay!" she said sarcastically.

"Get some sleep Jess." He started to strap on his armour and sparked up a cigar using the camp fire as a light. He watched as Jessica bedded down and the young woman climbing into Jessica's bedroll, clearly the young woman had been shook up by what had just happened. *I think you have found a friend there Jess.* He chuckled.

The sun started to rise, it was the priests turn to cook breakfast and he had pretty much burnt the eggs and jerky.

"I'm not a cook!" He said in a huff. Everybody humoured him and feigned delight about his prowess at cooking camp fire meals. Jess had wandered off into the desert counting the dead dogs that had attacked the night before. She counted twelve and Yolanda had been correct, if she had been by herself she would have died that night. Natasha woke to the smell of cooked food, she pulled up her undergarments and smiled at the thought of last night sleeping with Jessica. She had never been touched by a woman before, however she thought it was fascinating how another woman could make her orgasm. Jessica had been very tender with her and even though she wasn't attracted to women, the encounter had seriously opened her eyes. She knew it would be a one night stand but she couldn't help thinking of returning the favour. When she had sex with Joshua she had many orgasms, but Jessica was leaps and bounds when it came to kissing.

"Come and get something to eat, I don't think I've ever made breakfast for you, I've done your favourite, sunny side up eggs." Joshua said with a smile.

"Eat up and then we break camp!" Brae grunted while he munched down some fried jerky strips. Everybody rushed breakfast as Jessica returned to camp.

"A small trek across the desert and I think we will hit woodland by noon, as long as we stick to the bearing." Jessica said as she pocketed her compass. They all filled there canteens from the trickle of water from the spring, it took some time.

It was a little past noon and they had a hard trek through the woodland leaving the desert behind. It was humid now and the high sun had brought sweat to every brow. Brae sniffed his armpits and pulled a face.

"Not sleeping with you tonight Brae!" Yolanda said jokingly. They all felt unwashed but it was a long way to civilisation so they had to get with it. The trees were a cross breed of pines and maple, obviously due to the raised back ground radiation which most folks took as granted.

"We aren't far now, I think me and Yolanda should scout out ahead, do you agree?" Jess said looking to Yolanda for female support. Brae muscled in.

"No, Jess and me, Yolanda protects the folks!" Yolanda nodded in agreement.

"Brae and me then." Jess preferred being with a level headed ex-ranger, she only suggested Yolanda knowing Brae would counter the selection. Brae kissed Yolanda on her cheek and whispered something that Jess couldn't hear.

"You and me again, into the fray like always." He said patting Jessica's shoulder.

"Just get on point!" Jess said chuckling.

Jess and Brae knew each other's tactics and mirrored each other's combat prowess. They had both served in the Desert Rangers and gestured with hand signals to keep stealthy. They mounted the ridge which overlooked the location. Brae snatched the binoculars from Jess's hands and peered through the lenses adjusting to his own field of vision. He knew his vision was failing as the years went by but clearly Jessica's vision was like a hawk!

"The compound gate has been blasted open, it looks like it has been scavenged long ago?" Jess shrugged and snatched the binoculars and peered.

"Yeah, but I can see sun bleached skeletons in the compound!" The building in the clearing was littered with rusted up cars and the main entrance has sand bag barricades set in a maze like formation. The building itself was grey and drab, tall with concrete walls, which was marred with bullet holes.

"No windows?" Brae curled his lip and passed the binoculars to Jess.

"Yeah I saw that, I have a feeling that this used to be a pre-war military base of some kind."

"Dunno, I don't want to go up against another automated sentry gun, I know we are getting paid, but is this shit worth our lives?" Brae had his doubts.

"It looks quite so I think this will be easy money."

"It's your call Jess, I don't want to die outside Red town!"

"let's do this! Go and gather them up." Brae

nodded and cautiously headed down the embankment to bring the others up. Jessica tried her luck by walking towards the compound gates. The sun high in the sky reflected off the shattered glass of the many rusted cars in the compound, bringing a feeling of a lost civilisation. She got to the gate which had been blasted open. *Homemade dynamite!* She thought. It wasn't long before she noticed the party of travellers had reached the battered gate.

"This is it! This is where the Utopian said he had been!" Joshua said in a flourish of arm gestures. The priest was very over excited.

CHAPTER 4

Captain Ash sat in a bleak looking office which overlooked the ranger compound below. He had half closed the shutters just enough to cast an eerie stripped shadow on the mouldy plaster walls. He had his feet up on the side of his desk and he was dressed in plain clothing, his battle worn armour had been strapped to a wooden manikin that stood in the corner of his office but he always wore his side arm on his belt. He had an athletes body apart from the growing potbellied gut that came with middle aged folks. Mid-forties or somewhere-about, he had given up counting birthdays long ago, didn't have the time to worry about how old he could really be. Fort Charleston was a semi ruined pre-war shopping mall built near the old metro station. It had been fortified and housed the 26th ranger battalion, one of the largest contingents of the desert rangers. Most of the city had been nuked during the war but the outskirts of the city were still basically intact. Ash was in charge of the desert ranger stronghold in this part of the states, his rangers protected the farmlands and towns to the south-west always alert to the threats that wandered out of the ruins. Bandits, wild dogs and creatures that he couldn't even begin to describe on a full stomach wandered from the ruins. A battered old radio hissed and squawked sat on a filing cabinet to the flank of the desk. He listened to the seemingly endless live reports coming in from the patrolling and scouting rangers, however he had trained his mind to only pluck out the reports that often lead to conflict, the rest of the reports he ignored. It was just after noon when he heard a rap at the office door.

"Don't just stand knocking boy, get your ass inside!" He barked. The door opened and Sergeant Edwards wandered in carrying a bundle of heavy looking stuff in her arms. Ash kicked his legs off the table and closed his desk draw hiding a bottle of whiskey.

"Sorry Sergeant I didn't know it was you." He said embarrassed.

"Don't worry Captain, it's not the first time I've been called boy." She laughed as she set the heavy bundle on the Captains desk.

"What's all this shit?" Ash grumbled, he didn't like untidiness especially on his desk.

"Just got back in, bin' to Grain Town securing a deal with the farmers, bastards cut our grub share again by two percent, they were harping on about the dry summer and crop lice!" She wasn't laughing anymore.

"Well we will send two percent less rangers when they are in trouble next." He said it halfheartedly because he knew the farmers have had trouble with the season harvest.

"It grinds m' to the bone, while the farmers sit on their asses waiting for shit to' grow, we still bleed out tryin' to protect them!" She pulled up a chair and sat down leaning her assault rifle against the desk. Ash noticed a bruise under her left eye.

"You had trouble Edwards?"

"Yeah had ta' re-calibrate one of the new recruits, hell they wanna be rangers but they just don't have the same kinda ideals that a ranger supposed to have!" She ruffled her face up and touched the bruise. "The grunt sucker punched me, so I broke his wrist, fucker won't do that again that's for damn sure!" She shrugged.

"Give them some time sergeant, they will soon learn the hard way! We are doing gods duty here protecting the good folks of America." He shook his head and eyed the heavy bundle on the desk.

"Food tribute is two percent down, but they made up the tribute with this stuff." She said opening the canvas bundle. Circuit boards, wires and other electrical components spilled out of the bundle and scattered on the desk. Ash performed a quick appraisal of the goods and smiled.

"Goto hand it to the farmers they know we are struggling alongside them, this stuff will come in useful." He started to paw through the salvage and picked up an old giga-counter. He cranked the charging wheel as the apparatus came on line and started clicking away reading the back ground radiation. He looked puzzled.

"Did they say where they found this shit?"

"Naa, but I recon' they have more where this came from, fuckers are holding back." She winked before

Sickle Through The Sand

taking a swig from her canteen.

"Dress down a recruit, somebody they won't recognise as a ranger, see if they can find out where they got this stuff. It's probably salvage that scavengers have traded for food but we need to make sure." He commanded. "You never know the good folks might have come across an old pre-war bunker and have kept it secret from us." He leaned back in his chair and rubbed his salt and pepper beard, his dark brown eyes were cloudy and distant in thought.

"Ya' beard is getting unruly captain, you been getting any sleep of late?" She asked concerned about the black bruises under his crow feet eyes.

"Not of late sergeant, not of late, I think I've had about three hours kip per night in the last few weeks..." He sounded pissed off but he didn't wish to vent his anger on such an asset to the rangers but fatigue was clear on his face. "Something's stirring in the ruins hadn't pinned it down yet but the patrols have been finding dead bandits in the area and a lot of them!" He paused taking a deep weary breath. "Last week a deep ruin patrol claimed the old water station had been cleared out. Gutter's bandit clan had been butchered including Gutter himself. Whatever took that stronghold out must have had some real firepower, us rangers have given them a wide berth for months!" He kicked open his desk draw and pulled out a bottle of whiskey and took a few sips before offering it to Edwards which she declined.

"The Gutter's!" She whistled and shook her head.

"They were dug in good, we would have lost good ranger lives taking that nest of shit out." The radio crackled and they both listened to the live report coming in.

"Ranger deep patrol delta, we have found something, need assistance immediately! Recommend fire mission on the old library building grid sector..." Ash rushed to the radio and picked up, from out of the window below he could see rangers rushing to the bank of four artillery guns readying the howitzers for the grid reference.

"Stand down and dig in, I am coming with Alpha squad!" He clicked the radio to another channel. "Alpha squad you have ten minutes, meet me at the compound gates!" Edwards helped Ash strap on his armour.

"You sure sir? You are strung out, let me go in your place?" She peered into his bloodshot eyes but she knew his mind was made up.

"Edwards you're in charge in my absence, the fort is yours!"

"Yes sir!" She saluted as she locked and loaded his personal M4.

Alpha squad double-timed through the labyrinth of rubble strewn streets, in their mind eye they knew they had to get to a certain point quickly but had to navigate around certain sectors to avoid conflict from lairs of mutant creatures and radioactive hot zones. Ash had made a terrible but time saving decision which took the squad though a dodgy sector. Luckily it was daylight and the flesh eating cannibals that dwelled in this sector just peered and hissed through the broken windows of pre-war utility and shop fronts. Numerous masonry and rods of rebar were thrown at the small unit rushing though their claimed patch. Special ranger Heinrich had a broken arm from one of the missile weapons that had been thrown at them. When the squad left the area the medic crunched his humorous back into place and bound the wound. She did this so quickly that the squad moved out in minutes. They passed the 'Clay and Arts' building which was still weirdly unscathed? And then headed down the ruined streets towards Delta squad.

"Captain Ash!" The squad leader said and stood to attention saluting the captain. Ash, man handled the corporal back into cover. *They maybe brave, they may be loyal but sometimes they are stupid*, he thought.

"What have you to report?" Ash said looking over the rubble to a city square where bandit humans had been impaled on exposed rebar, dead and a testament to the new threat. The Corporal looked scared and was having to calm himself down.

"The Charleston blood bandits have been..." He composed himself but his lip was still wobbling. "They have been fucked over!" Ash knew the blood bandits had a stronghold in the municipal building in the ruined city square. The rangers had tried many times to destroy them but pulled out long ago in the fear of losing too many rangers in the dire conflict. *It was my order that the rangers didn't hit this place!* He remembered the order months ago.

"We have witnessed black armoured enemies coming in and out of that building and placing more corpses on the rubble spikes." The Corporal stated through excited bursts of airborne spittle. His dust respirator was dangling off his shoulder.

"Alpha squad is here now corporal, get your squad dug in and be ready for a fire fight!" He said gripping the Corporals wrist tightly. Captain Ash pulled out a set of binoculars and started to scan the building. He watched as two humanoid figures ventured out of the building dragging another bandit corpse. The armour that the figures wore was heavy metal and didn't have servos and hydraulics like the mechanised pre-war armour that the specialist soldiers had worn? He had encountered mechanised suits before but the occupants had been long dead and picked clean to the bone by natures agents. He couldn't imagine how heavy the suits must be to wear personally, without mechanised parts? *If they are human then they are incredibly strong!* He wondered. He looked to alpha squad and had a proud feeling rushing through his core, he could see the male and female elite all focused on the target ahead. He gestured with a flurry of hand signals to alpha squad and then looked to the nervous looking scouts.

"Alpha squad are going in, Delta squad dig in and provide covering fire!" He whispered as Delta squad readied their assault rifles.

Captain Ash and his elite squad scrambled over the

rubble as delta squad opened fire on the targets in a retort of gun fire. Most of the bullets hit and bounced off the heavy armour, giving the elite squad time to target head shots. The two targets were instantly downed in a mist of blood where their heads used to be. Ash and the squad rushed to the dead armoured folk. He made another hand signal to recover one of the bodies before Alpha squad rushed inside the building using the working end of their assault rifles to guide their way into the darkness... Two of the scouts quickly recovered one of the bodies and slowly dragged the body back to the strategic position. Just before they entered the building they clicked on their under slung flash lights.

"What are we up against Captain?" Sarah of alpha squad said, as she took point her flash light flickering around inside the entrance hall.

"Not sure, but be damned sure if it moves then drop it!" Ash said bitterly. Alpha squad moved quickly into a rotunda type hall where many human bandits hung on spikes, most of which looked withered and didn't have fluids dripping from them.

"They have been drained!" Richard said as he took in the carnage. This statement reminded Captain Ash about an encounter years ago where farm folks had been drained of blood.

"Fucking drainers!" He hissed shuddering and remembering old memories. He could see one or two of the squad making old religious gestures mentioning drainers but they still seemed steadfast.

"Contact!" Richard yelled as he started firing upwards. During the mayhem of torchlight, gun fire flashes Ash looked upto the ceiling and witnessed two heavily armoured drainers crawling on the ceiling above them. He combat rolled to his flank and then emptied an entire clip into one of the drainers cascading from the ceiling. Bullet casings scattered on to the floor to his side as he heard Richard yelping like a stuck pig. He got to his feet but it was too late, Richard was on the floor with his throat torn open as the drainer ravaged his elite companion. The other drainer hit the floor dead and heavy under the weight of its armour. The other squad members picked their shots and put another one down. Angel, one of the other squad members was trying to staunch Richard's neck wound which had pooled around him.

"Fucker...Got Me..." Richard gurgled as his lungs were filling with blood. Angel was trying her best to stop the bleeding as Captain Ash gestured for her to move away. He pulled out his .357 eagle and aimed at his head.

"Sorry son!" He said as he put two rounds in his head spattering blood and cranium all over Angel.

"Noooooo!" she shrieked and was about to attack Ash but another squad member wrestled to the floor.

"If he survived he would have become one of the Undead! Believe me I have seen it!" Angel got to her feet and wiped the tears from her eyes.

"I will never forgive you Ash... Never!" She wandered away cursing. Ash reloaded a clip and after a short while, when everybody had calmed down they searched the place entirely and found no more drainers apart from lots of dead desiccated bandits. They bagged items of use, like ammo and weapons they didn't already own and then left this place for nature to take back. Ash and Angel carried Richard's body back to the fort for a proper burial.

Back at the Charleston fort, Captain Ash commanded all off duty rangers to come to the mortuary where they stood looking at the drainer corpse they had carried back. The room were congested and there was a heavy scent of body odour, conflicting with the stench of a rapidly rotting corpse. Clearly the rangers that gathered were curious, scared and religious all of a sudden.

"The alert today was brought to our attention by delta scouts. And they did right! It seems we have a new enemy spawning in the ruins, in the form of drainers!" Most of the rangers gathered took a deep audible breath.

"Got your attention then?" Ash said with a chuckle. The rangers followed suit and started to laugh.

"This is no laughing matter!" He barked suddenly changing his tone. The gathered rangers all looked sombre.

"How do you suppose I became a Desert Ranger?" He peered around the crowded room. "Let me tell you a story then..." He took a deep breath. "I was fourteen..." He laughs and points at one of the younger ranger recruits. "Just like you!" The rangers looked to the youngling and laughed.

"But jokes aside..." Ash stretched and his old bones cracked and popped.

"My Papa and my Momma owned a farm stead..." He suddenly looked grim.

"One night when the moon was high, papa and myself, had just secured the hay under tarp. It had been quite a busy day on the farm and too be honest me and my pa was whooped out. We got back to the house and ma was just dishing out stew, we had just sat down when there was a knock at the door. I remember pa frowning and gesturing to me to go and get the rifle just in case. I grabbed the old twelve gauge from above the fire place and loaded it up. Pa opened the door to a drifter feller, he was dressed in a long leather duster and had a wide brimmed cap." Ash put his head down and sighed. "I'm not going to give you the gory details to how the drifter savaged my parents... Ones thing for sure, I dropped that son-of-a-bitch, put both barrels into the fucker." He sniggered and wiped his eyes which had filled up. "You know the rest, I joined up with the desert rangers a week later." Sergeant Edwards came to his side and put her hand on his shoulder to reassure her commanding officer..

"You never told me that before Ash, I'm sorry to hear such a heart breakin' tale." The rest of the off duty rangers all bowed their heads, some of them whispered a short prayer to the Bright." Ash steeled himself and looked to the drainer corpse which was rotting quickly than a dead deer under the sun.

"You get bitten by one of these mother fuckers then you better put a bullet in your head, because if you don't, I fucking will!" He growled. One of the braver rangers stepped forward.

"Captain are entirely sure the bite is that infectious? Isn't there something we can do?" Ash looked at the young ranger, he barely had hair above his lip.

"Not sure son, but I've seen folks come back from death, maybe not everybody turns but I don't wish to roll a dice on those odds. From personal experience I've always put them down." He looked to Thomas the scribe who was stood at the back of the room.

"Thomas, get your paper and pens out and document this abomination, find out as much as you can from this devils cock sucker!"

Morning had come quickly, Thomas had been up all night studying the drainer corpse. The corpse had rotted down so fast that there were just a bloodied skeleton and a lot of mush on the table and on the floor. He had covered his nose and mouth with a scarf due to the stench. He had removed the heavy plate armour and hung them on a wooden armour manikin which he had borrowed from the firing range. He rubbed his eyes and noticed how shadowed the room was, due to sleep deprivation.

"What is this symbol, I somehow remember it from somewhere?" He said to himself trying to jolt his memory. He walked to the suit of armour and traced his fingers around the red hammer and sickle motif on the dull black armour. His eyes grew wide when he remembered the symbol. He grabbed his jacket and rushed off across the parade ground to the out building where he kept his laboratory.

"It's here somewhere!" He said in a flurry, while he searched through his extensive bookshelf. He grabbed up a book 'Joseph Stalin on Chinese revolution' and on one of the worm eaten pages he focused on the symbol.

"Russia!" He said as he howled laughing. His mind was racing! He remembered seeing this symbol on American propaganda posters in underground subways. His blood was boiling in his veins and he suddenly stopped reading and looked to the cracked plaster ceiling. *This doesn't make sense?*

"Russian drainers?" He laughed so hard that he started to choke and cough. After coughing and spluttering he managed to sit down under the weight of his theories.

"Ash needs to hear this!" He finally whispered.

"So you're saying we are still at war with the Soviet Union?" Ash chuckled. Thomas frowned trying to get his point across to the captain.

"Too be honest I don't really know? Maybe these Soviet drainers are an expeditionary force of some kind? Maybe remnants of the post nuclear war, The USSR really laid waste to America! Maybe they are still acting on pre-war operations, or maybe they have just arrived and Russia isn't as devastated as we all thought?" Ash was still laughing.

"I'm sorry Thomas but it all seems a bit far-fetched. America to my knowledge still has no infrastructure, nor a government!" Ash said as his mind calculated the probability.

"A drainer would be the perfect soldier! They could walk casually across a radioactive wasteland and suffer no ill effects. I'm not an expert on the undead but in theory it's very possible?" Thomas was still fighting with his own mind about the theory. He had read Ash's mission notes when they encountered drainers a few years back on Hazy farm.

"I'm sorry to bring it up, but you yourself claimed drainers regenerate quickly, so their metabolism could absorb damaged cells." He said as he watched Ash's face sag.

"I can't believe you have brought up Hazy farm!" Ash said angrily. "We lost three good rangers putting down the undead I barely got out of there alive!" Anger had turned to furious anger. Thomas carefully picked his next words.

"I have read the mission notes and you were the only survivor and the people at the farm perished. But I suspect that drainers in the Ashland originated from a Russian project, hell they could have sent the undead before the bombs even fell, that would explain the drainer that..." Ash interrupted the doctors flurry of words.

"Killed my parents, is that what you was going to

say?" Ash's face was red with fury.

"Yes..." The scribe said avoiding Ash's piercing stare.

"Bullshit!" Ash levelled his finger to the door. "Get the fuck out and take your theories with you!" Thomas quickly gathered up his note papers and left the captains office as quickly as he could muster. Ash uncorked a bottle of whiskey and chugged about four shots worth. He felt the burning liqueur gush down his throat agitating his oesophagus, he coughed, his saliva glands worked over time and he nearly threw up his breakfast. However the doctor's words had got him thinking, the drainer that killed his parents must have already been in America. *Although could a drainer be a side effect of intense radiation, born of the bomb so to speak?*

Ash wandered across the compound watching the new recruits performing target practice under the ever watchful eye of sergeant Edwards. He came to her side as she roughly snatched the rifle out of a recruit's hand.

"You need to root yourself boy!" She barked as she kicked his feet into a steady firing stance. "Aim down the rifle and take a deep breath before you squeeze the trigger!" She barked. The new recruit was flushed and grabbed the M1 Garand rifle and did has he was tutored. The rifle retorted and the old U.S army helmet pinged off the target manikin. The sergeant clapped in applause.

"That's how you do it boy!" She hadn't seen the

captain come to her side.

"How the new recruits holding out sergeant?" Edwards craned her neck to look at the captain.

"Doin' fine Captain, just need to drum some sense into these fucks!"

"Good to hear." He smiled and shoulder bumped the sergeant as her cheeks flushed with blood.

"There going to make damn fine rangers sir!" She said as she watched young Lucy refilling the ammo boxes behind the firing range. Ash dropped to his knees in front of the young girl wearing a tattered old floral dress.

"And how are you doing Lucy? Has the sergeant kept you busy?" The young girl placed down a number of rifle clips and then stood to attention.

"Doing fine Captain!" She said while she saluted. Ash stood up and patted the sergeant on her back.

"Make sure young Lucy here gets a taste of that honey pot that the farmers sent up, give her double rations she deserves it." He said in a fatherly manner. Edwards smiled at the kid and nodded. "Will do Captain!" The girl grinned and then went back to work refilling the ammo for the target practice.

"How's the 30-06 ammo standing?" Ash asked, even though he knew they had shit loads in the ranger ammo dump.

"Lots of ammo captain, especially after we raided that old U.S army depot, still going strong sir!" She issued with a salute. The rangers practiced with old army surplus ammo and tended not to use 5.56mm ammo which fed the standard ranger M4 rifles, which they also accumulated when the rangers were out on scavenging missions. Every so often Ash heard the 'ping' of a range rifle depleted. The three ranger technicians collected the spent brass casings after target practice and refilled them in the firearm laboratory on the second floor of Charleston fort. They also found a shit load of gun powder at the U.S army depot, along with a massive amount of 5.56mm NATO standard rounds of ammunition.

Captain Ash watched as the food caravan rolled into the compound burdened with fresh corn, grain, preserved pig meat, vegetables and silver dollars. He personally inspected the shipment of tribute and his heart sagged.

"You're running short?" He knew the shipment would be lighter due to the poor harvest but it seemed the merchants were taking the piss.

"Another shipment will arrive tomorrow, this is all we could spare! We will starve otherwise!" The merchant said with a frown. "However we have acquired a shipment of 5.56 ammunition." He said uncovering an ammo case brimming with dusty old bullets.

"I hope you will still protect out farmsteads and villages, even though we are light on our harvest." Ash nodded seeing the stash of ammo the merchant unveiled.

"We will continue to protect you, but we need

food to feed the rangers!"

"Like I have already said, a wagon of root vegetables will arrive tomorrow, please continue our pact." The nervous and well fed merchant said. Sergeant Edwards appraised the wares and frowned.

"Where did the scavengers find so much ammo?" Ash tried his best to calm the sergeant down but he was already thinking in the same line of thought.

"The scavengers must have found a pre-war army depot, if you point it on a map we will go there in force!"

"We traded the bullets for food, the scavengers didn't mark any map location!" The merchant pleaded. Edwards was just about to punch the merchant until Ash stepped in front of her.

"Food shipment tomorrow or the rangers will leave you to the marauding bandits, is that clear?"

"Root vegetables and pumpkins arrive tomorrow, you have my word!" The merchant cried as he fell to his knees praying to the Bright. The off-duty rangers started to unload the bovine pulled wagons. The merchants disbanded from the caravan and took up lodgings in the ranger compound. As always the merchants brought strong liquor which satisfied the enlisted rangers. Ash knew there would be a party that night...

Sergeant Edwards staggered into the captain's office, she had a half drunken bottle of corn moon shine and gave a fully corked bottle to the captain. They could both hear the rangers having a booze laden party in the compound below.

"Is this wise?" He said as he used his teeth to uncork the rotgut.

"Allow them to blow off some steam!" She said as she staggered around trying to find a seat.

"Yeah you're right, it's been a month since they enjoyed themselves, but we still have to remain steadfast and alert!"

"I got you're back captain." She slurred as she staggered towards the office door. Ash chuckled for a while at the strength in her words, but he had his doubts, *if drainers have come to the ruins then this entire sector is fucked.*

CHAPTER 5

"We must go in Jessica, we cannot wait! We must find what the utopian has left for us." Joshua harped on like one of his sermons on Sunday morning. Brae had spotted the sun bleached skeletons in the main compound about fifty-foot from the main entrance.

"Jess what about th..."

"I've seen them, so what! Bleached bones, we see them all the time on every trail in every pre-war ruin." She interrupted.

"It's your call Jess?" He said still having doubts. Jess narrowed her eyes and stared at the bleached bones, the bones were scattered around, but that was normal due to wild animals feasting on flesh. But now Brae had put a hex on the situation she had her doubts too. Joshua could see the reservations on the gun-slingers faces and tried to remedy the state of affairs.

"I order you to continue, I have paid good coin and there is more to come on completion."

"You can order all you damned well like preacher! We hold position until we are certain." Jess hissed as she continued to evaluate the compound. The preacher was flustered and red faced with anger. He didn't like taking orders from piss-ant gun hands. *I'm the leader! I give the orders!* He could feel his heart hammering away and his blood felt like it was on fire.

"Come on everybody, there is no danger here, now come on!" He cried as he shouldered his pack and started to march into the compound like some kind of revolutionary. Natasha looked towards Jessica who had already started to laugh at the pathetic command. She was torn between staying with Jess or following Joshua who was still marching ahead through the mass of flanking rusty cars. Jessica noticed two small building segments articulating on the building, followed by two heavy auto-guns rising from manifolds below. The guns tracked the motion in the compound and opened fire. Brae quickly grabbed Natasha and threw her roughly behind the cover of the rusty cars as the others scrambled for cover. The din of the machine guns rudely broke the silence of the compound shaking them all from normality. Car windows and metal shards exploded all around them as the guns retorted in a sustained hail of hot lead.

"I fucking knew it! What the fuck Jess!" Brae yelled over the din. His face was pale and his eyes were wide in panic and remembrance of memories of robotic killing machines. Jessica's teeth were bared in the face of a wide grin, she could feel the adrenalin racing through her veins and her body cried for conflict.

"Oh yeah!" She howled as another volley of gun fire ripped up the numerous cars. Yolanda had unfolded the bipod below her rifle as she locked and loaded her high calibre sniper system. Jess could see the preacher cowering behind a busted old truck about forty feet up in the compound.

"Everybody stay put and don't make a sound! These bastards go off motion and sound." Jessica yelled before she covered her mouth from laughing out loud. The auto-guns had stopped firing and had shifted into search mode, even from cover they could hear the servos of the deadly machines working overtime trying to lock in on a target. Yolanda moved very slowly as she levelled her rifle out of cover, the bipod gained purchase on the bonnet of an old roadster.

"You got the shot Yo?" Jess whispered as Yolanda nodded slowly and waited for the command to shoot.

"Aim at the ammo belts!" She said, as Yolanda slightly shifted her target.
Jess looked to Brae who had his back to a car nursing his rifle in his lap. His dark hair was drenched in fresh panic born sweat.

"Brae, give me your rifle, I'm gona outflank!" Jess whispered. Brae looked to his rifle as though it was his own pet dog but he finally nodded and tossed the rifle into Jessica's hands. Jess started to crawl westwards using the available cover as she kept an eye on the auto-guns scanning for targets. As she crawled past Brae she said "Keep out of sight but get ready to bang on the car." Brae agreed and wiped the sweat from his brow, his eyes were glazed and distant, full of anxiety. When Jess got into position she did like Yolanda had done before and moved very slowly to take aim over the bonnet of a chunky looking pickup truck. She took a deep steadying breath.

"Distraction!" Jess yelled as Brae whacked the car

behind him. The two auto-guns first swivelled to Jessica's yell and then to the loud thump on the car.

"Fire Yo!" Jess yelled as she squeezed the trigger. The auto-guns started to fire again ripping up more cars and shattering windshields. The two rifle bullets must have hit home because the rapid auto-gun fire suddenly stopped, they had deftly jammed the bullet belts. A continuous clicking sounded from the robotic guns but no bullets were expelled from the steaming hot gun barrels. They waited a while behind cover as the clicking stopped. A yellow flashing rotating light came on line near the main entrance as the auto-guns descended into the buildings gun housings. The segments of the building articulated again hiding the dangerous auto-security. Jess wandered over to Brae and tossed the rifle back into his lap, she gave a thumbs up to Yolanda who waved back.

"I think we fucked 'em!" She said as she frowned at the alarm light rotating above the main entrance.

"Well done Yolanda!" She grinned as she watched the female sniper folding away the rifle bipod. She looked to the preacher who was still in a foetal position.

"You okay preacher?" She yelled trying to stifle a chuckle.

"Are they gone?" He mumbled as he peered around the side of the truck. He had his shotgun out shaking in his hand.

"Yeah, all done, but we must move quickly, the auto-guns have survived intact this long, maybe they have some kind of auto-repair system which might be going on as we speak?" Jess lied, as she tried to keep everybody on their toes.

The main entrance had old blast stains on the metal bulk heads which stood a jar. The party of looters were gathered around the entrance peering at the darkness inside the building.

"You think it's safe to enter?" Joshua asked, the previous bravado and leadership had been torn from the tone of his voice.

"Okay, so I'm the leader again?" Jess mocked as the preachers cheeks flushed with blood. Joshua mumbled a few curses under his breath which Jessica ignored. Natasha was still a little shook up, but Yolanda calmed her down with soothing words.

"Right, everybody get your light sources at hand and follow me!" Jess said as she strapped on a flash light to the armoured section of her left shoulder, once secured she un-holstered her twin 1911's. The others lit oil lanterns or turned on their own flash lights. Brae started to hand crack a wind up torch which seemed to take forever, but finally once charged he attached it to his rifle.

"Ready Jess." He said almost embarrassed about the performance. But before they started to enter Joshua planted a hand on Jessica's shoulder.

"How did the utopian get in here with those robotic abominations outside?"

"How the fuck should I know, maybe this 'Utopian' is one of those sun bleached bones in the compound?"

She shrugged his hand from her shoulder and pointed to the bones.

"But, one thing's for sure, those explosive blast marks on the bulk head doors tell me that some fucker made it this far." She said sarcastically. "Maybe your utopian friend had a security transponder that negated the security systems?"

"Jess is correct, when we ran with the rangers long ago we were issued with transponder cards that we wore on our armour. We accessed a similar pre-war depot's using the chip-set cards." Brae said recalling old memories. "The security cards must make the old systems stand down or something." Jessica started to get angry.

"Look your coin is good preacher! Let's find out what your utopian shit stain was doing in this pre-war installation!"

Jessica lead the way into the darkness of the building and the party of looters followed into a large hall like structure where many metal cases were piled high. Having scanned her torch light around inside, she had made up her mind.

"Looks like the occupants of the building were gathering up to leave!" She mumbled, not really wishing for the others to back up her theory. She looked to the many skeletons on the floor with tattered clothing, some still clutching army issue M16 rifles. She picked up one of the matt-black rifles and un-clipped the magazine.

"The dry climate has preserved this stuff, a bit of T.L.C and maybe some oil I recon these weapons could be used once again." She dropped the rifle to the ground and moved on to another metal crate.

"The ammo looks intact so I suggest field stripping this place." The party started to ransack the room, busting open crates and whooping when they found something that they could use. Yolanda found numerous crates full of canned food, the sell by dates were clearly out but the average Ash-lander knew tinned food stayed preserved. She personally bagged a number of tinned peaches. Jess found a several crates of LAW Rockets, she strapped one to her back pack. Having been a desert ranger she knew what this piece of equipment could do to a foe. Meanwhile Joshua was getting more and more angry.

"This stash of equipment and weapons is all very good, but we need to push on and find the path of the utopian!" He hailed as though he was the leader again, but they ignored him and continued the search through the stacks of equipment.

"Jess we are rich!" Brae sputtered in excitement. "We need to make a deal with a merchant caravan to collect this shit, we could retire!"

"We still can my friend, but we need to finish our contract with the preacher!" She could see her old friend fighting against the idea but finally he deflated.

"We can do both, but this utopian is intriguing me as well!" Jess stated and patted his shoulder, as she would to an excited heel hound.

"Too be honest Jess, I'm also intrigued by this legendary utopian feller…" He sighed. "So let's fulfil our contract to the preacher."

"Agreed!" Jess said before hugging the gun fighter.

The looters made a quick sweep of the area and found numerous doors, some were locked tight but other doors opened up into metallic corridors.

"I wonder why the occupants were leaving in such a hurry, hell they all died here, trapped in the main hall?" Yolanda said pondering.

"The main entrance may have been locked down, not sure why?" Jess assumed wondering herself. "Clearly they didn't starve to death having found all the canned water and food in those crates?"

"Maybe they ran out of air, sealed in or something?" Joshua decided. "The bones were in tact and no signs of melee or gun fire."

"Or disease?" Jessica said with a grimace. She wished she hadn't said that because the others were now thinking she could be correct.

"Look, let's just find this utopian thing and then get the fuck out of here!" She gestured to another corridor which had more side rooms, some of which had more crates obviously brought up here from an underground central store.

"This place must have been a place to ride out the nuclear war or something?" Brae said and gulped back some bile. With the mention of nuclear war, Joshua quickly ransacked his back pack and pulled out a giga-counter. He turned it on but it had no power.

"Fucking merchants jipped me!" He cried ready to throw the device against a nearby wall. Brae grabbed his wrist and explained that you had to crank the dynamo-wheel to build up a charge. Everybody laughed remembering Brae charging up his flash light. They waited for several minutes as Brae cranked a charge in the device.

"Here." He said rubbing his right arm from the exercise of winding up the device. Joshua turned the giga-counter on and it started to click away and it wasn't a back ground radiation kind of tick-tock ether.

"We can't stay here long, let's quickly locate this utopian thing and then get out of here before we don't have to take a lantern to take a piss in the dark!" Jess said with haste. Everybody agreed.

"This is the room the utopian described!" Joshua said dribbling foam at the corner of his mouth. The room was circular and in the centre was a reclining padded chair. Strange metal shiny spherical orbs protruded from the cylindrical metallic walls. Nobody dared to lie down on the chair, just in case something weird happened?

"The utopian came here! He lay on this bed!" The preacher said as he pawed the cushioned recliner.

"You're not really going to..." Jess sighed. As, Joshua leaped on to the recliner in a fit and frenzy religious bravado. Jessica frowned and noticed a battered old journal of some kind. She snatched it up as a bank of curved lights started to flicker into illumination. Brae grabbed her shoulder and pulled her out of the cylindrical room which started to arc with lightning. The party backed off covering their eyes from the arcs of electricity crackling and striking the chair like a summer desert storm. The preacher grabbed up some kind of metal helmet at the top of the bed and donned it like a crown of old. The illumination started to strobe, slow at first but it gathered up momentum until it was some kind of continual flashing light.

"I can see it..." Joshua started to breath, heavily at first as the arcs of electric picked up tempo.

"I see vast cities, cities constructed by man, as far as the eye can see..."

"I see automobiles and street lights, so many, too many to count..."

"I see flying objects coming into land, a field of guiding lights..." The others had retreated down the metallic corridor covering their eyes but they could hear the words almost augmented in their ears as they backed away from the intense light.

"Something's wrong, I see flying objects like the wing span of a bird, they are dropping dark objects and behind them I see other things, rockets falling from the skies..."

"Bombs, so many are falling from the flying objects, they are..."

"Too bright and it's thunderous, the rockets are burnt out now and falling, they are going to hit the city..."

"By the Bright! I see the most powerful illumination that I have ever seen, intense light, hotter than the sun! Flashes in the sky above the city. Buildings are falling and mankind is burning!" Joshua's heart rate and breathing only came in panic waves.

"The light is now a reddish glow, almost seconds... Is this how Mankind checked out?" His breathing is still in the throws of panic and anxiety.

"Darkness... A true darkness, no moon light, no nothing, just a void..." The cylindrical room fell into darkness. The preacher was silent for a while before vomiting over the side of the chair. Brae checked the giga-counter again, "Seems to be more radiation down here than the main chamber, we need to get the fuck out of here." Jess leaned over and watched the needle on the device tick away.

"Seen worse than that Brae! I've seen one of those bastards reading up in the red."

"Yeah but we had protective suits back then Jess!" Jess pursed her lips and nodded. "Good point, lets bounce!" She cupped her mouth with her hand and yelled down the corridor to the preacher. "We have to go now preacher!" He staggered down the corridor as though he were pissed, all the while he held his head as though he had a terrible headache.

"I've got a bastard headache!" He whined.

"Well you will sit on weird chairs in flashing rooms! I had odds on you not getting out of that light show alive!" Jess said shouldering his arm.

They arrived back in the main chamber full of skeletons and crates, already Brae was having a quick loot around before leaving.

"Best grab what you can carry, we ain't coming back any time soon." Jess reasoned. The others made a final sweep of the room, grabbing up ammo clips and bits of equipment small enough to carry, but also looked expensive to a merchants greedy eye. The preacher threw up again before they were done looting.

"Splitting it three ways this time Jess!" Brae growled referring to the stash of stuff. "We head back to town and round up some folks with wagons, then we come back here and collect the rest of this stuff, we are gona be rich Jess!" He was grinning like a kid with an icing topped cupcake.

"Split it up however you want Brae, I'm thinking of heading out. When I was back in Red town last I heard rumours of some heavy bounties up north, might try my luck up there." She patted Braes shoulder. He looked hurt and he shook his head.

"You gone fucking nuts Jess?" Brae tried to reason with her. "With this cut of the winnings you could buy a bar in Red town, settle down... You might even have enough to buy some whores to get down and dirty with in your retirement."

"That would be nice..." She said dreamily. "But, I'm an open road gal, the boredom would happen kill me, I just can't see myself sitting by a fire hearth with my pistols nailed up on the wall." Brae noticed the lantern fire catch her murderous green eyes and saw the truth in her words.

"When will that empty pit of a soul you have, be satisfied with enough killing?" He grimaced with disgust.

"The day my pistols have nothing left to snuff out." She countered with a wicked grin. With the talk of sharing out loot, Joshua wanted in on the bounty.

"The church of the bright will want a share of this too." Brae eyed the preacher and looked him up and down as though he was a steaming pile of shit.

"Me and Yolanda ain't sharing squat with you or your fucked up church preacher, when you pay us up full you can go back to your church and count your patrons. The contract will be through." Brae hissed and shoulder barged the preacher out of the pecking circle. He stopped and rounded on Jess again pointing a rough handed finger.

"And we are through too Jess, I hope one day when you're lying face down in the dirt, that you remember this day and our offer." With that said he grabbed up a tarp bag full of M16 rifles and started towards the exit. Natasha and the preacher grabbed up their loot bags as Yolanda shoulder bumped Jessica in a companion kind of way.

"You sure my friend, we could all sink our money into property and live out our days in Red town, stinking rich with no worries." Jess didn't wish to decline, she knew how persuasive Yolanda could be.

"I will think about it, now let's get this preacher and his whore back to red town alive so we can get paid."

They covered their eyes to the burning sun when they exited from the darkness of the depot building. They snuffed out lanterns and packed away torches as the unforgiving sun lifted heat trails from the numerous cars in the compound. They noticed the sentry guns hadn't reappeared so assumed they were either fucked or still being repaired by auto-systems. Jessica lead the way down the long drive way towards the busted gate, the numerous cars flanked her on both sides as the others picked up pace behind her.

"We heard those 'fifties' from miles out, we all wondered if somebody had finally got past those robot guns. We have sharp shooters so don't even think about going for your guns." A guttered voice issued from somewhere in the labyrinth of rusted automobiles. Jessica stopped dead and scanned around trying to locate the voice she recognised, but couldn't quite recall his voice. She also noticed two sun shining rifle scopes two o clock and ten o clock. *It seems they do have sharp shooters.*

"Well I will be damned! Is that you Jess?" The man laughed. A group of heavily armed folk started to fan out from behind cars in front of them. Jess sighed as she finally recalled the voice. Unfortunately the sun was in here eyes so she couldn't just make out the leaders face.

"How you been keeping William?" She said with bile in her throat knowing the situation was going to turn out bad. She deftly palmed a grenade from her gun belt and put her hand behind her back signaling to Brae and Yolanda. The grenades pin was out and around her thumb like some kind of fucked up wedding ring. She held firmly to the arming clasp ready to throw at a moment's notice.

"My names Bill, you know I hate being called William..." The leader growled as his heel hounds locked and loaded as though punctuating his words. They must also know that he had an angry tick when it came to calling him by his real name.

"You know these brigands?" Joshua said with fear in his voice.

"Yep, I know these fucks!" She half whispered in the direction of the preacher.

"Well it's been a long time no-see Jessica, when did we part last, can you recall?" The leader said with an angry facial twitch.

"Let me think now..." Jess paused long enough to add impatience to the fray. "Well it would have been the time when I left you to rot in the desert. Guess you were pissed that I took your share of the loot too." She said sarcastically.

"That's right, you left me for dead... But I survived bitch! Took me over a week to crawl out of that desert." Bill's eyes were narrow remembering the betrayal. "You didn't leave me much water either did you?"

"Nope, but you clearly are a tough cookie Bill, all's well that ended well, it seems." She said cursing the day by not putting a mercy killing round between his eyes. *Getting sloppy Jess*, she thought.

"Who are these people?" The preacher demanded in confusion. Brae punched the preacher softly in the ribs and whispered to him to shut up!

"So I'm guessing you found quite a haul in there judging by the laden bags. So, If you could all be so kind, just drop the shit and we will let you all go peacefully." Bill lied.

"That's not going to happen Bill you know that, besides which you will kill us anyway, so if we all go down here then we will all go down guns blazing. However, and hear me out." She squinted trying to read Bill's face. "There is plenty more inside, enough for your gang to get rich!" She waited for her words to sink in.

"Let us all go on our merry way and you can loot the shit out of the depot, nobody needs to die... But I promise you, if it comes to dying Bill, then you will be the first to eat dirt!" She said this with calm and matter-of-factly. Some of the brighter brigands saw sense in this and looked to Bill for solace, the others however were braying for blood and combat. Jessica could see the conflict working in Bill's mind, on one hand he would live and be rich and on the other hemisphere he could get rich and revenge providing he survived this encounter. But it didn't matter a shit, Jessica had already made up her mind. *I'm gona kill all you fucks!* She loosed the grenade while Bill was still contemplating; as soon as she threw the grenade Brae's shoulders sagged. The grenade bounced and then lifted from the ground bounced again and then rolled in almost slow motion and came to a stop ten feet from the gang of brigands. The grenade exploded kicking up dust, rocks and shrapnel, knocking most of the brigands to the ground in a rush of expelling hot fiery air. Jessica's 1911's were out and laying down covering fire as she combat rolled behind cover. The others had covered their ears due to the explosive retort and also rushed into cover.

The dust settled and several brigands (including Bill) crawled into cover behind the rusty cars, leaving several dead from concussion, airborne shrapnel wounds and a number of well-placed bullets from Jessica's pistols. The years of silence in this compound had been quickly converted into an angry exchange of live rounds.

"I'm going to kill you Jessica you bitch!" Bill cried in pain. He tried to hold his revolver correctly but noticed he was missing a finger and the other fingers were covered in blood and seemed not to work properly. His eyes were stinging and he tried to wipe blood from his eyes which was cascading down his scalp from a laceration on his forehead. "Fucking bitch!" He yelled as he heard more gun fire exchanging around him.

"We need to fire randomly to keep this position!" Brae cried over the gun fire as he watched Jessica rush left with her head down. "Jess is going to out flank them, just shoot, with anything you have!" Yolanda had her bipod out again and was shooting randomly over the bonnet of a car. Natasha and Joshua even though was shell shocked they did as Brae commanded and started to wild fire in the vain attempt to keep the enemies heads in cover. Brae rushed right and picked up position from the main group under heavy fire. Joshua had emptied his shotgun and was reloading as Natasha fired round after round from her revolver, not aiming at anything. Jessica had managed to circle around the brigands and was now shooting at the enemy flank. They could hear screams of pain and death somewhere down the rows of cars. Brae had also outflanked the enemy and started to fire at the angle, the enemy sharp shooters had already dived into cover due to the multiple angles that the bullets came from.

"By the bright gather up!" Bill said in vain, the blood from his wound had blinded him as he scrambled around in the dirt trying to find his gun that he had dropped. He could hear some of his brethren yelling in pain and sobs. He tried to ignore their doomed plights.

"I'm hit, I'm bleeding!"

"Please get my momma!"

"I can't see I'm blind!" Bill tried to manage the situation but he couldn't see shit either. "Pull yourselves together!" He cried as his ears rang with an up-tempo of his own heartbeat. He felt dizzy and the back ground noise was just a buzzing sound like an un-tuned radio.

"I will kill you Jess!" He cursed trying to get his breath back. He felt viscous fluids dribbling on to his busted up hand. He laughed and finally laid down face first in the dirt. He could hear less gun fire now but more weeping from his gang members. He tried with all his strength to lift himself up but his elbows buckled and his head pounded with pain. He settled down again to the dirt as something heavy slumped upon him.

"Boss... You... Okay... Ma..." He recognised the voice to be Hanz his right hand man and body guard. He felt the weight of his body guard grow heavier on his back and then felt fluids dribble down the back of his neck.

"Hanz? Please?" He whispered but the buzzing in his head was so loud he couldn't hear his own voice. The void came fast, the buzzing sound faded and he felt his body lighten.

"Let me see the son-of-a-bitch!" Jessica said biting back some of the anger she felt for this human being. Brae and Yolanda pulled away the corpse that was protecting Bill.

"Yeah, that's Bill!" She said with a grin, as she reloading one of her pistols. Jessica put the muzzle against the back of Bills head and he stirred a little and mumbled something.

"Fuckers still alive!" She backed off a little in alarm.

"Violent Bill is worth more to the people if we take him back for justice?" Brae said but noticed the rage of Jessica's face.

"I have already made that mistake once! I don't want to make the same mistake again!" Brae nodded and backed off as Jessica double tapped the back of Bills head. Blood spattered over Jessica's frowning face, she wiped away the blood on the sleeve of her leather duster.

"Jess, we would have been killed unless you evened up the odds with that grenade." Jessica nodded and together they gathered everybody and set off back to Red town.

Numerous days passed and the travellers reached Red town. The gun hands were paid in full as promised. The next day Brae was organising folks with wagon carts to take the trip back to the depot to secure the sizable stash of stuff on offer. Jessica made a bee-line for Roody's whore house to get her mind blitzed with alcohol and get her rocks off with the many hands of prostitutes. Due to the previous adventure Joshua and Natasha became ever-more closer, to the point where Joshua mentioned marriage. Later on that week Jessica traded the journal she found in the cylindrical room with Joshua, he moaned at the amount of coin she asked for it, but he begrudgingly paid her price. He was very eager to learn more about this so called Utopian man, he had the glimpse on the machine but he had so many questions he needed answering.

Brae and Yolanda spent a number of days tracking down free-lance merchants who owned sizable carts to make the trip back to the depot. It took a lot of negotiation before they finally had a party to make the trip. Meanwhile Jessica spent her hard earned cash on whores and hard liquor. She was clearly living it up for a while. A gun fighters holiday or sometimes called a 'respite'. She didn't think about her future even though her friends were securing some kind of future, a retirement so to speak.

CHAPTER 6

The sun started to crescent over the ruined city bringing with it a cool morning breeze. Captain Ash stood on the parapet of the fort overlooking the stockades in front of the fortified gate entrance. Sergeant Edwards ascended the make shift stair upto the parapet cautiously carrying a large mug of coffee, although she had spilt a great deal of the brew. She handed the mug to the captain while her eyes appraised the reddish sun.

"Thanks." Ash grunted not really paying attention to the kind gesture. Edwards linked her arm with his in a friendly companion way, which made Ash lean closer to her.

"I had a nightmare last night, a very vivid one at that." She waited for more words to follow and when they didn't she prompted him with an elbow nudge.

"Nightmare... So spill the beans?" She said. Ash chuckled and rubbed his eyes.

"Pretty fucked up really, dreamt the soviet drianers attacked the fort killing everybody, including me. I must have been floating as a spirit towards the back end of the dream when the Russian flag were pulled up the forts flag pole." He looked over his shoulder seeing the desert ranger flag fluttering on the breeze, just to reassure himself it was just a very bad dream.

"That's a ridiculous dream Captain, they would have a hard time taken us down but if we are over run, every single ranger will die fighting." The emotion in her face was clear but her tone was calm. Ash chuckled as he watched a group of rangers practising martial arts in the courtyard below.

"I have no doubt sergeant, no doubt at all, we would be back to back unleashing hell upon anything that tries to fuck with us." The sun was casting rays of light through the fissures in the ruined buildings of the pre-war city. It appeared peaceful and threatening at the same time, the creatures and bandits that lurked in the ruins were an ever present threat to civilization and mankind. He took a sip of the strong coffee which tasted gritty and full of crushed beans. The radio on Edwards belt crackled.

"Ranger team Charlie, we are holed up in the old Orange business building."

"What are you doing so deep in the ruins?" Ash asked with astonishment.

"Three AM, we followed a group of deer into the ruins, hoping to bag a couple, when we came across a large group of heavily armed soldiers. The black armour and motif is the same as the drainers you encountered." The ranger spluttered with an edge of anxiety in his voice.

"Calm down. Where are they now?"

"They are gathering in the car lot of the Ford factory, they are in great numbers, probably about one hundred maybe more.."

"Get back to the fort immediately and that's an order, leave no trace!" Ash's face had paled, *could this be our end?* Edwards had already set off running to organise the rangers.

"Wait... More are arriving sir." The ranger claimed.

"By the bright, how many corporal?" There was a long pause.

"Too many sir, we are coming back now!" The radio clicked and hissed into static. Ash's mind raced, *was my nightmare a warning?* He knew the howitzers didn't have the range that far into the ruins. He looked to the courtyard where angry nightshift rangers had been woken up and gathering up in formation, some only wore shorts and vests. Sergeant Edwards was still rallying everybody in the fort, including the cooks and servants. Ash quickly calculated the odds, he had a standing force around seventy rangers including auxiliaries. If the soviets came in mass the fortifications wouldn't hold, especially how the drainers ignored physics and could scramble up walls as though it was open ground. He just thanked the bright that Edwards didn't sound the alarm which would echo into the ruins. He quickly rushed down the stairs into the courtyard where everybody was gathered.

"We have a situation..." He sighed trying to fathom out the words to say without using the words 'we are fucked'. The rangers stood to attention and saluted, with a thumping sound from their boots.

"Charlie team is on their way back, E.T.A fifty five minutes if they rush and not attacked by abominations in the ruins." He looked at the brave faces of the rangers as his eyes filled up.

"The soviets are assembling en-mass, I have an inkling that the drainers we killed might leave a trail back to the fort." One of the corporals stepped forward and saluted.

"The fort stands stout sir! Everybody is ready and bolstered for combat!"

"You all need to be combat ready!" He looked to his sergeant. "Break out the pep-pills, it's going to be a long day and night!" Edwards nodded and glared at the resident fort doctor, Thomas nodded and began to head back to his surgery to ration out the amphetamines.

"We need everybody in combat shape. Now move your asses and get locked and loaded." Ash yelled as though it was some kind of speech from a pre-war movie. The rangers scrambled to the armoury, armed themselves and suited up in heavy armour.

By midday all the personnel of the fort had manned the parapets armed to the teeth. The artillery engineers had loaded the howitzers and filled the shell dump nearby the big guns, ready to reload. Ash spent about an hour checking the ranger's firearms and pep talking to bolster their bravery. The strong amphetamine pills previously administered, were rushing through the ranger's bloodstreams giving them an extra focused edge. Ash himself had an assault rifle slung over his shoulder and the leather holster on his gun belt was un-strapped with a .357 eagle begging to come out and play. Ash approached Angel one of his elite rangers, she noticed his presence as she readjusted her sniper system scope trying to ignore him.

"How you holding up Angel?"

"Still pretty pissed off with you putting two rounds into my companion's skull, but apart from that I'm steadfast!" She said with an unforgiving tone.

"Had to be done, but we are all sorry to lose an elite ranger like Richard's."

"Whatever you say captain, you are the leader and we are but grunts!" She said bitterly, trying not to recall the memory of her companion's blood spattered on her face.

"He would have turned into one of those undead mother fuckers, I had to make the choice, I can't allow my rangers to be compromised!" He tried to keep his tone calm.

"Just maybe, we could have saved him, I don't know shit about drainers I will admit, but there must have been something we could do?" She whispered and readjusted the sight on her rifle.

"Couldn't take the chance, you know that?" He finally said shrugging his shoulders.

"Well tell that to his wife and kids!" She spat. Ash knew he wouldn't be able to console her. Making a decision was one of those things you had to deal with being a leader, even though the decision you choose could have dire consequences among the fighting force, its shit like that only a leader had to deal with. He looked into her ice blue wolf like eyes and witnessed the hatred shining like an unforgiving light.

"I will be loyal for the cause Captain, but I will be the first to put a bullet in your head when you turn!" She whispered with revenge in her tone.

"Save the bullet and see what nightmare it could be when I turn into the undead and start ripping up everybody you know and love!" He huffed before heading back to his office. As he walked away he realised he shouldn't have said such a thing.

Ash sat in his private office. He palmed an amphetamine pill for a while, just staring at it. He reached to his desk draw and pulled out an unbranded farmers distil. The glassy bottle held an orange spirit. He upended the bottle and watched the air bubbles ascend through the potent looking liquid. His mind was racing through many scenarios and all the options came to one. *Should have been a farmer, concentrated on growing food or raising livestock, should never have been a leader!* He put the pill in his mouth and he could taste the acrid pre-war chemical on his tongue. The taste was unbearable so he quickly uncorked the rot gut and took a good swig which aided the transit of the pill down to his gut.

"Right then let's see how a pre-war soldier felt having taken such a pill?" He had never taken amphetamines before and assumed it wouldn't do anything. However, after about twenty minutes his gut seemed to explode, he felt a warming sensation rushing through his body, it was kind of nice too.

"Oh, this is odd..." He said as he felt his face flush. It somehow felt like a river rushing over his body, it started in his feet like pins and needles and then quickly rushed over his body like a tsunami. He stretched out his legs and noticed he was wearing his best boots. He started to giggle and tried to reach for the bottle of whiskey on the table. His hands were shaking and he only just grabbed hold of the bottle of whiskey. He took a swig but the drug was really working on him, he felt his heart beat accelerate and his mouth turning dry.

"By the bright?" He puffed out his cheeks, he felt very light headed. The door to his office opened and Edwards stalked in.

"Some of the rangers wish to check the area around the fort, to make sure we have the upper hand." She said as she peered at the rot gut whiskey bottle on the captain's table.

"No! We need to protect the fort!" He said harshly.

"Oh... That fucks it! I've already allowed Alpha team to patrol the area, sorry sir." Edwards stated with a salute even though she was regretting her decision.

"Don't worry sergeant. I suppose it is a wise call, now that I think about it... You're correct we need to have scouts to warn us of the eminent threat." He said idly filling a glass tumbler of whiskey. He tried to ignore the euphoric feeling racing through his brain. She frowned. "You okay?"

"Yeah, never better, you?" He said trying to sound sober, what he found really strange is he no longer felt drunk. The drunken feeling had been replaced by this strange chemical high. Edwards laughed and pointed to the pill packet on the table.

"You're fucking tweaking!" She laughed some more. "I took a pill about two hours ago, I don't feel tired at all!" She grinned.

"Stop laughing and get out of my office!" He said jokingly, but she did as he asked, all the while still giggling about the resident junkie captain. The room was quiet again apart from the back ground hiss of the ham radio. *Should of asked her to stay, I feel weird being high and all alone*, he thought. He had sent out some spotters earlier, solo rangers who preferred working alone, they were basically his eyes and ears in the ruins. They had taken up position in some of the high rises overlooking the main streets that lead to the fort. They would give the issue to fire the howitzers as soon as the soviets wandered into the dead zones. Ash had started to pace the confines of the office, he had so much energy and his mind felt like a computer, hot and calculating. He grabbed a 'walkie' and nearly ran from the room, he wanted air on his face. He wanted to run over hills as fast as his legs could carry him, it really was a strange sensation, but in his heart of hearts he knew the feeling would pass as the pill wore off.

Ash stood in the armoury with his arms held out as though he was being crucified. The quarter master was busy strapping on heavy ranger armour, basically a mixture of old pre-war riot armour and crafted pieces made on the forts metal forge. Andy the old quarter master still held the rank of sergeant but he was demobilised seven years ago after taking a shotgun wound to the leg. He never walked the same ever since, but he managed the entire forts inventory incredibly well. His left eye was cloudy with cataract and he levelled his good eye with Ash's.

"Were doomed aren't we." It wasn't a question it was more matter-of-factly having encountered drainers in the ash land before. Ash couldn't lie to the old quarter master.

"Yep, I'm still considering a tactical retreat, but if the rangers retreat then all manner of shit will be free to raid and pillage the farms and towns." Ash said bitterly.

"Yeah, it will be a butterfly effect, if the drainers had a free run then the bandits and abominations of the ruins will also..." Andy nodded as he logged out the armour segments in the ledger.

"It's not over yet, we still might have a chance but its odds on favourite that the fort will be over-run and the dead rangers will be but a perishable decoration." Ash said morbidly.

"One things for sure it's gona be one hell of a fight!" Andy issued, with lack of hope in his tone.

"We are done by the way, your good to go Ash!" He said ticking the last piece of inventory in the ledger.

"Look Andy, you don't need to die here, take a walk to Crimson farm, if it all goes to shit here, I will meet up with you there." Ash tried to offer the veteran a get out clause but when he looked at Andy he could see he had insulted him.

"Get the fuck out of my armoury captain, I will see you shortly on the field of battle." Andy began to strap on heavy armour, the kind of heavy movement restricting armour issued to support gunners weighed down with ammo belts and heavy machine guns.

"I Don't move quick anymore, I may as well be a tank." He said nodding over to the M60's strapped to the wall. Ash saluted him but couldn't find the words to thank the old veteran, instead he strode to the armoury door. He stopped and looked over his shoulder and watched the old man strapping on armour.

"I'm sorry it has come to this my old friend." He left quickly before Andy had chance to reply.

The fort courtyard seemed to be still busy, the parapets were full of rangers spying over the ruins, the engineers were ready on the artillery and Edwards had climbed the lookout tower spying through her sniper scope. The walkie had been quiet so Ash clicked it on frequency one.

"Alpha team, what is your position?" He waited and listened to the hiss for a click.

"We are just finishing our sweep near the old co-op building, no sign yet captain." Alpha team responded.

"Good to hear, keep tight." He said as he switched the radio to neutral. He looked to the sun and without looking at his time piece he estimated it was around 4pm. His thoughts came in chaotic pulses, doubts, hope and salvation. *Maybe the fort is not currently the soviet target?* He doubted his own mind though. His radio crackled.

"Solo Turrin, reporting..." The radio hissed for a few seconds. "I can hear gun fire coming from Soni square. Sounds like the soviets are being attacked by the wretched." She said referring to mutated ruin mutants that come up from the dark of the sewers. "The hunger must have drawn them out. It's rare they come up during daylight hours"

"Let's hope the wretched are culling their numbers." Ash hoped.

"Wait..." The solo cut off. "A small group of soviets have just entered the square, the dumb son-of-bitches are heading into our dead zone." She issued excitedly.

"Small group you say?"

"Yeah, six they are in skirmish formation, a volley would take them, it's your call captain?"

"Call the strike, if we take out a group of scouts it will confuse their command." Ash claimed.

"Calling it in now sir!" The solo said before cutting off the transmission. Ash looked to the engineers near the howziters, he could see they were receiving orders and pre-planned coordinates, usually marked with letters of the alphabet. The artillery retorted as the big guns rolled back under the momentum of the back power of the primed shells. Gun C and D were quickly reloaded by the engineers. Ash heard distant explosions hitting home from somewhere distant in the ruins. His radio crackled and clicked for a long time, he found he had taken a deep breath and yet to exhale. For what seemed like an age the frequency clicked back on.

"Report?" Ash barked with impatience.

"Hang on captain, I can't see shit for the dust and smoke, but it's clearing now!" He waited for the solo rangers report while sweat began to run down his cheek from the warmth of the helmet he wore.

"Targets down!" The solo finally said and even though he couldn't see Turrin's face he knew she had a smile on her face. Ash looked to the many rangers on the parapets and gave them a thumb's up. They raised their fists in the air and made a silent sound of victory. It was a small victory because Ash knew the explosions would have consequences. The radio had fallen silent again and he had a feeling this was just the start of things to come.

Night came quickly, the ruins turned into a place of dread at night, all manner of abominations and wild things stalked the ruins when darkness fell. Ash recalled Alpha team back to the fort to give them some respite and a decent warm meal. They reported the ruins were quiet and encountered nothing out of the ordinary but they did bring back two deer. Ash entered the kitchen as the cooks cleaned the carcasses, cutting off fine cuts of meat and boiling up the bones etc for stock. Ash smelt the fresh blood and cooking smells he knew his rangers would feast tonight. His heart went out to the Solo's who were still out in the ruins, but they excelled in those kinds of situations. They were solo's for a reason, sometimes they wouldn't report back to the fort for days. They were outfitted with night scopes so he knew they were still in over-watch protocol. Ash made his way around the parapets of the fort, he reassured the rangers hard wired on amphetamines and some of them were already taking a second pill to ride them through the night. *It will be a long night!* His mind contemplated. Bowls of stew were being distributed on the parapets by the auxiliaries and the meaty stew was being consumed with the occasional mmmmm nice. Ash's radio crackled yet again.

"Solo Greaves reporting." He was whispering so his voice didn't carry in the ruins and the silence of the night.

"Report?" Ash said quietly.

"Got a lot of skirmishing drainers heading towards the second dead zone, they seem to be very cautious, I suspect they have worked out what happened to the scouts in Soni square!" He paused. "They are armed with assault rifles, A.K's I think and some have heavy machine guns and R.P.G's which they are wielding as though they are light as toy guns?" Greaves reported.

"We need all the guns focused on dead zone Alpha!" Ash cried to the engineers manning the big guns. He watched as the engineers manoeuvred the guns into position, cranking gears to gain the trajectory.

"Battery A – D are standing by to level Alpha zone!" He whispered into the radio. "Just give the word!" The radio hissed and the wait began. Ash looked to the pale faces and wide eyes of the engineers arming the artillery. He could see the fear in their eyes and wished the threat would come to an end and get back to the normal threat of everyday protecting the farmlands. An engineer with a headset sounded the order to fire. The artillery thundered and the engineers were quick to reload sending another volley of death to the impact zone.

"Wait!" Ash cried as the engineers reloaded for another volley. He put the walkie to his ear, wishing for the shells hitting home. *Please, please, please!* The radio hissed against his ear. A minute passed and still the radio was void of a voice in the ruins. *Please no, please to the bright the soviets are but rubble and ash!* Another minute passed as he pleaded to the bright.

"We got 'em!" The solo cried through the radio. "It took a while for the smoke to drift away but we got them all!"

"Numbers? Numbers solo!" Ash yelled through the radio.

"Fifty maybe sixty, we fucked em' all up!" Greaves claimed through the communications. "Look I've been compromised here, I'm gona head back to the fort, I think Turrin should come back too sir?"

"Yeah, both of you get back to operations, but leave no trace!" Ash said stupidly, they weren't solo rangers for a reason.

"Solo Greaves coming back!"

"Solo Turrin coming back!" And then the radio turned back to a hiss.

Dawn broke, the sun started to rise over the ruined

buildings, a haze of dust obscured the sun slightly brought up by dust of the previous night of artillery impacts. Ash waited patiently near the main gates for the return of the Solo rangers. They must have met up at some rally point because they both arrived together. The rangers in the fort all clapped their hands when the solo's entered the fort. Ash couldn't issue any more ranks to the Solo's due to the next rank being the rank of captain. They were dusty and bandaged, apparently they were attacked by wretched mutants wandering around in the ruins but clearly the filthy encounters had been put down by hot lead. Ash bear hugged them both as the main gate closed.

"You have saved our skins again Solo's!" He pointed to the kitchen.

"Get yourself a hot meal and bed down for a few hours you have more than earned it!" They both smiled but he could see the distant stare in their eyes, it was almost predatory. Ash himself had been a solo ranger in his younger days and he knew how lonely and hard it had been not relying and working as a team with other rangers. *True hero's* he pondered. The solo's stopped in their tracks and then made a bee-line toward the engineers still manning the artillery. They spent a while shaking their hands and patting the engineers shoulders, pointing out that the engineers had saved the fort, as though it had nothing to do with the solo's risking their lives deep in the ruins. Ash also wandered over to the engineers to shake their hands.

"The fort stands stout due to your actions!" He

bolstered the Solo's affections toward the engineers. When the solo's left the courtyard Ash commanded the bugle player to sound the victory. A young ranger on the parapet lifted his battered old bugle and put it to his lips. The bugle sounded out the victory parade notes, while every ranger in the fort stood proud to attention.

"The rangers win again!" Edwards claimed as she clinked glasses of moon shine with captain Ash.

"Here's to living another day!" Ash agreed as he clinked her shot glass, nearly spilling her drink. She threw the spirit to the back of her mouth and grimaced as it burnt her throat. She coughed a number of times as her face reddened.

"Shit, we could go blind on this distil!" Ash nodded in agreement fighting the burn on his throat. They chuckled as the alcohol hit their bloodstream, making them shudder involuntarily.

"We have been lucky so far and I don't wish to be the witness of doom, but I don't think this is over." Ash said suddenly sober. Edwards sighed.

"I know, but let us take this day by the throat. Like you said we have seen another dawn, yesterday we were in so much doubt that we would ever see another sun rise." The door to the office knocked and without waiting the quarter master peered around the door.

"Sorry to bother you captain, merchants have arrived with more food, do you wish to check the inventory?"

"Sure, I will be there in just a tick." Ash said as he

donned his cowboy hat and snatched up his gun belt. He quickly caught up with Andy as he hobbled gingerly down the stairs.

"Odd, were we expecting another shipment?"

"Not sure, they probably had a rethink about the tribute that protects the farm lands." Andy pondered seeing the logic in his own words. They exited the building into the main courtyard, the merchants and guards were gathered around a large wagon covered with grey coloured tarp. The merchants wore roughly spun hooded gowns and some wore desert respirators and sun glasses. Ash noticed it wasn't the regular crowd that freights food to the fort. A bearded man who seemed to be the leader put out his arms as though welcoming the captain.

"We are the Mescal merchant's, would the brave rangers like to browse our extensive merchandise?" The merchant gestured towards the cart pulled by a gang of tried looking folks dressed in brown hooded robes. Ash approached the merchant studying his features, he noticed the man was sweating profoundly and he had a number scars on his face.

"I see you must be the leader of the rangers, good to meet you sir." He said shaking ashes hand with sweaty palms. His eyes were wide and he seemed to have a nervous twitch. Ash noticed he wasn't armed either, but not everybody is a gun hand.

"Never heard of your outfit boy, but we are always open to trade. What exactly are you trading?" Ash asked while he looked over the merchants shoulder to the tarp covered wagon. The merchant leant toward Ash and whispered something he couldn't quite hear.

"Speak up boy, cat got you're..." Ash didn't have time to finish his question, the tarp fell away revealing a small contingent of heavily armed soviets. They leaped out of the cart blazing away with pre-war Russian assault rifles. The hooded folk at the front of the cart threw back their hoods revealing pale bald faces with sickly colourer blood shot eyes, one of whom quickly engaged Andy tearing out his throat with its undead talons. Gunfire and chaos erupted around Ash, he managed to pull his eagle out and drop the first drainer that rushed at him. He saw the rangers firing back at the soviets but he could see a number of rangers all busted up on the floor near the parapets. He fired round after round retreating towards the door of the main building. The drainer on Andy was in some kind of blood frenzy lapping at his gushing jugular. Ash aimed and fired at the drainers skull, blowing it open like a ripe melon. Edwards must have heard the gun fire and had shattered the office window letting rip with her M4. Ash combat rolled into the shadows of the building and quickly reloaded a mag, while the cacophony of gun fire overwhelmed the ambience. Utilising the cover of the door frame he picked his targets knowing he only had one more magazine on his gun belt. *The fuckers Trojan-horsed me!* He thought desperately trying to upper-hand the situation. The slide of his eagle locked, he ejected the mag and quickly hammered home his last mag from his gun belt. Two brown robed drainers had targeted the captain and started rushing towards the building firing sub-machine pistols. Ash ducked into cover while the bullets ripped up the concrete. He rushed up the stair-well catching a ricocheted bullet to his thigh. He ignored the pain and ran as fast as his legs could carry him to the office on the second floor. Edwards was reloading her M4 as he scrambled towards his assault rifle bracketed on the wall behind his desk. As he locked and loaded the rifle, Edwards fired another full auto volley down into the courtyard, she looked focused and professional. He grabbed up a magazine belt and tossed another mag towards Edwards, she caught it and reloaded.

"Stay your ground sergeant I need covering fire, I'm going back into the fray." She heard him but she was busy picking targets to shoot. As he turned toward the door the two brown robed drainers leapt into the office, hissing and cursing humankind. Ash managed to drop the first, nearly cutting the fucker in half when he went full-auto, however the other one flanked right and then pounced on him. It felt like a bull hitting him at full pelt, he cascaded over the desk under the power of the impact, his rifle scattered on the floor. The strength of the drainer was unbelievable he was like a rag doll in the hands of an angry child. *This is it. This is how I check out!* He wondered if that was going to be his last thought as the drainer clawed at his arms trying to land a coup-de-grace. His own blood splattered on his face from the lacerations on his arms as the drainer punched and clawed its way toward his neck. Ash was done, he had made up his mind. It was hopeless to struggle against such ferocity. And then it stopped, his ears were ringing almost deafened, his eyes half blind due to the blood in his eyes. He felt the weight of the drainer slumping on his battered body nearly taking the wind from his chest. Edwards kicked the dead weight away and put the muzzle of the carbine to his forehead.

"You bit?" She screamed pushing the gun hard against his head. He could only just hear her voice over the ringing in his ears.

"Don't think so? I'm pretty fucked up though!" He gurgled spitting out blood from his mouth. Edwards poked around his neck area with the end of her gun, but with all the blood she couldn't work out if he had been bitten or not.

"Protocol is to put you down captain, you know that." She said as her eyes welled up, her hands shaking fighting back emotion. Ash lifted himself up and Edwards backed off as though he was a leper.

"I'm not bit sergeant!" He wasn't too sure himself but he had no pain around his neck but the drainer could have bitten his arm in the heavy melee. He shook his head trying to reassure himself.

"Nope I'm not bit, pretty sure!" He lied. The gun fire had stopped in the courtyard below, Edwards took a peek out of the window and saw Rangers milling around, all the while she still had her gun trained on Ash.

"Think we won captain, but I'm sorry, you are

under quarantine!" She looked at his gun belt.

"Gona need your eagle too!" Ash agreed and unbuckled his gun belt sliding it over to her feet.

Ash was taken to the brig, it used to be a paper-stand kiosk of sorts which the rangers used as a prison because the roller shutter door was still functional. He was given water to wash with, bandages and a couple of apples. A ranger stood guard outside. Even though the rangers had overcome the attack they had taken many losses. Edwards had explained the situation with the captain and a few of the rangers wanted to put him down, but the majority vote wished for quarantine. Later on that day, Thomas the medic persuaded the guard to let him see the captain. He entered carrying his doctor's bag, he looked at the bandaging on Ash's arms.

"Made a mess of that didn't you cap'? He chuckled and started to unravel the bandages.

"Try and bandage yourself up with busted up arms." Ash sneered and then chuckled. "Nice to see you Thomas, glad you survived."

"Well to be honest with you, as soon as the gun fire started I pushed all the furniture against the door, I am definitely not a hero, but I'm definitely a survivor." He grinned.

"How long am I going to be a prisoner?"

"Not long, usually symptoms come on quick. Are you feeling thirsty?" Thomas asked suddenly professional as he properly bandaged up his arms.

"I wasn't bit Thomas and we are wasting time

having me locked up!"

"Now, now, now... We must follow quarantine rules, we can't have you tearing up the place in a feat of bloodletting." Thomas said laughing. "With all that said, I'm pretty sure you are okay, just ride it out, I will see you in the morning." He winked and pulled out a small bottle of distilled spirits.

"For medicinal purposes only, doctors' orders." He placed the bottle of rot gut on the floor. Before Thomas left the brig Ash thanked him.

CHAPTER 7

"Astonishing?" Joshua cried, he had started to read the utopian man's journal that he had purchased from Jessica and he simply couldn't put the damn thing down. This Utopian man seemed to be very intriguing, however he did write about a lot of mundane things as well as side notes written from the mind of somebody clearly insane. But he also wrote about hidden places in America, bunkers, habitats, radioactive ruins. Joshua knew that Washington used to be the capital of America, obviously pre-war, but this fucker who claimed to be the utopian had been there, he had walked the radioactive ruins and documented some of the interesting buildings that still stood.

"Listen to this" He quoted from the journal "I wandered into a place called Green camp, a ramshackle camp site inhabited by wretched settlers scraping a living growing corn and other farm produce. I traded a giga-counter and a few medicals in exchange for food and lodgings. He must be referring to Grain town, up north, but back then it was a mere campsite???" Natasha peered up from darning some socks with a frown.

"Tomorrow is Sunday Joshua and you haven't prepared your Sunday sermon." She said trying to change the subject.

"Sunday sermon... Oh I will muddle through it somehow." He claimed, not really giving a shit. She dropped the sock and darning needle to the floor and put her hands on her hips, he could see she was pissed off.

"You have a duty to your flock and you waste your time reading about some long dead traveller! Have you abandoned the bright?" He put a book mark in the journal and placed it down on his study table.

"No I have not abandoned the bright, what nonsense do you speak of?" He noticed that she had been getting more and more religious by each day that passed, ever since the sojourn to the old military depot.

"Natasha this is the truth." He claimed patting the journal. "But I suspect this was written on his death bed, thoughts, places, encounters, they are all jumbled up, no time line, no order to which he writes. One page describes a settlement in Alabama, the next page mentions a ruined place called New York? It goes on and on, jumping from place to place without any chronological order."

"Well its all lies, that journal belongs in your vault of religious books, locked away from prying eyes." She hissed as she pulled out a flash light from the folds of her gown, clicked it on and shone it on his face in a religious gesture to the bright. He fanned his hands and retreated from the torch light.

"I am still a priest of the bright, but Natasha you didn't see what I witnessed, the bright, even though doctrine claims didn't cause the fall of humanity.

Mankind did! Governments of old armed with atomic weapons. I know this because I saw it with my very own eyes in that room!"

"That room changed you Joshua, I see it in your eyes, the bright sees the lies as well." She slapped him hard across his face a real back hand slap, she had never laid a violent hand upon him before. The strike shook him up and being the high authority in Red Town he was not used to such action. He rubbed his cheek as she levelled her gaze meeting his eyes.

"It's bullshit and lies Joshua, pull yourself together and start writing tomorrows sermon!" She barked showering his face with spittle. The slap had rattled him and he felt like a child once again.

"Get out!" He yelled as his eyes welled up with tears. Natasha stormed out in a huff slamming the door behind her. He grabbed his holy flash light and threw it hard against the door making a dent and smashing the glassy front of the torch. He had never felt such emotion and rage. *Bitch! She hasn't seen what I have witnessed!* His hands were shaking and he had to take some deep breaths to calm himself down. He looked to the journal and could feel the magnetism toward the hand written notes.

"There will be no marriage if you keep this up! You... You fucking whore!" He yelled at the door. Natasha on the other side of the door tried to hold back tears as she cowered up in a foetal position rocking back and forth, her eyes cascading with tears.

Joshua had been up all night reading the journal, Natasha left him some supper behind the door as an apology but he refused to eat. One of the random pages described a place which Joshua assumed to be in the Kentucky area. Apparently the utopian man mentions a clue about his father? The journal often described his father as a survivor of the nuclear war. He was some kind of government official who survived the bombardment deep underground. The journal was vague but clearly this utopian man looked up to his father as a true son. He turned a page and was baffled about the randomness. The utopian man was somewhere up north crossing a radioactive wasteland of ruins, in his description he was wearing some kind of mechanised armour and he was travelling with folk from the Iron core? Joshua had to re-read the section of the journal trying to work out who these Iron core folk were? A hand drawn sketch depicted a large group of tall, bulky armoured folk travelling through a ruined city of some kind. No dates and no time line, but Joshua was under the assumption that it was late on his life due to the sub-note describing his father as very old, sporting silver hair. Joshua could feel the pull once again. He needed to find this clue about the utopians father on the land map called Virginia. *But, what of the church?* He pondered. He made a decision he must marry Natasha, he could not travel alone and he wondered if the Deacon would take over the running of the church in his absence? He snuffed out the candles and pawed his way to the door in the darkness, he assumed it was early morning. He wandered among the wooden pews and grimaced at the sun rise shining through the stained glass windows. The Deacon was busy laying out the kneeling pillows in front of the pews.

"We will do Sunday service as usual but you will be giving the sermon, I have wedding plans to negotiate." The Deacon dropped a pillow he was holding.

"Wedding? You are to marry Natasha?" His voice shuddered with torment and anguish. The young man started to weep.

"Why? Why would you marry such an angel?" His words floundered he was broken.

"She will never marry you Deacon... Besides which I am planning a sojourn. You will have full custody of the church in my absence." He waited until his words settled with the Deacon. The tears ceased flowing and the Deacon stood proud like he was a Titan rising up from the Mediterranean sea, like the Greek mythological stories.

"I have two hours to write a befitting sermon for Sunday service." He said before rushing off to his study in a fit of excitement.

The streets of Red town were quiet but the morning sun had already started warming up the land bringing with it the stench of latrines and out houses. Joshua pulled up his cravat to try and mask the stink away. He circumnavigated around the bars and saloons in order to avoid the drunken farmers being kicked out from a night of heavy drinking. It had been Saturday night and he knew the bars would have been full. He made a mental note to chastise such behaviour but then he remembered he wasn't doing the Sunday sermon. *The Deacon can do that shit!* He crossed the wooden bridge over the stream of water that came from the mountains. The stream was a mucky brown colour washing away the raw sewerage from the towns filthy deposits. He got to the foot of Roodies whore house, several drunks were lying prostate in the dirt outside, very likely thrown out this morning. He picked his way up the wooden steps towards the swing door, making sure he didn't wake the drunken unconscious farmers. The tap room stank of hard liquor and unwashed bodies, some of the bar patrons were fast asleep still nursing the last remnants of bottled whiskey. Roody came too and tried to stand up, but his knees gave way and he then settled back on the chair behind the bar. He looked through squinted eyes and recognised the preacher.

"You doin' you're sermon in my house today preacher?" He slurred as he rocked back and two.

"Nope! I'm here to see Jessica, is she in?"

"Jess, hell yeah she is upstairs with one of the whores..." The owner tried to stand again but give up half way.

"Wanna a heart starter preacher?" He said trying to string together words as he reached for a bottle of whiskey.

"No, just need to see Jess, if she is available?" The owner paled and jettisoned his guts on the wooden floor, coughing and spluttering. Between throwing up he apologised to the priest.

"What room is Jess in?" Joshua asked when Roody stopped spewing out last night's whiskey. Roody tried to gather himself up and reached for a bottle of whiskey taking the hair of the dog.

"She's in room four, she's always in room four, it's her room for bright's sakes!" He burped and raised up his hands in a plea. "No offence preacher, I'm sorry to take the lords name in vain!"

"The deacon is doing the Sunday sermon today, make sure you are there and you can apologise to the bright yourself!" He said in a huff before ascending the rickety stairs to the upper floor glaring at the whore house owner.

Joshua wandered down the bank of rooms on the upper floor, he could hear muffled sobs and head boards banging against the walls of the whore house. He got to the foot of room four and put his ear to the door, he couldn't hear a sound so assumed Jessica was sleeping. He rapped quietly on the door and waited but nobody responded. His patience grew thin and he pushed the door open. Jessica was spread eagled on the bed naked holding the back of a prostitutes head, pushing her head between her thighs. Jessica was breathing in short powerful breaths, her eyes were closed and her other arm was holding the back of the bed frame, as though anchoring herself. Her dark hair was ruffled against the pillow and he could tell she was about to orgasm. He averted his eyes from such debauchery and waited for Jess to climax. When she audibly came and her panting returned to normal, he coughed to announce his presence. The prostitute looked over her shoulder wiping her mouth with her wrist, clearly alarmed by the intruder.

"This is a private room, if you wanna get off, then talk to Roody, this ain't no peep show!" The prostitute yelled as she threw the bedding blanket over herself and Jessica. Jess opened one eye trying to stop the room from spinning due to the booze she had consumed the night before.

"Joshua? What the fuck!" She clambered out of bed naked and started to dress herself. The preacher averted his eyes but he had taken a good look of Jessica's slim body and noticed she shaved downstairs, probably to make it preferable to go down on her. The blonde haired prostitute had rolled a cigarette and sparked it up, puffing out plumes of smoke while Jessica got herself dressed.

"What you want preacher?" Jess said with a tone of irritation.

"Need to hire you again." He watched as Jessica pulled up her leather pants and tried to think of mundane things and not to get aroused, all though he could feel himself hard against his rough spun robes.

"I told you the last time we met. I'm heading up north to collect on some bounties!" She claimed as she buckled up her gun belt.

"One hundred coins." He paused. "And another

one hundred when we get there unscathed?" He gambled. Jessica looked him up and down and grinned.

"You can do better than that preacher! I'm the best gun fighter in the territory, you know that, you were there, your bastard ass would have been smoked if I hadn't stepped in!" She said arrogantly referring to the army depot, the auto guns and the encounter with the bandits.

"That's why I'm here Jess, need a gun-slinging bitch like yourself to protect me and my soon to be wife!"

"Wife? You getting married preacher?" Jessica laughed.

"Yeah, and you're gona give Natasha away at the ceremony!" He grinned.

"The hell I'am!" She spat..

"I was thinking this Monday?" He frowned and continued. "Do you recon Brae and Yolanda will come along?"

"Maybe, depends if they salvaged the depot?" She grinned. "I will put my feelers out and rally up our old mates. One hundred each sound good for you?"

"One hundred each but make sure you have them on board!" He made a religious gesture before heading on back to the church. As soon as the door shut Jessica threw some more coins on the side table and started to undress, winking at the whore.

Jessica had three queens and two ten's, she took another shot of whiskey and threw in a few coins to the pot. The rest of the gamblers folded apart from some jumped up prick called Derrick, who was fresh in Red town. Derrick eyed his cards and counted up three kings.

"Raise you, two coins plus another coin!" He said cockily eyeing the pretty brunette. Jessica feigned surprise to the raise and reluctantly put in another coin.

"Call!" She stated. They showed their cards and Derrick went for his gun. Jessica couldn't even be bothered pulling her gun, instead she grabbed the barrel of the revolver and snatched it from Derricks hand, breaking his trigger finger with a twist.

"You broke my finger you bitch!" He cried holding his broken trigger finger. Jessica spun the revolver in her hand and stopped it spinning as she grabbed the firearm like a knuckle duster.

"Time to check out!" She said and then punched him in his eye using the revolver as a melee weapon. Derricks nose burst open gushing blood all over his shirt and his eye socket fractured, probably blinding him forever in his left eye. Derrick slumped unconscious under the table as Jessica pulled the pot toward her.

"Cashing out guys no hard feelings?" The others that folded just looked wide eyed at the aggressive female and made their polite goodbyes. Jessica sat counting out the coins and filling up her purse. It's when somebody tapped her on her shoulder. She was like a rat out of hell, she combat rolled to her flank and stood up with both her forty fives locked and loaded. Natasha cowered in a crouching position covering her face with her hands.

"Don't shoot!" She cried. Jess recognised the lass and holstered her firearms.

"What's up love? I'm sorry that I scared you" She said sincerely.

"I am too be married and soon..." She claimed but Jessica could see Natasha's heart wasn't truly ready for that path. Jess gestured her to sit and poured two shots of whiskey from the bottle the kind gentlemen had left in a hurry.

"I'm not supposed to drink." She giggled and chugged it, Jess waited while she coughed and spluttered.

"So you and o'l Joshua getting hitched, eh." It wasn't a question more a conversation starter. Natasha looked in her eyes and slowly nodded her head.

"Most brides get nervous about getting hitched, it's the natural order of things. You see the way I see it, women love cock and they worry about settling for one cock when they could have many." She paused and sniggered. "I'm the kind of woman that don't fit in that category because I like... Well, you have had firsthand experience of what I like." Jess noticed she was confusing Natasha more and waved her hand.

"Probably be better off..."

"Should I marry Joshua?" Natasha interrupted as though it was a weight lifting of her. Jess shrugged and started weighing up the pros and cons.

"He is well paid, he has a steady income, he owns property, he is a leader in the community and if you don't mind me saying but he is a handsome man for his age."

"So I should marry him?" She asked wide eyed. Jess puffed out her cheeks and looked to Natasha's laced up red leather shoes.

"How the fuck should I know?" Jess shrugged. "Too be honest I thought I might of tempted you to the other camp." Again Natasha stared with her head cocked like a dog, confused but interested.

"Other camp?"

"By the bright, I mean when we shared a bed roll." Jess simulated vulgarly using a cupped hand and several fingers.

"Oh no, I'm sorry but I prefer men if that's what you're asking?" Natasha said flushing.

"I wasn't being serious, it was a joke. Gee liven up won't you?" Jess said pouring another shot. A fight had started in the tap room near the bar, bringing with it outbursts of foul language, smashing bottles and flesh being punched. Natasha was holding her arms, cowering on the chair.

"They ain't gona bother us love, drink your whiskey your safe with me." Jess said as Natasha shuddered with all the crashing sounds in the next room. The fight calmed down as Roody brought out a baseball bat and vented out some anger on the brawlers. When the tap room fell back to a background chitter-chatter Natasha leant forward and touched Jessica's knee.

"I have decided I will marry, but I want you to give me away." Natasha half begged. Jess removed her hand from her knee and huffed.

"What! I'm supposed to be your father figure all of a sudden!" She hissed "Round up somebody else to give you away." Jessica bit back the anger rising in her belly and knew the little girl better scarper. As Natasha backed away from the table and gained enough ground between them she whispered. "Think about it." Before turning on her toe and rushing from the bar.

Jessica went for a walk to clear the whiskey from her head, the streets of Red town were bustling by now and the burning sun brought up the dust from the dehydrated streets. Among the crowd she spotted Yolanda and Brae, it seemed they were in mid-argument over something and Yolanda had started to attack Brae in a physical lovers tiff. Yolanda was crying and lashing out towards Brae who countered her punches using his gun bracers as a shield. Brae looked up and saw Jessica standing in the throng of people, she was smirking. He appeared even more angry having seen Jessica.

"I don't want to see you Jessica!" He barked as he left Yolanda crying in the streets and barged past Jess nearly knocking her to the dust. Jessica tried her best to be incognito but it was too late Yolanda rushed to hug her. The strong lass bear hugged her and wept against the nape of her neck.

"He is a bastard!" She sobbed. Jess feigned consoling her as she curled her lip, she couldn't stand seeing a woman crying. *Weak!* She thought but the mothering instinct pushed through the tough wall in Jessica's mind.

"Come on let's get a drink and you can tell me all about it." She voiced monotonously patting Yolanda's back. She grabbed her hand and pulled her to the nearest bar which happened to be 'The Corn head tap room'. The bar was full off relaxing farm hands drinking corn beer. The stench of animal shit and sweat was quite overpowering in the bare board tap room. She seated Yolanda and headed off to the bar to purchase some beers. When she returned with beers she noticed Yolanda had stopped crying, her cheeks twitched battling back more tears.

"Brae sunk most of our cash into the enterprise of looting that army depot. But some bastard outfit had already looted it by the time we got the wagons and labour up there." Yolanda said with an onslaught before Jess had time to sit down.

"That's a bitch!"

"I know, do you recon there were more of those bandits that you seemed to know?" Yolanda asked, her eyes bloodshot from the tears she had shed.

"Probably... William had quite a retinue of scum working for him, even back in the days when I ran with them." She shrugged. "But it could have been the gun fire that drew others to the depot when we journeyed out?"

"You're right Jess, could have been a passing merchant outfit with enough wagons to clear the place." Yolanda said sadly. Jess narrowed her eyes all business like.

"Changing the subject, I have landed a job, it's dangerous and I wouldn't mind you guy's coming along for the ride. It pays well too."

"We are nearly broke Jess. Brae was trying for us to retire but that's gone to shit. What's this job you speak of?"

"Another one of the preacher's sojourns, he seems to be all fucked up and focused on this Utopian man from the journals." Jess sighed. Yolanda waved her words away and took a sip of beer in disgust.

"The last time nearly got us all killed Jess! I was thinking about what you said, heading up north and tracking down some bounties."

"Fuck the bounties! The preacher has hard coin to waste on tracking down this utopian loser's father or something?" She grinned. "The way he harps on, it's like he is tracking down god. The fucker hasn't been the same ever since lying down in that weird electrified room."

"That room was pretty screwed up!" She giggled and took another swig of the sweet corn beer. Jessica put her hat on and got up to leave.

"Meet up with Brae, explain what is going on and then meet at the church tomorrow." With that said she strode off confidently to the dusty streets.

Joshua had cleared the holy alter dedicated to the god of the bright, he unrolled an old pre-war map that had seen better days. Some of the creases in the map had perforated over time and revealed the stone work of the alter below it. Yolanda and Brae had just arrived and was shown to the alter by the Deacon where Natasha, Jessica and Joshua stood peering at the map. They all greeted one another as though they were long lost friends meeting for the very first time.

"Before we get down to business let us talk coin preacher." Brae stated as though he was some kind of general of an army. Joshua rolled his eyes.

"Of course, but payment has already been agreed with Jessica, I take it you wish for more coin?" Joshua said in disgust at the mercantile statement.

"We." He said referring to himself and Yolanda. "Are in a bit of a pickle as it comes to wealth. If we are to be enlisted on this 'amazing quest'." He mocked "Then you need to get your coin purse out to purchase supplies and equipment. Jess has already filled me in on some of the..." Jessica shook her head and interrupted.

"What my friends are trying to say is; we will need respirators and radiation capes, like the attire of the deep desert merchants. The target zone you speak of will take us through a number of radioactive ruins. Some of which we can navigate around but some of the ruins we will be forced to cross due to the tactical bridges and subways." Joshua sighed and agreed as he mentally calculated the extra coin.

"Things have changed..." Joshua paused and watched the gun fighters faces melt into a frown. "Natasha and myself will be married tomorrow, I will pay you a further one hundred coins to get us back to Red town." Jessica gripped the preacher by the scruff of his neck.

"It's a one way trip for you and your wife, you pay us up when we arrive and then you're on your own! Once north, me and the gang are heading off to collect on some bounties! That's for sure!" Joshua appeared upset but finally agreed.

"Okay one way mission for you... You dirty un-godly mercenaries!" He yelled sending spittle into Jessica's face. Jessica let go of him and gestured to the map. The quested party spent a few hours pondering over the old map, questions and solutions were raised but Brae and Jessica smoothed out the worries due to them knowing the land because they had spent many years travelling the ways with the desert rangers. The meeting ended around 2pm, everybody seemed satisfied about the quest and agreed upon Monday being the wedding, Tuesday gathering up equipment and nursing off a hangover and Wednesday, the date to set off. They all shook hands and went their separate ways.

Joshua had persuaded, with heavy coin, for Jessica to give away Natasha at the wedding. About a third of the township of Red town turned out for the wedding. The church pews were full and Joshua waited impatiently at the holy alter for his bride to arrive. The ambience in the church, were a mixture of happiness and hushed disappointment about the preacher and his new wife leaving soon. It seemed very few of the parishioners were looking forward to the Deacon taking over Sunday sermon in the preacher's absence. Some of which were quite audible about the temporary change. Mrs Armatige started to play the wedding march on the churches organ. She eyed the harlot as she wandered in accompanied by Jessica who had rented a suit from the undertakers. Jessica appeared quite dapper in her two piece suit, but it was spoilt by the gun belt she had refused to relinquish. Natasha wore a faded but bleached pre-war white wedding gown, which was also rented from the undertakers. The gown she wore was in the fashion of ancient Greece. Probably the fashion just before the bombs fell? Jessica elbowed her gently.

"You sure you want this cock?" She joked as she peered through the faded veil to Natasha's sparkling eyes.

"Yes, I'm sure, thank you so much for giving me away." Her eyes tearful but, her mouth was a beaming smile. As the wedding march played on the organ, Jessica guided her down the main line of the pews. Every face of the parish upon them, most of them smiling and emotional, but others, frowning due to a woman giving a girl away. She handed the bride to the groom and took a step back. Joshua leaned toward his bride to be.

"I thought you might of backed out my love?" He said wiping tears from his eyes using a brightly patterned handkerchief. Natasha shook her head, the veil seemed to catch on an unseen breeze.

"Of course I am here Joshua my soul mate." She

grabbed his sweaty hand to reassure him. Jessica over heard this and nearly vomited. *Get a room!* She thought. The ceremony went on, blessed by the deacon in his ceremonial gown, it was a bit long and everybody could tell the Deacon was winging it out due to it being the first wedding ceremony he had ever done. Joshua had chosen Brae to be his best man and Brae was lapping it up presenting the wedding rings. Joshua had purchased the best rings available in Red town, the rings were salvage from pre-war fingers but he covered the ridiculous cost from the churches stash of contributed coin. Jessica even though bored throughout the ceremony thought it was indeed a well-established event.

"How you doing Jess?" Brae asked as he swayed around on two feet offering a bottle of half drank wine. The church was full due to the after party.

"I'm... Doing okay Brae, how are you?" She snatched the bottle and drank a quarter of the bottle, wiping her mouth with the sleeve of the rented clothing. Brae was about to continue the conversation when an old buddy shoulder bumped him.

"Hey, I remember you, we fought side by side at..." The drunken man tried to remember the battle even though Brae didn't recognise him, Jessica definitely did.

"Burgstill Town?" Jess said trying to stop the room spinning even though she was sat on a church pew. The feller stopped his wondering and focused his gaze on Jessica.

"By the fucking bright! Jess???" The conversation were no longer on the male, but the pretty female that he somehow remembered during the past battle.

"Burgstill Town, yeah I remember now." The ex-ranger sat down next to Jessica and he was no longer happy in the memory of the battle. He seemed to sober up all of a sudden.

"I owe my life to you Jess, I remember I was hideously wounded and you dragged me off to safety... But you left the other rangers..." He was bawling his eyes out. "I wouldn't be here if it wasn't for you Jess!" He continued to cry but Jess thought it might be the beer talking. It's when Brae sat near Jess and put his head against hers. "He is right, you saved him, I was manning the walls, I tried to look for you on the field but it had turned to melee by that time." Jessica could only remember bits of that battle, but she remembered dragging off a wounded ranger.

"Yeah that was back then when I had a heart!" She put her head down and whispered. "Back then, when I gave a shit!" Jessica went off to find another drink and left the two veterans to swim in remembrance.

Jessica awoke she peered round the room and recognised, through phased intoxication that she was in her own rented room in Roodies whore house. A plump red haired prostitute was out for the count and had her arm over her shoulder. She twisted her body as the prostitute groaned and shifted position in the bed sheets. Her gun belt was on the bed side table and she vaguely remembered throwing some coins there but they were now absent. She climbed out of bed noticing the pink flesh of Macey. She had vague recollections of the night previous. She remembered a lot of red hair cascading in her face but nothing much more. She climbed out of bed and her mind cried out as though there was a tumour in her head. She patted the shoulder of the whore and she stirred.

"Let me sleep... You have paid me already..." She whimpered attempting to sleep though a hang over. Jess shrugged and started to dress she had a long day at the market with Joshua, they needed many supplies and she would be damned if he wasn't going to offer up coin. The blood rushed to her head making the head ache worse, her head span and she rushed to the 'jerry' to puke. She finally collapsed in the corner of the room still holding the 'jerry', just in case she vomited again.

Several hours passed, Jessica started to come around, she ventured off to the market square and met up with the preacher and Brae who were coordinating the purchases. By the time Jessica had stopped throwing up and wandered to the market, it seemed the boys had already purchased what they needed. She blundered through the bags of purchases and eventually gave a thumb's up to the inventory they had purchased. (Radiation protection stuff)

"Yep, it's all here..." The market square was spinning in her head and she felt bile rising. "I need to go!" She claimed before rushing off to an alley way in the township. Dribble cascaded from her mouth as her body made the way for her to be sick. Luckily the guys didn't witness her disgorging her innards behind the hay stacks. It was truly a terrible event in her mind's eye. When Joshua asked Brae to see how Jessica is doing, Brae declined knowing that his mate had drank far too much the night previous and could be inconsolable.

"Nature must run its course!" He reassured the Preacher, while grimacing at the noises coming from the alleyway.

CHAPTER 8

Ash took the last swig from the medicinal spirits, when the roller shutter door rolled up. Three rangers lead by sergeant Edwards marched into the cell wearing full combat gear. He noticed the safety were off there carbines.

"Suit up we are leaving!" Edwards said in a commanding tone. The other rangers started to dress the confused captain in heavy combat armour and in their haste they weren't being gentle.

"By the bright watch that arm you sons-of-bitches!" Ash yelled as one of the rangers strapped on a heavy bracer. He looked to Edwards and saw she had a mean look in her eye.

"What's all this nonsense about leaving?"

"Not your concern, I am the temporary leader until you have been cleared!" There was little emotion in her tone, almost monotone like a robot.

"We can't just leave, we have a duty to protect the farmland, this fort is..."

"Did I not make it clear Ash? I'm in command and we are fucking leaving right now!" She hammered it home by prodding his chest.

"Are the soviets at the gate?" he asked. She answered by shaking her head.

"We have the tactical advantage by keeping the

fort sergeant!" He tried to intimidate her by stepping towards her but the other rangers pushed him roughly back to the cell wall. *What's with these guys?* He thought.

"Aren't you going to at least arm me if we are to travel at night?" He noticed the lack of a gun belt on his armour. "At least give me my eagle!" But his words fell against a stone wall.

"You ain't gettin shit until we know you are still human!" Edwards pointed to the exit. "Now move out!" Ash was manhandled out of the cell, as one of the rangers strapped a heavy back pack on him.

"Sorry sir, but while you are a prisoner you may as well be helpful." The courtyard was floodlit and Ash could here generators humming. Rangers and auxiliaries were busying themselves filling hand carts with supplies and ammunition. *Got to hand it to you Edwards, you have certainly been a busy bee.* He was still a bit pissed off that his own sergeant and best friend hadn't filled in the details about the abandonment of the fort. He watched as the ranger flag being reeled down from the flag pole. He felt anger, confusion and sadness all at the same time, a proper melting pot of emotions rolled into one. *The bastards!*

Two rangers flanked Ash as they travelled off south west into the night. He looked to the auxiliaries dragging hand carts and wondered if they could keep up with the half jog the rangers had set pace. One of the wheels snagged on heavy bracken other rangers rushed to free it up and then joined formation almost leaving the auxiliary behind. Luckily the moon was full which swept the land in a lunar glow. He could just make out Edwards leading the front of the exodus. *Oooo I can't wait until I'm back in charge! Edwards my friend, you are going to be drilled to hell.* He quickly changed his mind, she wasn't stupid, she probably had a very good reason to abandon the fort. Behind them several explosions illuminated the land, he heard several nearby rangers sniggering. Goatie, one of the rangers flanking Ash, shoulder bumped him in a friendly manner.

"It sounds like the soviet cock suckers have found our booby traps." Another explosion ripped through the night air, Ash could see debris being scattered around the distant fort. Fires were burning bright under the full moon, the fort had been ruined. *My beautiful fort! What have they done?* Ash had been in charge of that fort for such a long time, it had been almost a family member.

The sun started to rise colouring the landscape in reds, oranges and yellows, the rangers had stopped to rest. Ash could see the axillaries t-shirts were soaked with sweat but he could see determination on their fatigued faces. Lookouts had been placed in a circle around the camp, some used binoculars to scan the landscape while others used scopes attached to their rifles. Edwards sat down next to him, she put her arm around his shoulders and gave him a little squeeze.

"I'm sorry captain, I had no time to explain. The soviets were marching in force, their numbers are double what the scouts reported. I had no choice." She put her head down as though she had been defeated. "Trust my luck when I become the leader and I give the order to abandon the fort." He could see very little spirit left in her eyes.

"With the sounds of things you made the right decision, I would have made the same call."

"Yeah well, I'm hoping we got a lot of those sons-of-dogs when the bobby traps tripped. The bright save us if we hadn't at least halved their numbers." She pulled out a half full canteen and took a swig, she didn't offer Ash any water worrying about the quarantine. She looked into his eyes and he could see they were glazed, gone had the sparkle that usually furnished her eyes.

"This is bullshit!" She stood suddenly and marched to Ranger Goatie who was having a piss up against a cactus. Ash couldn't hear the exchange but she marched back and gave him his gun belt with his nickel plated eagle in the holster.

"Thanks." He looked up shading his eyes to see Edwards smiling.

"The sun would have started to react on your skin if you were a drainer." She took a step back, saluted. "Captain Ash is now back in charge." She yelled making sure the entire camp heard her words. He stood and bear hugged the sergeant.

"I relinquish supreme leadership!" She howled over his shoulder hugging him tightly. One of rangers was distant on the sand and was running back to the rudimentary camp.

"Formations!" She yelled, it was Angel from Alpha team. Ash let go of Edwards and his body sagged. *So soon!*

"Combat nine! All rangers to Angel" He yelled. Remembering the ranger code to form a battle front. The rangers quickly gathered in two lines, front line kneeling while the second line stood. He was surprised how quick his rangers filed into formation. He borrowed Edwards binoculars and scanned the North east landscape. At first he couldn't see anything, he refocused and to his horror he could see a large skirmishing number of soviets wearing heavy armour and metal helmets, rushing toward the camp. It still bothered him how strong the drainers were? No human could run that fast wearing heavy metal armour. Ash ran to one of the carts.

"Everybody arm themselves, this is going to get messy!" He cried as he picked up a G3 battle rifle and slammed home a magazine of twenty bullets. Edwards was already at the front line her right leg anchored and her rifle facing forward. The bastards were running quick. The naked eye could pick up the soviets, even with the heat trails rising from the sand. Angel joined formation kneeling on the front-line, she had fixed a bayonet to her rifle and was already cursing the undead. Ash looked down his scope, the enemy group were still half a klick away but covering ground quickly. Ash needed to bolster his rangers, if they felt impending doom like himself then the battle was already over.

"Front line! Take single shots when the bastards get in range, second line go full auto on my command!" He peered over his shoulder and noticed the auxiliaries had gathered up the carts in a defensive line. They were still in sweat soaked t-shirts but had armed themselves with pistols and melee weapons in their off-hand.

"When the second line goes full auto, I want the first line to rally back to the camp behind the carts. I will stay with the second line!" His hands were shaking and he wished to hell he hadn't consumed that spirit the night previous, even though it had numbed the pain in his tattered arms. He looked down his scope and witnessed the dull black metal armour of the soviets, the armour so dark and dull that it didn't catch the sunlight. The front line was already firing, nervous un-aimed out of range shots.

"Hold the line!" Ash cried as he open fired with his battle rifle. 7.62mm casings spun in the air from the ejector port as he aimed true taking down one of the soviet targets. The front line combat rolled backwards between the second line, they got to their feet and started running to the cover of the carts.

"Fire!" Ash yelled as the second line went full auto, depleting magazines within seconds, but taking down a good number of the charging force. Gunsmoke obscured the battlefield as the first drainer leapt into melee. Ash dropped his rifle and whipped out his eagle sending hot lead into the skirmishing ranks.

"Retreat!" His pistol had locked and he just

managed to slam in another mag when a heavy armoured soviet bowled him over with the impact of a freight train. The air was knocked from his lungs and his nose burst open when the soviet head butted him in the face. His vision tunnelled quickly and he felt the embrace of unconsciousness riding up and down his spine. He vaguely remembered firing his pistol several times against the flank of the drainer before his vision cascaded into darkness.

He tried to open his eyes, but the sunlight was too bright. He tried to lever himself up but his arm was too damaged. He gave up and wiped crusted blood from his very sore nose. Throbbing pain in his head took over and he wished for the sanctuary of sleep. He distantly felt probing fingers around his neck.

"The captain isn't bit and he is alive!" A female voice sounded distant but it was comforting. He tried to speak but the pain in his chest stopped him short.

"I think my ribcage is busted." He whispered somehow ignoring the pain. He felt his lips were chapped and the sun was hot on his face.

"You need water Ash." He felt his head being cradled and warm water trickling into his mouth, but dreamland came in force.

A scraping sound woke him up, he covered his eyes from the sun and peered around. He was on a makeshift cot, being dragged through the sand, under the labour of Angel who he recognised by the tattoo of a leaping horse on her left arm.

"How long have I been out?" Ash managed to say through chapped lips. Angel halted and set the cot down.

"Stop the column, pass it on!" The elite ranger said to the ranger in front of her.

"The good news is, you weren't bitten. The bad news is we are approaching the grass lands." She chuckled as though it was bad news. He tried to get up but his busted ribs and arms stopped the meagre effort. Angel pushed him back onto the cot.

"If I'm gona drag your wounded ass through the desert, then you need to relax, can't have you bleeding out on me!" There was some comfort in her words but she still had the undertone of hatred toward him. *Still not forgiven me then!* He thought. The column picked up pace again and it wasn't long before sand replaced grass. Long lush water fed blades of grass. He put out his hand and felt the long fronds of grass tickling his palm. It was a nice feeling bringing memories of his childhood when he used to play in the fields around his mother's farm. The cot started to bounce around a little as it was dragged over a rough uneven trail. He opened one eye and recognised the path. *We are nearly at Apple wood farm*. He could see the orchard in the distance and recalled the bulging fruit grown here. It was strange because apple wood farm was on the cuff of the desert. It held fertile soil because of the two rivers that ran through the farm. The desert however drank up the rivers and replaced lush soil with unforgiving thirsty sand. He smelt the fresh smell of lavender, a small field on apple wood farm, kept by Mrs Drydan. She tendered the small grove due to the healing powers of lavender which she ground up to make healing poultices and liquors. Every now and then merchants outfitted the fort with tonics manufactured from lavender.

The sun shined through the muslin curtains, as Ash reached for a tumbler of water on the bed side cabinet. Solo Greaves grabbed the glass and placed it gently in Ash's hand.

"You feeling better cap?" The rugged looking solo asked softly. Ash felt tightly bound bandages around his arms and chest and when he shifted in bed he smelt the strong smell of lavender, which brought back a cascade of child hood memories.

"Nice to see you Greaves. I would have thought Edwards would be beside my bed." The mere mention of sergeant Edwards made the solo ranger bow his head.

"Is she okay?" Ash asked, as the solo narrowed his eyes and shook his head.

"Sorry Cap, she..." The solo covered his eyes with a calloused hand. "She got bitten, she took your pistol and wandered out into the desert. We heard a gunshot when we moved out. She took her own life on her terms." Ash shuddered, the pain in his ribs were distant as he fought back tears.

"It's what she wanted captain." Greaves finally

said. "She couldn't compromise the rangers. She is with the bright now." He smiled but clearly the solo was battling emotions against the loss.

"And the others... What of my rangers?"

"We have been thinned out! We barely have enough man power to fortify the farm stead. The battle took many of our brave warriors." The solo laughed halfheartedly. "But, we survived and we are steadfast!" The solo grabbed Ashes hand trying to console him, he knew Edwards was his favourite.

"It's not over captain, I fear we might be attacked tonight, the soviets move quicker under moonlight. But we will make a stand at apple wood, you have my word that we will take at least three to our one!"

"I need to get back on my feet, where is Thomas?"

"Thomas is tending the wounded in the barn, he is very busy."

"Get me on my feet Solo, I need to talk to Thomas." The solo sighed and nodded. "Are you sure cap, your pretty fucked up?" Greaves couldn't ignore the order even though he thought it may indeed kill the captain. He threw back the bed sheets and shouldered the captain out of bed. Ash tried to ignore the pain grappling his body as the solo 'fireman-lifted' him to the door. Ash tried his best to cancel the pain which came on like a tsunami. He felt broken bones in his rib cage grating against his lungs. He felt every step down the stairs as the elite solo shouldered the burden. The strong man carried the weight toward the barn, every now and then he voiced his opinion but Ash wished to carry on, even though he was in agony and short of breath. Thomas had set up a surgery, using bounded hay stacks as beds, it was bloody and audible with pain. As Greaves took Ash down the makeshift beds, Ash could see many wounded, mostly bullet wounds. Thomas was midway through sawing off Ranger Coulding's arm. Coulding had a length of leather in his mouth, biting back the pain as two auxiliaries held the ranger down. Thomas had a poker face but Ash could see torment there. When the hacksaw had finished the bone Thomas quickly used a bowie knife to finish the last strand of flesh. Some of the farm hands grabbed up a hot plate, burning hot off the brazier and cauterised the amputation. Screams like you wouldn't believe punctured the ambience of the clinic, bringing forth a stench of grilled bacon.

"Sorry son but we needed to take the arm, I haven't got very much antibiotics, I'm sorry." Thomas wandered over to the next patient with a worried frown. Greaves sat Ash down in a vacant chair as Thomas tried to find an artery in the bloody wound of the next patient. Ash felt nauseated and needed to lie down.

"I've seen enough, take me to my bed, I thought I could do something but I'm too damned wounded." He opened his arms to Greaves who lifted him up and carried him leaving the carnage behind. *Too weak, too fucking weak!*

Ash woke up, it was night time and he saw a

shadow at the bottom of the bed, he pulled the blanket upto his nose. The shutters to his room were open and the muslin cloth billowed slightly under the force of a night time wind, moon light dimly illuminated the bed room along with a feminine figure stood at the foot of the bed.

"Oooo Ash my kin?" The figure sang. The shadow crawled up the length of bed towards him. Moon light caught an oval face which he recognised.

"Edwards? But you are dead!" He whispered, he tried to shift his body weight but his body screamed in pain.

"Ash my darling." The washed out pale face of the sergeant said while cocking her head to one side, leering over him. He could feel her fetid breath on his face, she had fed recently he could smell the blood.

"Chicken out did you? Couldn't take your life, instead you have selfishly added another disease ridden drainer to the world!" He said through gritted teeth. Edwards grinned her canines weren't fully extended yet, but in time they would be prominent. She dropped the grin and suddenly looked sad.

"I was sitting alone in the desert with your pistol in my hand and..." She tried to find the words. "I just couldn't! It was something like the urge to survive took priority in my mind and then later it was curiosity more than anything else, the chance to see and feel what it is to be dead but not dead." She was whispering, she knew a guard had been posted outside the door, she was surprised Ash hadn't screamed for help yet?

"So have you made contact with the soviets, I'm assuming you are hedging your bets with them now?" He tested. Her hand stroked his throat and her thumb depressed on his wind pipe semi-choking him, enough to bring panic.

"What do you take me for, I might have gone to hell, but I won't align myself with those fucks! Becoming a drainer doesn't wipe your memory." She stopped choking him and he sputtered and coughed for a while.

"But they are now your kin, don't you want to run with your own species." He questioned having got his breath back. She pondered this, he could see the moonlight dancing in her eyes. He noticed the scar on her left right cheek had vanished, he remembered the day she got that scar. She had been lucky, the bullet damned near took her head off.

"Too be honest I don't feel any inner urge or wanting to be with other drainers. I'm guessing in time that may change, loneliness might set in. I'm unsure at this point in this new way of life."

"Human?" Ash asked referring to what she had just dined upon. She shook her head slowly from side to side still eyeing him like a predator looks at prey.

"Coyote, three of them. I feel as good as new after that feast." She smiled seeing Ash's distaste. "Yeah, I'm glad you didn't see that, it was feral and bloody and the poor little doggies didn't stand a chance." She finished with a custie-custie tone, almost mocking before she stifled chuckles.

"Captain?" A muffled voice issued from the door.

The guard rapped a few times. Edwards hissed barring her teeth like a rabid dog, she leapt like an acrobat off the bed and landed softly on all fours, before diving through the open window. The silence and speed in which Edwards shifted, un-nerved Ash more than the fact he was unarmed and could had been killed easily by the night caller.

"Erm... Hi yes, could I have a glass of water?" Ash said nervously looking at the open window.

"I suppose so." He could hear the guard regretting asking.

"Wait... Forget the water please could you close the window shutters, its bloody freezing in here." The door opened and the guard thumped in. Ash recognised Ranger Sanding, he wasn't his favourite ranger by any standards and he wondered how he had survived all these attacks? If anybody was going to die under his command it would have been him. *Maybe I miss-judged him?* He thought. The ranger looked out of the window and peered into the night before shutting it fast.

"You sure you don't want some water?" Sanding asked looking to the nearly empty tumbler of water. Ash could see now, it wasn't out of laziness or reluctance, it was fatigue.

"How long since you last slept?" Ash asked feeling a little guilty. The Ranger shrugged and sighed.

"Too long captain." A gunshot rang in the night startling the ranger, followed by more gun shots. Sanding pulled his sidearm and thrust it into Ashes hand, alert and wide eyed.

"Thanks, now go and see what is going on!" The ranger locked and loaded his carbine and rushed out of the room leaving the captain shivering in bed, the cold steel in his hand.

Time passed like an age, as he heard mumbled voices outside the farmstead. Ash had managed to lever himself upto a sitting position as Sanding returned, almost breathless.

"We are gathering in the hearth room captain, I think its best if you hear what Greaves needs to say." Sanding shouldered Ash up ignoring the winces and moans of pain. He half dragged him into the warmth of the main hearth room. The fire had been stoked back up with fresh logs bringing a not unpleasant burnt apple wood smell to the spacious room. Farmhands and rangers had gathered and they all looked grim and worn out. He spotted Angel holding a portable radio set, she was busy giving coordinates and speaking with another ranger outfit, possibly Captain Harris of north watch.

"The fort has been taken and the east is compromised?" The radio crackled.

"Affirmative!" Angel concluded.

"We haven't encountered any drainers or threats carrying a pre-war Sigel?" Ash could hear the doubt in Captain Harris's words.

"I need to speak to Captain Ash, get him on comms!" Harris stated. Angel looked to Ash being manhandled into the hearth room.

"He is here Captain, I will put him on." She held the

radio out at arm's length as though it was a bag of fresh dog shit. Ash fumbled for the radio set and clicked the speak button.

"It's true, the fort is gone, it was compromised by a pre-war soviet force, which we believe to be Drainers." Ash stated biting back the pain in his ribs. A long silence descended and the radio just hissed with background radiation.

"Drainers? Are you sure Ash?" It was a question but his tone was that of dread.

"How is north watch holding out?" Ash asked trying to glean information.

"North watch has been quiet, has been for months. We had some bandit activity about three months back but it's been boring ever since." Harris still sounded doubtful.

"We are fortifying Applewood, we are going to use this as a base of operations and hope to fuck the soviets don't bypass us and attack the other farmsteads..." Ash took a deep painful breath. "We need rangers down here old friend and quick." The radio fell silent once again. Ash assumed the other captain was conflicted and in deep discussion with his sergeants and personnel.

"We are abandoning north watch, we will rally on your position in four days, hold fast Ash. We are coming!" The radio bleeped and then hissed. Ash gave the receiver back to Angel and peered around the room. The farmhands and the Drydan family owners of the farmstead, all appeared glum. He could see defeat on their faces and their world turning upside-down as every second passed.

"Will we hold out for four days Mr Ash?" Mrs Drydan asked as she gathered her young children to her skirt. Ash could see fear on the young faces, the youngest had started to weep.

"Solo Turrin! We need to warn the other farmsteads in this area." Ash looked at the anti-social ranger cleaning her gun near the fire hearth. She looked up and met his gaze. Her face had no emotion what-so-ever, her eyes were glazed from conflict and too much time alone in dangerous environments. Her hand swept over her crew cut blonde hair as she stood and nodded. She was a predator and had no fear, humanity had long since sailed from her broken but focused mind.

"I will warn the others." She whispered, as though she was deep in enemy lines. She picked up a G3 battle rifle and checked the ejector port before shouldering the heavy rifle before marching out. Ash grabbed her hand as she passed, she instinctively swiped her hand from his grasp like a dog with a sore paw.

"I said I will warn them, no pep talk for me captain!" She said angrily. Ash nodded and saluted at the same time.

"Bright speed Ranger." But it fell on deaf ears. Before she left Solo Greaves hugged her, followed by a silent exchange of words that was out of earshot. Turrin opened the door and left quickly shutting the door almost silently. Greaves had his head down for a while before joining the meeting.

"You all heard, we wait it out and stand fast here, remember we die to protect the civilians that is the code of the rangers." Even though Ash tried to reassure the farmers he could see the anxiety levels were high.

"What is the supply situation?" He asked referring to ammo and weapons more than basic needs such as water and food.

"We have enough to make a stand captain." Tina the auxiliary claimed. She had taken leadership ever since the quartermaster had perished. Her vest, pants and auburn short hair were clinging to her athletic frame due to the sweat and worry of the default leadership. Her hands were shaking but Ash could see fire in her belly. Ash looked to the farm hands armed with double barrelled shotguns.

"If we have assault rifles to spare, then issue them to the farmhands, shotguns are good, but in a fire fight we need an almost continuous barrage." Ash turned his gaze to Mrs Drydan.

"Those shotguns are better in the hands of your kin, which will be holed up in this room with me." Mrs Drydan tried to mouth her complaints but she bit back her words understanding the peril which could come at any given second. She snatched a shotgun off one of her elder sons and checked to see if it was loaded.

"I've been on this farm all my life, I will be damned if somebody is going to take my farm from me!" Mrs Drydan was tall and sported a middle aged body that had more scars carrying children than the average combat ranger caught in battle. Ash silently applauded her bravery.

"So it is settled, we make a stand here and we will send anything that attacks this farm, back to hell!" Ash Yelled at the top of his voice, through the sheer pain of his broken rib cage. He tried to stand but the pain sat him back down. One of the farm hands approached with a shot gun over his shoulder.

"A drainer scout was in the grounds of the farm, I tried to shoot it down, but it ran like the wind!" It was the eldest son of the Drydan family. The muscular man palmed two spent shot gun cartridges. Ash looked at the spent shotgun rounds and wondered if the farm hand had witnessed Edwards fleeing the farm.

"Did you hit it?" Ash hoped not.

"Dunno it was dark, but I guess we could pick up a trail tomorrow when the sun rises." The eldest son claimed. *Run my rabbit!* Ash thought.

Dawn came quickly casting long red shadows around the farmstead. Ash had commandeered a Shepard stave to aid his progress wandering around the extensive farmland. It was beautiful seeing the sun rise and the morning breeze on his face, fragrant with the sweet smell of apples and lavender. When Edwards came to him the night before he thought he would never see another dawn. Fatigued looking rangers were busy making stockade out of logs, fortifying the north east of the farm. He could smell meat being cooked and lavender tea brewing on the open camp fires dotted around near the stockades. Thomas had tried to give him pain killers but he opted for the apple moonshine brewed and distilled at Applewood farm. The pain in his ribs and arms were nothing but a back ground throb due to the alcohol in his bloodstream. He held a berretta in his off hand, that ranger Sanding's had given him the night previous. He missed the reassuring weight and calibre of his desert eagle but he remembered that Edwards had taken his pistol to end her life. *Could have done with my old pistol Edwards!* He cursed. He wanted to tell the rangers about the visitation of his former sergeant but he didn't wish to cause panic. *She could have killed me but she didn't, there is hope?* He wondered if she would come back and visit him, maybe fight alongside him as she had done so many times before.

"If you're out there my friend, please come back to us, we need you now and be fucked if you are diseased!" He whispered nursing the bottle of moonshine. He hadn't noticed Solo Greaves sit down next to him. He had obviously overheard his whisper.

"So she lives?" He eyed the captain with his ice blue unforgiving eyes. The solo passed him a cup of lavender tea with a questioning stare.

"She lives but she walks in the night." Ash said solemnly, caught out.

"And you didn't tell us?"

"Edwards was a fine ran..."

"Fuck that! She is one of them now, why would you keep that from us?" The Solo Barked. "Protocol is to put them down, you know that captain, by the bright it was your doctrine!" The solo spat.

"I know, but it somehow feels different, if she wanted to compromise the rangers then she would have killed me!" He said, but his mind was conflicted between saving Edwards or killing her.

"That's on you captain." He poured the last remnants of tea to the grass before storming away angrily. *Yes that's on me!* He watched the elite ranger plod away towards the main stockade where tired looking rangers manned the fortification, with rifles at the ready.

Later that day Ash sat at the long farmhouse dining table, a place where only farmers ate their meals after a hard days graft in the fields. Mrs Drydan's daughter spooned out stew into each bowl present around the table. The stew smelt of pork and vegetables and had the consistency of a chunky midnight drunken puke. Her eldest daughter Cornelia was an un-married spinster of thirty years. Her parents had tried their best to marry her off but to no avail. Ash couldn't work out why she hadn't been married off. She was a bonnie-lass, with long reddish-blonde hair a little bit buxom, but in a nice way. However, when they ate the meal he noticed she was very shy and a little bit 'off' when she spoke. *Spoilt child*, he thought. The meal was nice and there were plenty of corn bread, better than the rangers got at the fort, but on the other edge of the sword it was hard to make meals from the rations the farmers provided to the fort as tribute. Ash had never been religious but he respected religion especially the common religion Bright. But when the farmers finished the meal and blessed the taking he couldn't help thinking they were all pissing in the wind. Cornelia, had placed herself across the table from Ash, during the end of the meal, when they brought out a sugary pudding, he couldn't help feeling Cornelia's foot caressing his leg under the table. He had shifted three times but still she found his leg to caress. When Mrs Drydan clapped her hands, to clear the table she looked to Cornelia. The old woman gave the captain a focused and direct stare in disagreement, as though she knew what had been going on. The consumed booze had more than numbed the pain in his arms and ribs and he quickly made his apologies before retiring to bed. Ash made his way through the labyrinthine of corridors and rooms in the farmstead and finally found his bedroom. The intoxication had thrown his senses and balance off guard, but he managed to back shuffle, closing the door to his room and then collapsed on the bed barely having the strength to cover himself up with a blanket. The room span for a while before sleep found him and the abyss engulfed him in to darkness.

CHAPTER 9

You could just make out Red town from the top of the hill, the party had headed due north east and it was around noon when they sat down for a rest. Jessica sat with the back to the party staring intently on Red town and all the liquor and whores she was missing out on. *Could have been getting fingered by Mary-lou right now*, the thought crippled her. Brae had appointed himself the leader of the group, Jess didn't care a shit it was time he stepped up and cut her apron strings.

"We should hit Targ's trade house by sun down, where we can bed down for the night, its relatively cheap a coin each and Targ has guards so we can rest soundly and don't need to rota a watch." Brae pointed at the map with his finger.

"I will pay, it will be good to get a goodnight's sleep before we hit the real trail. We have such a long way to go." Joshua agreed. Natasha was sat nearby tugging and pulling on the armour straps as though it was an uncomfortable bodice.

"Its too heavy Joshua, can't I take the armour off, its hot and making me sweat." She moaned.

"We all have to wear armour sweetheart, we are going to be travelling in some lawless places where armour will save your life." Joshua patted her softly on her arm. He had made a very expensive purchase and bought Natasha a customised carbine, it had fifteen point forty fives in the magazine and it was light due to most of the carbine had been made from carbon fibre (some kind of pre-war shit).

"We aren't in lawless territory yet Joshua can't I just bag it for now and put it on when we leave civilization?" She pleaded. Joshua got real angry.

"You wear the damned armour! It's my duty as a husband to protect my wife!" He growled. Natasha pulled a face and sulked with her arms folded across her body armour. Yolanda wandered out from a bunch of shrubs pulling up her trousers.

"If anybody needs a piss, then beware of rattle snakes, there must be a nest of the fuckers in those bushes. But I think I scared them off." Jessica pondered for a while out of all the times on the trail with Yolanda she hadn't once glimpsed a flash of her lady parts. *Bet it's hairy!* She thought, as she dismissed the imagined blonde haired bush. Jessica preferred the maintained and shaved pussy of a whore. She was feeling horny again thinking about the prostitutes she had recently slept with at Roodies, Mary-Lou was her current favourite. Yolanda wasn't her type, too masculine she preferred her girls pretty and feminine, god only knew what Brae found attractive in Yolanda. Brae was a good looking feller, Jessica had slept with him a few times years back when they ran with the rangers, but it was more out of curiosity because she did prefer women.

"Right everybody up, if we don't set off now then we will be wandering in the dark before we reach

Targ's." Brae announced before shouldering his heavy back pack. The party moaned and groaned as they picked up their belongings and marched out of the temporary camp. The patches of poverty grasses soon became sandy desert as the party leant into the dusty wind following a bearing on Brae's compass. The sun was unforgiving, they found a few water holes frequented by roaming cattle drivers and stopped to boil water to fill canteens. Brae had been correct; they managed to get to the trade house just as the last of the sun silhouetted the dunes. The trade house was an old fortified filling station, the road that must have lead here had been long engulfed by the desert. The battered old sign stated 'Amoco' and numerous guards were patrolling the parameter.

"Here to trade?" One of the rough looking guards asked armed with an old army issue M16.

"Gona trade and hole up if you have room?" Brae said as he clicked the safety on his rifle.

"Get yourself in from the night, we have rooms and food on the hot plate. Hope you like pork, we have a lot of juicy pork?" The grizzly looking guard stated.

"Pork's just fine. We have a preacher with us if you wish to have solace?" Brae said hoping for a discount. Brae could smell the pig pen at the back of the building before he even laid eyes on it.

"We ain't bright folks, no offence preacher. But we do respect your faith."

"I will pray for you this night." Joshua said, but his words fell on deaf ears.

Jessica pulled out her battered old fob watch and peered at the time. It was ten o clock and the guards started to lock down the trade house. They closed the shutters on the windows and chained and locked the main fortified door.

"Expecting trouble?" She asked. The guards ignored her and carried on locking the building tight. Targ the owner was a short potbellied man wearing a grease stained apron and a troubled frown.

"We got an old pre-war bunker several klicks west of the trade house. It's full of 'Rotters', they come out at night, they do no harm but they sometimes wander this way and knock at the door." Targ said bitterly. Jessica and Brae had encountered 'Rotters' before, they were basically long living humans that have very little in the way of lateral thinking. Mindless almost, but they often carried out daily pre-war activities. They seemed to get aggressive when they encountered human beings, attacking out of jealousy or something?

"Why haven't you cleared them out?" Jessica asked. Targ shrugged.

"We feel sorry for them, it ain't their fault. Too be honest we cull their numbers every so often, but the bunker must have housed thousands of people. I don't know how they have lived so long since the nuclear war?" Targ said with sorrow in his voice.

"We have seen 'Rotters' before but they usually dwell in radioactive city ruins, like you said Targ, not sure how they have lived so long, maybe some kind of disease or something?" Brae added. A knock at the door alerted the party, Jessica pulled her pistols and started to walk to the door. Targ stopped her by grabbing her wrist.

"Leave them be, they are no harm to us, just ignore them. They will be gone by sun rise." He smiled and let go of her wrist. Jessica put her guns away and nodded to the guard standing near the door.

"You give me a shout if they bust that door down." The guard just chuckled and rapped three times on the door.

"They will move on soon, it takes them a while to reach here, most of them pretend to fill up imaginary cars and then wander off into the desert to eat bugs and rodents. This happens every night we are used to it." Jessica tried to remember and realised she had never come to Targ's before.

"It's time to turn in." Joshua stated as he stretched and yawned. The party agreed and headed off to the rooms they had paid for, all apart from Jessica who ordered another round of whiskey, which she shared with Targ and a number of guards.

"A game of cards?" She said as she rummaged through her pack revealing a leather pouch of chips and a battered old deck of cards.

"I will warn you now, the Jack of diamonds is missing." She said as Targ and a group of guards pulled up stools around her table, tossing in a coin for the pot.

Even though it was early morning, the desert had

started to heat up to an uncomfortable heat. The sand had changed from packed sand, to loose deep desert sand when every step drained you. Joshua had a large pre-war golf umbrella in his hand and Natasha was hugging close to him seeking the shade. Jessica pulled off her wide brimmed hat and looked upto the blue cloudless sky. The sweat on her brow evaporated within seconds. Brae stretched out a moth eaten map on the sand and checked his brass nautical compass for a bearing. Jessica peered over his shoulder and chuckled.

"Remember when we got lost in the desert and we followed captain Ash's bearing and we found out his compass was fucked?" Brae looked over his shoulder and grinned.

"Yeah I remember that. Gee we were so lost and dehydrated. We thought we would die out in the ash land until you pointed out the morning dew on that cactus stump." Brae began to laugh remembering the memory. Jessica knelt down and shoulder bumped Brae. Yolanda sneered at the old buddies bonding.

"Old times." She sighed. "We got a north bearing from the dew on the cactus and managed to get to the oasis spring that saved all of us." Jess said, with fond memories. Yolanda shoved Jessica out of the way, eying her while she sat next to Brae pretending to get involved with the map.

"We are approaching a ruined city, but we can camp there." Yolanda stabbed her finger on the moth eaten map. "We camp up and then get our rad-capes and respirators to traverse the ruin." Jessica had backed off from the jealous female.

"We need to keep our wits about us, when we cross that city, unfortunately that is the only bridge for miles, crossing the wide river. Unless we double back and head north?" Brae said.

"We will use the bridge in the city to cross the river!" Yolanda said as she hugged Brae and sneered at Jessica. *Leave my man alone, bitch!* Jessica took the hint and wandered over to Natasha and Joshua who were in deep conversation.

"It won't be long until we find out the utopian man's lineage. His father's notes will lead us to Utopia!" Joshua said as Natasha huffed in the mindset that he was wasting everybody's time.

"You should have stayed in your church Josh, your flock needs you." She said having built up the courage to make him see sense. Joshua agreed but his quest was strong in his mind.

"If we find the utopia then I could lead my people there and we can live our lives in peace!" His words were strong and without doubt. He gazed into Natasha's eyes. He witnessed innocence and the sparkle of love.

"The bright will guide our way Joshua my love." She embraced him and her hand reached down to his crotch rubbing at his groin, as she kissed him passionately.

"We will all be safe when we reach utopia." He whispered ignoring the landscape around him. He couldn't wait until they camped down so he could make love to his wife.

"We head for Red-hands oasis!" Brae stated as he grabbed Yolanda's hand to lever her up. He folded up the map and placed it in the pocket of his back pack.

The sun was going down but they could see tree's scratching a living around the water hole in the distance. The party double timed it, ranger style and arrived at the oasis just before the sun light disappeared, casting the desert in to darkness. The oasis smelt of mould, even though the sun should have dehydrated the land. Large mushroom blooms were gathered under the palm trees along with bulbous, spiky cactus plants.

"We camp here!" Brae said as a command, as he unrolled out his bed blanket. "We are deep desert now, so we need to stay on watch. I will take the first three hours, Jess could you take the second? And Yolanda you take the third watch!" Everybody agreed as Natasha and Joshua bedded down and started petting each other and then fucking. Jessica bedded down. She didn't sleep until Joshua and Natasha 'came' and then the darkness cascaded into forgiving hug of sleep.

"Jess, it's you on watch." Brae grabbed her hand as she moaned and groaned as sleep fleeted from her.

"I'm up for fucks sakes!" She said, trying her damned best, not to get pissed off and wake the others. She kicked off her bed roll and reached for her gun belt. Jessica stood up and buckled up her belt, it's when she noticed numerous humanoid shadows creeping up the hill towards the camp.

"Get everybody on their feet Brae!" She howled pulling both of her forty fives.

"Alarm!" Brae cried into the night. Yolanda was up on her feet with her rifle in her hand, while Natasha and Joshua fumbled their way out of the camp bedding. The bandits had heard the alarm cry and started shooting into the night. Bullets whizzed past Jessica's head, as she flanked right, firing a volley from both her pistols. Bullet casings cascaded to the ground around her boots. Yolanda combat rolled to a safe position behind a cactus and quickly aimed and fired. Her night scope was coming in handy now. A mist of blood erupted after she squeezed the trigger. *One down at least!* Yolanda thought as she witnessed more bandits coming up the hill. The night sky erupted in a blaze of gun fire, audible and illuminating for a second or two. Brae wild fired into the night depleting a magazine of thirty bullets, before he reloaded. Jessica had reloaded both of her pistols and managed to sneak down to the bandits flank. The entire party were wild firing into the dark as the bandits found sanctuary in the bluff of the hill.

"Leave the Silver and move on, we will let you live!" The bandit leader said even though bullets were punctuating his words, in a bad tense.

"We are rangers and you are fucked, law breakers!" Brae cried, as he peered down the scope of his rifle looking for targets He aimed and fired, as one of the bandits head popped open showering blood and bits of cranium over a nearby bandit. Before the bandit had time to think, Jessica had already out flanked them and quickly put them all to sleep in a rage of her pistols. Jessica reloaded her guns and scanned the carnage, she was alive. That's all that mattered. *Fuck the rest!* She thought. A number of the bandits had fled off into the night when the odds weren't stacking their way anymore. Brae was stood over one of the bandits poking a bullet wound in the young mans shoulder using the muzzle of his rifle.

"Where you camped up scumbag?"

"Please, I beg you, I didn't fire a bullet, check my rifle, I didn't want any of this..." The young man started to sob and whimper. Brae kicked him hard in the side of his chest, knocking the sob from him.

"How many and where is your camp?" Brae pried again fearing they might re-group and attack again.

"We are part of a wide patrol operating out of the ruins, we crossed Clifford's Bridge this morning." The bandit wheezed. Brae slapped him hard across his face using the back of his hand.

"You still ain't answered my question?" The young lad had started to cry again, but this time it was incredibly hard to understand him.

"A lot of us, leave me alone!" He sobbed. Jessica had finished off the other wounded bandits with her knife and had come over to see what Brae was doing to the young bandit feller.

"He, telling the truth?" She asked, eying the blubbering bandit suspiciously. Brae nodded and made the old ranger sign to break camp quick. Jessica nodded, pulled out a pistol and put one round in the young man's head. The sound of crying halted immediately and the night was quite once more.

Before they broke camp they quickly looted the corpses for anything they could use, ammo, food and a seemingly abundance of coin? They fled into the night making a bearing north of the bridge, they had agreed to hole up north and send Jessica to check out the bridge. Joshua and Natasha were complaining a lot as they marched in the night but were very thankful that they were still alive thanks to the gun fighters. Brae and Jessica had taken up the lead.

"They had a lot of coin on them, it was almost as if they had nothing to spend it on?" Brae said quite perplexed.

"Either that or they have a different economy in these parts? Consider this; imagine if they had busted open a bank?" She Paused and stopped to stretch out her aching limbs. "Well, if the bandits had found so much coin in 'said bank', then prices would go up for the average produce or service."

"That's very deep Jess." He smiled. "But, I suspect they have been raiding merchant wagons like fuck and got the coin that way. Makes sense, possibly why they were on this side of the bridge. They were clearly looking out for opportunities."

"Opportunities like us you mean." Jess said grinning. Brae chuckled and nodded, gesturing for Jessica to get moving.

The sun started to climb into the sky, they had made good headway across the desert sands and to the south east they could just make out using binoculars, the massive bridge spanning the river. Due to the locality of the river, the sands had started to change to poverty grasses and other plants. Jessica dropped her heavy pack and took off her heavy leather duster.

"Right, I'm going for a look see, if you hear gun fire, stay put, I will lead them out in the desert and then meet here later on when its night time." She said as she grabbed up two canteens and a bundle of extra ammo.

"You sure you don't want me along for the ride?" Brae asked with genuine worry in his voice. Jess shook her head and jogged out of camp following the river down to the far away bridge. After about twenty minutes or so, she stopped running and started to shift cautiously through the plants and grasses growing by the river bank. She could see the bottom of the river until about fifteen feet out and then it got dark. The river was clean, man hadn't polluted the river for so many years and nature had taken back the reins. However, being so close to the ruins it was probably not a good idea to drink from it, isotope wasn't her favourite flavoured water. She had shifted closer to the toll bridge buildings on this side of the river, using the plants to stay in cover. A large group of bandits were gathering and preparing to move out into the desert. She could smell un-washed humans and rank breath on the desert breeze. The group were heavily armed and had large packs, where ever they were going and judging by the bags and equipment it was far from here. She waited a while until they got themselves sorted and moved out into the desert on a bearing of south west. When they had covered enough ground she broke cover and ran back to camp. *Lucky break for us it seems.* She wondered hoping they hadn't left a kettle on and doubled back. A few guards had stayed back among the toll buildings but they wouldn't cause too much of a threat.

Having gathered up the party they followed the river bank to the toll buildings and dug in among the plants and long grasses. Brae and Yolanda had opted to take out the guards leaving Jessica to protect Joshua and Natasha. She hadn't been too chuffed by the decision but she was fatigued and needed the rest. Brae and Yolanda shifted forward and took a stairwell upto the main bridge. The bridge had clearly been retro-fitted years before the war, it must have been a stone built iron affair but later converted into a suspension bridge to take heavier traffic. Jessica watched as Brae and Yolanda took out the guards using stealth and knives. She heard no cries of alarm or gunshots. Brae eventually signalled from the top of the toll bridge building having cleared it out.

"Move out, the coast is clear!" Jessica said as she shouldered her heavy pack. Natasha and Joshua grumbled for a while as they made their way to the stair well near the river bank. Two old rowing boats were moored by the stairwell, stuck fast on the mud of the river bank, they hadn't been used for many years. Funnily, one of the little row boats had 'The lady Jessica' in faded yellow paint down the side of its hull.

"You have a boat Jess." Natasha said through giggles. Jessica laughed seeing the funny side. She hadn't owned shit in her life and made a mental note that if ever she retired she would come back for this cute little row boat. She didn't dwell on the idea of getting the boat to wherever she had decided to retire in the land, but it was a nice thought all the same. As they ascended the dark stairwell she nearly tripped over a number of fresh corpses which had been thrown down here by Brae and Yo after their murderous spree. They got to the top of the stairwell smelling that fresh copper-iron stink of fresh blood. Yolanda was sat on the bonnet of an old rusted up car which looked like an old Dodge charger, she was busy cleaning the blood from her knife. Brae had his binoculars out scanning the way across the bridge. Jessica assumed merchants had shifted the many cars to the side of the bridge leaving a clear run for the wagons between. It must have taken them an age and probably done a long time ago. Jessica approached Brae still transfixed, spying using his binoculars.

"Anything?" She ventured with a little hope to see some conflict. Brae put his binoculars away shaking his head.

"Nothing, looks like a clear run. I think the bandits only guarded this side, which makes me believe their stronghold is close to the other side of the bridge." He didn't know for sure but his wits were still about him. Jess put down her pack and started to pull out equipment and attire.

"Everyone get suited up in your rad-capes and respirators, we will be crossing a nuked out ruin, best be protected, this city looks like it took a big one!" She said referring to a proper city smashing nuke. Everybody agreed and began to do as they were told. She assumed this city was a strategic enemy target, probably due to the many foundries and manufacturing complexes it held. Brae switched on his giga-counter, it clicked away softly but everyone assumed it would hiss as they crossed the central part of the ruined cityscape. Yolanda started to pep talk Joshua and Natasha, warning them about radiation and the constant threat from abominations that dwell in ruined cities.

"The radiation from the bombs has changed all life dwelling in the ruins, be it plant, animal or human. Be on your guard, they will not be how they seem!" She tutored to the new travellers in the Ashland. Brae stepped forward as though he was a university lecturer.

"Try not to touch anything unless we tell you it is safe to do so. Flowers might look pretty but they can be incredibly poisonous. Structures might go at any second bringing down..." Jess put her hand on his shoulder and squeezed hard.

"We aren't here to shit you up or tell you tall tales. Touch nothing and do what we do and before you know it, we will be camped down on the other side of the ruins laughing about our journey." She said sternly bolstering Brae and Yolanda's words.

The rad-capes and respirators narrowed vision and felt heavy and encumbering as they made their way across the bridge toward the skeletal city ahead. The itchy capes were sweaty and the mid-day sun added to the claustrophobic confines of the protective attire. The tall buildings on the other side of the bridge, leant, sagged and crumbled visibly. Windows were shattered and structural columns of concrete groaned in the desert breeze bringing up clouds of ash and debris. Dust devils whirled around the foot of the bridge as Jessica wondered how anybody could make a living here. She kept looking at Brae's giga-counter and watched the needle climb and flicker as the device counted the various radiation pockets in the area. Jessica never wanted kids, but she still worried about the damage to her body from all the radiation she must have soaked up over her travels, especially travelling through numerous radiation hot zones during her life. She was glad she preferred the physical company of females, if she had been heterosexual then that might have been a different story.

They got to the foot of the end of the bridge and the ruined city loomed in the horizon.

"It's now or never, we need to move quickly through the city and I advise everybody to keep up with me!" She mumbled through her respirator. Everybody agreed and took up a ranger like pace down the ash strewn ruined street ahead. The ruins were foreboding and seemed to lean on each side bringing anxiety and fear to the travellers. They had plenty of sun light but they needed to get through the city before sun down, to avoid the ever present threat to their lives.

CHAPTER 10

It had been three more days and the soviets hadn't attacked Applewood farm, Ash had hoped the farmstead had been overlooked by the soviets. *Maybe there is hope*, he pondered. He clambered gingerly out of bed checking his dressings. Thomas had been administrating some pre-war steroid to aid his body to knit up the wounds. He was no longer in so much pain, in fact apart from stretching he felt okay. He picked up an empty syringe from the bed side cabinet, it was labelled 'F.A.S.T'. He didn't understand what the abbreviations meant, but whatever it was it was working. Thomas opened the door and wandered into the bed room opening the shutters.

"It's noon sir, but that stuff knocks you out as one of the side effects." He went through the routine of checking his pulse and listening to his chest using a stethoscope.

"You're going to make a full recovery captain. I'm happy to say." He smiled and cocked his head as though he was startled by how good the pre-war medication had worked.

"This stuff looks like it was supposed to be administrated to pre-war race horses?" Ash said peering at the empty syringe, recollecting old pre-war flyers.

"Yes, it's quite a cocktail of drugs. Apparently

F.A.S.T was the latest field medic drug given to the wounded towards the close of the war. Not sure about the side effects, didn't think they had time to wonder about such things as the bombs fell." Thomas shrugged and began to rub the bronzing blood from the cuff of his stained white gown. "But you're feeling okay now, yes?"

"I Feel a lot better now Thomas, thank you."

"I'm sorry, but I need to give you another dose. You will feel sleepy again and maybe miss another day, but your wounds will heal quicker and your busted ribs will knit back together quickly. We need our captain back on his feet!" Thomas broke the plastic seal and pulled out another potent looking syringe. Ranger Sanding's stood at the side of the bed and tried to pull a positive face, but he was riddled with doubt.

"It's for the good of the Rangers Sir, I will watch over you if you don't mind?" The ranger asked. Ash grimaced as the doctor rolled up the sleeves of Ash's long johns.

"Do it!" Ash said as he looked away from the needle he had seen several times by now. Ash felt the spike and then the drug rushing through his bloodstream, it was too late to turn back, he felt sleep coming down hard on his mind. He looked upto Sanding's grim looking face as the ranger held his hand.

Ash managed to get to the stoop of the farmstead and sat down on the stair, one of the farm hands of Applewood farm started to play a banjo. Ash felt out of breath but his wounds felt incredibly better. He realised he had been out for the count for at least two days, the farm hand was playing an old song, singing the pre-war song as though it had been recorded before the war..

"I see a bad moon rising… I see trouble on the way." Ash listened to the song and started to mummer some of the words He remembered listening to this song long ago on a wind up stereo-set that the rangers had found deep in some ruined city. He couldn't remember where? But he recalled it had a catchy tune.

"Don't go out tonight, because it's bound to change your life…"

"There's a bad moon on the rise!" He joined in and smiled and chuckled at the words because they were so apt to what was going on in the farmstead. He was about to join in on the next verse when a female ranger rushed through the gaps of the stockade and thrust up her fist.

"Northern watch approaches!" Ranger Edding cried in a hysteria of happiness. She looked happy but full of sleep deprivation around her eyes. Ash Stood and he had to politely push Sanding's arms from lifting him.

"Captain Harris?" Ash stood on tip toes trying to see the arriving ranger entourage, even though stretching hurt his ribs in excitement. A large contingent of rangers arrived, they were dusty from desert travel and looked to be worn out. Through the crowd Ash spotted old Captain Harris making his way to the water barrel near the stockade. Ash quickly made himself presentable and walked toward the stockade with a grin on his face. Harris spooned several gulps of water from the water barrel and spotted his old friend Ash.

"By the Bright we have arrived in time!" Harris said wiping water from his almost white beard. Ash threw his arms around the old warrior and hugged him even though his body cried out in pain.

"Good to see you old friend." Ash chuckled against the nape of the old warrior's neck, squeezing him tight.

"I heard you abandoned the fort!" He barked suddenly serious. Ash was lost for words, he couldn't counter such words.

"We fell captain and rallied to Applewood." Ash claimed with sorrow. The old warrior grinned and hugged Ash tight.

"You had reason my kin, you wouldn't have abandoned the fort without proper reason!" He pushed Ash away and put his head against Ash's head.

"We have come to fortify the farm lands my fiend. My rangers are yours!" The old grizzled old veteran stated.

"Welcome to Applewood you ol' bastard!" Ash said trying not to laugh and unstitch his wounds.

The new arrivals dug in with the other rangers. A meeting had been called in the main room to outline what had gone on. Ash wasn't looking forward to announcing the retreat, but he hoped the old captain would understand. Before the meeting started Mrs Drydann threw up her hands and wished to speak. To be fair it was her land and her farm.

"The farmstead can't support such numbers, food

will run out quickly. We have plenty of water, but that is all!" The elderly woman that had seen so many winters and appeared more grey than her actual age. Ash understood and tried to calm the situation down. He was tired and the drugs were still trying to repair his body.

"We need to leave a contingent of rangers here and distribute the rest of the rangers to support and protect other farms. This is a crisis which we didn't foresee!" The room erupted in debate and doubt as the farmstead folks tried to salvage a logical solution to the present state of affairs. Harris lifted his head in a noble stance.

"My rangers will protect Applewood and use this land as Ranger central. Ash and his rangers will separate and protect the other farmsteads. Tributes from other farms will arrive at Applewood!" He looked to his personal female scribe, who noted down his words in an old pre-war notebook. Ash recognised Sarah the scribe who was at least ten years older than him, sliver haired but still kept her figure.

"Wait... I was to remain at Applewood?" Ash pleaded.

"No! You will take the last of your outfit and fortify neighbouring farms, I'm sorry son, but I outrank you, my word as first captain will ring clear!" Harris claimed haughtily.

"Yes, sir. We will move out at dawn!" Ash sighed, feeling deflated. It was true, Captain Harris outranked him by several years and he had to adhere to the ranger rank.

"You heard the captain, start gathering up equipment and provisions we move out at dawn." Ash bit back his own thoughts but understood they couldn't all stay at Applewood farm, just in case the soviets navigated around Applewood and attacked other farms.

Later in the afternoon Harris found Ash in his room packing up gear into a backpack. Ash tried to salute but Harris grabbed his arm and stopped him.

"Bollocks to that Ash! Look I have thirty good rangers, I will take two teams and the rest will now be under your command." He paused and sighed "There ain't a lot of us left now, the calling of the ranger has been thinning over the years."

"We are partially to blame for that though." Ash countered.

"How so?" The old man asked.

"The rangers protect the farms, the farms are now comfortable and safe. Who in the right mind would wish to join up and risk their lives for others?" Ash questioned as Harris sadly agreed.

"Where did all the good folks go, it seems to be all about profit margins, trading and commerce... Arg I'm old hat, what do I know about economics." Harris cracked his knuckles with a worried frown.

"Ones thing for sure, the comforts and protection will be replaced with fear and survival once the rangers are killed."

"Like the good old days!" Harris chuckled, not

really meaning the old days where actually good. Ash stood peering out of the window, the sun had started to head down towards the desert in the distance casting long shadows on the grass.

"Thanks for the extra men old friend, our numbers have been cleaved." However, Harris had already left the room. Ash finished up packing and returned to the window. He could see Harris organising more fortifications to the farm. He wished he could remain at the farm it would have been better for the farmers. They wouldn't like Harris's new rule at all and knew the farmers would be quickly drafted as auxiliaries. Applewood would be annexed by the rangers and Mrs Drydan would be relieved of master of the farm, probably become a cook of some sorts. He shook his head as he watched the old captain ruthlessly preparing for the takeover. He wouldn't have gone down that line and kept the farmers happily cultivating crops and livestock while the rangers dealt with the protection. With that sorrowful thought he headed to the dining room and ate a basic meal before turning in for the night. It would be a long day's travel the next morning and he hoped his body would hurry up and heal.

Ash and the rangers headed out at dawn. They had split into two groups, one group headed to the Orangery farm to the west under the command of sergeant Nerris (one of Harris's elite) and Ash, his twenty rangers, Thomas and ten auxiliaries headed south west to Main-Bridge farm where they would cross the silver river via the pre-war bridge. The three farmsteads would become the buffer between the enemy and the other farms that lay behind. The three farms would be fortified quickly and become drafting stations and subjected to split tribute from all the other farms. Ash had already wondered who would keep track of the logistics, so he promoted Mortima a heavy set auxiliary from the fort. He hoped he could keep track of the movement of food and equipment supplies. He had in the past asked Mortima to become a ranger in the fort a few years back, but Mortima had claimed he wasn't a killer. Back then Ash saw that as a waste of a good resource, but then understood the humanity which Mortima adhered too. He never once pressed him again and respected his chosen path. Ash remembered reading an old pre-war army manual and one of the sections touched on 'conscience objector'. What good would it be to draft Mortima as a ranger if he refused to kill! He had decided long ago that it would be no good for other enlisted men and women who put their lives on the line. Harris would have seen this differently and forced him into enlisting. Ash was glad he wasn't an old barbarian like Harris.

The land had patches of arid land dotted with grasslands where small hamlets scraped a living. He worked out that it would take two days to get to Main-Bridge providing they weren't attacked. Mortima was labouring a hand cart of supplies keeping up pace with Ash. The big muscular man was focused and stern faced on the objective, he saw no fear in his eyes, in fact Ash found solace in his determination.

"It's not long to the next hamlet, I'm pretty sure the Mc'Rose family will share provisions when we camp in their land." Ash said trying to keep the auxiliaries spirits up.

"For what good it will become!" Mortima muttered. Ash sighed and halted the group by putting up his fist.

"We aren't finished yet brother?" The travelling group came to a welcome stop, some folks sat down on nearby stones and chugged water from canteens.

"Together we will pull through this bump..." But Mortima got real angry.

"I saw what Captain Harris was doing at Applewood. They are simple farmers not everybody are killers like the rangers!" He barked sending spittle in the air.

"Son, we are in this together, we all have our station and the rangers are doing their very best to keep civilization a float!" Ash tried to keep his voice calm.

"And I'm not your fucking son! If you want to pep talk, take it elsewhere!" Mortima hissed. Ash cautiously put his hand on Mortima's shoulder and levelled his eyes with his.

"I'm just trying to keep the equilibrium and calm through the ranks, I'm sorry Mortima. I wish I could console you, but our present situation requires steadfastness, courage and above all companionship against an enemy that doesn't sleep."

"Stick all that up your ass, Ash. It's not going to bring Vera back!" Mortima's eyes had started to fill up, Ash had forgotten that Vera (one of the auxiliaries) had been killed in the retreat from the fort. He had forgotten that Vera and Mortima were lovers. *Fuck I forgot about that, the poor bastard is grieving*.

"I'm very sorry for your loss, we all are." Ash said sombrely." Even though Mortima was a conscience objector, it wouldn't stop him from punching Ash. Ranger Sandings had moved into position just in case the auxiliary tried to take a pop at the captain.

"Captain Ash was unconscious when we buried Vera in the desert!" Sandings said grimly, readying himself for a fist fight.

"I will never be able to tend her grave, I'm no ranger!" Mortima said before shuddering with tears. Ash backed away wishing he had been conscious for the burial.

"I'm very sorry..." He was going to add that many folks died that day during the desert battle against the soviets, but he thought it would be best to leave it be. Ash allowed some time for Mortima to console himself before ordering the group to move on.

The travelling group arrived at the Mc'Rose family hamlet around six. The hamlet was a stern pre-war concrete building, possibly a pre-war highway service station. The hills around were lush with grasses, corn and the audible brae of livestock, mostly chickens and the odd goat. Guard dogs met the group first, they stood to attention growling and complaining at first before one of the owners heeled the animals.

"We are Rangers and I'm captain Ash, would it be okay if we camped in your grounds, we have items to trade for food?" Ash said calmly as more rough looking family members came out armed with shotguns. Ash knew the hamlet was under the umbrella protection of the ranger force, but he also knew most hamlets were not required to tribute. The leader seemed to be a middle aged man, he sported scars on his face and bandit type tattoo's on his neck. Ash recognised the tattoo's but they were faded and obviously this fellow didn't run with gangs anymore.

"Feel free to camp here, I've heard about the fort being attacked! We kinda liked the protection the rangers provided." The leader of the Mc'Rose, family said with a guttered voice. The leader chuckled and holstered his revolver.

"My family will bring food and water to your camp, with thanks for your protection, you need not pay!" His face became stern. "You keep to your camp mind, you have no business coming up here to the hamlet!"

"Thankyou Mc'Rose." Ash stated as he began to organise a temporary camp and a watch rota. The grizzled looking scar faced leader saluted and wandered back to the hamlet accompanied by the vicious looking guard dogs.

"I will be down in a minute." The ex-bandit said while he wandered away to the main building.

The sun went down and the grassland became cold, dew was already forming on the blades of grass as the ranger contingent made camp fires. A number of various aged females came to the camp bringing firewood, food and heavy kettles of cold water. They introduced themselves as Mc'Rose family members, some of them sported faded black eyes and abuse, but once they delivered the hospitality they quickly rushed off to the old building. Bedrolls were rolled out and several rangers remained on watch as the travellers dug in for the night. The moon was full and the sky twinkled with uncountable stars. The leader of the family came down to the camp 'clinking' many demijohns of moonshine liquor. The leader sat down next to Ash and began to share out the moon shine.

"Haven't seen your outfit in a while, we get the odd ranger outfit now and then just camping over and such." The leader of the Mc'Rose family stated with a sinister grin.

"I'm Richard Mc'Rose and I'm pleased to meet you captain?"

"Ash." They shook hands. Richard poured a number of glass tumblers with potent looking alcohol and gave the first to the captain. He accepted the drink and sipped at the full tumbler. It burnt his throat like a son-of-a-bitch but it was to be expected.

"I heard the fort has been evacuated, one of your solo-rangers said as much."

"Yes… It's unfortunate but it's not in vain, we killed a great number of them before retreating into the farm lands." Ash claimed with gritted teeth. Richard nodded grimly and filled up Ash's tumbler.

"Well I'm glad you guys survived. I'm not an educated man but I know if the rangers fall then it will be back in the old days like my father, where every home was a fortress against..." Richard drifted off.

"Against the threat of civilization, my friend." Ash added. Richard agreed with a knowing nod.

"Where are you guys heading?"

"Heading to Main-Bridge, going to try and fortify that area against the new threat!" Ash said while he watched the embers burn in the camp fire.

"Main-Bridge? Okay... It's quite a hub of trading down there, we trade frequently with them. It's quite a town ship now. It's got its own whore houses, bars and merchant barns full of stuff to trade." Richard claimed. Ash wondered, it had been several years since he went to Main-Bridge, he thought it was still a farm stead.

"Township?" Ash questioned.

"Sorry buddy, but Main-Bridge is now a town, it has its own militia and everything. In the last few years it has become a stronghold of trade?" Richard was now beside himself with laughter.

"It seems the merchants that were supplying your fort kept that fact as a secret." Richard started to howl laughing by now leaving Ash in dismay. Richard peered into Ashes eyes and witnessed the betrayal.

"So while we risked our lives everyday, the folks of Main-Bridge were busy outfitting a township!" Ash was really pissed off, especially with all the lives that had been lost recently.

"I need to see this town!" Ash said finally with a scowl.

"The town is run by a council of merchants, they have grown rich under your protection and you never knew this fact..." Richard had stopped laughing realising the upset caused by the truth and Ash was now comprehending.

"The mother fuckers!" Ash whispered into the night as he watched the firewood crackle and burn on the campfire.

The sun started to rise, Ash thanked the Mc'Rose family for their hospitality and organised the rangers and axillaries to move out on his compass bearing. He felt ruined inside due to the concept of merchants getting rich on the protection of rangers lives. It wasn't long before they picked up a well trodden trail which sported the indentations of numerous hand carts and bovine driven heavy carts. Ash needed to see this township, he wanted to storm out into the wilderness and scream at the top of his voice, the rangers had been fooled! They travelled across fertile grass land seeing numerous fields of crops, grain, corn and orchards, cultivated by numerous out-landing hamlets. The majority of the hamlets were not providing tribute to the ranger's protective hand.

"We have been bitched!" Ranger Sandings said with a scowl.

"All these years and they have grown strong, as we

laid down our lives to protect them" Ash hissed bitterly. He was on the border of continuing south and allowing the Ashland to fend for itself. But a niggling in his mind pushed to stay steadfast, they were rangers and they had a job to do. *They will pay for their secrecy!*

It was midafternoon when the ranger contingent arrived at the bridge over silver river. The bridge was a four birth pre-war highway crossing the river. Rusted cars had been pushed to the side of the bridge leaving a clearway run between. As the ranger contingent approached they were met by a numerous guards wearing a mixture of pre-war combat armour and fortified leather. They were armed with a mixture of rifles and shotguns.

"Here to trade?" The cocky leader said while drinking from a demijohn of hard liquor. The leader had two pistols on his gun belt and his armoured shoulder plate still had a faded 'Blood Raider' motif.

"I'm Captain Ash of the Rangers let us past!" Ash said angrily to the guard leader. The leader sparked up a cigarette and narrowed his eyes at Ash.

"This is a trading hub, I see you have carts so you must be here to trade!" The guard leader grinned as he took a heavy drag on his cigarette, blowing out blue smoke around his face.

"We are here to fortify your township, we are rangers god-damn-it!" Ash cried. The leader of the guards flicked his cigarette over the side of the bridge and appeared pissed off.

"Rangers of what? We don't need your protection here! We have our own outfit to protect the township. You can come in but remember rangers are not welcome." Ash could hear the debate going on behind him, Mortima leading the voice.

"I told you, Rangers are no longer needed in the Ashland!" The muscular auxiliary claimed. Ash needed to get on top of this situation.

"The rangers protected you as your township became strong! Let us see this township that we laid down lives to protect!" Ash yelled, trying not to shake his voice.

"Like I said, you can come in for hospitality and trade, but rangers have no rule here." The guard leader said while chuckling. Ash was beside himself in rage, he couldn't believe what he was hearing.

"You can either enter or fuck off back to the desert!" The leader kept his pistol holstered but he locked the pistols hammer to punctuate his words.

"I recognise you!" Ash said bitterly remembering a raider gang which used to frequent the ruins near the fort.

"Indeed you do sir. I was the one who you set free to take a message back to the blood gang raiders. Just after you put bullets in my friends!" The leader was scowling remembering himself being on his knees watching the rangers put to death a number of his fellow gang members.

"Should have put a bullet in your head that day!" Ash whispered, the guard leader didn't hear. Ash looked to his fatigued squad and waved them forward to cross the bridge. He had nothing left to say to the cocky guard leader and he didn't want a gun fight this day.

Main-Bridge had indeed grown since Ash had last been here, four years back. The farmsteads had expanded and many buildings have been erected and fortified against attack. Some of the corrugated wood/iron buildings had flags dancing in the slight breeze. The flags had the blood gang motif, a red skull crying blood on a field of white. Ash cursed himself for being lapse and comfortable in the fort, not knowing that an evil raider gang had taken over one of his settlements. The mains street was awash with mud and shit, both human and animal. It fucking stank to high heaven. Trade houses, saloons and whore houses flanked the main street. He couldn't believe how established a farm could become in such little time. The rangers followed the signs to a large building which claimed to put up travellers and merchants for the night. Empty hand carts were brimming at the back of the hostel, so much so that they had trouble finding spaces to house their supply carts. He organised a quick guard roster and headed into the tap room with Sandings and Angel. The tap room was half full of merchants and rough looking guards and its smelt of stale beer and effluent. The wooden boards were damp from the shit and piss that had been dragged in on folk's boots, frequenting this place.

"What can I get ye?" The bar tender asked,

sporting a stained apron. Ash felt like he was in an alien world, he wasn't used to trading in coin, the rangers had relied on tribute to survive and he hadn't had time to collect the stash of coins from the fort. He had a few silver dollars on him for keep sakes, mostly kept for the pre-war date stamps. He started to rifle through his back pack to get the coins when Angel placed a number of coins on the bar. Solo's frequented the new world so they knew about coins and trade.

"I got it Cap." She said smiling seeing Ash was way out of his league.

"Thanks Angel." Ash said sincerely.

"We need food, lodgings and beer, will this cover thirty four of us?" She said pushing the pile of silver dollars to the bar tender. The bar man counted the coins and gave one coin back.

"That should cover two meals each, beer and lodgings for the night." The bar man looked chuffed and Ash could see they had over paid. A number of scantily clad waitresses began to prepare the order, pouring pitchers of beer and preparing food. Ash and his body guards retired to an empty table and began to drink from the shared pitcher of beer.

"What happened here?" Ash said shaking his head in dismay.

"Progress sir, civilization flourishes when conflict sits on the back burner." Angel said with a wink. Sandings was still on watch scanning the exits and the bar patrons like a true ranger.

"Did you know of this new township?" Ash

questioned peering into Angels wolf like pale blue eyes.

"Naa, never really went so far south for years, last time I was here it was just a farmstead run by the Greenwood family. It seems the family have done well, but I'm pissed off that they have joined up with a notorious gang!"

"Me too Angel, maybe the rangers are finished, maybe we let the chips fall as they may?" Ash said with sagged shoulders, knowing the rangers could be on the last legs.

"The rangers aren't finished yet, if the soviets pile down here then this township will goto fuck!" Sandings said with a stony face.

"We will move out tomorrow, maybe head to Corn fields. With any luck the farm will still be a farm and not a fucked up place like this!" Ash downed his beer and headed out to the stables to make sure his entourage where being cared for. As Ash exited the bar he witnessed two drunken fellows exchanging gun fire, the combatants were so drunk that they were missing every shot. A passer-by got winged by a bullet and fell to the floor. Ash pulled out his pistol and started to walk toward the battle but the township guards had moved in swiftly and broke up the scuffle. By the time he had wandered over, one of the town guards shoved him back.

"Nothing to see here, go about your business!" The scarred faced guard said. Ash nodded and wandered back to the stable. *They maybe gang members but they seem to keep the peace, they might be hope yet!* Ash pondered.

CHAPTER 11

Jessica took up the lead at a steady ranger like jog. Brae took up the rear protecting Natasha, Joshua and Yolanda. Jessica stopped at an old faded weather beaten metro sign. She traced her finger on the old map of the city spotting a bridge ahead. The subway would have bypassed the river underground, but she knew there must be a bridge that crossed the polluted river.

"On my bearing!" She pointed to a ruined hospital building. "You need to keep up, if you fall behind then you're on your own!" She growled through her respirator. Joshua took off his respirator and held up his hand.

"You're running us ragged, we need to stop to rest!" He rasped trying to catch his breath.

"We need to cross the ruins by sun down! Fuck resting, keep up!" Jessica commanded, knowing that the monsters frequent night.

"Jess is right we can't stay here, my giga-counter is hissing!" Brae cried with anxiety in his voice.

"Rotters!" Yolanda cried as she raised up her rifle firing a couple of shots. The retort of the rifle echoed along the ruined buildings, a dinner bell for abominations. Jessica saw a group of wretched survivors shambling out of the shopping mall to the flank.

"Yolanda! That will bring more down on us, you stupid bitch!" Jessica yelled as she emptied both of her magazines towards the mob of Rotter's staggering toward the party. Yolanda gave Jess the finger between gun shots as she backed off from the numerous and murderous crowd of wretched survivors.

"We need to go now!" Jessica cried as she reloaded her pistols. They double paced it toward a city square where mutated plants flourished bringing one of the many green spots to the ruined city. The city square had a statue of a woman reading a book and water still flowed from worn down stone holes in the statue. The water must have been a spring from the river and somehow survived the nuclear missile that devastated the city. Natasha was doubled over trying to catch her breath. She ripped off her respirator and gulped at the air like a pond fish out of water.

"I Need to rest, I cant carry on at this pace!" She pleaded. She sat down on the side of the fountain folly.

"Put your respirator back on, we need to move out now!" Yolanda said as she pulled the respirator over Natasha's face. Some of the Rotter's had entered the rubble strewn square, wandering like drunken folk towards the group. Jessica was busy firing both of her pistols against them.

"We need to go my lover!" Joshua said while he shouldered Natasha. The group rushed across the square and headed down the main street strewn with rusted cars, leaving the slow walking atomic folk far behind.

The group rushed along the ruined ash laid streets, kicking up radioactive dust with every foot fall. They stopped to rest for a while at a sector that hadn't been maimed from the nuclear strike that had destroyed the majority of the city. Brae looked at his giga-counter and gave a thumbs up.

"We head for the north bridge, my giga-counter is clicking slow so we must be in a clean zone." Brae announced to calm everybody down. They headed north through the ruined city away from ground zero where the atomic bomb had impacted it's smite. The buildings in this area were still intact, standing proud against the devastation of the city. A solace and quiet descended and the travellers felt at ease. It's when a shop front glass window shattered, showering broken glass into the street. Long rubbery, purple like tentacles reached out from the confides of a perfume shop. The tentacles were feeling the rubble and broken glass at first and then the bulk of its aquatic body revealed itself. A huge, bulbous, fleshy creature slid its way out of the building thrashing its long tentacles towards the group of travellers.

"Abomination!" Yolanda yelled at the top of her voice. She fired a couple of rounds which just pissed the huge creature off. It was more like a wasp sting but the sting of several 7.62mm bullets. Jessica took a deep breath watching her team mates firing on the huge creature, the bullets seemed to do no harm against the fleshy creature. She dropped to her knees and unhooked a LAW rocket launcher from the side of her backpack. She ejected the safety housing which dropped to the asphalt below. She took her time peering down the iron sight of the weapon and took a deep steady breath. Down the iron sight she saw the abomination sliding out of the municipal building in all its fucked up glory. She squeezed the trigger and felt the kick of the rocket expelling from the housing. The fiery trail of the rocket made a bee line to the gargantuan creature, the rocket impacted against its bulbous flesh, penetrating deep inside. There was a slight delay, before the man made fuse burnt out its short lived life. Chunks of flesh showered over the street, the street looked like the interior of a slaughter house. The creature tried to bolt back inside the building but its life gave out. The huge aquatic looking creature slumped outside the building, half of its weight had been taken off by the rocket and was scattered in fleshy lumps in the ash bound street.

"Well done Jess!" Brae cried putting his fist to the sky as though he was some kind of Greek god. Jessica stood up and threw away the spent rocket housing which was still smoking.

"The bridge, we need to get to the east bridge before sundown!" Jess said with passion in her voice as she strapped her backpack and gear on.

By late afternoon they arrived at the ruined hospital building, the large dusty faded sign still stated 'Saint Catharine's hospice.'

"Half way across!" Jessica mumbled, more to herself than anybody around her. She looked at Natasha and Joshua who were now lying down near the entrance of the hospital, they looked fucked. She knew they couldn't carry on at the pace she had set and knew if they didn't move at her pace, then night would fall in the city and things would go from bad to terrible. Brae gave her a look and shook his head, he was thinking along the same lines.

"Fuck it! We hole up here and hopefully we will still be living tomorrow." Jess covered her eyes from the sun and peered up the sides of the multi-story building, she noticed that at least one of the fire escapes were still intact and retracted from the ground level. She looked to Joshua and Natasha who looked forever thankful for deciding to rest.

"We need to get to the roof of the hospital, that way we can see what comes and escape using the fire escapes on the side of the building, if we are attacked. She looked to Brae. "How's the rads?"

"Good, not high but we still need to wear capes and I advise keeping on respirators when not engaging in conversation. But to be honest when we get way up high, the air should be a lot cleaner." He smiled, but Jessica scowled. *As if you know if the air is clean or not, you're no scientist!* She thought.

"We move quick through the hospital building, ascending where we can until we get to the roof of the building. Jess and I will take up the front and Yo, you take the rear." Brae said trying to show some aspect of leadership. *Prick!* Jessica thought. As Natasha and Joshua got to their feet with jelly like fatigued limbs, Brae and Jessica entered the gloom of the building. They entered what seemed to be the main reception area, banks of waiting rooms had been set in zones all labelled with letterers of the alphabet. Many skeletons still sat on benches or lay on the dusty floor, which were strewn with trash and old rotting medical consumables. Many corridors exited the main foyer but they took the main stairs. Luckily the pre-war design of the hospital had several main stairways to the upper floors, most of them however had been barricaded long ago with heavy furnishings and equipment. Light from the many windows still shined with daylight but the stairwells were dark and foreboding. Brae had turned on his flashlight which was under slung on his assault rifle. This provided the way forward some element of illumination. Joshua had used his initiative and lit an oil lantern and seemed okay to be the main bearer of light for the group. Jessica noticed they had been quite a battle in the hospital at some point, it wasn't recent but it was definitely post war. They encountered dead bandits still clutching firearm's, the group quickly ransacked them for tinned food and ammo and collected quite a stash. Jessica chuckled as she packed away three food cans, the faded label stated 'Heinz beans and sausage'. It was amazing how tinned food was still edible and nourishing after all this time. The group had ascended eight floors and skeletons of the dead were now sparse. Jess reckoned they had another six floors to the roof to climb. She was quite surprised and almost disappointed in a 'tactical way' that they hadn't encountered anything so far. The bandits that had used this place as a stronghold had long since perished. She estimated that staying a night here would be okay as long as they didn't draw too much attention. Most of the very upper floors were baron, picked clean long ago, the group finally got to the last stairwell and came to a fire escape type door which were locked.

"Brae, get your shoulder against the door with me, let's see if we can force it." Jess said as she leaned against the door trying out if it was locked or it was just barricaded on the other side. The two warriors strained against the door and the door gave a little, which meant it was locked and not barricaded. Yollanda pushed to the front of the group and inspected the lock, she pulled out a small leather bound case of lock smith tools from her backpack.

"Let me try. Brae get your light on the lock." She said as she probed the lock using a slender tools. She set to work and deftly picked the lock, she was surprised how easy it was to infiltrate the pre-war lock.

"We are in!" She claimed with a smile. Jessica shoved her out of the way and kicked the door. Daylight half blinded the party as the door slammed open revealing the spacious roof section of the hospital. They moved out quickly securing the roof which gave a vantage over the cityscape. When everyone was satisfied that the area was safe, Yolanda re-locked the door.

"No fires and we must be deadly quiet!" Jessica whispered as she returned to the group setting up camp under the hospital water tower. Brae was checking his giga-counter and he seemed happy with the reading, having shaken it a few times to make sure it was reading correctly.

"Rads are low up here in the fresh air. I think we have found a damned good place to ride the night out." He said bagging the apparatus.

"I'm fucked, fight it out between you for first watch, I'm gona get some Zzs!" Jessica said referring to Brae and Yolanda as she climbed into her bed roll nearby the others. Yolanda and Brae had decided to take the first watch together so they could chat and bond.

"How you feeling Yo?" Brae asked looking at his lover's fatigued look in her eyes.

"I'm great it's just like old times." She said cocking her head and smiling feeling butterflies in her stomach. It had been quite sometime that Brae had been loving towards her. She levelled her rifle and looked down the scope and she could see the distant east bridge, she felt her shoulders sag knowing they were still in the shit. Brae rested his head against her shoulder and she could feel his smile, even through her heavy leather armour.

"Once we finish this mission we should have enough money to settle down for a while, maybe purchase a bar in Red town?" He said. She had heard this promise a number of times before and each time it had failed. She didn't hold the circumstances against Brae it was just how fate dealt its cards.

"Yes, that will be paradise." She said trying to make her words sound positive.

Overlooking the ash strewn streets Brae noticed movement in the streets below.

"Give me your rifle!" He whispered. Yolanda passed the scoped rifle to him. He peered down the scope toward the street below and witnessed a contingent of rough looking bandits heading across the city. One of the scouts stopped and started to search near the entrance. He couldn't hear what the scout said but he could imagine that the scout had picked up some kind of trail. Brae bolted back and gave the rifle back to Yo.

"Those bandits we killed on the bridge... It looks like they have picked up our trail!" He whispered. Yolanda started to shake her head.

"Do you think they will search the hospital?" Panic in her voice. He shook his head and cautiously looked over the wall of the roof-top and looked down below. The bandit group counting twenty strong and armed to the teeth seemed agitated and bored.

"They would be stupid to hole up in the city, they will be heading for the bridge!" The rough looking leader said, pulling his scouts back in line. The Bandits moved on down the street as Brae sighed in relief.

"We live another day!" He finally whispered.

Night had fallen, bringing with it the sounds of the

abominations from the city. Due to the darkness they couldn't make out what was going down in the city below, but whatever it was, it was fearful and noisy. Jessica, had woke up due to the noise and joined Brae and Yolanda over-looking the streets from the vantage of the hospital roof. Yolanda tracked a large aquatic like creature, similar to what they had seen in the main square, sliding and feeling its way down the ruined streets.

"Bet you don't have another rocket to kill that?" Brae said chuckling. Jessica shook her head.

"Nope, I spent the rocket on the last mother fucker. We need to be very cautious from now on!" She said as she disassembled her pistols, cleaning them on an old cloth rag stained with lubricating oil. As she assembled her pistols and loaded them with fresh magazines, Brae knew they had a fight across the ruined city as soon as dawn reared its warm illuminating head. That's when the door to the roof started to bang and bulge. Brae quickly and silently roused all of the travelling party.

"We have been compromised!" He hissed. The sleepers kicked themselves out of their blankets and armed themselves. All of them looked toward the roof top door which were banging and crashing against the lock.

"We need to form a firing line!" Jessica barked, it was no longer silent. She pointed to the roof top fire escape. "Yo, take them to the escape, Brae and I will fortify our retreat!" Jessica said with panic in her voice.

The others rushed towards the fire escape as the sun started to illuminate the top of the building.

"If we get separated meet at the east bridge, rush east and do not stop!" She said raising both of her pistols as the door to the roof smashed open...

Jessica and Brae made the distance towards the roof top door firing round after round as shambling 'Rotters' as a mob, disgorged from the below. While Brae fired his assault rifle he kept looking over his shoulder to make sure Yolanda and the others made their escape down the fire escape on the side of the pre-war hospital building.

"It's just us Jess!"

"Yeah, but this time we don't have hard core rangers backing us up!" Jess said as she fired both her pistols at the shambling fucks that exited on the hospital roof space. The undead started to pile up near the door making a rotting barrier of corpses.

"Run now!" Jessica cried as she backed away towards the fire escape. Brae had spent his magazine and tried to reload. Jessica grabbed his shoulder armour and used her strength to pull Brae towards the fire escape.

"Go now, I will lay down cover fire!" She said through gritted teeth. He broke combat and rushed towards the fire exit on the side of the building as Jess fired both her pistols in retreat. They got to the fire escape and rushed down the steps, the entire roof had been compromised by wretched survivors. By the time they had reached the steps of the fourth floor they looked up to see the 'Rotters' making their way down the rusty steps, some of the undead had started to fall from high, landing in bloody heaps in the streets below.

"Fucking abominations!" Jessica yelled as she emptied her clips. She reloaded and armed both of her pistols, clicking them in place. The sun had started to rise, cascading a welcome sun light over the streets of the ruined city.

"Jess!" Brae yelled. "We need to move to the bridge and quickly!"

"Yes we do!" Jessica said while trying to catch her breath having descended the fire escape from the hospital. She looked to Natasha and Joshua and saw they had new spirit, the spirit of survival. Everybody picked up pace, the rising sun probably gave them exceptional vigour. The party stopped for a reprieve and donned rad-capes and respirators even though radiation readings were minimal. The group had made it past the radioactive hot-spots from the city, but in the back of their minds they worried about procreating, all apart from Jess who dint give a fuck about being a mother.

The east side of the city didn't seem as harsh. They made good head way through the outskirts of the city. The buildings seemed relatively intact too, it was almost as if the bomb hadn't touched this side of the city. The high risers started to dissipate, replaced by suburban houses, some of which the gardens had outgrown the houses. The party had settled to a calm trot, enemies seemed fewer on this side and the only menace they encountered was a few rotter's shambling around the cul-de-sacs. They left them be and avoided conflict, knowing that bullet fire brought more enemies. Jessica thought they had been lucky really, the last time she crossed a ruin was with rangers and even that was a struggle. The party had taken off respirators and rad capes due to the low readings on the giga-counter and the fact that the sun was fucking hot. Joshua caught Jessica up and fell into a stride by stride trot with her.

"You want something Joshua?" She said without looking at him.

"I wanted to thank you, for saving our lives again."

"Don't mention it Joshua, but remember your paying for that privilege."

"Even so… We still are very thankful. If I had known it would be this treacherous, I don't think I would have risked our lives for such a perilous journey."

"But, on the other-hand, I bet you feel better for the journey so far, the adrenalin in your blood, the options of fight or flight. Not to mention the scenery, you wouldn't have seen ruined sky scrapers, deserts and water holes sitting on your ass in the church." Jess said with a smile.

"Your correct Jess, I do feel more seasoned and more worldly-wise. Many thanks to you, Brae and Yolanda for that." He said sombrely with his head down.

"Too be honest Joshua, I didn't think you would

have survived so far, so you're doing pretty good." She said not realising how harsh and hurtful her words could be. Joshua stopped and gripped her arm.

"Do you know? You can be such a bitch at times!" He said angrily, letting go of her arm and spitting on the floor to his side. Jessica looked him in the eye and cocked her head.

"Been called a bitch a lot of times, but spitting..." She quickly flanked him and punched him very hard in his cheek bone. A proper, full extension of her arm, knocking him to the floor, very likely unconscious. Natasha screamed and rushed towards Jessica flailing her fists at her. She sniggered and just backed off away from the pathetic blows. Eventually Natasha gave up her assault and rushed to Joshua side, who was indeed, out for the count.

"You bitch!" She rasped as she cradled Joshua's head, tears forming in her eyes. Jessica shrugged and started to laugh. But she stopped laughing when Brae went to see if Joshua was okay, scowling at Jess. Yolanda made a bee line for Jess. Jessica put her arms up in salute, she had never gone toe-to-toe with Yolanda and the thought crossed her mind that she might loose the fight.

"What the fuck is wrong with you Jess?" Yolanda yelled in her face as Jessica backed off a tad.

"Sorry, my bad."

"We have enough enemies in this fucked up world!" Yolanda spat. Jessica had seen her mad before, but not this angry.

"Like I said, I'm sorry, he should have..." She noticed Yolanda had balled fists, ready to lash out.

"Not good enough, he probably has a concussion and that's bad for travelling, what was you thinking?" Yolanda was calming down but still ready to go at a moments notice. Jess bit her lip and didn't answer, thinking she might escalate the situation by saying the wrong words.

"He is coming too." Brae said as he dabbed Joshua's face with water from his canteen. Brae recalled the memories of this happening before, back when he and Jess were rangers. Many times Jess had knocked out a ranger that had come on to her in the field.

"We are here to protect them, they aren't rangers or combatants!" Brae said referring to Natasha and Joshua. Brae helped him to his feet, but Joshua's knees were like jelly. He placed Joshua's arm over his shoulder to bolster him from falling back down.

"Shame on you Jess!" Brae said bitterly.

"It was my fault, I insulted her." Joshua mumbled as he fought to try and stay conscious, as he rested his spinning head against Brae's shoulder.

"We are near the bridge, can he walk?" Jessica said trying to change the subject. Yolanda eyed her with an unforgiving stare before wandering back towards Natasha who was in a fit of tears.

"I want to go home Joshua, I don't feel safe." She whimpered through a cascade of tears.

"Soon my love, we don't have far to travel now, we are nearly there." Joshua tried to console her while fighting against the pain bulging on his left cheek. He could feel his left eye lid closing up, narrowing his vision. Yolanda took up point and Jessica was banished to the rear of the group as they headed off towards the east bridge.

The east bridge seemed un-guarded. The bridge spanned a wide discoloured brown river which had a scattering of floating stuff on its surface. It was an old suspension type bridge. Everybody wondered how it had survived so long? The bridge was strewn with old rusted cars and as they made their way across the bridge. Brae wondered about the bridge and couldn't understand how bandits had not outfitted this area as a toll bridge?

"We have made it!" Brae laughed, a proper chuckle type of laugh, deep from his stomach.

"This is the East! Desert Rangers patrol this sector so we should be okay!" Jessica claimed. Brae remembered all those years when Jess and Brae ran with the desert rangers keeping law and order among the farmsteads and settlements.

"I wonder if Captain Harris is still the keeper of this province?" Jessica said, hopefully.

"Gee, Captain Harris, looked after me and thee!" He said remembering old times. Jessica became suddenly stern.

"We have a mission to find the utopian, let us find his records!" She nodded to Joshua who was kissing Natasha tenderly.

"We head east towards Virginia!" Jess said as she placed a point forty five round in the chamber of one of her pistols. Brae spread out a moth eaten map on the grassy floor. He took some time trying to find out where they were, using a nautical brass compass.

"We need to head east, following the old high way road, until we get to the grass lands, which isn't that far from here!" They made there way down the cracked and broken asphalt and passed a number of trade posts, which were protected by rough looking guards. The land started to get more hilly and green and the party witnessed cattle being driven by ranch hands who tipped their hat in greeting. As the sun started to go down they stopped at small farmstead just off the highway. The buildings looked old and made from battered wood, but the owners seemed hospitable.

"Looks like you have been on the road far too long travellers." A young man said dressed in rough leather armour.

"Are these lands still patrolled by Rangers?" Brae said to the young man.

"Rangers are mostly up north, but now and then we see the odd Solo stopping to purchase provisions. I hear the rangers have had trouble up north"

"Trouble?" Brae questioned.

"Yeah, I heard the Rangers have abandoned one of the forts! Retreating south, but that's just hear say." The young man said lighting up a cigar.

"Are we okay camping up with you folks, we have a long journey tomorrow?"

"Hell yeah, get yourselves upto the farm house, it would be nice to have company. And don't be camping, we have rooms for you to stay. I see the stride of rangers." The young man said noticing how Brae and Jessica appeared.

"Yeah, we used to run with the rangers, but we got disbanded a number of years ago, politics man!"

"I hear ye." The young man chuckled and pointed to the building up on the grassy hill where cattle mooched around.

The farmstead looked to be a ramshackle group of buildings, outfitted with a number of barns to house cattle. The group settled in nicely, but had to share rooms. Natasha and Joshua took the small room on the west wing of the house and Brae and Yolanda took the other spare room, leaving Jessica sleeping on the floor of the living space. She didn't mind, in fact she thought it was better that she was alone, due to the stunt she pulled and everybody hating and distrusting her. The sun had gone down and all the farm folk gathered around the dining table in the main room. The ranch hands weren't used to taking on guests, so most of the party felt like a fifth wheel. The eldest man took the head of the table as his daughters dished out a robust beef stew. Brae wanted to pay for the lodgings but the head of the house didn't want coin.

"Where you heading?" The old man said as he brushed back a full head of white hair.

"Heading to the old army depot, east of here."

Joshua said between mouthfuls of bread and beef stew.

"The bunker?" The old man said with a frown.

"Yeah, it's just over the way, not too far a few days travel.."

"Be wary, there is a gang of thugs camping near there, they don't bother us, but they sometimes raid the merchants travelling in that sector, be on your guard!" The old man said between dragging on his tobacco pipe.

"We will try to avoid them." Brae said, as he looked to the others around the table.

"Best beef stew I have ever had! Thank your daughters and your hospitality." Jessica said, as she spooned up a large roast potato from her bowl of stew. She eyed up the eldest daughter, the one with the dark hair and freckled face. Jessica winked towards her and the young woman blushed, however she seemed to have her eyes focused on Brae. Jess looked to the rugged looking square jawed man and cursed her sexuality. The old man finished his meal and mopped up the last of the stew with a cob of freshly baked bread.

"Don't mind me, I'm old so I will have to retire to bed, take care on your travels tomorrow and keep safe." He gingerly got to his feet using the heavy wooden table as support before wandering off to his room. As he was passing Jessica he placed a withered old hand on her shoulder and leant down to whisper.

"I have an old friend in my bedroom, I want to give it you." At first Jessica was on guard thinking he was coming on to her, but she realised he was being genuine. She followed the old man to his bed room making small talk. The bed room was Spartan, simple but functional.

"I used to be a ranger like yourself, my daughters didn't take up the gun, so I present this to a fellow ranger." He said as he ruffled through his bed bottom locker. The old man produced an old moth eaten wooden case. He opened it and placed a heavy set pistol in Jessica's hands.

"That was my old side arm, when I ran with the rangers, probably before you were even born." He smiled as Jessica felt the weight of the Nichol plated desert eagle. "The ammo might be hard to find but I have a few clips to go with it."

"Thank you." Jessica said with astonishment.

"Point forty-four." The old man said before climbing into the folds of his bed. Jessica grabbed up the three clips and aimed with the pistol testing the weight. She smiled and leaned in and kissed the old man on the cheek, as he settled down to sleep.

CHAPTER 12

At dawn the Rangers moved out of the township towards the 'Corn fields' south-west of the settlement. As they gathered up the hand carts the locals spat on the floor issuing an un-welcome, 'glad to be gone'. Ash aided one of the cart bearers as they exited the township. He unfortunately witnessed some of the Blood-gang guards mouthing disrespect to the rangers as they headed to the outskirts of the town.

"And don't come back!" One of the grizzly looking guards said as the rangers exited the township. Ash bit back his lip, wanting to kill the guard that issued such hatred towards the rangers, who kept them safe for so many years.

"Leave them be!" Angel said, as she felt the same hurt that Ash felt.

"I feel like it has been a running joke?" He had his head down and dearly needed a hug, to make it all go away.

"Civilization moves on brother. When the soviets arrive they will be begging us to sort it all out!" Angel said bitterly.

"I have to admit, they seem to have a strong set of guards, maybe this will work in our favour. A bolster, against the coming enemy." The solo looked Ash up and down and came to the conclusion that Ash was weak.

She noticed that the captain was still wounded and lame. She tried to ignore her thoughts, but she was niggled by the fact. The rangers powered through the landscape, over hill and dale towards the corn fields. They had to stop twice to rest due to Ash wishing to stop.

"You need to catch up buddy, we can't keep stopping because you need a break!" Angel stated, as she thought about the groups safety. The ranger column halted at a watering hole to fill canteens. Angel peered down the scope of her rifle and cursed silently.

"You have to be fucking kidding me!" She raged.

"You need to see this captain!" She said as she passed the rifle to the captain. Ash peered down the scope and thought he saw a female running into a wooded area from a nearby wheat field. He put the scope down and squinted at the land, but he couldn't see anything moving.

"Was it a woman?" Ash questioned. Angel rolled her eyes.

"You know damn well who it was!" She barked, as Ash realised who it could be. He peered down the scope again and this time he saw her. Edwards was stood in the tree line, she was grinning and staring back with sickly bloodshot eyes. She was still wearing her ranger gear and wide brimmed hat. *Fuck!* He thought, he hoped she would have back tracked to the fort to join her kin. Angel noticed Ash's face drop.

"How long have you known?" She said with malice in her tone. Ash had to own up, he couldn't lie to a fellow ranger. The entire rangerhood had been built on truth and justice.

"Since Applewood..." He whispered, ashamed that he had kept the dark secret. "She visited me one night while I was still hideously wounded. I was unarmed so couldn't do anything. But even if I was armed I probably wouldn't have been able to lift a pistol." He felt Angels rage building so he continued to look down the scope spotting Edwards waving to him. Angel snatched the rifle back and threw it over her shoulder and started to head off in the direction towards Edwards.

"No!" Ash cried and grabbed her arm.

"Get the fuck off!"

"No, not like this, please don't shoot her down like a dog. Let me do it, I will go out and meet her and I will put her down, after all she was a good friend of mine." He pleaded. Angel shrugged his grasp off her arm and pointed in his face, her eyes were narrow and her lips were trembling trying to bite back anger.

"Do it now!" She said calmly, still ready to attack the captain.

"Not now, I will head out at dusk, meet her and then put her out of her misery." He claimed as Angel shook her head in disapproval. She walked back to the group as though she had washed her hands off the captain.

"The sun had started to go down, casting the last of its light on the clouds, turning them dark reds and purples in colour. The ranger contingent had camped down on the top of a grassy hill overlooking grass lands and sparse woodland. Angel eyed Ash while he drank a cup of tea. He had started to clean his pistol trying to ignore Angel's perpetual and unforgiving stare.

"I'm going to have a scout around before the watch is set." He said rising to his feet and holstering his pistol. As he strolled out of camp, Angel followed him.

"Do you want me to shadow you, just in case?" At first Ash was going to say no, but he was going up against a Drainer who was also a fearsome ranger too!

"Think it might be best if you do Angel." As he began to wander down the hill he swore he heard Angel calling him a 'pussy.' He ignored the comment mainly because she was correct, he was a broken man and due to be even more ruined having to put his friend down. He was already beginning to choke up and his eyes were as wet as a whores cunny. He attempted to go over the words that he would say to Edwards and wondered at which point should he shoot her? He hoped that she had thought long and hard and didn't want to be undead anymore, so that he would do her a favour of sorts. The grassland stopped at a small beach wood, the moon was out but cast very little light in the woodland. Upset had quickly turned to fear. *Drainers move fast and Angel doesn't have a night-scope on her rifle!* He thought as he backed away from the foot of the woodland. Some kind of light source flickered in the woodland ahead. It looked to be in some kind of grove far in the distance between the trees. Ash plucked up the last bit of courage left in his broken bones and headed off towards the light. *She must have lit a candle so that we can meet?* He wondered, but tried not to think about traps and ambushes. He clambered over a fallen tree covered with moss and stepped on a few twigs purposely to alert Edwards he was coming. He thought if she was following the rangers then she would be close but out of sight in this small wood. As he made his way toward the light he could see it was an oil lantern placed on a tree stump in the middle of a small grove. He couldn't see much in the way of movement and he hoped Angel was close watching his back. He got to the lantern and looked around, sweat had beaded on his temple even though the night air was still and cold.

"Edwards?" He nervously whispered as he looked to the half moon shining down from above. Twigs started to crack from behind him, the way he had come? He turned and saw Angel walking out into the grove towards the light, she had her hands behind her back and she didn't have her rifle.

"She has me Ash!" Angel said bitterly as Edwards pushed her toward the grove where Ash stood. By the bright! He knew Edwards is quite the combatant, but to take down a solo would have took some doing.

"You can both relax, I'm not here to kill you. I only wish to talk." Edwards said grinning, her reddish eyes glowing in the moon light.

"Kneel down bitch!" She said as she kicked Angel to the ground.

"Grownups need to talk, sit still, be quiet or I'm

going to kill both of you!" She stated to Angel more than Ash. Edwards had two rifles slung over her left shoulder.

"I don't blame you Ash, you are the leader and you needed to act..." She sighed. "I'm still a ranger, even though you think I've joined up with Satan."

"Nobody said that Edwards!" Ash tried to counter.

"Is that so? Is that why you brought a solo to back you up, so you could murder me out here in the woods?"

"Abomination!" Angel hissed. Edwards placed her boot on her back and pushed her gently to an almost praying, prostrate position. Ash could see Angel was bound with cable ties around her wrists.

"Silence Bitch!" Edwards shrieked, her evil looking eyes bulging with rage.

"You both need to listen to me very carefully and Angel you are going to love this, believe me!"

"Fuck you! Undead whore." Angel said trying to get back to her knees. Edwards chuckled and allowed her to sit up, removing her boot from her back.

"Ash, you have been ignorant all these years, you don't just turn from a bite. Do the fucking math... If that was so the Ashland would be overrun by the mother fuckers!"

"And you know this for sure?" Ash rolled his eyes and huffed.

"I do actually. I must admit there is a slight chance of turning, it's more to do with how injured and close to death you are if bitten. Like me, I was bitten and I was a goner. If you were say just bitten but in full health, it's very likely you would remain human." Edwards patted Angels head knowing that she would be hurt by this.

"So you're saying Richards wouldn't have turned!" Angel said remembering how Ash put down her best friend back in the ruins in the drainer nest. She tried to get to her feet so that she could attack Ash, but Edwards kept her boot in the crook of Angels knee, stopping her attack.

"No! Chances are we could have patched him up and he would have healed." Edwards said sadly, almost feeling the rage building in Angel.

"Rubbish! They all turn if bitten!" He tried to think back, but he had always put a bullet in those who had been bitten... *Maybe I was wrong!* A sickly feeling sank in his stomach.

"We all went toe-to-toe with those creatures and we are human. They are quick and strong but if you recall, they couldn't shoot for shit. In fact most of them were just savage and tried to get into melee combat." Edwards placed a cold hand on Ash's arm, she peered into his eyes.

"The thing is old buddy, the soviet drainers, were bandits, scum and mother fuckers, who wished to be turned. They were obviously keen for the cause and power that they would gain. And they would no longer be sickened by radiation?" She let her words settle. Ash felt sick, he could feel bile clawing its way up to his throat. His head span and he doubled over and threw up his lunch.

"So if they aren't bitten how did they turn?" Angel asked. Edwards shifted around to Angels flank and cut her bonds with a combat knife.

"I don't know for sure but I think they drink blood from somebody who has already turned. Or like me, bitten and was on deaths door. Either way it seems to work." Edwards shrugged.

"Look, I captured some of the guards back at Main-Bridge, while you lot bedded down for the night. I dragged them out into the wilds, tied them down and bit them both. I waited a long time and neither of them turned, even when the sun climbed the next day, they were both still human. I needed to test my theory a kind of stupid experiment..." Edwards settled on the tree stump next to the lantern. She hugged her knees staring into the night.

"Did you let them go?" Angel asked.

"No... I killed one and asked the survivor if he would join me."

"And?" Ash asked.

"He lapped up the blood from my wrist after I ran my combat knife across it." She started to rock on the tree stump remembering the ordeal. "He turned and it was quite quick, at first he went into convulsions and then laid still, dead I thought, for at least an hour."

"Then what?" Angel said eagerly wanting to know.

"He turned... He broke his bonds and attacked me, but I had been prepared."

"Bullshit!" Ash hissed. "He could have turned

from the original bite."

"I don't think so. He turned by drinking infected blood!" Edwards said shaking her head. Angel looked to Ash and her face was contorted in rage.

"You fucking bastard!" She yelled before lashing out towards Ash. Edwards caught her fist as though catching a base-ball, she held her tight until she calmed down.

"It's no fault of Ash, he was ignorant to the truth when he shot Richards, he was thinking about the safety of the entire ranger contingent... But he knows now." Edwards claimed calmly. Ash slumped to the ground in a foetal position and shuddered.

"What have I done!" He repeated many times curling up tight into a human ball on the mossy floor of the wood.

"You murdered Richards, that's what you did!" Angel said as she spat on the floor. However, Angel wondered at the new truth, her thoughts were bouncing around in her mind.

"So the drainers we have encountered are but levies. Untrained, desperate bandits and scum bags joining up with the soviets for extended life and power?"

"Yes Angel, that is indeed so." Edwards agreed.

"So the real soviet drainers, the trained, elite soldiers..."

"Are creatures that we have yet to encounter." Edwards finished her sentence.

"When all you lot were holing up at Applewood

farm and I was left for dead in the desert. I encountered a small group of soviet scouts heading toward Applewood farm. I attacked them and too be honest they didn't put up too much of a fight. Okay they were quick, strong and ruthless, but they were no match for a ranger armed with the knowledge of martial arts, gun training and tactics like an infected ranger. Just like me!" Edwards, gave Angel her rifle back and winked.

"If you're going to kill me, make it quick." She held up her arms as a form of surrender. Angel put the working end of her rifle to Edwards forehead, her hands started to shake.

"Please no! Edwards has spoken the truth!" Ash cried, he had no more fight left in him. Edwards placed her mouth over the end of the rifle.

"Do it!" She mumbled. Angel narrowed her eyes and gritted her teeth, but finally she clicked on the safety and lowered her rifle.

"You are a fellow ranger, I can't murder you." She put a balled fist to her mouth and bit her trigger finger, the slight pain countered her anger.

"What do we do Ash?"

"I don't know yet, but let us sit and work this out." Ash said as he prised himself up, aided by Edwards helping hand.

They discussed the situation for an hour, bouncing ideas off one another, but the conclusion was to keep Edwards as a ranger, a solo, a secret scout who would be a guardian angel over the retreating ranger force.

"I'm happy with that." Edwards agreed.

"But we need to work out how we will welcome a drainer into the rangers, obviously altering the doctrine." Ash claimed. "It is going to be incredibly hard to gain the trust of the rangers."

"I know and if it was me being a human, I wouldn't stand for it at all." Edwards said chuckling at the idea of introducing an enemy into the ranks. "I wouldn't blame them for being cautious."

"Time is on our side my friend." Ash said finally.

"We need to head back to camp Ash, the rangers will be worried by now." Angel claimed.

"Yes, we do." He hugged Edwards and kissed her cheek. "You take care buddy." He whispered in her ear, before marching off towards camp with Angel leading the way. He had hugged the sergeant many times before but this time she had a strange smell, a kind of smell you would associate with your grand-mama's house, instead of the lovely feminine smell you associated with a lover, which he had been accustomed to back at the fort.

The ranger column moved out at dawn. It would be a good three days travel to the corn-fields farm, which Ash wasn't looking forward to. Each day of travel he regained strength but he still felt weak due to his wounds, but he was happy that his body was getting better. Every night when they camped down he and Angel looked to the east and witnessed a tiny lantern illuminating in the distance. *My friend sergeant Edwards.* By the third day of camp Angel started to nudge him to announce we have a guardian angel in the form of abomination. However, he felt the rangers were not ready for such things. They decided, once they settled down at Corn-fields they would both reveal the truth. The ranger contingent mounted the great hill that over looked the Corn-field farm. It was a beautiful sight to behold, rows and rows of fields of yellow/green fields practically obscured the large farmstead below in the natural basin of the land. The rangers began to sing a ranger song having seen the bounty of food and sanctuary.

"Guns in arms, as we travel down the trail."

"Wishing for comfort, but all we hear is pain."

"We hole up for a time and everybody sounds our praise."

"Because the rangers are coming, safety in our minds."

"Because tomorrow we bring sanctuary and all there is hope!"

"And by the hour, we make happy to the folks." The song continues until they get to the main gate of the farmstead. The farm hands spotted the rangers coming and recognise the song and started to chant some of the words they know, but it seemed not everybody knew the song, but the song was catchy. One of the farm hands armed with an old army issue M16, lowered his firearm and hailed the rangers as they arrived at the corn-fields. It seemed, they hadn't been corrupted by what had happened to Main-Town and instead they recognised Angel. (Who was some kind of local hero)

"Angel is here!" The young farm hand cried as several younglings rushed off toward the main building. Angel didn't lap it up, instead she stayed focused and haughty as she marched through the main fortified gate, made up from scrap metal from pre-war car doors and side panels.

"I didn't know you ventured this far from the fort?" Ash said while smiling.

"Now and then I doubled back here. This is where I grew up as a girl." She admitted with a grin.

"By the bright I didn't know that Sister." Ash said feeling the ambience of praise around the rangers.

"You never asked you dick!" She said before rushing off to hug an older man which maybe her brother? Her brother, Big Tom, hugged her and grinned stupidly at the rangers.

"You are welcome here my brothers!" He claimed through giggles of excitement.

"I wanted to be a ranger too, but..." He bowed his head and sighed. "But, I'm the eldest and had to look out for out ma and pa."

"Angel, is one of the best rangers that have ever been under my command!" Ash claimed augmenting the solo ranger.

The rangers were welcomed inside the large extensive farm buildings which must have been a pre-war gas station before the war, but over the years many wooden out-buildings had been constructed, creating a very large farmstead. The eldest folk who owned the farm must have been in his seventies or more, frail and old, leaving the running of the farm to the eldest son. Ash had noticed that many of the corn fields had gone to seed, a clear sign that this farm wasn't harvested to its full potential due to lack of labour. The rangers settled in easily due to the amount of out buildings that were abandoned. He had a brief talk with the senile old owners of the farm and the eldest son present.

"Really, you are welcome here, my sis is a ranger and if you wish to stay then so be it." Malcolm said with a happy tone. Even when Angel warned her eldest brother that things might change on the farm with the rangers stay.

"We will be protected and we can add labour to our fields, we have more food here than most farms." Malcolm stated happily.

"If we stay then you will have your labour in the fields." Ash claimed as he took a swig of corn brewed beer. Angel was slightly miffed by the new order, but she contemplated the wrath of the soviets and then welcomed the idea. Some of the hard core combatant rangers were annoyed by the new order, but they wondered about the romantic idea of settling and living their lives in peace. The majority of the ranger auxiliaries loved the idea and opted for a better life.

Ash took a wander around the farm outstretch

accompanied by Angel, the sun was going down and a watch had been established among the rangers.

"Too be honest I like how fate has played out, but promise me, we will keep this farm safe!"

"You have my promise Angel, we have food, water and meat from the pigs your brother rears on the farm. We will fortify and hope the soviets don't get this far!" He said with a worried brow. Ranger Sanding's approached and waited for the commanding rangers to quit talking.

"All rangers are settled in captain. Have you any more orders?"

"Let them settle in and tomorrow we will begin to fortify the farm, could you send a runner to the top of the hill." He pointed to the only hill nearby the farm.

"Set up the radio, I need to contact Captain Harris."

"Yes sir!" Sanding's darted off to the farm.

"Your thoughts?" Ash said to Angel.

"All is good captain!" She took a pace backwards and saluted, before wandering off.

Ash sat at the flank of the dinning room table from old John the owner of the farm. Ash sat across form his wife Carol who had really gone to town on her appearance using pre-war lipstick, makeup and a floral dress. Her hair, white and tied up in a bun.

"My daughter is a ranger do you know?" She said as she spooned a mouthful of corn and onion soup, which dribbled from the sides of her mouth.

"Yes, by far the best ranger under my command!"

He repeated as Angel kicked his leg under the table and gave him a scowl. Ash laughed it off though. The door to the dining room opened and in walked ranger Neris.

"Sir, you need to come to the radio." Neris eyed the folk around the table and tried not to alarm anybody seated having their dinner. Ash patted his face using a cotton woven rag and followed ranger Neris out of the farmstead.

Cool air assaulted his face as he followed the ranger up the hill to the radio emplacement.

"Report?" Ash said sternly.

"Just follow me." Neris said almost out of line with his tone. Ash nodded and climbed the hill towards the lantern light where the radio equipment had been set up. A Ranger and a couple of axillaries were sat cross legged around the pre-war radio equipment, which was crackling, hissing and buzzing.

"Not getting anything from Applewood!" Auxiliary Daniels stated with stress in his voice.

"Let me try!" Ash said budging Daniels away.

"Are you sure?"

"Yes captain, I think Applewood has fallen!"

"Nonsense! Captain Harris would never allow that!" Ash fumbled with the radio settings trying to establish contact to Applewood. However, each time he tried it was but a hiss of background radiation.

"By the bright Applewood must have fallen!" Daniels said with a sob in his tone.

"Harris! Harris! God-damn you pick up!" Ash

yelled into the radio. His plea fell far into the hiss of unknowing. Finally after several more attempts Ash settled back.

"Applewood has fallen... I can only hope that some rangers retreated, but I'm not holding my breath. I know Harris, he would stand to the last man!" Ash picked himself up and wandered down the hill toward the farm building. He knew Main-Bridge would be next in the firing line of the soviets. He got back to the farmstead building and while everybody was rejoicing in a fine meal he had to make the call.

"Rangers! Applewood has fallen, we require everybody to be steadfast and ready!" He went on to describe what had beset the Ashland and Angel fortified his words.

"Tomorrow we fortify this farm and by the bright hold our flame!" He felt tired and retired to bed. Thomas gave him another injection, but it was a low yield steroid, so that he could wake the next morning fit as a fiddle.

Ash awoke, he had a series of nightmares, which he couldn't recall, but remembered they were all bad. He kicked himself out of a sweat ridden blanket and marched his way to the front of the main building where all were gathered.

"I need to tell you what is happening in the Ashland. We abandoned the Ranger fort and rushed across the land to Applewood, where we established contact with other rangers. Rangers fortified

Applewood and it seems they have been compromised. In between us and the enemy gathering in the ruins. There is one more stronghold, which is in Main-Bridge. The township is protected by heavily armed gangsters, I hope they stand true, because if they don't, the enemy is coming our way. We have guns and training so we should be okay, however, we need to make procedures to allow innocents to escape while the rangers take a stand here!"

"We will stand with you rangers!" Malcolm stated as he looked to other farm hands to bolster his words. Ash waited for the others to contemplate staying or fleeing. Discussions among the farmers seemed to get quite heated. But, finally they all decided on an outcome.

"We are with the rangers!" Malcolm cried at the top of his voice which made Ash ash's arm hairs stand on end.

"So be it!" Ash growled. Ash knew time was at the essence so he made do with the time he had to fortify the farmstead.

Days passed swiftly as the folks and rangers of Corn-fields, fortified the buildings against a horde of attack. Everyday, folk became more and more religious, praying to the bright, hoping the sun god would protect them. Stockades were established, windows of the buildings were boarded up leaving slits to fire through. The sun started to rise, cascading beams of bright light around the farm. Ash took a long walk around the outside of the farmstead, shaking hands with rangers and farm hands. He had banished the axillaries to the main building so they could drag wounded etc inside. Ash stood next to Angel who still had a bugbear with him.

"How you feeling?" Angel asked with a frown.

"I'm going to head out and establish contact with Edwards, we need an alarm."

"By the bright bring her in!"

"Really?" Ash said worryingly.

"Bring her in, we need her with us, I just hope she don't go all feral on us." Angel stated. Ash nodded and wandered down the way, away from the farm. He borrowed a sniper rifle from one of the rangers and sat down peering down the scope. After a while he saw Edwards stood in the middle of the corn field. She must have noticed the reflection from the scope shining in the sun. He used the shinning scope in a ranger fashion, bringing the palm of his hand on and off at intervals. Ash sent a message, 'ranger style', using the scope of his rifle. Within minutes Edwards appeared standing under an old oak tree. Ash approached cautiously.

"You ready to come in?"

"Hell yeah!"

"Walk with me! We will get challenges from the rangers!" Ash covered her with a blanket and made his excuses taking the drainer into the farm building so they could talk. Some of the rangers were scowling as they walked past the stockades and defences. Somehow he managed to get to his private room in the farmstead.

Ash brought her upto date about Applewood falling and the drainer very nearly shed tears, but found it was damn near impossible.

"So how are we gona roll with this, Ash? You can't keep sneaking me back and two covered in a blanket."

"Really? Oh no, because I'm all out of idea's." He said feigning a puzzled frown, before laughing out loud. "But your right, we need to tell the others what you are." His frown retuned for real this time.

"I have an idea..." She grinned revealing an evil set of pointy teeth. "Why don't we say, yes I'm a drainer, but some kind of mutation of its form?"

"Like, retaining all the goodness of the ranger you were?"

"Might work, but we need to get them to trust me." She crouched down on the floor and folded her arms over her knees, staring at the rough spun floor mat.

"We have Angels backing, that's a start..." A knock on the door hushed the conversation. The door opened and Angel popped her head around the sturdy wooden door.

"Shit!" Ash sighed. "Thought you might be one of the other rangers! That would have set off one hell of a shit storm if they noticed who was in here with me."

"I heard my name!" Angel said shutting the door behind her.

"How long you been listening at the door?" Edwards asked, but she knew the answer all ready.

"Long enough, but your plan is floored. If you

need rangers to trust you, then you need evidence, proof, etc."

"What are you suggesting Solo?" He asked, hoping to fuck it did not involve Edwards biting somebody.

"She bites me." Angel shrugged with a stony face. Ash threw his cup across the room. "She ain't biting anybody, didn't you listen to Edwards??? There is still a chance of infection!"

"Angel's correct, we do a test in front of everybody, she is fit as a fiddle, she ain't gona turn!" Edwards said, not doubting her own words having seen the test with her own eyes. She seemed excited by the idea, very likely a trait with all drainers. Ash didn't like the idea one bit.

"No! They must be another way!" He barked and started to pace the room.

"We are doing this Ash, it's the only way to prove Edward's stay among the rangers." Angel claimed. "We do it tonight!"

That night, Ash and Angel called a meeting, they explained to all present about the theory of the test and the chance of success. Edwards stayed in Ash's private room, ready to bolt out of the window in case of an uprise. It took some persuasion and a lot of discussion until the majority of the rangers and farm folk decided to perform the test or kill Edwards.

"The majority vote is for the test." Ranger Sanding's finally said. A small percentage were still ready to shoot her on sight, but it was clear that it was for the good of the rangers survival to gain back sergeant Edwards, who was still respected in the ranks.

"We do this properly. We tie both the recipients down and if anything goes wrong at least we can pull the plug!" Ash said grimly, knowing he might be forced to shoot both of his companions in the head. Again it was a majority vote. Neris, was one of the doubters, so it was only fair that he got to tie down the would be prisoners. He spent more than twenty minutes securing Angel and Edwards down with tight rope bonds, but finally he nodded.

"Do it Edwards!" Angel whispered cocking her head and revealing her neck to Edwards, who appeared quite vulnerable and fearful if the test went horribly wrong. Edwards leaned in close and bit her neck, slurping on the blood that welled up from the wound. Angel shuddered at first and then leant into Edward's dire embrace. This brought a shocked gasp from the audience. Some of the rangers locked and loaded their carbines ready to shoot at a moments notice. Ash involuntarily grabbed his own neck and pulled a face of disgust, but most of the folk gathered were either curious or looked away from the macabre spectacle. Edwards pulled away and leant back in the bonds of the chair.

"Now we wait…" She whispered, tasting the wonderful blood on her lips. Minutes passed and the air could be cut with tension. After twenty minutes folk started to wander away, leaving a group on over watch.

Dawn came, the sun started to caress the cold windows with warmth and illumination. By now the group had thinned down to Neris, Sandings and Ash keeping watch.

"If it was going to happen, Angel would have turned by now!" Edwards broke the silence and tension. Sandings woke up, he had fallen asleep.

"Is she okay?" He asked, as he stretched the sleep from his limbs.

"I don't feel any different if that's what you are asking." Angel said with a smile. It had been a very tense ordeal and she looked knackered.

"Ash, feel her brow, if she is cold then you can shoot both of us right now!" Edwards said with a poker face. Ash walked over to Angel and felt the warmth he expected from a fellow human.

"She is warm to the touch." He said after a very tense few seconds. He then reached over and felt the brow of Edwards. He pulled his hand away in shock.

"Cold... Cold as a cucumber." He laughed nervously looking to Neris who had a scowl of doubt on his desert beaten face. Neris gave his rifle to Sandings and mimicked what Ash had already done. Satisfaction washed over his face.

"Untie them!" He whispered before grabbing his rifle and wandering away.

"It seems like the test has been successful. Let's get these bonds off you." Ash said fumbling with the rope knots.

"It will take some time before they fully trust you Edwards, but you have my backing." He said as he released Angels bonds. Angel stood up and stretched the cramp from her body.

"I need a piss!" Angel finally said, before wandering off toward the latrines. Ash released Edwards and collapsed into a soft chair nearby.

"By the bright that was an ordeal I never wish to do again!"

"Me too!" Edwards said as she rubbed at the rope marks on her wrists. "Me fucking too!"

"Angel, is the bravest ranger among us. Hell I wouldn't have done the test." Sandings said chuckling.

"Indeed she is! Such sacrifice too!" Ash said, knowing also, he wouldn't have had the marbles to do what Angel had just done for a fellow ranger. He silently cursed his own fortitude. *Am I such a coward?*

Later that morning, Ash, Neris and Sandings began to organise the fortification of the farm. Angel and Edwards had been temporary banished to Ash's room, until everybody felt at ease to the events the night previous. By mid-day and all hands on deck, the rangers and folks of the farm had already made head way into the fortifications. Derick, the trader had been told to move his trade-post within the farmstead grounds. Utilising one of the un-used rooms inside the large farmhouse. The auxiliaries aided the merchant carrying trade stuff to the new appointed trade-house, inside the fortified security zone. Ash even leant a hand with the fortifications which gained him some admiration among the rangers who were now touching the void of ranger moral. By sun down they had secured a watch and fortified the farm enough to sleep easy that night. Ash had a quick supper and then retired to bed, fatigued but steadfast. Angel and Edwards were moved to a secure out-building just in case. They didn't complain and they understood the reason why two rangers stood guard outside the out-building with safety switches off their carbines.

CHAPTER 13

The sun had peaked just past noon and even though they had all just had a good nights kip, the stress of the ruined city had taken it out on the questing party.

"We need to head north to the Corn-fields, a settlement half a days trek north. There we will purchase provisions, ammo, a hot meal and a bed for the night. We need it!" Jessica said, while they stopped for a rest. They had been travelling east over the grasslands, navigating around the small woodland area's. The family at the farm house had prepared a nice breakfast for them all and wished them a good day's travel.

"We go east to the old army bunker!" Joshua said with a bite in his tone.

"We need ammo Joshua, what good are mercenaries with empty guns?" Jessica said in a huff.

"She's right Joshua, crossing that ruin has seriously depleted our ammo reserves." Brae said in agreement.

"Well I'm down to my last five clips, if we come up against bandits like the old fuck warned us about, then we are all fucked!" Jessica growled.

"Well I'm not dishing out anymore coin, buying ammo for all you lot, ive paid out enough in this venture!" Joshua hissed.

"I'm sorry Joshua, but needs must, to be honest I'm with Jessica this time. I'm nearly spent up on rifle ammo." Yolanda said trying to calm the heated discussion.

"Sorry old man, we head on Jessica's bearing, we need fresh food and ammo and don't worry the Cornfields is a safe settlement and has a good trade-house, bar and inn. Me and Jess has been there a number of times before over the years" Brae said with a shrug. Joshua grumbled his curses and then fell in line as they headed off north. He kept looking east to his goal. He wanted so much to find out more about the father to the Utopian man. It was nearly in his grasp. Natasha linked his arm and cuddled him, trying to subdue his rage and wanting.

"We are still going Josh my love. Allow the experts to keep us all safe." He stared into her innocent eyes and could see the wisdom in her words.

"Fine, lets head fucking north!" Joshua said bitching.

Brae and Jessica had been correct, by six-o-clock they started to see the grass land change into fields of overgrown corn. The sun had begun to sink, bringing a cool and welcome breeze from the heat of the day. As they approached the farmlands a group of heavily armed rangers approached.

"They look like rangers, but be on your guard!" Brae said narrowing his eyes and watching the two rangers approaching with carbines at their chin. Joshua started to get agitated and pushed his way to the front of the group.

"We are travellers and seek hospitality and trade in these lands." Joshua announced to the coming armed warriors.

"Trade house has shifted inside the farm building, but if you seek sanctuary and trade we will follow you in!" One of the battle hardened rangers announced with doubt in his words. The rangers moved quickly into position, flanking the group, weapons hot. It's when one of the rangers lowered his weapon with a smile.

"Is that you Brae?" Brae pushed the priest aside.

"Remmy? Is that you? You son-of-a-bitch!" Brae said recognising the elder of the two rangers.

"Shit on me, how you doing Brae?" Remmy said slinging his carbine over his shoulder. The grey haired ranger opened up his arms, grinning like a Cheshire cat. Brae bear hugged his old friend from the rangers.

"By the bright! How have you been keeping my old buddy?" Brae asked, at arm's length from the hug.

"Up and down my mate, but better for seeing you!" Remmy hugged the mercenary again and then spotted Jessica.

"No!" Remmy started to laugh. "No way that's you Jess!" Jessica chuckled remembering the old days running with the rangers. She joined in the hugging.

"Glad you're still kicking Remmy... Shit how long has it been?" The ranger was still shaking his head in disbelief.

"Too long my friend, gee you must have been but

twenty?"

"Yeah, something like that." Jessica pulled away and looked to the others with a wink. Brae felt a little side tracked as their old ranger buddy focused on the pretty woman.

"Ooo this is a bit awkward, didn't you once try chatting me up?" She said with a nervous smile, remembering she had knocked back Remmy's advances to her, during one of the ranger missions.

"By the bright, fuck all that, I'm sorry for coming onto you back in the day." The Ranger said biting back some embarrassment.

"I'm so sorry. I didn't know you batted for the other side, shame on me!" He said chuckling. The group followed the two rangers into the fortified settlement. Brae was the first to pick up on the fortifications.

"You expecting trouble?"

"long story mate, but lets get you up to the trade post and get a hot meal down you guys!" Natasha looked in bewilderment of the unfolding scenario.

"You know these guys?

"Yeah we do!" Brae and Jessica said, while Yolanda, Joshua and Natasha felt like a fifth wheel.

As they wandered up to the main farmstead, they all noticed that the farm had been fortified with stockade, kill zones and sniper positions on top of the farm building where rangers stalked around with precision rifles.

"It has changed since we ventured these parts. It's

as though you are expecting trouble?" Brae asked Remmy, who was walking and matching his stride to his flank.

"Got a lot of shit going down at the moment buddy, but don't worry the rangers have this area sealed!" Remmy said with conviction. Two more rangers levelled their guns and tracked the entourage entering the secure zone.

"Are they merchants?" One of the rangers on the stockade asked while he took off the safety on his carbine.

"There with me, some are ex rangers and I know them!" Remmy said with a stupid grin on his face.

"Who is in charge here?" Jessica asked as they wandered past the stockade.

"Captain Ash is in charge... But we have a weird situation going on, but its none of your business. Please let us get you to the trade-house." Remmy assured them. They wandered past numerous elite looking rangers into the main building. Remmy took them past the main living space, which had been doubled up as a kitchen and ranger mess hall. Old Derick were taking inventory on the stock as the party entered the trade depot. The grey haired old man put his palms on an old farm house table, he appeared ready to trade with a merchant smile.

"What can I Get ye?" The merchant said with a guttered voice, quite like the accent of a bandit, of the Ashland. Jessica started to chuckle and put her gnarly long fingers on the table.

"You got point forty five ammo?"

"As it happens I do... How many bullets do you wish to trade?" The shop keep was one of those survivor types probably gun running to the highest bidder, be them rangers, merchants or bandits, he clearly didn't care!

The party spent some time trading coin for bullets and the merchant seemed to have plenty to sell. Joshua and the collective funds of the party managed to outfit their weapons with a serious amount of ammo for a quite cheap price. Jessica wandered off with twenty magazines worth of bullets for her colt 1911's. She also purchased some fresh provisions and a bottle of corn whiskey before retiring to bed in a common room where the rangers slept. The others did the same, purchased ammo and then shared a small room together where they could bed down for the night. They had all agreed to have an early night so they could re-vitalise themselves. Several rangers guarded the hospitality rooms even though some of the rangers knew them by face and not name. Natasha and Joshua started to get frisky in the dark, at first Brae and Yolanda tried to ignore the affections they heard which sounded sexual. Lots of sobbing, moaning and groaning, going on in the dark. Yolanda grabbed Brae's hand and moved it down between her legs. He felt the wetness and he could feel the warmth of her body against him, his hand was moist with her wanting. He was at first put off by the sexual sounds that Joshua and Natasha was making, clearly Natasha was having a very good time. He had to man up. Yolanda kissed him passionately, her tongue sliding against his. He doubled over, under the bedding and parted her legs, pushing his tongue against her. She sobbed softly, not trying to compete with the other sounds of passion in the dark. He felt her hand grabbing hold of his hard cock and then sliding her tongue over the end. He felt the warmth of the full embrace of her mouth. He moved his tongue against her clitoris and lapped against it, now and then moving his tongue downwards and penetrating her for a few seconds. He felt her shudder and stifle back a sob, so he lapped hard again against her, she felt every lick of his tongue as her body went into spasms. He could feel the suction of her mouth around him, licking, sucking, caressing spirally. They were both in the zone and he felt the roaring and buzzing sound in his ears as he came into her mouth. His pulse rate was through the floor but he wanted her to come to, so he set about her in a manic assault. He lapped and licked against her until he could feel her about to come. Her legs outstretched and toes curled as her body went into orgasm. He felt his lips warm and wet as she came. They rearranged each other to a facing position and cuddled before sleep took them both. Kissing silently into the night.

Jessica was up with the sun and wandering around the grounds of the farmstead catching the first rays of sun on her face. She sat on a hay bale and gazed at the sun slowly rising over the corn fields. She loved times like these, no hustle and bustle of townships and no bullets whizzing over her head, just the peace and calm of a good sun rise. She uncorked a bottle of corn whiskey and took a gulp, the biting liquor warmed her throat as the acrid tasting liquid flushed to her gut.

"Well shit on me! Is that a grown up Jessica Ryding?" A voice she recognised but couldn't place. She peered over her shoulder and grinned when she saw that it was Ash, her old commanding officer.

"I heard mention you was here somewhere, I went looking for you last night but you had gone to bed. How you doing sir?" She said remembering to use 'sir'.

"Cut all that nonsense out! You aren't under my command anymore." He frowned seeing the bottle of whiskey.

"You starting early Jess?"

"Yep!" She said turning to face the sun again a little pissed off, she did what she wanted when she wanted.

"Well, it's too early for me, but I'm not going to let one of my old rangers drink alone." He picked up the bottle and took a few sips, pulling his face a little.

"By the bright they should only make whiskey out of grain, this corn stuff just doesn't sit right on your palette."

"Out in the Ashland you get what you get." Jessica said through a smirk. Ash suddenly turned serious, she could see it in his face and she almost knew what he was going to ask.

"Why did you leave Jess? You were one of the best rangers I ever had under my command and since then I've had some damned good rangers. You were a fucking natural."

"I think it was the shit pay… But deep down I think it just wasn't for me, it was all a bit goodie-two-shoes for my liking." She chuckled knowing he wouldn't like that answer.

"We protect lives Jess, if it wasn't for the rangers I don't think humanity would have got to where it is today. Townships, civilization, before the rangers, there was chaos, murder and constant threat. At least now a feller can come home from a hard days work and relax in his chair and not worry about bandits, abominations and drainers…" He silently cursed himself saying that last word, he really didn't want Jessica to know what was really going on.

"Drainers? Haven't heard that word in a very long time."

"You know, scum in general." He said trying to distract her, it seemed to work.

"The rangers did a fine job in the Ashland, but again it wasn't for me."

"Heard you ran with some bandits, I was sorry to have heard that, cut me all up inside. Knowing you had joined up with those evil fucks" He spat on the ground.

"Yeah, ran with some real mother fuckers, pay was good, but mostly I stayed in the gang due to a girl." She made a rude gesture with her tongue and two fingers to punctuate her words. Ash screwed up his face with disgust.

"Where you heading?" He asked changing the subject.

"Got a contract, with a religious nutcase. Taking him and his missus, to some secret pre-war military base. Not very far from here, as it happens. Must be secret because I've never heard about it before and I've been all over the Ashland."

"Military base?" Ash suddenly intrigued.

"Yeah, apparently some dead feller's father had left some evidence to where utopia is, or some such shit. Pays good and we are still alive so that's all dandy to me."

"Would you mind me tagging on, we could do with some military equipment, if it hasn't already been pecked clean?" He asked hoping she would say yes. *A real fortification. A place to rally against the coming storm.* He wondered.

"You wanna come with us?" She said questioning and surprised.

"Yeah, might be able to get some good heavy equipment, we could do with a fifty cal, maybe some rocket launchers. You can find all kinds of shit that is helpful to rangers at old military depots." He grinned.

"You roll with us you drop your rank. That was another reason I dropped the rangers, couldn't do with all that yes sir bull shit." She warned.

"I will be under your command Jess, if that is what you wish?" He put his hands out palms up.

"Then get your shit together we roll out after

breakfast."

"Who are these people?" Joshua said scowling at the male and two females dressed in the garbs of rangers.

"That's Ash and the other two are Angel and Edwards. They are tagging along, they are hoping to bag some supplies from the base." Jessica said not giving a shit if he liked it or not.

"I'm not happy with this situation Jess, can't we mark it on a map or something and they can go after we have been there?" Joshua pleaded.

"With the sounds of things we are going to run into a very dangerous bandit gang, we could do with the extra guns and what better to have on your side, than rangers?"

"Well I'm still against them tagging along!" He huffed.

"Too be honest Joshua, you can curl up in a tight little ball and eat your own shit, because they are still coming with us."

"Then I will share the contract among them as well." He bargained.

"You can do that Josh, but you would be missing some teeth if you don't cough up what you owe me." With that she wandered over to Ash who was chatting with Brae about old times and ranger shit.

"You ready to head out?" Jessica said while peering at Edwards who was wearing a bandana around her mouth and sunglasses. Something seemed odd with her and it didn't settle right with Jess. She nodded at her and Edwards nodded back, they both had an understanding that neither trusted one another.

"Right then lets go." Brae said as he patted Ash's shoulder. They both took the lead as Jessica idled at the rear. She fell into a steady trot flanking Edwards. She could almost see a smile under the bandana, as though Edwards knew Jessica was onto her.

"See that you have the stripes of a sergeant." Jess broke the ice.

"Yep, earned them too..." Edwards bitched. "I heard you ran with the rangers and then joined up with a notorious bandit gang. That seemed to be a wonderful career change. Bet you felt great killing hard working innocent folks for coin and supplies." She said bitterly.

"Yeah it did!" Jessica stopped and faced her, fists balled. Edwards stopped and looked Jessica up and down.

"It wouldn't be worth the effort to kick your ass!" She said before catching up with the group, leaving Jessica behind, angry and pent up for a fight.

The group had travelled all day following the dirt roads from the merchant carts criss-crossing the land. They camped down in an old abandoned filling station, some of the asphalt still showed and wasn't overgrown like most of the pre-wars were. Yolanda started to laugh at the faded sign for the filling station that stated 'Bumble Bills gas station'. It had a cartoon style painting of a man smiling with a bushy beard.

"Bet Bill didn't look like that painting." Jess said as she came to Yolanda's side.

"Yeah I bet he was a fat bastard, who wore dungarees, quite like those old photos we found a few years back." She giggled. Jessica grabbed her arm and leaned close to her ear.

"Keep an eye on Edwards, the last time I got this feeling, it turned out it was an assassin after my bounty."

"Didn't know you had a bounty Jess?" Yolanda said, it was no longer funny.

"Yeah I did, but I paid it off. All two hundred silver dollars of it. It's when I left the bandit gang and went bounty hunting myself."

"The more I find out about you Jess, the more I dislike you, but don't take offence I still have your back!" Yolanda said before heading into the gas station. Jessica plodded up and down outside the filling station, she could smell a camp fire being started and the sun had disappeared behind a low hill in the distance. She sat on an over turned battered old litter box and pondered. Her mind delved deep into her memories. There was something familiar about Edwards. *Have I met her before?* She wondered. The bandana obscured most of her face and the sunglasses didn't help, she could always remember a persons eyes. With that thought she headed in, the smell of cooked pork sausages made her gut groan. The room where they camped used to be the main garage space where they fixed automobiles. The camp fire burnt low and Joshua manned the spits. Ash sat crossed legged next to Natasha eagerly waiting with a tin plate with fresh uncooked pork sausages, which they had purchased from the farm. She eyed Edwards and un-rolled her bed roll well away from Edwards who had her head down cleaning her carbine rifle. Angel nearby unscrewed a hip flask, she was about to take a sip, but instead she offered the silver flask to Jess.

"You look troubled lass, take a hit." Jess smiled and took the flask and glugged a good shot.

"If I'm not mistaken, you look like a solo?" Jess said passing the flask back to Angel.

"It shows don't it." Angel chuckled and shifted closer to Jess. "We can't all be pretty, especially if most of my life I have slept rough."

"Sorry I didn't mean it that way..." Jess tried to apologise but Angel put her hand up.

"Pay no heed, and you need not be sorry lass. I've had a hard life and it shows, I can live with that." She passed the flask again. Jessica couldn't tell her age, the solo had a weather beaten face of an old farmer wife. But her eyes sparkled with wisdom. She estimated that she was in her late forties. Angel started to unbuckle her armour and took off her green shirt. Angel was top heavy for a ranger, Jess had always been jealous about other women with large breasts, because she had small little bumps, hardly worth noticing at all. Angel had already sussed out Jessica's sexuality, she didn't mind being appraised she seldom had in the past. It was just a shame that it was a female appraising her. Jessica rummaged through her back pack and pulled out a half full bottle of corn whiskey. She un-corked it using her teeth and then passed the bottle to Angel.

"I went solo for a while, it wasn't for very long, a few months maybe more. I was part of a recon group of rangers. I didn't like the loneliness, the fact that nobody had your back and if you got into trouble your team mates were too far away to aid you." Jessica said while taking off her leather duster and armour. She placed her gun belt beside her bed roll and kicked off her boots.

"I remember once I got into a real situation where bandits found my hiding place, a gun battle issued and I got properly shot up. Luckily they left me for dead and moved on. Stranger still they didn't take my gun or any ammo, I think they were in a hurry to leave because as I faded away I could hear more gun shots in the distance." The sparkle in Angel's eyes faded as she recalled the event, it was like she suddenly had cataract infecting her eyes.

"Been there and done that sister." Jess said comically as she climbed into her bed roll. The temperature had dropped in the night air, she shivered and rubbed her flanks to stay warm. Angel watched over Jessica as her eyes closed gearing up for sleep. She reached over and pulled the bed roll tight against Jessica, in a motherly way.

"Sleep tight Jess, I have your back, even though being a solo I seldom have any body looking over me."

"The name Angel suits you." Jess finally said as

she faded into sleep.

Jessica stirred in her sleep, she half opened her eyes and smelt and saw the low burning camp fire. She fumbled around in her pants pocket and pulled out an old pocket watch. The radium paint stated quarter past three. The others were fast asleep and she noticed Edwards standing at the window peering out into the night. Her rifle slung over her back and she was still in her full ranger get up. *That bitch don't sleep!* She thought. As she reached for her gun belt, Edwards reacted to the noise and peered towards Jessica. Edwards eyes glowed yellow in the darkness, she couldn't work out if it was the reflection from the fire or her eyes actually glowed. She cautiously pulled out one of her pistols and slowly pulled the slide locking a bullet in the chamber. She cursed silently when the gun made an audible clicking sound.

"I'm not your enemy Jessica!" Edwards whispered. Her eyes glowing in the dim light. Jess feigned sleep but her eyes were open, watching Edwards every move. Her mind raced and then focused on a distant memory. *A fucking drainer!* Everything seemed to fall in place now, it was the smell, that sickly almond like smell that her mind had associated with drainers. *Is Ash insane? Why would he travel with the undead?* She was about to attack, but Edwards raced towards her using unearthly speed. Edwards grabbed Jessica's throat with the strength of a bear, her knee fast against her gun hand.

"Yes I'm a drainer, but you have no idea what is going on my friend!" Edwards said grinning showing razor like teeth, her sharp finger nails digging into Jessica's throat.

"Easy now!" Angel whispered as she put Edwards into a choke hold, her combat knife fast against Edwards throat. Angel had stealthy climbed out of her bed roll and come to Jessica's plight. "As you said, Jess don't know the full story. I suggest we all stand down and discuss this matter tomorrow. We all need to sleep." Angel said tightening her grip around Edwards head. Edwards put her hands up in surrender and began to chuckle.

"There you go Jess, you do have a guardian angel." Edwards cautiously got to her feet and pushed Angel aside.

"If It's okay with everybody, I will continue my watch, seeing I don't require sleep like you humans do." Edwards stated cockily and wandered back to the window to stay on watch. Angel pulled her bed roll nearer to Jess and felt around in Jessica's bed roll until she found the pistol. She pulled the pistol from her hand and replaced it with her own hand. Angels hand was callused but warm and comforting.

"Tomorrow I will inform you. But for now get some sleep and trust Edwards, she might be a drainer but she has our back!" Angel whispered.

Breakfast was cooking on the camp fire and Jessica took a morning stroll around the vicinity of the gas station. Everybody had slept in and the sun had started to heat up the land. Jess ate a plate full of fresh scrambled eggs and pork meat jerky while she sat on a trash bin. Ash sat on the available space and also had a plate of scrambled eggs, but his had some kind of red sauce dribbled over the smashed up eggs.

"Sorry Jess, should have been honest with you from the start." He scowled, but it was more of a scowl for himself.

"There is shit going down, which I didn't wish to inform you about. But I should have done, so that on me." He used his fingers as a comb to brush back his salt and pepper hair.

"I guess it has something to do with drainers!" Jess said with a frown.

"We are on the run Jess, the Rangers are all but finished!" Ash went on and filled in the gaps, he told Jessica about the coming storm, the soviets in the form of drainers. The fortress falling, Applewood and all the shitty details.

"That sounds really bad Ash! Knowing you, I suspect your going to use this military base as a stronghold for the rangers." Jessica had worked it all out, she was bright and tactical.

"You read my thoughts Jess, are you one of those rad-children we came across back in the day? Those nomadic people, that could foresee the future? Remember when we geared up for that battle at lost ridge?"

"The time I dragged your wounded ass back to the

fortifications. Yeah I remember" Jess grinned.

"But they were right Jess, we did win, those abominations swarmed our position and we had a major victory." Ash smiled and his eyes faded in remembrance.

"So you need me again?" She sighed, looking down to the ancient asphalt.

"I need that victory again and if we can find equipment at this so called secret army base, then it may just turn the tide of the storm heading our way." Ash pleaded. Jessica took a deep breath and a swig of the last dregs of the corn whiskey.

"I'm in, but it is conditional. You pay my way in coin and then I will join your cause!"

"If coin is all you wish then we will pay..." He said shaking his head in antipathy.

"Then I'm in!" She finally said while she shook his hand.

Another day passed without conflict or strife. The party had gathered enough ground toward the secret pre-war installation, but knew they were on borrowed time. The savage bandits in the area had already picked up there trail and were hunting them down. Brae had tried his best to hide there passing but every time they stopped for a rest, in the distance they could see armed groups following the trail. They broke camp in the morning and headed south east as a bearing using Brae's compass. Yolanda stood on the ridge peering down into the natural bowl of the landscape using binoculars.

"They are catching up..." She moaned. "We need to find a place where we can dig in!"

"We carry on, we must carry on!" Joshua barked even though he was utterly exhausted by the harsh travel over the terrain. Brae noticed Joshua was feverish and Natasha was lopping around like a rotter. Brae pulled a face when Natasha fell to the ground.

"We need to rest, our contract is to protect them. They can't carry on in this state!" Brae said angrily. It was when Yolanda spotted a building off the broken road.

"There is a house on the ridge there!" She pointed up the hill towards a small house. "Maybe It's abandoned?" She wondered.

"We head there and be quick about it!" Ash ordered. Seeing the coming threat they all double timed it up the hill toward the house. When they reached the house the ranger contingent secured the main area.

"Clear!" Angel yelled, as she looked down her rifle scope. Jessica was first to the door of the house, she had her guns out and gestured to all the party to move in quick. Brae kicked the door with a heavy boot nearly knocking the door off its hinges. Jess backed him up in the sweep of the building. The others fanned in behind her.

"Clear!" Jessica yelled as she stormed into the living space sporting a rotten old couch and a busted television. She heard many more 'Clear' chanting behind her as the others searched the other rooms. The house was quite spacious and even had an evaporated swimming pool out the back of the premises.

"Bet this house belonged to a high roller of some kind, maybe an actors house?" Brae said as he finished the sweep of the upstairs rooms.

"Big ass house!" Jessica added.

"We need to dig in, those bandit groups are hot on our trail!" Ash said in a commanding tone. He looked around the interior and his mind started to calculate the best defences.

"I'm going high with Yolanda, we have high velocity rifles, give us an edge on over watch!" Brae said before racing upstairs with Yolanda, Joshua and Natasha in tow.

"I will be out in the field!" Edwards said rushing out of the door. Jessica usually did that but she wanted to stick close to Ash and Angel.

"Looks like we get downstairs!" Jessica stated as she pulled out the Nickel plated point forty four desert eagle. Ash spotted the pistol and held his up.

"Snap!" He nodded. Jessica looked to the barrel of Ash's gun and smiled.

"Not snap... Mine is a point forty four!" She winked and smashed a nearby window and got herself ready for and attack. Ash looked at his pistol and frowned.

"Didn't know they came in higher calibre, always thought the three fifty seven was the beast!" Ash seemed bugged off.

"Where the fuck are they?" Angel whispered, it had been over an hour by now and the bandits still hadn't attacked.

"Maybe they don't like the fact we are dug in and fortified?" Jessica added.

"At least they can only come at us from one direction. But on the other edge of the sword if things go bad for us, we will die here because I can't see any bolt holes due to the rocks enclosing the house." Ash, said half-heartedly. Movement in the trees brought them back on guard. Two whistles came from the tree line followed by an owl sound.

"It's Edwards!" Ash said as she appeared from the tree line. She strolled toward the house seemingly with all the time in the world. When she entered she shrugged.

"They are camping down below that bluff, they have a few scouts out but none of them have ventured very far up the hill."

"How many?" Ash asked.

"Thirty eight of them, some better armed than others..." Edwards paused and pulled a puzzled face. "If I'm not mistaken but I suspect they fear this place?"

"What's to fucking fear?" Jessica chuckled.

"Like I said I'm not sure. But one thing is for sure, the bandits seem a little backwards, like savages. A bit like those nomadic groups in the north Ash." Edwards looked to Ash.

"Superstition?"

"Yeah, a kind of sacred place or place where bad

spirits dwell? That kind of thing." Edwards said as she sat down on the busted couch.

"If your right Edwards, we could use that as a tactical advantage." Ash said pondering.

CHAPTER 14

"Suns going down. Shit! We are gona be up all night on guard." Jessica moaned, as she watched the sun riding down from the sky slowly. Edwards had been fluttering in and out all day checking up on the savages camping down the hill from the house. She returned again, shrugged and nodded.

"Same old, they haven't moved." She looked at the folks and noticed they looked tired. "Look I will stay on watch, take it in turns to nap down. It's probably better that way because my eye sight is a lot better in the dark." They all agreed and set up a rota. Jess made sure she was on a different watch than Angel, so when she slept, Angel had her back. Just in case the drainer turned feral. Jessica fell onto the couch and curled up to get some Zzzs. Ash had already nodded off sat awkwardly on a busted up dining room chair as Edwards and Angel took the first watch. A similar watch had been established upstairs with Brae and Yolanda taking turns to sleep. Joshua and Natasha were already tucked up in their bed rolls fast asleep, oblivious to the guardians around them protecting the house.

About midnight Angel roused Jessica to take the next watch. She looked to Ash who were snoring his bastard head off, his head lolled back in the chair.

"Leave him be, he looks like he needs the rest." Jessica said as Angel tried to wake him up. "I'm sure me and the drainer can keep watch."

"Less of the 'drainer' bitch!" Edwards snarled showing sharp teeth like a feral dog.

"I mean no offence... Drainer!" Jessica said deliberately trying to wind up Edwards. Edwards made a rude gesture toward Jess using her middle finger, a smile forming on her pale face.

"You two play nice now!" Angel chuckled before collapsing on the couch feeling the warmth where Jess had laid.

"Any movement?"

"Nope, not a sausage." Edwards said shaking her head.

"They are waiting us out, they don't fear this place, they know we will have to come down to them eventually." Jessica said bitterly. The moon was full in the clear dark sky casting strange shadows in the interior of the building. She noticed a glow from upstairs and assumed Brae had lit a lantern.

"Keep watch, I'm gona check on the others."

"You do that... Bitch." Edwards said with a smirk on her face, giving Jess a taste of her own medicine. Jessica bit back rising anger and climbed the rickety stair following the glowing light in the upper rooms. Brae was fast asleep slumped against the wall near a window as Yolanda used the night-scope on her rifle to scan the tree line through the shattered window.

"Everything okay up here Yo?" Jess asked.

"Tickety-boo." Yolanda whispered as she continued to scan the tree line. Jessica approached and sat down next to Yolanda, she pulled out a full bottle of corn whiskey, uncorked it and offered it to her friend.

"I'm on watch Jess!" She said with a bite in her tone. But she grabbed the bottle and took a swig.

"Thanks Jess, things are so damned serious, we just don't have time to chill out anymore. I can't wait until Brae and me settle down and we can put all this bullshit behind us." She slumped down next to Jess and took another swig.

"You're probably going to hear through the grape vine. So I will tell you now. I've decided to run with the rangers again… After, we finish this contract with Joshua."

"Good for you Jess." Yolanda had happiness and hurt in her voice.

"Ash convinced me, I can't carry on the way I've been running my life. I will just end up dead in a gutter in front of a saloon or a whore house. I might as well do some good again. Give something back to the Ashland. Which, I have reaped for so long." Jessica said with a half-hearted laugh.

"That's if we get out of this shit!" Yolanda chuckled swigging another gulp of whiskey.

"I hear you sister." Jess laughed and nodded at the bleakness of the situation. Two owl calls came from downstairs, Jess raced down the stairs gun out peering into the darkness. Edwards was at the foot of the stair, her glowing yellow eyes wide and her arm outstretched pointing to a back room. Not pointing at the front of the house where the attack could be imminent.

"Seen something?" Jess whispered. Edwards shook her head and pointed to the back room again.

"I can hear things below the house!" The statement seemed wrong and confusing. Ash and Angel had woken up and were peering through the windows.

Ash left Edwards on watch and lit a lantern before entered the spacious backroom, which had been decked out to be a pre-war kitchen. The group began a more detailed search of the other rooms, until finally Angel found a trap door which had been covered with a moth eaten rug. The room had once been a storage space, shelves of bottles, jar's, etc lined the walls and the hidden trap door smack bang in the middle of the room.

"What do you think?" Angel said eyeing the empty produce jars.

"I recon we have a bomb shelter below us, I've seen them before in out of the way houses probably belonging to rich paranoid folks." Jessica said staring at the heavy set iron trap door. The door didn't seem locked but it had a hinged bolt on this side.

"Naaa, if it was a bomb shelter the bolt would be on the other side." Ash huffed.

"Then the bolt was added after the war..." Jess finally said. Ash held the lantern over the trap door and made a hand signal to Angel to open it, while Jessica aimed at the floor door. Angel crouched and cautiously unbolted the door. Ash showed a count down on his fingers. When his index finger touched his little-pinky, Angel threw open the door. When Ash put the lantern over the hole, they could see a metal rung ladder heading down into the darkness. They all leapt back away from the trap door when they thought they saw something passing under the ladder.

"Shit!" Jessica yelped, peering around wide eyed to the others.

"Yep, I saw that too, there is definitely something down there moving around!" Ash whispered. Angel handed her carbine to Jessica and drew her side arm.

"Last thing we need is something attacking us from behind while we defend from the front, we need to clear it out!" She barked not caring what was listening below.

"No! You need to stay, I'm going down there and whatever it is, I'm gona kill it!" Jessica said throwing the carbine back to Angel. Ash agreed.

"Jess is right, I need you up here defending the house, you are best at range and Jess is better close quarters with her pistols." He remembered Jessica was also the best tunnel rat in his squad back in the day. Jessica switched on her flash light and hooked it on to her shoulder plate using a Velcro strap, securing it tight. She grinned and tested her weight on the rung ladder before descending.

The rung ladder was cold and damp on her fingers as she made her way down the ladder. Rusted steel ducting made up the wall surrounds and below she could see her flashlight reflecting off the surface of murky looking water. On the last rung before the water she tested how deep the water was, it seemed to be about two foot deep. The metal clad corridor went east and west, she scanned both of the ways but headed east, following where the shadow had gone. The ground felt un-even under her boots as though rubble had fallen. She scanned down using her flashlight but she couldn't see past the surface of the dark water. She pulled out her eagle and a combat knife in her off hand, just like she had done in the past, when she had been ordered to clear out an underground section. Her boot snagged on something that nearly took her balance. She reached down through the filthy water with her knife hand and lifted up a human rib cage.

"By the bright!" She cursed.

"Jess, you okay, what you found?" She could hear Ash's voice echoing down the tunnel head.

"I'm fine shut up, let me focus!" She responded tilting the knife allowing the bones to fall. *Those savage fucks have been feeding rotters!* She thought with bile clawing its way up her throat. She suspected that's why the savage bandits hadn't attacked! She assumed this was some kind of ancestral place? She bolstered herself and gritted her teeth, moving on toward an open metallic clad room. The room appeared to have once been a living quarters, half submerged padded seating flanked the room and a rusted mushroom ridden wooden dining table had pride of place. The water exploded in front of her, she managed to get two good shots off with the powerful pistol, she was sure it would drop the creature but it bowled her over. The cold water rushed around her shocking her body, she scrambled under the weight of the abomination and felt its sharp claws digging through her armour. She held her breath under the dark water and lashed out with her knife frantically into the flank of the creature. She panicked as the mass of the creature went limp, a dead weight upon her. She kicked and gargled as she tried to scramble from under the deathly embrace. She managed to lever her leg and push the creature's body to her flank, alleviating the drowning peril. Her mouth broke the surface of the water and she took a deep breath of foul air, giving her enough strength to kick the body away. She stood and screamed at the top of her voice. Her heart pounded in her chest and her veins were full of adrenalin as the murky water cascaded from her armour.

"Fuuuuuccccckkk!" She screamed again, attempting to purge her body. She heard splashing sounds behind her, she spun around and levelled her pistol to the door way. More splashing footsteps came as fear started to rise again in her bones. Angel came to view, her face stern and her eyes wide taking in the room.

"You okay Jess?" She panted, still scanning the room for threat.

"Yes, but it was close. Thought I had been bagged there. Fucking abomination!" She cursed as she lifted the heavy creatures head out of the water into view.

"Us solo's call them 'Rakes'." Angel said appraising the kill. "They usually dwell in the sewers of ruined cities. I suspect they were once human riding out the bomb underground, but over time radiation and inbreeding turned them into abominations."

"Too be honest, I've never had the pleasure before!" Jess laughed and almost wept at the same time. She used the rotting old table as support and rested her head for a while.

"Fucker nearly had me." Jess mumbled through panic ridden laughter, trying to expel the drowning memory from her psyche.

"Don't worry! In an out way place like this. It has probably eaten the others to remain strong." Angel said as she started to search the room for things she could use.

"I think the savages have been feeding this fucker for a long time, the floor to this place is riddled with bones of the dead." Jess said as she holstered her knife and pistol.

"I think you were right, this place used to be a bomb shelter of some kind!"

"Let's get out of here!" Jessica pleaded. She made her way back to the rung ladder as Angel made a final search of the bunker.

"Lot of bones down there, too many which makes me think the savages were feeding the Rake." Angel stated as she emptied out her back pack in the living space above. An abundance of pre-war tins of various soup, beans and sausage, tinned tomatoes, tinned fruit and tinned meat, spilled out on the floor. Everybody knew pre-war food, even after all the years still tasted pretty damned good.

"We have enough food to wait them out!" Ash said appraising the cache of tinned food.

"There is more down there. I just couldn't fit them all the tins in my back pack." Angel conceded.

"I wondered what happened to the folks who owned house? You might have thought they would have eaten the last tin?" Angel pondered.

"Maybe, the leader of the household thought they were better off in the Ashland?" Jessica concluded.

"Maybe?" Angel said peering at a tin of peaches. She reached out and picked up a tin of syrup fruit. "I need to taste this bastard!" She hummed a tune as she pulled out an old tin opener. Ash recognised the tune, it was an old ranger song. He smiled and grabbed up a can of preserved fruit and eagerly waited to borrow Angels can opener.

The sun started to rise, Edwards made a small field trip to check on the encampment of savage bandits. She had been gone for a very long time and Ash worried about the safety of his friend. As the group had a breakfast of perishables, Edwards pushed through the tree line followed by a nervous looking savage woman. She was tall, her hair were golden set in dread locks, she was in her mid-thirties and dressed in treated animal hides. Most of her body was covered in tribal tattoos, set in geometric lines and shapes.

"Guns down!" Edwards stated. "She is here to talk and talk only!" Ash looked to the others and nodded.

"This is my bag, I will sort this!" He said before walking out to meet the savage looking woman. Yolanda had the savages head in her cross hairs of her scope, she was eagerly awaiting the order to fire.

"Speak!" Ash said abruptly.

"She speaks our tongue, but you must speak words very slow, otherwise she will not understand you." Edwards warned.

"We no longer wish to raid you! We will give you safe passage from here as long as you leave this sacred place!" The savage woman outlined. Ash held his hands up in salute and nodded. Over his career as a ranger he had placated tribes, bandits, merchants and scum. With only a few words, but bullets usually worked best.

"Move your camp to the west and you will give us safe passage to the east. These are our terms!" He said sternly, staring with his fearless blue eyes into hers. The tribal woman bowed, Ash took the opportunity to bow also.

"We have heard the wisdom of your leader..." She made another bow in respect. Ash follows suit and bowed deeper. "We will move camp but you go quickly!"

Ash knew she was in plight of the savage's council and knew this must be adhered or conflict would follow.

"We will move out now while the sun shows our

path!" Ash said trying to adhere to their fucked up religion. As the savage woman wandered away, Ash tried his best to get on top of the situation.

"We move now, gather up all equipment and let's get the fuck out of here!" Ash cried as he rushed back to the stronghold of the house. When he got to the house the group had heard his words and started to pack up.

"Finally! We go to the secret army depot!" Joshua said with a grin on his face. They all met up outside the house where they thought they would be killed and probably scalped.

The group quickly descended the hill passing the small enemy camp fire smouldering low. The smell of charcoal and cooked meat still fresh in the air, disturbingly they noticed an abundance of rat bones and small wooden spits.

"The dirty bastards!" Joshua said covering his mouth, his face paling. Natasha looked in the same way.

"Such savages dining on rats, its making me feel sick!" Natasha said puffing out her cheeks. The others however had all suffered lack of food out in the ashland at one time or another and resorted to eating undesirable foods. Jessica caught up with Angel and fell into her stride.

"I'm curious, what's the worst thing you had to eat?" She asked with a grin on her face. Angel shot her a glare and sniggered.

"The worst thing has to have been..."

"Quiet back there and keep up!" Ash interrupted.

The women stifled grins and their cheeks turned rosy, it was like being scolded by an angry parent. Angel winked and mouthed the words, 'tell you later on'. They had got back down to a beaten trail, probably frequented by the primitives. Ash wasn't stupid, he asked Brae to watch the rear, just in case the savages were tracking them again. So far though it seemed the bandits had stood by their words. By noon they had come to the foot of a rocky bottom stream, where they filled up their canteens and filled their bellies with water.

"We need to head south east from here, but that means going over and through that woodland." Brae pointed out the large woodland sloping up the land. He started to pack his compass and map away while the others checked their gear and secured their canteens. Angel returned from a small scouting mission, she had doubled back half a klick to see if they were being followed.

"They aren't following us." She answered Ash's question before he even asked.

"Look we have to be careful though, that was just one group of savages, by what I've heard they have quite a strong hold in these parts and their numbers are in the hundreds." Ash warned. Angel started to laugh, Ash frowned at her.

"Got something to say solo?"

"What you have heard and what is real are two entirely different things. Believe me, the savages do not number in their hundreds, for the simple fact; we haven't passed any farm lands, natural food etc." Angel chuckled some more "I recon the group we encountered were a third of their numbers and they clearly rely of hunting rather than raiding."

"Your probably right Angel, we looked like an easy target, they are probably nothing more than opportunists, rather than blood thirsty bandits." Ash agreed seeing logic in her words.

"If they were bandits, they would have never allowed us to pass!" Angel said finally. Brae was stood on a rock scanning the terrain up to the woodland.

"The road to the army base must be on the other side of that woodland. I can't see any dips in the land that nature might have claimed back." He said distantly as though he was talking to himself and not the group.

"Yeah that figures." Jessica said pulling a silly face to Yolanda which made her laugh.

"Brae, you take point, Angel take up the rear. Let's make good of the light we have before sun down." Ash said as he threw his back pack on.

The woodland trees were old, a mixture of ash, birch and pine. Animal and human trails were sparse and it was hard to navigate through the thick wood. The hot sun made travel a humid hell, as they picked their way through the woodland. They encountered small streams and springs bursting out of the undergrowth and had to avoid the occasional patches of large insect infested areas. Now and then the party had a brief spectacle of large yellow hide deer roaming around the forest. Some of the bucks were seven feet tall and stood their ground long enough for the does and fawns to escape before they fled off.

"By the bright? Those are big animals." Joshua noted. He grimaced at the thought if one of those big bastards turned nasty and attacked.

"Don't get too close, because they will attack if threatened." Brae warned over his shoulder. The rangers all knew how dangerous these beasts could be, the pre-war text books claimed quite the opposite.

"Wait!" Brae said he raised up his hand, palm vertical. Everybody halted in their tracks. Jessica made her way to the front of the group cautiously and spotted what Brae had seen. The woodland ahead had some kind of blight in the form of almost luminous orange/yellow mould clinging to the trees and ground level ferns.

"We might need to navigate around this area!" Brae said as he rummaged around for his giga-counter. He turned the device on and was shocked that it was reading a steady back ground radiation.

"What you think Jess?"

"I think you are right, let's not disturb that mouldy stuff." Jess said pulling a face of disgust. Brae suddenly crouched to his knees and everybody did the same.

"You see that?" He whispered. They all took a deep breath and scanned the strange looking area.

"See what..." But as soon as Jessica said the words she noticed one of the tall yellow/orange fuzzy trees seemed to move and not in a natural windblown way, it shifted? Firearms raised they watched in horror as the tree shifted again, it was jittery in its movement, but a rooted tree couldn't possibly move that distance.

"What in the fuck is..." Joshua cried, his face pale with terror. The seventeen foot tall tree began to stride out toward them, thrashing out with its mouldy tree limbs, smashing off nearby tree branches and crushing ferns in its wake. Gun fire erupted around Joshua as the tree creature creaked and swayed bringing a sickly, earthen mushroom like smell. Jessica ducked under one of its sweeping extremities but it hit Brae squarely in his chest, cascading him down the hill cursing. By now everybody had put enough lead to down the sinister creature, but it marched on smashing Ash to the ground. Joshua ran forward up the hill and aimed at one of the limbs of the tree, blasting it off with both barrels of his shotgun. A milky white liquid jetted from the broken limb showering unfortunates below with slimy tree sap.

"Aim for its legs!" Jessica cried as she opened fire, concentrating her pistols on one of its thrashing root like legs. Everybody followed suit and aimed at the roots, firing and smashing the root system. The creature started to topple over in the path of Ash who was trying to get his breath back. Edwards raced quickly to Ash and pulled him away from the tree fall and accidentally dislocating his shoulder. The tree smashed against the ground and started to roll down hill, while its still tried to thrash out with its long limbs..

Natasha, Yolanda and Angel were in the firing line. They looked in horror as it came quickly toward them. As luck would happen, the tree hit a small bank in the landscape, which ejected the creature into the air. They cowered up in foetus positions as the main body of the tree missed them by inches. The tree creature carried on rolling down the hill.

"Brae!" Yolanda yelled, she scanned the woodland below her and tried to pin point where Brae had fallen. The tree creature shattered lots of trees going down the hill and then finally came to a stop in a natural bowl in the land.

"Brae!" She yelled again, tears filling her eyes as she dropped her rifle and raced down the hill to find her lover. Ferns, bushes and small trees had been annihilated under the force of the falling tree. Yolanda wiped the tears from her eyes using the cuff of her sleeve, she picked her way down the hill weeping and repeating her lovers name.

"I'm here." Brae said coughing and spluttering through laboured breath.

"Where?" She howled, scanning the forest floor.

"Up here!" He gurgled and tried his best to smile. She looked up and saw Brae wedged in the bough of a tree, limp and bleeding but had a smile on his face.

"I think I've busted a couple of ribs, but I'm okay." He wheezed.

"Can you walk?" Ash asked appraising the bandages around Brae's chest. It had taken a long time to get him out of the tree without him bleeding out from splintered chest bones.

"I will be okay, just can't wear armour for a while." He grinned biting back pain.

"You had us all worried there you son-of-a-bitch!" Jessica said nervously chuckling, as Joshua continued to bind and wrap his chest with fresh bandages.

"He will be okay, as long as he doesn't do anything strenuous, or stupid!" Joshua said as he placed a number of medical safety pins to secure the bandages.

"Really, I'm okay, I've had worse over my career, come on lets head up there while we still have light." Brae said bravely. Ash looked him up and down and heard the guy labouring for breath.

"Are you sure?"

"I will be fine but I'm sure Natasha and Joshua will help me up the hill." He smirked and then reeled in pain for a few seconds. With aid from the folks around him the travellers moved on. Brae was the kind of guy that didn't want to be a burden, but in the state he welcomed help from the others. They navigated around the infected area and reached a clearing at the top of the woodland hill where they all decided to rest for the night. Natasha, Joshua and Jessica gathered up fire wood to camp, while the others stayed on guard. It was a long night, but Joshua slipped Brae some pain killers in oral form. The pills came from a bottle called Ibuprofen, in which he had a double dose of. Brae fell asleep and had some horrible nightmares due to the exceeded dose of pain killers.

The travellers headed across the plateau and stopped when Jessica pointed her finger southwards from the vantage point.

"Its there!" She claimed. Angel, Ash and Yolanda came to her flanks and borrowed her binoculars.

"I see it! That is definitely a military base. I can see the pill boxes on the broken road heading upto the installation." Ash smiled as he handed the binoculars back to Jess.

"Let's hope it's kitted out with a medical facility, Brae needs medical attention." Yolanda said hoping.

"Pretty sure it will be. We can't always have bad luck." Ash said grumbling.

"We need to move down there quick!" Yolanda stated as she looked over her shoulder to Brae who was being pampered by the others.

"Yes we do!" Ash added. They broke camp and made their way down towards the installation which looked to be a compound of low concrete bunker like buildings. Even from the vantage point Ash could see it could be well defended, a series of out buildings heading toward a primary building which he calculated to be an underground bunker of some kind. The woodland had thinned on this side, the terrain turned from woodland to a sharp rocky landscape, sparse with poverty grasses. When they made the final distance Ash called the group to a halt.

"We don't know this place and if it's a Pre-war installation then it could have robotic defences. I hope to the bright that is not the case!" Ash worried.

"Everybody be on your guard!"

The group arrived at the compound wire criss-cross fence. A faded sign stated 'FORT ANUBIS, U.S ARMY PROPERTY, TRESSPASSERS WILL BE SHOT' Angel pulled out some bolt cutters and made a hole, large enough for them to pass with a wounded comrade. They performed a quick inventory and it seemed they had plenty of food and water, fortified by the tin food they had found at the old house.

"If pre-war defences go hot, then we need to all pull together and take them out." Jessica looked to Brae who raised up his rifle. Jessica doubled back and grabbed the rifle.

"I'm just borrowing it my friend!" She said as she inspected the barrel and bullet port of the assault rifle.

"I will take care of this buddy." Jessica assured him. Ash and Joshua were both eager to get to the fortification.

"Come on we go now!" Joshua cried as he took up the lead. Natasha followed suit as though she would follow Joshua into the gates of hell. As a group they headed into the compound of the Pre-war army installation. And all seemed quiet. They moved in and out of cover toward the main building. The doors to which seemed locked.

"What now?" Joshua yelled with balled fists at the locked bulk head doors.

"Wait, let me think..." Ash said as he brushed sand off the door terminal control. He stood for a while racking his brain for the code to get inside. In between his thoughts he tried a number of combinations on the terminal, which still had power?

"Wait..." He rummaged through his rucksack for his little black book and started to study every flick of the page, but he couldn't find any reference to Fort Anubis?

"Wait, I think I know the code!" Joshua stated. "Let me try!" He had read the journals of the utopian man. Joshua pushed his way to the front and typed in 'XD206' into the terminal. The code seemed to work and the double steel door started to clink and turn mechanically...

CHAPTER 15

The double steel blast door started to jolt open, the lubrication of the military door struggled but eventually the door opened. Flickering light inside the installation began to come on line. Everybody looked to one and another and smiled as the ancient code worked.

"Let it be said, if it wasn't for Joshua we would never have found the code to enter. When I looked though my little black book of pre-war codes..." Ash sighed. "I don't think I had the code to get in to this instillation. Hail to the scholar!"

"I'm no hero! I just read and gathered up information." Joshua said as he swam in the praise and words of a ranger commander.

"Right! Everybody on me, we do this ranger style and check every corner!" Ash said as he un-holstered his desert eagle and went in first. At first the installation illumination seemed dim, but as seconds passed the bulk heads above gathered momentum and illuminated the way inside.

"The depot still has power?" Jessica said peering around the foyer.

"It's either nuclear, or geo-thermal power, that has kept this installation alive?" Ash wondered, not knowing the truth.

"Nuclear?" Brae said while spluttering and coughing due to his busted up ribs. He turned on his giga-counter and watched the needle fluctuate.

"It's not radioactive, so the power source must be geo-thermal." He said trying to read the giga-counter through one eye focus due to the pain in his chest.

"It still could be nuclear, it's just not compromised the installation." Ash said wisely.

"Maybe?" Brae agreed through a fit of coughing up pinkish lung blood, into a paisley cloth. Ash looked at Brae and shook his head.

"Yolanda, stay with Brae, Edwards, Angel and Natasha. Me, Jessica and Joshua will move on?"

"We stay, but don't be long inside, find some medicals and come back soon!" Yolanda worried, as she tried to comfort Brae who looked to be in a very bad state even though he tried to say he was okay.

"We need to find some medicals for Brae!" Jessica said as she looked toward her companion in dire straits.

"Secure this area and we move on!" Ash ordered. The flickering light in the corridors leading out from the main chamber started to maintain a steady light. The commando group moved on down one of the corridors labelled 'Command centre'. An auto sentry gun dropped from the ceiling and tried to fire, but its ammo housing had long since been depleted. The robotic gun clicked mechanically for a few seconds before standing down. The metallic corridor, they entered had numerous skeletons scattered on the floor, rusted firearms still in the grip of skeletal hands.

"Quite a fire fight happened here, I guess that utopian feller lost a lot of his minions here!" Ash said bitterly. Joshua was beside himself in rage.

"The utopian was trying to locate his father. You can't blame him for the carnage that happened here, robots have no soul!" Joshua announced angrily.

"That maybe so, but he lead them into a pre-war death trap!" Ash countered.

"The dead are dead! Its pointless trying to justify how they died!" Jessica grumbled, not really giving a shit. The team moved on down the rusty metallic corridors encountering a number of depleted robotic security guns and more skeletons. They finally reached the command centre which was an open planned area obscured by numerous banks of off-line computer terminals and screens.

"I guess this was the room where the U.S army watched the final countdown to Armageddon." Ash said, as he tapped a few buttons on a nearby terminal.

"Front seats to the nuclear war, I bet they were pissed off!" Joshua huffed. He had long since thought the devastation of mankind was the fury of his god, but not no more. Mankind was its own enemy!

"There!" Joshua pointed to a side room. "The father of the utopian was the leader of some kind!" The rusty steel door was at a jar and they could just make out that one of the terminals had power. Joshua raced to the room eager to find out more, he stopped at the door and rummaged through his back pack and found a small device which he called a pen drive. The others looked at each other and shrugged, wondering why the priest was so excited? Joshua sat himself in front of the terminal which was thick with dust. He spent a moment brushing the dust off a qwerty type keyboard.

"So close, so fucking close!" He said with excitement. He pushed the hand held device into one of the ports on the terminal.

"The pen drive belonged to his son, I'm sure this will reveal the location of utopia!" The terminal started to chug and growl excepting the pen drive. The green screen monitor started to cascade with unknown codes and writing and finally settled down and stated audibly in a robotic female voice.

"Welcome agent Sundance. What can I do for you today?" The terminal stated. Joshua grinned like a child opening a festival present. He typed in a number of codes referred from his notebook.

"Certainly Agent Sundance!" The terminal stated and offered up a number of files on the green screen monitor.

"I need to find out where utopia is?" Joshua said, not knowing how to access the files on offer. The terminal clicked and whined for a number of seconds before its circuits settled down.

"Voice recognition activated. Utopia..." The terminal spoke. "I have a file designated Utopia. Please feel free to browse." A map of the united states of America up loaded on the green screen showing the borders of each pre-war state. An 'X' mark appeared on the map.

"Project Utopia... Classified... Accessing... A garden of Eden, constructed as a failsafe... A place where humanity lives on!" More chugging and weird clicking sounds came from the terminal.

"Network error..." Joshua looked to the others, disappointment on his face.

"Re-routing... Accessing... Utopia is operational... Eighty five percent solar power... Last update... Twenty fifty three... Director Kenly... Accessing files... Last message." The terminal downloaded the last message, it wasn't an audio file.

'The crops are growing strong. Everybody here seems to be in good shape. Radiation is a little over background which is due to the all-out nuclear war. Food and water is optimal. We have also grown opium plants to combat pain through child birth and medical functions. Everybody seems happy, but a few wish to leave the habitat. I have set up a S.O.P for folks wishing to leave the habitat, I can't blame them. Humanity has a natural curiosity to explore, that's what makes us human. Director Kenly signing off.' They all took turns reading the last message.

"Joshua, the last message was years ago, something happened during this time?" Jessica pointed out.

"Nonsense, the network is down all over the ways of America. The folks are still surviving in Utopia!" Joshua claimed un-doubtfully.

"We must go and become accepted in this utopia. I plan to have children with Natasha. And, what better place? A utopia where there is no conflict, a place where food, water and power is in abundance!" Joshua pleaded.

"That's your dream Josh! It's not ours!" Jessica huffed and wandered away. Joshua down loaded the files and location to the pen drive. He pulled out the hand held device and tossed it around in his hands. Ash shook his head.

"Are you sure you wish to pursue this?" Ash said shrugging. Joshua had a face of steel.

"Damned right I will pursue this!" His face stern, unrelenting to the truth and fortified by religious doctrine. Ash caught up with Jessica and continued to sweep the installation, leaving Joshua to his madness.

The installation was huge, numerous corridors, stairs that went down to other levels, large lifts for transporting equipment and supplies around the base. They had to bypass many locked off areas, not knowing passwords or failing a retinal scan. They found armouries, they discovered an enormous amount of preserved tinned foods, still good to eat. They discovered the installation had its own spring and had filtered water, best tasting water they had ever tasted. They came to a large horseshoe shaped room with a bank of windows. They tried to peer through the windows but the seemingly huge room beyond had no illumination.

"There's a breaker box there." Ash pointed to the wall nearby Jess.

"A breaker what now?" She looked to a large grey metal box on the wall.

"The red handle on the side Jess pull it down." He gestured with his arm. Jessica did as she was told and pulled the metal lever down. A series of loud bangs, clicks and other strange sounds flowed.

"What the fuck have you just done Ash!" Jess said wide eyed listening to the scary noises as she backed away from the breaker box. Lights started to flicker on in the room beyond, which was vast. Ash peered through the window and estimated the room was fifty foot deep from the room he stood in and another fifty foot high. Jessica came to his side and watched as numerous upstanding missiles came into view. The missiles stood over seventy feet and they were in two huddled groups to the east and west, each group comprising of six missiles. A rail track ran down the centre of the huge room to a cylindrical section about three hundred feet north of the windowed room.

"It's a fucking ballistic missile silo!" Ash's mouth fell open. "But surely they would have used these during the war?" It bothered him and he wondered if this station had been abandoned in the run up to the nuclear war. It would figure due to the enormous amount of food supplies they found. In their wonder and bravado they hadn't heard the robot wandering into the room behind them.

"Do not be alarmed!" The robot stated in a male robotic voice. Jessica had already combat rolled to the flank and had both of her pistols out aiming at the strange robot who had its arms up in surrender. Ash not very quick on the draw had his pistol up as well aiming at the robot which looked like a plastic/metal human with lenses as eyes wearing a stained and faded lab coat.

"I mean you no harm, I am Doctor Kienz, please do not shoot." It said. "I'm unarmed and have been programmed to aid and save humans, not maim or murder."

"Where did you come from, we searched every niche and cranny!" Ash asked as he held up his hand to keep Jessica from totalling the fucker.

"I have come from the laboratory section which was locked off to humans such as you." It answered.

"Stand down Jess, I think it's telling the truth." Ash whispered, trying to calm Jessica's instinct to shoot.

"Fuck that! Keep talking robot!" Jess narrowed her eyes and cocked both triggers.

"I'm the head surgeon and doctor at the Anubis installation, I provided medical assistance and surgery when required for the people of 'Vengeance twelve.' The code name of this pre-war installation."

"Go on!" Jessica prompted, still aiming at the robots head.

"Years ago, Agent Sundance made a managerial decision to stand down as mankind tore itself to pieces using nuclear missiles. In the aftermath he was branded a hero, he saved incalculable enemy lives by not sending these missiles to the targets in Europe." The robot allowed the humans to ponder its words. Ash and

Jessica frowned at each other and then continued to aim firearms at the robot.

"Agent Sundance and the people of this facility waited for several years locked away from the fallout and nuclear winter. When the sun came back, they performed an exodus to Utopia. Agent Sundance oversaw the exodus." The robot continued to keep its arms raised.

"Why didn't he send the missiles?" Ash asked, he didn't understand the logic by not annihilating the enemy.

"At the time America had twenty five percent more nuclear warheads than the enemy not counting the long ranged bombers which were already in the air heading to targets. He figured the enemy was all but wiped out already. But the off chance of saving human lives, even enemy lives meant something to him. Small pockets of Europe still had a chance of surviving however bleak the percentage was." Jessica and Ash lowered their guns as the robot continued. "Agent Sundance gambled there could be other likeminded leaders out there in the world, that also could have stood down. He wanted to give humanity another chance of survival.

"So these nukes were destined for Europe?" Ash asked.

"Yes, if you turn on the main terminal it will display the targets for each missile standing in the silo." It nodded robotically. "The targets were all pre-programmed all Agent Sundance needed to do was activate the program and they would have set off one by one and death would follow." The robot paused. "Please if you allow me to show you?" It waited patiently.

"Please do." Ash said as he backed away from the robot wandering to the main console. Jessica eyed the creature, it looked man like with rubbery sections between articulated plastic. It moved un-human like, quick and jolty but precise in its operations. She kept her guns handy and her legs ready to spring into action. The robot deftly tapped in some codes as a large screen above the windows came on line showing a digital map of the world. Numerous dotted lines traced the missiles and there destinations in Europe. A side screen listed names of cities which Ash and Jessica had never heard of before, odd sounding names like Budapest, Hamburg, Bordeaux, etc… Twelve destinations! Which would have been reduced to ashes.

"He was a god-damned traitor!" Ash huffed, not knowing what was going through Sundance's mind. Jessica kind of understood, but was still fighting at the idea of saving enemy lives over American lives.

"Not a traitor sir. Agent Sundance was a humanist, he claimed he couldn't live with the loss of so many lives, women, children, elderly people… Humans… Men!" The robot said with no emotion in its tone.

"Maybe…" Ash said, his mind racing. "I suppose it would have been a big decision, do they live or do they die?"

"Exactly! Sir. During the run upto the atomic

exchange, a lot of innocent countries got caught up due to America, China and Russia placing military equipment, troops, missile silos, bomber aircraft in allied zones. It was the biggest melting pot of war since world war two." The robot stated.

"What year is it?" Jessica asked out of the blue. The robot looked toward her and moved away from the console.

"My internal clock says its 2098. But I'm unsure, my circuits could be corrupted. I have been on-line for a very long time. Sometimes after I power up I have noticed some lag of time passed so that figure could be wrong. I would surmise it's minus five or plus five years to the figure I stated?" The robot said with a blank face. "I wasn't manufactured to last this long."

"By the bright 2098, that's nowhere near the Ranger calendar!" Jessica frowned at Ash, who looked away, red cheeks blooming.

"You're a doctor right? Then come with us, our companion requires your aid!" Jessica said sternly.

It took a while of explaining to the travellers why they had a robot claiming to be a doctor, but eventually after a serious argument Brae allowed the robot to appraise his wounds.

"Numerous rib bones have been compromised, your right lung is punctured that is why you are struggling to breath. Let's take you to the medical wing, I will have you back on your feet in no time soldier." The robot said in a strange male cheery tone. Brae agreed and Yolanda aided him towards the medical wing of the installation. With that out of the way Ash called a meeting.

"My fellow rangers." He said referring to Edwards, Angel and Jessica. He paced up and down for a while picking his words.

"This installation has enough food for hundreds of people to survive here for many years. I haven't done an inventory but I think I'm correct." He looked to Jessica.

"Lots of food, lots of water here." Jessica agreed.

"We also have found a weapon we can use against this soviet menace. But this is not a clear cut situation. We need to find out how to operate the missiles we have found and where to target them."

"Missiles!" Edwards said wide eyed.

"Yeah, one of the missiles should wipe the soviets out, if we could locate the soviet strong hold." Ash answered with one eye brow raised and growing smirk.

"We have missiles?" Angel said trying to stave off laughter, the promise of a quick death to the enemy was like winning at Texas hold'em.

"We have a lot of preparation to do, but first of all, we need to shift the rangers here along with all the farmsteader's and survivors to this base. We need them to bring seed and anything useful they can muster." He looked to the robot.

"Has this installation got a radio set so we can contact our friends?"

"Of course, this installation has radio, satellite

uplink and many other forms of communication." The robot seemed to shrug which the humans found disturbing.

"Then let's manage this situation to the full. Phase one! We shift all operations from the corn farm to this base of operations!" Ash pulled at his over grown salt and pepper beard as his mind calculated Phase one.

"Angel please accompany Dr Kienz to the communication room and start the ball rolling."

"Yes sir!" Angel said as she hooked her arm around the robot and pushed it toward the communications, even though she had no idea where it was in the installation. Joshua arrived to the meeting. His eyes were wide in the wonder of finding Utiopia. He ignored the discussion between the rangers and grabbed Natasha's hand and pretty much dragged her away to the war room section of the base.

The robot accessed a ranger frequency and allowed Angel to communicate to the corn farm. Once the radio frequency had been acquired and Angel was relaying orders to the ranger stronghold, the robot made its way to the medical wing to aid Brae. The medical unit was attached to the laboratory section of the installation. It found Yolanda putting on a brave face at the side of a clean bed where Brae was fighting to stay conscious.

"I will take it from here, but if you will be willing could you stay and comfort the patient as I perform my duties."

"The doctor is here my lover, he will make you better." Yolanda stifled tears and tried to stop her hands from shaking.

"I will need to sedate the patient, but require you to stay and help. I used to have human aids when performing surgery." The robot stated. Yolanda nodded and held fast to Brae's clammy hand. His eyes were rolling to the back of his head and perspiration dripped from his chin. The robot set up a saline drip and attached it to his left arm. The robot then pushed a tube carefully down his throat and gestured to Yolanda to pump the artificial lung.

"I will sedate you now my friend." The robot said monotonously as it injected a potent looking syringe into the drip housing. Within seconds Brae started to mumble things as though he had drank two bottles of whiskey. Seconds later the patient was out.

"Keep squeezing the bag, count two seconds then squeeze and do this throughout the operation." The robot stated gesturing to the artificial lung. The robot took out a sharp looking scalpel and set to work...

Ranger Sanding's got the message over the communication. He raced through the farmstead organising everybody to travel. At first he got a lot of rejection from the farm hands. They had no wish to leave the farm which they had strived to cultivate all those years. But after a lot of warnings about other farm-stead's falling to the soviets, they got on board. He waited near the old trade house as everybody gathered up, back packs and carts full of seed, food, water and equipment to farm.

"We leave this place not out of love but out of survival. The soviets are coming and they will kill all of us!" As the farm stead folk and rangers gathered up. Ranger Sanding's shed a single tear.

"We go with the promise of fertile lands, a safe haven with enough preserved food to last us many years, enough for us all to start again cultivating herd animals, crops and fresh water!" He heard a lot of dismay and emotion from the gathered folk.

"We travel to be safe, nobody wishes to fall to the enemy, like Applewood farm, we have time to make this right!" He yelled, trying to bolster the folk. He watched as elderly folk climbed on top of hand carts, accompanied by food stuffs, seeds, farm equipment and vats of water.

"We are not finished here, once the enemy has been purged from this land, we will return to pick up the pieces!" He said finally, before giving the heads up to move out, with an armed force of mean looking rangers vowed to protect the exodus.

"By the bright protect us!" He mumbled, before taking up a ranger jog to the front of the column.

A few days later, Brae was back on his feet, bandaged around his chest but his breathing was no longer laboured.

"How you feeling Brae?" Jessica asked as she offered a bottle of preserved brandy. He took the bottle and chugged a good gulp, which made him cough and splutter for a few seconds.

"I feel okay, the robot gave me some kind of injection that makes me feel like a raging bull!" He laughed and coughed a few more times but this time he wasn't dribbling pink blood from the sides of his mouth.

"Good to hear Brae, I'm gona miss you." She reached in and hugged him, not a tight hug just in case she busted his ribs again.

"You're staying with the rangers then?"

"Yeah, Ash has promised coin, but the coin is just a bonus, the bonus is aiding the rangers again..." She looked into Brae's eyes and chuckled. He started to laugh too.

"Yeah I'm gona miss you too Jess. Joshua has already set up a contract with Yolanda and myself. Gona get better then head out to this Utopia place. The money is good Jess, surprised you're not picking up the contract?" He said grinning with hope.

"Nope, gota do good this time, it seems Ash and I have a mission, to save the Ashland..." She took a swig of rot gut brandy and smiled. "Gona die protecting the folks this time, I can't die in some fucked up whore house, don't want to check out like that!" Jessica said with a frown on her pretty face.

"When all this shit, is out of the way. Let's all meet up in Red Town and have a drink!" Brae winked.

"Definitely my friend." Jess said with an ear to ear smile. Jessica spotted Yolanda entering the room. She eyed Jessica up and down before coming to Brae's side.

"How you feeling honey?" She put her arms around him and gave Jessica a frowning look. A jealous look as though she would kill!

"After that last shot that fucking robot gave me, I'm ready to take on a horde of bandits!" He said hugging Yolanda in a loving embrace while winking at Jessica.

"I will leave you lovers in peace." Jess said as the couple kissed. Jessica wandered away with a smile knowing when Brae shagged Yolanda that night he would be thinking of pretty Jessica, very likely eyes closed and mental image.

Jessica found Ash in the missile command room, the robot was in mid-discussion about how the missiles worked.

"Let me say again, I don't think you have understood for the third time?" The robot said.

"What's not to understand?" Jessica said as she wandered into the room swigging a bottle of brandy which she had taken from the installation stores. The robot turned around and gestured to Jessica.

"I've been trying to explain how the missiles work, at the moment we don't have a true satellite link. The only way we could use the missiles is to take a portable laser guidance system to the target... The person which did that will have to sacrifice themselves unless they had protection. And I mean serious protection!" The robot concluded.

"That could work! What kind of protection do we

need?" Ash said willing to sacrifice his life.

"Follow me, I know of such protection!" The robot stated. Ash looked at Jessica and shrugged. The robot took the two rangers down many corridors and finally after many stairs down to the deep of the installation where the lights were dim. The robot stopped at a locked door labelled 'E.C.A STORAGE'. The robot stopped and looked to Ash and Jessica.

"I will show you!" The robot tapped some kind of key code into a terminal and waited. The double mechanical door hissed and clinked on old pre-war gears. The doors opened revealing a chamber beyond. At first the light flickered on, Ash witnessed large metallic humanoid objects beyond. Jessica had her gun out and was already cursing the robot.

"Jessica be calm, I am here to help your cause!" The robot snapped before striding into the room confidently. Ash and Jessica took an involuntary step backwards as they saw rows and rows of bulky robotic, very tall armoured units inside.

"Suits... Not robots, suits that humans can wear!" The robot attempted to console the humans.

"By the bright, I have seen pictures in pre-war magazines. These mechanical suits were outfitted by the united states army for the front lines before the war!" Ash gawped, shaking his head in amazement.

"These suits of armour are outfitted with a plutonium battery, similar to the satellites which humanity sent into orbit as power sources for satellites." The robot stated.

"They still work?" Jessica asked before Ash had time to question.

"Yes they do!" The robot said in a weird childish algorithm.

"Thank you for showing us this Dr Kienz" Ash said while grabbing Jessica's shoulder and pulling her away from the sheer spectacle of the advanced armour. Ash for some reason no longer trusted the robot...

"When Agent Sundance announced the exodus, why didn't you go with them?" Ash asked, his eyebrows high in questioning.

"I'm a robot, my network is tethered to this installation. It is a whole with my parameters. I cannot leave this place. If I did my network would fail and my internal battery would explode. It's one of my many, directives! Along with aiding and not, harming human kind." The robot stated and almost shrugged in a human like fashion.

"Did you persuade agent Sundance, using your protocols?" Jessica questioned.

"Yes, in answer to your question lady Jessica, I think I may have swayed his vote in saving human lives. I must admit, it had taken many days of persuasion. But I'm synthetic and I can be a pain in the ass. Is that correct in a manner of speaking?" The robot asked.

"Yes! I have only known you for about a day and already I want to put a bullet in your main frame." Jessica chuckled.

"I trust that you won't do that lady Jessica." The robot said as though it had emotion or life preservation in its code.

"I guess you need to show us how to operate these kick ass mechanical suits!" Ash said with a cheesy grin.

"Indeed I shall, Captain Ash of the desert rangers." The robot said in a blank tone.

It was over a week before the rangers and farm folks arrived at Vengeance twelve. The travellers where weary and a lot of them were wounded and bandaged. Ranger Sandings approached Captain Ash and saluted.

"You look like you have a lot of wounded!" Ash said peering over the shoulder of the tall ranger.

"Yes, sir we ran into those primitives you warned us about. We killed them all, a good bunch of them too."

"I'm sorry to hear that Ranger, but we have a doctor in the installation. Please don't be put off by its appearance, it is a robot but it's a very good medic."

"Robot sir?" Sandings appeared alarmed, even un-slinging his carbine.

"Yes, it is a robot, but it's on our side. It has even aided our cause by outlining how to use mechanical armour and how to use the missiles we have claimed in the installation. The soviets are soon to be history my friend!" Ash claimed with a wink.

"I hope you know what you are doing captain. But if you back this robot, then I will make sure everybody follows suit." He saluted again then rushed off to aid the hand carts.

"How did he take it?" Jessica asked as she approached Ash.

"Not sure, but I'm hoping in time the folks will adopt the idea of a robot aiding humans."

"It will take time, but I suspect once the robot proves itself, I think everybody will grow to love the synthetic pile of shit." She smiled to reassure him.

Many days passed as the rangers and the farm folk settled into the new habitat. The farmers started to plant corn, tomatoes, and other crops in the fertile land that surrounded the installation. The many streams and rivers had already been siphoned off and re-routed to the new crop fields. Everybody had settled in and the installation robot became a person. The robot had helped the wounded and aided as much as it could muster, in pain management to the wounded and pregnant farm girls. Brae was back on his feet, healthy and ready to pursue Joshua's contract. Jessica went out to meet the travelling company before they left. She hugged Brae and Yolanda and patted the heavy packs they had burdened themselves with.

"You got enough ammo and provisions?" She smiled, trying not to shed tears.

"Yeah we are ready to move out!" Brae said as he looked to Joshua who was packing a number of books into his back pack.

"Are you sure you're not coming with us Jess, we will need another gun hand?"

"My time is with the rangers old friend, you take

care now" Jessica said punching his shoulder.

"Meet back at Red town then, look us up. Me and Yolanda will have purchased a bar by then." Brae said as he kissed Jessica's cheek. Jessica noticed Yolanda was in mid conversation with Natasha, so she grabbed the back of Braes head and kissed him properly. At first Brae was shocked by her affections and struggled a tad in the embrace. But seconds later his tongue met hers as they settled into each other's embrace. Jessica waited and watched as the travelling party marched out. She laughed as she saw Joshua complaining about the amount he was carrying.

"Good luck!" She whispered before heading back inside the installation. She waved for a while but they didn't see her gesture.

CHAPTER 16

A number of days travel passed as they made their way north, following Joshua's bearing. They didn't encounter anything of note, just the standard travelling over hill and dale. They had avoided the radioactive hot spots which Brae had pointed out on the map and circumnavigated around bandit zones. Brae being an expert and a ranger in the Ashland, he would be fucked if he would lead them into strife. All the while Joshua was ever eager to step foot at utopia. The promised lands which he had read about following his notes dictated by the utopian man's son. The travelling party came to the foot of a wide river.

"We need to cross the river and we aren't doubling back to that bridge in the ruined city." Brae said with a defying tone.

"Okay, but we must cross this river!" Joshua said as he estimated the breadth of the river and peering up river he could make out a building on the other side.

"I think I can make out a hand painted sign. I'm hoping it says ferry service?" He put his binoculars away and pointed up river.

"Right, we need to be cautious, they might be good folks or the sign might be a trick to draw innocent travellers into a bandit trap." Brae warned and ducked into the long grasses near the river bank. The others followed suit and kept themselves out of sight, using the natural cover. After ten or so minutes of crouching travel, Brae called a halt. He took out his binoculars and started to scan the other bank. There was a building and a large hand written sign had been nailed to the side of the building stating 'Ferry Service $1 per head'. A large raft like vessel had been moored on the small jetty. Not very far up-river was another small jetty on this side of the river bank.

"It's a bit steep, but I suppose they wont get many customers out this far." Brae said more to Joshua who pulled a face.

"I'm not paying for everybody am I?" He looked to Natasha and she just giggled.

"Son-of-a..." Natasha put her finger over his mouth to stop the priest from cursing and frowned. Brae and Yolanda often wondered how much coin Joshua carried, it was certainly a lot. Mind you it was a good deal less after the hired guns had been paid out taking him to the old army depot.

"What do you think Brae, do you think they are friendly?"

"Not sure until we ring that bell on the jetty." Brae pondered for a while and rescanned the building. A door opened and a bare-chested man wandered out drinking from a demijohn. The man had a full beard and didn't sport any tattoos that he recognised to be bandit or gang related. The man went to the river bank and dropped his pants. Brae put the binoculars down and rubbed the bridge of his nose.

"What?" Yolanda asked, knowing there was something wrong.

"Nothing. Just a guy taking a shit, I didn't feel like watching." Brae laughed. Yolanda shoulder budged him and laughed too.

"Hey Natasha, have you still got that low calibre pistol with the suppressor, that Josh bought you in Red town before we left." Brae asked, he hadn't seen it since, because Natasha seemed to prefer the snub-nosed revolver. She nodded and started to rummage through her rucksack, after a while she pulled out the small pistol with the long cylinder attached to the muzzle. She handed it to Brae. Brae checked the clip and chambered a round. He looked back at Natasha.

"You got plenty of ammo for this, I don't want to waste the last bullets if you haven't many left?" He asked. Natasha shrugged, I got a small box of little bullets, I don't really use that pistol so use however many bullets you need." She said uncaring, clearly she didn't like guns, even if they had saved her scrawny arse all this time. Brae took aim and squeezed off a single round. The bullet hit the bell making a dinging sound. He repeated this until he emptied the little pistol. He then picked up his binoculars and had another look. This time there were three men all dressed in the same scruffy garb. The eldest still holding the big bottle was scratching his head and looking towards the other two men, which could be either sons or maybe brothers. It was hard to tell from this distance. He noticed the other two were armed, but they were standard rifles, that any folks carried around in the Ashland. Brae finally got up and started to wander to the bell waving to the other bank.

"On your feet I think they are friendly." He said.

The ferry took quite a while crossing the river, the two brothers/sons rowed while the older man steered from the rear of the large raft. Every so often the older man waved. It was a strange kind of crossing, they seemed to aim up river to compensate for the current taking them down river. After what seemed to be an age, the raft finally moored against the jetty. The older man came down the jetty to meet.

"You folks travelling north, there's a lot of hunting going on north and there's a number of townships and trade houses."

"Yeah heading north to 'clear springs', you heard of it?" Brae asked.

"Stranger, there is a lot of places north called 'clear springs' and I only been to one, but that's not very far at all, in fact that's just due north-west of here as a crow flies." The bearded man chuckled.

"I'm sure I've travelled around this area and I don't remember seeing this ferry service."

"That's because it's only been here for two... Or is it three years now Hercule?" The bearded man turned to face Hercule, who had clear family resemblance, Brae figured eldest son.

"Nearly three and a half years pa." Hercule said spitting out brown spittle mixed with chewing tobacco.

The sons eyed one another which Brae and Yolanda spotted, they both had sinking feelings in their gut. Both the sons were staring at Natasha now. *Shit!* Brae thought.

"Well I count four of ya, so that's a shiny coin for each, if that's okay sir." The father asked opening his palm to collect the money. Joshua hadn't seen the danger and counted out a number of coins, placing them in the ferry man's hand.

"Well we are good to go." The ferry man grinned and gestured for all to get on board the raft. Once everybody got on board the two sons began to cast off across the river.

"I'm Billy-Bob and these are my sons Hercule and Zack, Ol mama is across the way cooking up stew. She has made plenty if you wish to stay for dinner?" Billy-Bob asked.

"That's very kind sir, but we are heading north, need to use all the day light we have for travelling." Brae said as he eyed the two burly sons labouring on the oars. When the ferry got to about mid-point across the river, Billy-Bob cocked his head as he looked Brae and Yolanda up and down.

"Don't mind me asking, but you two look like rangers?"

"Your correct sir, we are ranger scouts. You will have more coin for the other rangers following us up, they should arrive later this afternoon if you are still in business hours?" Brae lied. Billy-Bob looked to his sons and they both nodded and appeared a bit glum.

"More business, hell that's what we are here for, aren't we sons? Come rain or shine, night or day, the ferry will be of service." Billy-Bob said with a feigned grin his shoulders sagged. Brae thought his lie had made them stand down, clearly they had other plans for the travellers.

"Don't get many rangers travelling up these parts, but we have seen the odd ranger solo over the years." Hercule asked with a sinister looking grin.

"Captain Ash is expanding operations, he wishes to bring law and order to the north." Brae lied again and kept his eye on the ferry folk.

"No offence to the rangers, but the 'northern folk' probably won't take kindly to rangers moving in on there territory!" The other son Zack claimed. The father sighed and scowled at his son.

"Now that's a crock of shit Zack, You keep your fucking mouth shut! The north is law abiding and we welcome the rangers. The south does okay in my book with the protection of the rangers." Billy-Bob was trying to calm the situation down before it got out of hand. However, Brae suspected falsehood.

"Pay no attention to Zack, he don't know no better. If the rangers came up here, business will be good for our family!"

"Sorry pa!" Zack put his head down and dug in on the oar. Clearly his father beat him from time to time.

"In the north, do you praise to the bright?" Joshua asked as Brae covered his face and shook his head. Typical Joshua being from the safety of a township, hadn't read the thin line they were all treading.

"We also revere the bright up north!" Billy-Bob said angrily as though the priest had insulted their intelligence. "We have our own priest at Trinty Town, he makes the journey to our house at least once every eight weeks to bless our family."

"Trinity town you say, I would like to meet with this priest." Joshua said looking to Brae.

"We can alter our journey and goto Trinity town to meet the priest Joshua." Brae said wide eyed towards the priest, mouthing the words 'shut the fuck up!' Joshua nodded and fell silent as his mind had finally worked out the trouble they were all in.

"We are civilized folks up here!" Hercule barked as he stopped rowing, eyeing the priest with daggers.

The raft had nearly crossed the river by now and the party was eager to get away as fast as they could before trouble started. Yolanda had her pistol in her hand under the folds of her leather duster and Brae was ready for trouble. The conversation had calmed by now and Billy-Bob had begun to tell of wonderful hunting grounds to the north a place called 'Grey wood' not too far from Trinity town.

"Grey wood has beaver, deer, bears and wild cattle. Trinity town only takes a certain amount of pelts and meat hunted so that the wildlife is not over hunted. Often or not if they have a lot of pelts coming in they don't offer any coin." Billy-Bob rambled.

"Good to know, as a ranger humans need to

maintain hunting grounds or they will become barren." Brae agreed, which got smiles and nods from the ferry folk.

"That's a nice bit of iron you have there." Hercule pointed to Brae and Yolanda's assault rifles. Brae could see the wanting on his inbred face.

"They are standard issue ranger rifles, each ranger passing the tests gains one of these bad boys. The rangers are always looking out for potential soldiers." Brae said proudly without bragging. He failed to mention that Yolanda and himself, had found the rifles and had not been earned by becoming a ranger. Too be honest he saw the two sons wide eyed at the concept of becoming rangers. That was his good deed of the day it seemed. The raft hit home on the jetty. It seemed the ferry folk had changed their minds and now revered the travelling folk in the hope for more coin coming their way in the form of many rangers wishing for passage across the river. Brae made a mental note to go back south a different route to avoid confrontation.

"Are you sure you don't wish to stay for dinner, Mama has cooked up a mighty stew?" Billy-Bob asked genuinely.

"I'm sorry but our resident priest wishes to goto Trinty town. Could you mark its location on our map?" Brae asked offering the map to Billy-Bob and a pen.

"Sure I can, anything for more business." He chuckled. The older man studied the old moth eaten map and put a small X on the oiled surface.

"Thank you sir. Take care and be ready for the

rangers following." Brae said folding up the map and pocketing it on a pouch on his armoured breast plate. He browsed at his nautical compass and then back at the map for a bearing and set off. Yolanda took up the rear, peering over her shoulder pistol ready just in case the fucks made a move.

They travelled north-west as a bearing and sent Yolanda back on the trail to see if they were being followed. After the second time while they stopped for a rest Yolanda came back and shook her head, smiling.
"Your lie worked, they aren't following so we are okay to camp."
"Josh, if you wish to see Utopia then follow my lead and next time we encounter some ruffians keep quiet, blend, be the silent type. Yolanda and I will get you through the situation!" He chastised. Yolanda nodded and gestured to zip his mouth shut. Natasha must have noticed the situation even though Joshua didn't. Natasha went on to give him a silent telling off, outlining that she was in real danger back there. Joshua profoundly apologised and agreed.
"Your right I should have kept my mouth shut!" He said putting his head down in shame. The party camped up and selected a rota to keep watch. The next morning they set off and headed for Trinty town, it would be a good place to purchase provisions and get information about the wild north. By late afternoon after several stops for rest they came to the foot of a fortified township, not dissimilar to Red Town. Guards

on the parapet fortification asked them why they wished to enter town. Brae used his charm which allowed access to the township. The main street was dirty, pretty much an open sewer running down the street, full of urine, human and animal sewerage. They found an inn called 'Trinty Rest' and entered into the tap room. The bar was empty apart from a number of folks playing dice in one of the cornered off booths. They noticed the town had its own militia in the form of deputies run by an overlord type sheriff. They seemed okay and none threatening but Yolanda and Brae noticed the place was more than a little corrupt. A pretty standard township, where you needed to keep on guard and tried not to break the law. Whatever the fuck the laws were? Joshua was already consulting the bar man about the resident priest. The bar man gave him directions to the church, but took a coin for the information.

"By the bright Joshua, I could have found the church and it didn't need coin!" Brae chastised. Joshua paid for a night's stay, a room where they all could sleep safely and together. Yolanda and Natasha went to the room to rest while Joshua and Brae headed over to the church to meet the local priest. Brae thought it might be best if he went with the priest just in case it turned violent. Just before they left they paid for food to be taken to the room.

The church seemed to be bigger than the church at Red town but clearly it was in disrepair. Maybe? Due to the lack of tribute from the dwindling worshiper's of the bright? Joshua assumed. They entered the main chamber of the church and the resident deacon approached, she wore a Sunday dress that had seen better days. The cuffs were stained and the trim was quite tattered.

"Welcome my children, how can the church of the bright be of service?" She asked eyebrows raised and a smile you would only get from somebody who walks in the path of the bright. Joshua had seen that ridiculous smile many times before, hell he often had such a smile. But not no more, due to his present mind set on the world.

"I'm here to see the priest. I am a priest of the bright myself and would love to chat with the resident champion of the bright!" He smiled as he had been taught. Brae was busy looking for exits just in case this building was a trap.

"Of course, priest of the bright, I will go and fetch priest Phillips." She bowed and rushed off towards the vestry of the building. Brae and Joshua waited patiently for many minutes before a robed priest exited a side door and pulled up his robes to quickly make passage toward them.

"I'm Priest Phillip's, I believe you wish to speak to me?" She said slightly out of breath.

"I have passed many of whore houses and places where you can slurp from the devils cock!" Joshua said with vehemence, referring to the many taverns in Trinity Town.

"I have done best as I can muster my fellow priest, but folks need vice, I try to push them down the path of the holy bright but my church does not offer debauchery!" The young priest claimed sorrowful. "The church competes with dens of sin at every approach!" The young woman got on her knees and kissed Joshua's travel worn boots.

"Forgive me!" The poor priest pleaded, kneeling on the floor before him.

"Child, you need to try and comfort the sinners like I did in Red Town. I found if you make friends with the wives and tutor them in the bright, then the wives do most of the holy work!" He said as he patted the priests head.

"Times have changed my holiness. Only a few come to service on Saturday or Sunday. It's but a pathetic few. I Guess your church was full of bright parishioners?"

"Yes and still is my friend, I have left my deacon in charge while I lay the path way to the holy lands!" Joshua said like a king of old times. He stood proud with chin high in victory.

"Deacon!" She slurred? "You have left your second in command in charge or sermons?" She stood up levelling her eyes with the priest.

"Yes I did, due to I'm on a holy quest to find the Utopia!" Joshua claimed before backing off away from her gaze.

"What is Utopia?" The female asked. Brae grabbed hold of Joshua and pulled him away.

"Keep this church holy and true, I need to take this fellow priest to Utopia. I'm sure he will send word once we get there!" Brae said as he dragged Joshua from the church.

"Drink up we have a nights stay and our gullets are full with beer and food!" Brae announced as he got to his feet in an unsteady manner.

"All hail to Joshua paying for our rooms!" Brae said staggering away through the tap room up the stairs to his room. Yolanda followed him upstairs to the secure communal room they had to share. Yolanda locked the door and slipped into Braes bed and cuddled around him. In the darkness she could hear Joshua snoring and Natasha purring, they had gone to bed earlier, probably to fuck. She found solace quickly, her eyes heavy from the miles they had travelled. Her dreams fluttered in and out of things she had done recently to obscure moments from her past. Her dream settled and she remembered a tree swing, playing with children her own age. When it came to her turn a rough boy pushed her hard and she felt panic as the swing went far out. The creak of the tree limb made her more frightened. She looked back during the arc and saw the evil boy ready to push her again. On the way back she braced herself and then at the right moment she lashed out with her foot. She leaped off the tree swing and stood and watched the boy wailing on the floor, blood squirting from his burst nose. When she looked up she witnessed fear in the other children's eyes. From then on she knew she was different to what she considered to be, normal folks. The dreamscape fluttered and she felt her body drifting like the feeling of going down river laid on your back on a wooden raft. Sun blazed in her eyes and she elbowed herself up and smiled. It was the time Brae took her for a riverboat picnic. The food he brought was rudimentary, mostly jerky meat and soda bread. But he did bring something else. He asked her to close her eyes, she did, smiling like an excited child. A small box had been placed in the palm of her hand, she opened one eye and saw that it was a faded pink little box, with a faded red velvet heart on the top. Brae muttered something, it sounded important but being a dream it was vague. She knew what was inside the box, it was a gold bracelet, pre-war and whoever owned it last had also been called Yolanda, because it was engraved so, in fancy writing. She opened the box and inside was a gouged out eyeball, the heavens above moody and the sun was long gone. She was still on the raft but Brae was nowhere to be seen and the river was picking up momentum. The white water river swirled and hissed as the raft swayed back and forth and lurching over large banks of water. She held on tight and in the distance she could see the edge of a water fall coming quicker than her heart beat, the thunderous noise booming against her ears, the raft tilting over the falls...

"No!" She Yelled. Sweat ran from her neck and trickled between her breasts. She looked to the bed and

Brae wasn't there. "Brae?" She screamed.

"What's the matter, I'm over here having a shit?" Brae rolled his eyes and continued his toilet sat on an uncomfortable looking wooden bucket. Yolanda collapsed back into bed, her heart beat bouncing against her rig cage.

"I thought you had left me." She whispered.

"Don't be daft, we are lifers, look calm down I'm nearly done." He grumbled.

"It was close back there, the tree nearly killed you." She continued to whisper, he could here upset in her voice.

"Yeah, but I survived... Anyway It's going to take more than a psychotic tree to end me, that's for sure." He chuckled, but Yolanda didn't see the humour. She turned over in bed, her back to Brae and pulled the blankets over her shoulders. She stared blankly for a time at the bare wooden latched walls.

"You had a bad dream girl. That is all?" Brae said softly.

"Maybe, not sure? Something to do with an eye ball and a fierce white water river."

"Probably that river we crossed, maybe playing on your mind, we got away from a gun fight there. Remind me when we head back to Red town, we don't cross by ferry. Those brothers will be angry about my lie and will want blood." Brae said comforting with an ounce of logic.

"Yeah it could be that, but the eye was piercing green, just like Jessica's?"

"Calm yourself love, we did go mad on the booze last night, beer and spirits can cause all sorts of manic dreams." He climbed into bed and hugged her, she was hot and sticky. She complained because his body was cold but after a few seconds he felt her bum wiggle against his groin. He thought it best not to make a move, she needed a cuddle more than a rampant fuck. He squeezed her and settled his face against the back of her neck. He could feel her drifting off to sleep again, her pulse rate was steady and calm, like a slow military drum beat. She started to snore quietly and he noticed her sun bleached hair had got unruly. He ran his hand through his own hair and grimaced, he needed a haircut too. He made a mental note to get their hair cut before they set off, the last thing they needed was hair in their eyes when they were aiming rifles to put some son-of-a-bitch to a dirt nap. He felt his eye lids falling and sleep found him fast.

Joshua and Natasha had got up early to organise provisions for the travel, he bartered with a greasy looking merchant and knew he was being ripped off.

"By the bright can't you cut us a deal?" He moaned as Natasha tapped her foot impatiently, her arms folded neatly below her pert young breasts.

"Prices have gone up recently due to the pig flu!" The sweaty merchant mentioned not trying to hide a smirk. He needed to save enough coin for the journey and the township merchants were all claiming the same pathetic lie, even when they shopped around.

"Okay, three for the jerky and two for the bags of corn flour." Joshua grumbled, handing over the coin. He shoved the other items away from the deal in a huff. However, the merchant changed his mind quickly, knowing a deal needed to be made.

"Right you win, three more coins for the sundries and that's my best offer." The merchant said pushing the items back to the barter circle on the merchant stand.

"Two coins and we have a deal." Joshua said with a poker face. The merchant pulled a conflicting face and then finally nodded. Natasha gathered up the items as Joshua forked out more coins. As they wandered away Natasha patted her lover on his shoulder.

"Well done Josh, he was clearly trying to bleed every coin from our purse."

"Shit heads, it would have been half that price back at Red town." He moaned. By the time they had shopped around most of the morning had been wasted. They met back at the tavern and sat impatiently watching Brae and Yolanda tucking into a late breakfast.

"New haircuts?" Joshua said noticing the gun fighters had been cropped. Brae had a skin head and was clean shaven and Yolanda had a short blond chin length cut.

"Got to keep up appearances." Brae chuckled and forked a large slither of omelette into his mouth.

"Well hurry up, we are late leaving this shit hole as it is." Joshua snapped with a scowl, not seeing the regular folks frowning about him referring to the town as a shit hole. It was around ten thirty by the time the group had packed up and left the township. They headed north satisfied with the knowledge they had at least three weeks food between them as long as they didn't get greedy. The grassy hills turned to flat rocky wilderness, pin pricked by large free standing cactus and small juniper bushes. The stream they had followed north came to dusty sand, the land was thirsty and drank up the stream. From then on they relied on finding small water holes frequented by strange desert like animals, most of which had been friendly.

A week passed quickly and foot hills of grass appeared on the horizon dotted by sparse looking trees. They filled canteens at springs and small streams before heading into deep forest. They had been travelling off the beaten path so didn't encounter many folks. Occasionally they passed small groups of scavengers and traded ammo and sundries for very little coin. They knew they still had far to travel so they used any opportunity to trade. Brae and Yolanda found it unbelievable how folks lived so far from civilisation and without the protection of the rangers. However, the people they met were of a different calibre to the folks of the south. They were hardened folk, left to fend for themselves in such a harsh climate, often sporting primitive ways and equipment. They camped down with a small group of hunters deep in the forest, at first appraisal you would assume they were bandits or cut throats but they seemed friendly enough.

"More Ember flower tea?" A dusty looking woman called Sara asked as she padded around with bare feet wielding a hot kettle of tea.

"Yes please." Joshua said with a smile holding out a battered old camping cup.

"We are heading south east tomorrow, good hunting grounds to what we call Amber wood. She claimed pouring tea to the brim of his cup. Joshua couldn't help but stare at her bare breasts, the only clothing the hunter gatherer's seemed to don was loin cloths and tattoos decorated over their muscular bodies. One of the burly males sat next to Brae leaned in and eyed Joshua for a while.

"Your priest has the urge with Sara, yes?" He asked Brae.

"No, he is married to Natasha the blonde girl tending the fire." He pointed at Natasha and tried to reassure the hunter that Joshua was not used to seeing the world or half naked folks.

"Aaaahhh, I see." The hunter burst out laughing. "A pandy foot, yes?"

"Yes a pandy foot." Brae agreed and laughed with the hunter. Brae had encountered many tribes during his travels so he was used to nakedness.

"He needs a tattoo, to keep away evil spirits." The hunter said with a smile.

"He has his own religion and way of life, but feel free to ask." Brae said covering his mouth as it formed a grin. Yolanda grinned too and elbowed Brae.

"That's naughty Brae!" She giggled. A number of

the hunters stood up and started to move in on Joshua who was light headed from the strange tea that Sara had been pouring into his cup. Joshua's face was a picture when the hunters man handled him to the campfire, he was complaining all the way as Yolanda and Brae started to howl laughing. Natasha noticed what was going on and started yelling at them to stop. But after a few winks from Yolanda and Brae she calmed down and watched the hunters preparing ink.

"My god will not like this!" Joshua cried as he tried to escape from the many hands holding him down.

"Just go with it Joshua, it is their religion." Brae chided.

"Fuck you Brae!" Joshua groaned as several females started to prepare ink, tonic and brews by the camp fire.

"You're in for quite a ride buddy." Brae laughed as he rolled up his sleeve showing a faded ink tattoo just below his shoulder. "It's a warrior tribal tattoo, me and Yolanda have a similar tattoo but not of this tribe." He said trying to calm his friend and benefactor down. Natasha seemed interested and laid down next to Joshua, holding his hand.

"Me next." She simply said with a smile. Brae and Yolanda knew this was going to take some time so hankered down into their bed rolls. They noticed some of the hunters were stood proud on watch, they were safe in the hands of the hunters.

Morning came and the sun started to rise through the canopy of the trees bringing a humid heat. Brae and

Yolanda tucked into a breakfast of forest meat provided by the hunters. They thanked them and sat with them telling stories of the south and the rangers. The hunter folks listened to the tales as Natasha and Joshua sat naked at the edge of the camp watching the sun rise. Their arms were around one another taking the morning chill from their bones. Both sported a small tattoo of a rabbit on their fore arms. It was hard to tell but Brae assumed they were pretty chuffed. After a number of bear hugs and back slaps, the hunter folk broke camp and allowed the travellers to witness a new dawn. Brae and Yolanda brought blankets to the naked people and a cup of hot coffee that Brae had brewed. They sat and felt the warm rays of sunlight filtering through the forest canopy.

"Are you enlightened Joshua?" Brae asked, stony faced, but dying to laugh when he saw the fresh tattoos.

"It was quite the experience... But I'm glad we did it. I understand now, how small gestures could make the Ashland so bright." Joshua said through a clouded drug induced film over his eyes. Natasha giggled and hugged him closer.

"It was wonderful." She said still giggling from the last dance of the drugged tea.

"Take your time guys, it is still very early, enjoy and in a few hours we set off north." Brae said grabbing hold of Joshua's wrist and winking.

"Thank you Brae, that was such a new experience and I'm glad you looked after us while we dreamt of fantastic things. I'm not used to intoxication so we will have to set off later than planned." He smiled and shook Braes hand.

"I thought you would enjoy that Joshua, a vision into other religions, just a taste." Brae smiled. Brae and Yolanda busied themselves breaking camp. Yolanda had time to head off and gather berries and nourishing roots while Brae stayed on guard, keeping the others safe. By the time they were clothed and ready for travel it was at least half an hour till noon. The potent tea had subsided and they all headed out north using Brae's compass as a bearing. It would be a long and hard day's travel and none of them felt like they were up for it. They plodded through the thick forest, navigating a path through the dense fawner and bypassing the odd giant mushroom. Keeping any kind of fungus at arm's length, due to the previous attack that nearly killed Brae. Moral was up, because Joshua kept everybody's spirit alive with the idea of Utopia is not that far away. Brae had his doubts because they still had a long way to travel across landscape Yolanda and Brae, had never traversed so far north. The hunters claimed there would be a number of lonely trade houses to the north, even pin pointing them on the map. Brae estimated they could easily bypass the trade houses due to the vague coordinates. He wasn't holding his breath to find these places and calculated each camp with enough time to hunt and gather, providing the land held animals and plant life to eat. It wasn't the end of the earth though and he figured there would be farmsteads and places where humanity gathered in small villages. He just hoped they would not be hostile.

CHAPTER 17

Ash watched as Jessica, Angel, Edwards and Sandings attempted to master the hulking armoured suits. A number of weeks had passed. He had set up a run outside the army base, to train them. Dr Kienz the robot stood next to ash and even the robot put its mechanical hand over its visual sensors when one of the pilots fucked up and smashed its way into the ground.

"Again!" Ash yelled through a mega phone. "Jessica get back on your feet!" He shook his head watching the Armoured suit trying to get to its feet, kicking up dust and sand. The hatch on the back of the grounded Environmental combat armour opened and a sweaty and pissed off Jessica leaped out in an angry rage.

"Fuck this shit!" She screamed into the air, the veins on her neck prominent. She tried to march off in a huff when an auxiliary grabbed her wrist and pointed to the embedded E.C.A.

"Give it another go Jessica don't give up." Zoë the auxiliary said with a positive tone. She pushed Jessica back to the grounded machine.

"It's un-controllable!" She barked spitting at the boot of the female auxiliary.

"You're not going to master the E.C.A by being a bitch, now get back in there and get control of the unit."

Auxiliary Zoë stated in a calm voice. Jessica balled her fist and was ready to punch her out, until a hulking E.C.A stomped towards her and opened the escape hatch. Angel leapt down from the machine and smiled at Jessica.

"Do as Zoë suggests and get that hunk of junk back on its feet, with you commanding its progress!" She was harsh but loving in her tone, kind of like a parent chastising a child.

"Fuck you I need a drink!" Jessica hissed, as she strolled towards the habitat. Ash noticed what went down and un-corked a bottle of bandy and made a bee-line to intercept.

"Drink up Jess, calm your nerves!" He offered the bottle to her and she snatched it out of his hands and gulped at the pre-war spirit. Her legs gave way and spilled brandy all over her face as she landed on her arse.

"Can't we just 'rad-cape' up and walk to the target?" She giggled as the alcohol hit her blood stream. Ash peered over her, he wasn't pleased at all, she clearly had been drinking before the training begun.

"The E.C.A's can cover so much land, by-passing dangerous zones. Not to mention radioactive ruins, which you will have to pass!" Ash sighed and shook his head as Jessica took another gulp of brandy.

"Training session is over, everybody back inside there is a storm brewing!" Ash said as he looked to an angry cloud front coming from the east. The Auxiliaries climbed inside the E.C.A's and piloted them back inside the habitat as the rangers followed Ash inside for a debriefing meeting.

"What I saw was piss poor, we have been at this for days and by now I would have thought everybody would be on line with the workings of the E.C.A's." Ash was pissed off, with the progress.

"Our friend Dr Kienz, has outlined how to work these armoured suits, what kind of malfunction are we dealing with here people!" Ash aimed it more to Jessica, but the others hadn't handled the armoured suits very well.

"Too be fair, these suits of mechanical armour are not how we operate normally, it's new to us so give us a little leeway here!" Angel said as she hugged a pot of hot coffee. "We are ground folk, surveying the land as we wander. It's what we have all been trained to do. Mechanical armour is new, so give us some time Ash!"

"I will be damned if I get in one of those fucked up contraptions again!" Jessica said with a sigh. Knowing she should master the suit before the mission.

"You have one more day to master an E.C.A, if you don't then our contract is finished!" Ash said to Jess before heading towards his personal quarters.

"Maybe I should head back to Red town?" Jessica said with defeat in her tone. As she tried to walk away Edwards grabbed her.

"You and me, back in the E.C.A. There is enough room for two, so I will show you what I have learnt so far?"

"What now?"

"Yes right this second buddy!" Edwards said with a smile.

"Fuck you Edwards, I'm not getting inside a confined space with a fucking drainer!" Jess hissed. Edwards laughed, she knew what Jessica would say and how she would react.

"Angel you up for a night walk with Jess, teach her to operate an E.C.A?" Edwards grinned towards Angel.

"I'm shattered Edwards!" She moaned and then looked at Jessica's defeated face. "Son-of-a-bitch!" She got to her feet and gestured for Jessica to follow her.

The night air was chilly and skies were clear with the sparkles of the milky-way. The E.C.A that Jessica had grounded was still stuck fast in the sand where she left it. The axillaries clearly couldn't be arsed putting it back away or couldn't get the mechanical creature back up from the ground. Jessica opened the hatch and climbed inside the bulky suit, clicking a few switches to bring the suit on line. Angel looked down to the hatch and shook her head.

"It's going to be pretty intimate in there looking at that confined space."

"Let's just get this over with!" Jessica said irritably. Angel climbed into the suit behind her and shifted around until she was basically lying on top of her. She smelt the female musk of Angel's body from the day's exertions and wondered how she would smell too. Angel placed her knees behind her knees and gripped both of her wrists and moved her hands towards the mechanical grips.

"Right, we need to self-right this bitch. Move the grips forward like you would do a press-up." Jessica cranked the grips and the suit sprung to life.

"Not too hard Jess, do it gently or the suit will fling itself backwards on to its back. Remember small movements and the suit will take the strain." Angel chastised. The E.C.A got to its knees and wavered a little, its powerful mechanical arms grabbing air trying to keep its balance..

"No! That's wrong, use control. Think mechanically, the suit has a self-balancing protocol so don't try to compensate."

"Okay." Jessica said with a frown, she was trying her best, but it was hard to think when Angel had her body pressed against her. She could feel Angles breasts squashing against her back. Jessica shuddered a little which made Angel nervous.

"Oh by the bright Jess, you're not getting off on this, are you?"

"Me??? No, not at all!" Jessica lied. Angel had her doubts and could swear Jessica had a major crush on her.

"Right now, manoeuvre your right knee and pull up your right foot into a lunge like position." The exo-armour followed suit to its sensors and got to its feet.

"That's right, you did it." Angel said with pride in her tone. Now that they were standing up in the suit, she brushed Jessica's hair out of the way so she could see the heads up display. The camera on the suit was a little fuzzy and she made a mental note that this suit was slightly damaged. She pushed closer to Jess and like a string puppet she used the woman as an extension through the controls of the E.C.A.

"Let's open the beast up. Remember small movements and it will walk, if you push a little harder then it will run. Let's try running, but be careful not to hit those cars." The E.C.A started a steady trot and then broke out into a swift jogging like motion, thundering across the sandy ground.

"Perfect Jess! Now slow down before we hit that wall." Angel said. Jessica felt her breath against the nape of her neck and tried to concentrate on the task at hand, dismissing thoughts of having sex with the woman. The mechanical creature slowed to a walk and then flung itself around and picked up pace again back towards the habitat. Now that Jessica had come to the idea where you only make small gestures with your body, she seemed to have control of the armoured suit. Angel let go of her wrists and hugged her arms around Jessica's waist to brace herself from the motion of the E.C.A.

"You're doing great Jess, keep it up and before long you will master the suit." She said like a teacher congratulating a child. Jessica had an ear to ear smile on her face, the controls seemed simple now. The inside of the suit was getting hot with another person inside which brought more feminine musk to her nostrils. She tried her best not to get horny but it was hard not too having a warm body embracing her.

"One more run and then we call it a do." Angel said, bringing a sadness to Jessica. The armoured suit rushed again towards the outer limits and then rushed back to the habitat, stopping suddenly near the large doors. She flipped a few switches to put the E.C.A into standby mode and then craned her head to put her cheek against Angel's cheek.

"Thank you so much Angel, I think Ash would have cancelled my contract if I couldn't master the E.C.A. It would be a shit thing for me not to go on the mission, especially now that I'm trying my best to do something Nobel and not looking out for number one as usual." Jessica said with determination in her tone. Angel gave her a squeeze of reassurance around her waist which made Jess bite her lip. She took the gesture and shifted around in the suit to face Angel.

"What you doing Jess?" Angel asked with a judging frown. She peered into Angels ice blue eyes and traced Angel's jaw line with her index finger. Angels frown softened and her pupils dilated in the soft light of the interior of the suit. Jessica reached around Angels back and pulled her closer to her.

"This is weird Jess, I'm not a lesbian. I'm not really anything. Sex is a thing that goes on in the world and seldom comes my way, being a solo." She confessed.

"Sex is a release Angel. It has kept me alive all this time through the bad times and the good times." Jessica whispered as she reached forward to kiss her. Angel had her eyes closed and a face of distaste, fleeing from

Jessica's affections. But then she relaxed and felt Jessica's lips touching hers. It felt strange but inside her mind she thought what the hell, try it. She felt Jessica's tongue slide inside her mouth, she hadn't kissed anybody properly or passionately before. The only kisses she had to her memory were on her cheek or a quick peck on her lips. She tried to stay calm and joined her tongue against Jessica's, sliding and caressing. It was like time had stopped and she got caught up with the tempest. Jessica's hand was now on the nape of her neck pulling her towards the embrace of the passionate kiss. She felt like a child again, not knowing what to do, but Jessica seemed to have the upper hand now and she followed her lead. Jessica's hands was un-buttoning her pants and reaching into her knickers to caress her. Angel shuddered it had been a very long time since she had masturbated and Jessica seemed adept of touching all the right places. She tensed up and was about to push Jess away, but she felt the warmth rising from her groin, rushing up to her chest and the tingles in her body washing over her. She stopped kissing Jess and hugged around her shoulders kissing Jessica's neck as her lover worked her magic on her clitoris. Angel's breath came in bouts of gasps and soft moans until she finally came wet against Jessica's fingers. She yelped and collapsed on Jess, her knees turning to jelly. Jess laughed and hugged her kissing her cheek.

"It's been a long time then?" Jess asked, still laughing.

"A very long time Jess." Angel suddenly looked

stern. "This is a secret yes?"

"I'm not the kiss and tell type. But you know where to find me if the urge gets strong." Jessica had stopped laughing now and hugged Angel to her.

"I think we best get back to base." Angel said flushed and a little bit embarrassed to what had just gone on. They popped the hatch and the cool night air rushed into the confines of the E.C.A. They clambered out and leapt to the sandy floor noticing a woman stood near the shadows of the doorway of the habitat. Angel recognised the woman dressed in a simple blue boiler suit, she looked pissed off and had her arms folded across her chest.

"Zoë?" Angel asked squinting in the dimness of the night.

"That's right, surprised you acknowledge an auxiliary?" Zoë said with a frown.

"Oh yeah that's right, you are in charge of maintenance in the base?" Angel said fanning her flustered face with her hand. Trying her very best to appear inconspicuous.

"Ash put me in charge of engineering due to my skill set." She paused and appraised the two females with her large hazel eyes, her eye brows slanted in a questioning look. "Does Ash know you have been messing around with one of the E.C.As? Training is supposed to be scheduled for tomorrow?" Zoë tapped her foot waiting for a pathetic excuse.

"Jessica was struggling today, she has a binding contract to fulfil, the only way she can go on the mission is to master an E.C.A!" Angel said trying to console the engineer.

"Well you better not have damaged the mechanical suit. I don't want to spend all fucking day trying to fix it up back up to working order!" The auxiliary said as she made a bee-line to the E.C.A standing in the grounds of the base. Jessica and Angel headed into the base leaving Zoë to inspect the mechanical beast. They could hear her cursing and inspecting the mechanical monster under the bright illuminated moon. Jessica and Angel followed the metallic corridors down to the rooms they had been granted by Ash. Angel paused when she got to the door of her room, she wished for Jessica to join her but she didn't want to be the subject of idle gossip. Jessica stole a quick kiss and strolled away to her quarters.

"Room fifty five if you're interested?" She said without looking over her shoulder. Angel sighed and opened the door to her room, she laid down on the Spartan type bed and drummed her fingers on the mattress for a while, her thoughts cascaded to the sex she had just had. She looked at the wall clock and it stated twelve fifty. She suddenly stood up and exited the room, she marched down the corridors towards room fifty five. The door wasn't locked and she entered, Jessica was naked sat at the bottom of the bed, she was smiling.

"I knew you would come."

The next morning, the volunteers for the mission

were hard back at it, training in the E.C.As. Ash was surprised at Jessica mastering the armoured suit, had his warning paid heed to her physiological make up? He appraised her technique and made a mental note that she was back on the mission. By dinner time the armoured suits came to a standstill and the occupants wandered toward the picnic table Dr Kienz had set up. Proper boiled eggs taken from the chicken coop the farmers had established at the base from the farm. The table was laid in finery with tinned tomatoes and fresh baked corn on the cob. Ash took the head of the table and started to tuck in to the meal prepared by the robot. He noticed Jessica seemed in high spirits, it was a far cry from her mood yesterday. Edwards stayed by the armoured suits, she didn't require nourishment like regular humans. He finished a plate of food and wandered over to talk to Edwards.

"You ready to take on the mission?" He asked sternly.

"Of course sir!" She saluted and stood proud.

"Any hesitation, about the people who will follow you into battle? After all you still retain rank and will be the team leader." Ash asked as he read her face.

"No sir, it is a good team, a strong team, sir!"

"It has taken many days to train up the squad are we battle ready sergeant?"

"Yes sir!"

"No doubts then?" He hesitated and waited for a reaction.

"No doubts sir!"

"Then fall out and get ready for tomorrow." He said before heading back to the base. The others finished up their meal and took one last run in the E.C.As before heading back to base. By the time the sun started to go down, everybody gathered in the common room. Ash stood like a sentinel with his hands clasped behind his back. Jessica, Angel, Edwards and ranger Sandings sat around a circular table drinking whiskey shots.

"As you all know you are to perform a mission for the greater good of the rangers and human kind. Rangers are now thin on the ground and god only knows how many settlements have fallen to the soviet enemy. Applewood and Captain Harris haven't replied to our radio messages, so we can only assume they are now dead." Ash paused and wandered back and forth at the head of the table. "Its now in our hands to bring justice to the Ashland and take back what humanity strived to protect! We know not where the enemy dwells, but one thing is for certain they have a base of operations somewhere out in the Ashland."

"Last point of contact was at the old fort captain!" Edwards stated.

"Yes and that's going to be your bearing. Go to the fort and follow the trail into the ruins." Ash said sorrowfully. "From there you will pick up the trail and find where those draining mother fuckers operate from. You will..." Ash stopped as Dr Keinz the robot wandered to the table carrying some kind of gizmo.

"This is a laser guided spotter. You will pin point

the target using this device. It is heavy so we will strap it to one of the E.C.As you will be utilising. Normally the missiles find the target using satellite uplinks, but the satellites have long used up their plutonium batteries. So you need to do this manually." The robotic creature stated.

"So we still don't have a target?" Jessica said frowning at Ash.

"Your correct Jess, the mission is to find the target so we can nuke the shit out of the soviets." Ash countered. The robot moved further toward the table.

"Your mission at first is recognisance. The E.C.As have a built in transmitter, so you will be in full radio contact to this base. Ash will direct you once you have established a target!" Jessica got to her feet and shook her head.

"Are we done? Because it sounds like you haven't a clue how this is going to play out!" She barked, before storming away towards her quarters.

"Jessica!" Ash Barked. "Sit the fuck down, I'm not finished yet!" He could see she was about to tell him to get fucked or maybe something worse, instead she strolled back to the table and sat down in a huff.

"Our robotic friend has a surprise for you all." He grinned and gestured for the robot to speak.

"As you know this facility is outfitted with lots of standard and advanced military equipment." Dr Keinz spun around on one foot and clapped its rubbery hands. On cue two axillaries wheeled out a manikin dressed up in some kind of armour? The armour looked jet black and made up of thin looking carapace like plates, quite like a bug.

"Towards the end of the war the American government had been developing all kinds of light weight combat armour to maintain front line troops." The robot pivoted back to face the group.

"This particular design was based on the version six, battle armour. This armour saw service in Europe, India and other countries that the soviets and red army had attempted to invade, running up to the nuclear exchange." The robot paused and mechanically shot its strange lenses like eyes from blank face to blank face, he needed to dumb it down.

"I will skip the material science which is wasted on your post war education." The robot tapped its foot for a few seconds.

"Basically, it is a very light weight armour which can stop a standard rifle round. It will down you and it will probably knock the wind from you, but it shouldn't penetrate you're..." The robot wanted to say 'pathetic biological flesh' but decided not to.

"Its erm... Kick ass." The robot said finally choosing a pre-war word for something amazing.

"Has this armour been tested?" Ash inquired.

"Yes, the material has been vigorously tested. I suppose we could demonstrate. Ash if you would?" The robot pointed to Ash's pistol. "Empty your clip against the armour. Ash pulled his pistol and walked towards the manikin aiming.

"Everybody stand well back." He waited until the

axillaries shifted away from the manikin and then opened fire. The bullets either penetrated or glanced off the armoured plates. Everybody's ears were ringing due to the retort of the pistol, all apart from the robot. Jessica and the others went to inspect the armour while Ash reloaded his pistol.

"I'll be fucked?" Edwards grinned as she poked her finger against one of the bullets that protruded from the armour. She instantly shot her finger away because the bullet was still hot.

"Ow!" The drainer yelped and laughed at her silly mistake. Ash pushed his way through the crowd to inspect the armour himself.

"By the bright we could have done with this kind of armour when we were bringing law and order to the Ashland." He sighed, thinking of all the rangers that had perished in gun fights against those who brought murder and terror to the land.

"Unbelievable!" Jessica hissed. "All those souls that died and right on our doorstep we could have had this armour to protect us!"

"The Ashland would have been an entirely different place if the rangers had found this technology earlier." Angel said as her eyes filled with tears.

"The fortress wouldn't have fallen that day, that's for damn sure!" Ash claimed as he put his arm around Angels waist and leaning his head against her cheek. Dr Keinz put his robotic arms up in a flurry.

"Let us not dwell in the past. We must look to the future." He tried to console the rangers but clearly his words fell on deaf ears. *Humans are far too emotional*, the robots circuits wondered.

"How many of these suits do we have in the base?" Ash asked.

"There is enough version seven armour, to outfit the current strength of rangers here at the base and enough for the next generation of rangers, if needed. When Agent Sundance performed the exodus, very few took the armour with them. They clearly wished to travel light to utopia." Dr Keinz claimed.

"You didn't answer the question?" Ash turned to face the robot and stared into its weird mechanical eyes.

"Oh, I see. Then we have one hundred and seventy two version seven combat armoured suits in this base." The robot computed.

"Axillaries! Outfit every combat ready person at this base with this new armour, do it tonight." Ash ordered as the two axillaries nodded and raced off toward the stores. It would be a long night for them but at least lives would be saved. Jessica, Edwards, Sandings and Angel followed the axillaries to the stores to claim a suit for themselves, leaving Ash and Dr Kienz to chat.

The E.C.As stood proud as the sun started to rise. Zoë the auxiliary had already strapped the laser pointer to Edward's armoured suit. The ranger auxiliary did a final check on the E.C.As before saluting to captain Ash.

"Ready to go Captain!" The auxiliary stated as she winked to the captain.

"Good Job Engineer." He said as he wandered around the hulking suits, noticing the shoulder mounted guns were full of ammo, the water vats and food stuffs, stowed nicely on the storage points. He was impressed, he patted the auxiliary on her shoulder and grinned.

"Double rations this week, you have earned it Zoë." He said as he wandered towards the group of dark armoured figures gathered near the door of the base. They were busying themselves doing a final pack. Jessica had opted for a battle rifle rather than a carbine.

"What's with the G3 Jess?" He asked. Jessica traced his eyes to the automatic rifle leant up against her backpack.

"I've opted for the higher calibre, seven point sixty two. When I put one of those mother fuckers down, they will stay down." She said absent minded as she continued to pack her gear.

"Five point fifty six don't cut it for you then Jess?" He said laughing. "I have to admit I prefer the G3 over the M4." He grinned knowingly.

"What it lacks in ammo, it makes up for its stopping power." She stated. Ash noticed the others had opted for the standard carbine rifle which had more ammo in the magazine. He conceded that rangers didn't always wish to kill, more maim a target so the enemy was compromised into making a decision of who to save and who to leave. He gritted his teeth and thought Jessica could be correct, drainers didn't have a habit of worrying about wounded fellow drainers. He had always chosen the battle rifle for its stopping power.

More now if he had to go toe to toe combat against those unholy mother fuckers. He watched the mission group stashing packs and ammo onto the E.C.As and he looked to a male auxiliary cooking a breakfast fit for hero's on a barbecue stand. The smell of gammon and boiled potato's being cooked was a heavy scent in the morning sunrise. A table had been set for four and he could see the dew forming on the legs of the aluminium table and chairs. Dr Keinz stood at the head of the table spooning pre-war freeze-dry coffee into a large pot bubbling on a small electrical hot plate. Ash felt proud, he wanted to climb inside an E.C.A and follow his friends into battle, but he knew he had to stay to organise and manage the facility. Keep law and order and protect the farm folks, keep them safe at the new base. He peered to his pistol belt and sniggered knowing he would lay down his life to protect the people. He would be damned if he didn't! The robot dished out the meals and then joined Ash on the side line, well away from the breakfasting hero's.

"You..." The robot peered into Ash's eyes with its shiny lenses like sensors. "You love them?" The robot finally asked.

"I do!" Ash took a deep shuddering breath. "I do my friend."

"I see people performing a task, I have no emotional response in my network. But my sensors see happiness and comradeship." The robot said as it tried to understand humanity. Ash could see the hero's chatting, laughing, having a cooked meal, smiles, nods and now and then fear and doubt on their faces.

"They are scared, but they are using this snatch of time to forget the world as it is and the dire mission they are to perform... They are brave and strong and I wish I could do more for them, but I cant." Ash said a little bit choked. The robot placed a synthetic hand on his shoulder.

"I see strength, passion and willing!" It said as it patted the captain's shoulder. Ash smiled and wiped a tear from his eye.

"So do I." Ash said as he caught Edwards eye and saluted to her. Edwards stood up proudly and saluted back to her captain. He feigned a smile but deep down his love to Edwards was like a drifting ship, far away. He gritted his teeth and cursed his rank, they should have been lovers, but it was never to be, nor would it ever be now that she was a drainer. He had contemplated back at Apple-wood farm, to become a drainer and run off into the wilds with her. Ever since, he had dreamed of the adventures they would have had, the freedom, togetherness and immortality. But recently he had pushed that dream down into the depths of his psyche and foregone love to be what he is, a ranger captain! He watched as the hero's finished their breakfast and then clambered up inside the confines of the hulking armoured suits. He waved stupidly knowing they couldn't see him waving. Tears cascaded down his cheeks as the armoured suits filed out at a steady trot and within half a minute all he could see was dust and sand brought up by the heavy stomps of the suits and the prevailing desert winds. He waited until he couldn't see the E.C.As through the clouds of dust before headed back inside the base. Dr Keinz followed Ash in.

"We have all done our best! It's now in their hands..." The robot said as its mechanical arm comforted Ash around his shoulders. Ash grumbled and tried to steady himself as he made his way toward the base door.

"God-speed!" He whispered before heading inside the habitat.

CHAPTER 18

"It's not far now, we should reach a trade house by sun-down." Brae said looking at his compass. They had all decided to veer off north/east towards a friendly trade house. Brae had outlined that it wasn't far off the trail towards utopia. Joshua stood at the top of a grassy foothill which had wild growing wheat. However the wheat plants were larger and more robust than any wheat plant he had ever seen.

"Why are the plants so big?" He grumbled as he rummaged through his pack to find his giga-counter. He scanned the overgrown plants and the giga-counter clicked above the back ground radiation which he had been used to reading. The wheat grass stood five feet tall and had bulbous seedlings fruiting. The wheat seed was nearly as big as corn seed.

"Not sure if we could eat this, the plants are registering above back ground radiation." Joshua said with a shrug. The others stood in the obscuring fields of wild wheat and shook their heads in dismay.

"This must be a rad zone!" Joshua claimed as he rifled through his pack to get out his rad-cape.

"Yeah, Joshua is right, don't pick this cereal and everybody get respirators on and rad-capes!" Brae watched the others donning radiation attire before he clambered inside his rad-cape and donned his respirator.

"Follow me!" Brae mumbled through his respirator. When everybody got suited up, they made a bee-line across the field of mutated wheat plants.

"Keep up!" Brae commanded as the journeying folk rushed though the tall, grass like plants. They headed through the tall mutated crop at a steady pace and stopped at a clearing. Four muscular, tall, strange looking farmers, armed with shotguns gathered in the clearing. Brae called a stop and lowered his rifle. The bald headed, muscular, mutated folk grinned as the travellers arrived. Brae being a ranger had already pin-pointed the leader, who seemed to have another half head growing out of his own head. Brae could feel bile rising when he saw the mutated looking farmer.

"We are lost." Brae said innocently. "We are heading north, I'm sorry that we have crossed your lands." Brae took a side glance at Yolanda who had already had her berretta in her gun hand. Feeling slightly safer he narrowed his eyes. The farmers started grinning and fanning out.

"We seek north only, but if we die this day, then so be it!" He claimed as he was ready to level his carbine against the mutated, inbred folks.

"Hey we can all be friends, can't we!" The leader looked towards his inbred, mutated kin. The likes of which was pretty gross on the biological scale.

"Drop your weapons and come with us!" The leader stated through both mouths which sounded like a stereo system. The other farmers were leering at the two females.

"Cant do that friend, we are heading north, I was thinking maybe we could give you a few coins for passing your farmland?" Brae said, but deep down he knew this was going to come to a fire fight. As the leader tried to speak, Brae interrupted.

"Fuck this! You go all hell and we go all hell and we all die this day, do you want that?" Brae had already shifted his feet into a firing stance, aiming his rifle at the leader.

"Are you ready to die?" Brae said as he aimed at the leader's heart with his M4. The leader threw out his arms and laughed.

"What you're failing to see! Is my siblings have out-flanked you and you have guns on you all around." The weird looking leader claimed, his arms outstretched like he was Jesus on the cross. Brae made a decision and hoped the others were on board. He squeezed the trigger of his rifle taking the multiple heads off the leader. He then combat rolled to the ground. The leaders head burst open like a log against an axe, showering brains, blood and cranium bits all over the corn fields. Shotguns fired wildly as more gun fire whizzed over Brae's head as he leaped into the cover of the tall wheat grass. He noticed Joshua un-loading his shot gun and cutting a strange looking farmer nearly in half. Brae knew he had twenty eight rounds left. He rolled and opened up his firearm sending a bullet through the head of a nearby assailant. Natasha didn't duck, instead she spun around on her heel and unloaded a bullet into one of the farm hands, taking the back of his skull out like a cat door in the wind. The dust seemed to settle and the combatants were scanning around for another kill. Two of the farm hands had thrown there shotguns to the floor in surrender. Brae stood and aimed putting a round in each of there heads, dropping them to the earthen floor.

"Anybody wounded?" Brae yelled as he got to his feet.

"We are good!" Joshua said scanning around seeing the dead. Yolanda walked forward and put two more rounds in the head of one of the farmers that was moaning.

"We take the farm house now!" Brae hissed as he pointed to the building beyond the corn fields. They all filed in rank behind Brae who was clearly angry.

"What of the shotguns?" Natasha said staggering around the corpses.

"Leave them! Let's hole up at the farm stead!" Brae spat with adrenalin rushing though his veins. As the travelling group approached the farm house building they could see females armed with shotguns gathered around the door.

"The sun is going down, we wish for shelter!" Brae said as he aimed his rifle towards the females. The strange inbred, females dropped their guns and allowed them to enter their farmstead.

"Yolanda you keep a gun on them, while we establish a place to hole up!" Brae couldn't remember the last time he was this angry, the fuckers attempted to kill them, for no reason at all. The farmstead building was quite big. It had a main living area and many other rooms reaching out from the main room. Brae did a sweep of the rooms as Yolanda kept the females occupied with the working end of her carbine.

"All rooms are clear!" Brae stated as he spooned a bowl of broth from the kettle cooking over the fire.

"Corn and some kind of meat stew?" He said as he tasted the broth.

"You gona be nice?" Brae directed his question to the three females huddled in the corner.

"We are nice." One of the females said as she licked her lips, in a sexual manner.

"We are going to hole up here for the night, you even think about hurting us then..." Brae pulled out his pistol and angled it to catch the flickering fire light.

"Then my little friend will put out your lights, forever!" He said as he put the pistol in his side holster.

"I will be on first watch, get some sleep and we switch in the next four hours!" Brae said as everybody agreed and bedded down.

Yolanda groaned and tried to turn over in her bed roll.

"Let me sleep, I'm so knackered." She moaned. Brae thought it was about time the others stayed watch so he clambered over to Joshua's bed and woke him up. He noticed Natasha clamped around him.

"Joshua, it's your watch!" Brae said harshly. Joshua growled and then rubbed his eyes and nodded.

"Yes it's my watch!" He fumbled around for his shot gun in the dim light of the lantern before grabbing up the trusty firearm.

"Get some sleep Brae, I will keep an eye on these ungodly creatures!" He climbed out of the bed roll and eyed the farm hand daughters, before cranking both barrels of his shot gun, levelling it towards the inbred females. Brae collapsed behind Yolanda and put his arm over her to hug her close to his body. Joshua nodded to the females hugging each other in the corner.

"Your brothers were unholy!" He said eying the young women. He bit his lip to try and stave off sleep. A bit of pain always wakes the senses.

"Have you any coffee in this un-holy house of yours?" Joshua asked, he needed a caffeine boost to stay awake. The eldest woman nodded and pointed to the tub on top of the shelf near the fire.

"Make myself and your sisters a cup of coffee!" He said slapping the side of his cheek. "But I'm keeping an eye on you so no silly business!" He warned. The middle aged woman got to her feet, her knees creaking on her bandy legs. They were all rake like and sported rashes and boil like growths on their flesh. Not one of them had a full head of hair, they looked like mangy dogs. He aimed the shot gun on her while she began to make coffee.

"We got no sugar!" She said looking over her shoulder towards Joshua.

"I don't care, just make it strong."

"You look like a preacher? Are you a godly man?"

She asked.

"I used to be..."

"Now that's a darned shame, we need preachers in this world. The world is full of hate..." She drifted off as drool dripped from the corners of her inbred mouth. She came out of her day dream and set about making the coffee pot. He kept his eye on her to make sure she wasn't slipping poison into the coffee pot, bubbling on the fire.

"Is they all dead Mr?" One of the younger daughters asked, her face innocent but her eyes looked to have seen terrible things.

"Yes, they are all dead. They were bad men. They had no right to live on earth with good folks." He said as though giving a Sunday sermon.

"But you killing the bad men, does that make you bad men?" The youngest asked as the older daughter to her side was slowly lifting up her dress and opening her legs with a dirty grin on her scabby face. He tried to ignore her and focused on the question.

"Yes, it's quite a paradox really, we are evil ourselves by taking a life, but if somebody didn't then more good lives would be lost." He nodded to the girl in appreciation too her valid question.

"Mr, they were bad men, they often beat on us and grunt up and down on us. They deserve to die for their sins." She whispered.

"Are you of the bright?" He asked the youngest, trying not to look at the other women slowly fingering her vagina and licking her lips.

"Yes sir, I have the book of the bright under my pillow." The younger said with a smile. The other sister slapped her hard against her face.

"Shut up Mary!" She shrieked. She looked to the preacher as Mary started to sob.

"What's the matter Mr, you never seen a pussy before?" She was real angry and clearly couldn't understand why the man wasn't paying attention to her. She tried to get to her feet but Joshua stood up quickly aiming the shotgun at her.

"Are you one of those gay boys, is that it? Is that what you are Mr?"

"Sit the fuck down!" Joshua yelled, waking the others.

"Susie, sit back down like a good girl." The eldest woman said while trying to pour coffee. Susie shot the older woman a glare and sat back down, elbowing Mary in her ribs to gain more space in the corner of the room.

"You folks have been a god send to our household. They were very bad men, they raped their own daughters regularly. I ain't even going to bury those..." She tried to swear but swearing was bad in the house when the men were around. Instead of swearing she passed the coffee cup to Joshua.

"I'm Beth, I was married under the bright to my husband Thomas. But he won't be going to the bright will he preacher?"

"No, he won't, that's for sure." Joshua nodded to affirm his authority in religious matters. He waited for the others to drink coffee before taking a sip. He looked to his friends and they had gone back to sleep, purring like pussy cats.

"Nice coffee." He said raising his mug to the hostess.

"We trade farm stuff to get the best coffee, Thomas did love his coffee." Beth said sitting down near the fire hugging the mug of coffee with both hands. He could see a burden had been lifted from the household. The only sour puss was Susie who clearly enjoyed being fucked by her father and brothers. She sat hugging her bony knees staring at the mould ridden wall.

"The farm will be a lot better now the men have gone." Beth said slurping her coffee. She had a bright smile on her face. She looked at Mary and smiled.

"Go and get your good book for the preacher, maybe he will read a sermon for us?" Beth said in a cheery tone. Joshua wasn't keen on the idea of the young girl leaving the room. He toyed with the idea that she might bring a firearm back.

"Be quick about it Mary, just get your book and come back as soon as you can." Joshua said pointing his finger at her. Mary smiled and rushed off to her bedroom to get the book of the bright. He watched her leave and relied on her innocent manner, gambling the lives of his own life and his friends. She came running back holding a moth eaten book. He quickly searched her for concealed weapons.

"You're a good girl Mary." He said as he took the book from her. He sat down and flicked through the pages to his favourite story. He placed his shotgun on his lap and started to read.

"David the traveller had travelled the land of Columbia and seen many things. He stopped at a small settlement where everybody wore simple clothing salvaged from the ruined city nearby." He eyed the three females and could see they were all looking at him wanting more words. "The people of tent town had sought shelter underground to survive from the fire and purging of the great bright. David saw these people as bright folks, clever folks who revered the great spherical god. Many days passed as David brought the words of god to the survivors and established a larger tent as a church to the bright one..." Joshua read on into the night, captivating the small audience, including the sex hungry Susie.

"Best nights kip I've had in ages." Yolanda said stretching out the sleep from her body. She eyed the three females sleeping in a bundle of blankets near the fire. Joshua had dark bruises under his eyes, he must have stayed watch all night.

"Thank you Joshua, I think we all needed a good night's sleep. Tonight you sleep like a king and the rest of us will stay on watch." Yolanda said as she began to massage Joshua's shoulders. Brae was busy stoking the fire back up to prepare and cook breakfast. Natasha was still fast asleep snoring like a ranger.

"Any trouble Josh?"

"No trouble at all, in fact our hosts enjoyed my sermons read from the book of the bright. Isn't it fascinating that the book of the bright has reached to these northern parts." He said with a cheery grin.

"That's great Josh, thanks for staying watch, Yolanda needed a good kip." Brae said winking at Yolanda. He cocked his head to one side and smiled at Joshua.

"You look like you have found the bright again?"

"I must admit, it was nice to read those words again, I kind of miss the church."

"Well you can set up another church when we reach utopia." Brae said absent minded as he placed strips of pork on the spit to cook.

"That would be nice, but unfortunately I know the truth now and I've abandoned the very thought of a higher power." Joshua said bitterly. Brae stopped what he was doing and appraised the man. Joshua looked weathered and worldly travelled, he wasn't the pathetic creature that he first met, by a long shot. Brae even contemplated on the idea of persuading him to become a ranger.

"You're a good man Joshua and it's a shame that you have turned your back on religion. I still gesture the sign of our lord before going into battle. The bright god is a ranger in my eyes. It protects the good and destroys the evil." Brae claimed, remembering the ranger doctrines.

"I still look to the sun for hope, but nowadays I just see the sun and not an intelligent being with supreme power." Joshua said as he wandered to the door.

"Think I might take a stroll, the morning sun will re-energise me I think." With that said he left the farm house. Brae woke Natasha up and they all tucked into some breakfast while the hosts still snored near the fire.

"It's still early and the coffee is nice, we should hang around for a few hours before setting off, what do you think?" Brae asked.

"It would be nice to relax for a while. We have been hitting the trail hard for the last month or so." Yolanda said between mouthfuls of cooked salted pork.

"Then let's stay and recharge out batteries." Brae said with a grin.

Joshua had wandered back to the clearing where they nearly lost their lives to the bunch of unholy bastards that owned the farm. He sighed as he peered over the carnage, seeing the corpse of the young lad that he put both barrels of his shotgun into his guts.

"Sorry son, you backed the wrong dice." He whispered as he reached down to close the young lad's eyes. He was about to make a bright gesture and then shook his head.

"No more bullshit!" He said to himself. He heard a rustling sound from behind him. He turned to the noise and saw an angry looking skinny man rushing toward him brandishing a large calibre revolver. He attempted to grab his pistol from his gun belt but the man bludgeoned him in the face with the heavy steel of the pistol. His eyes illuminated for a brief second and he felt some of his teeth un-lodge as his knees buckled to the floor...

"You awake preacher?" He heard a voice in the darkness of his vision, light filtered in and out as his body fought for consciousness. He felt cold steel in his mouth and an iron like taste in his mouth.

"What the fuck?" Joshua managed to mumble but his tongue couldn't articulate the words, due to the pistol muzzle in his mouth. He opened one blurry eye and felt the weight of a man sat on his chest, leering down toward him. The man had a withdrawn face, his left eye cloudy with a film of cataract.

"You killed my brothers you son-of-a-bitch!" The angry man yelled as foul smelling spittle showered his face.

"You got'a gang up there? At the farm house?" The angry man said as he pushed the barrel of the gun deeper in his mouth making him gag and cough. Joshua slapped the pistol out of his mouth and tried to get to his feet. But the weight of his assailant kept him fast on the floor. The angry man put the working end of the pistol to Joshua's forehead.

"Speak up bitch?" The scabby faced man yelled.

"Your brothers tried to kill us last night. We barely walked away with our lives!" Joshua yelled, hoping his friends would hear his plight.

"How many mother fucker?" The man covered Joshua's mouth with an unwashed stinky hand, as he nervously looked around the clearing, deep in the wheat fields.

"Rangers!" He managed to mumble through the

palm of the nasty man's hand.

"All I can see is my father and my brothers are all dead!" Tears cascaded down his withdrawn cheeks, his good eye red with salty tears.

"You're coming with me!" The man said as he pulled Joshua to his feet. Joshua noticed his pistol lying in the dirt, as he was dragged toward the farmhouse.

"I ain't seen a fucking ranger for years! The last ranger that came all up here is buried in the wheat fields. But not before we had our fun on him!" The evil man said with a grin. Joshua couldn't believe how strong the withered man was? It was like he had super human strength. After a while as they approached the farm stead the man had let go of him. Now and then kicking Joshua forwards and spinning the barrel of the heavy pistol, mocking him.

"They are good people!" Joshua said while spitting out teeth and blood.

"Fuck you preacher, they are all gona die for what they did!" The man spat. They had come out of the wheat fields and could see the farmstead. He felt the barrel of the gun on his back nudging him forward. As they got to the foot of the door, Joshua felt an impact on the back of his head. His vision tunnelled and his last vision witnessed the floor coming quick with a crunch before darkness shrouded his mind.

Brae looked up from his breakfast plate as the door of the farmstead nearly came off its hinges. He was quick to combat roll forward pulling out his side arm. A silhouette of a man stormed into the living space firing wildly, with a noisy revolver. Yolanda flew through the air as a high calibre bullet hit her square in the chest. Brae watched in almost slow motion as his lover smashed against the dining room table, splitting the table in half under the momentum. He just raised his side arm, when Natasha unloaded two rounds from her snub nosed pistol dropping the foe. The assailant landed in a heap at the door, thrashing around due to the agonising pain in his abdomen.

"Is that all you..." The man gurgled and vomited up blood around his pale face. He lay there for a while fighting off death. The man put up quite a battle before he laid still. Brae pointed at Yolanda, blood had pooled around her.

"Yolanda!" Brae shrieked as he crawled his way toward her. Yolanda wasn't breathing; blood had stopped pumping from the wound in her chest.

"Natasha!" Brae cried he was doubled up in the agony of loss. "Do something!" He looked. But even when his words left his lips he knew Yolanda was dead. He cowered up into a foetus position, hugging his knees and rocking back and too and forth.

"She's dead Brae, I'm sorry." Natasha said, as she held her fingers against Yolanda's neck.

"No... No... No!" Brae cried as he rocked back and forth. "She wasn't supposed to die like this!" He sobbed. Natasha sat down next to him and put her arm around him.

"She is in the bright now. No pain, no combat, just

heaven in the warm sun." She claimed tying to console him. "She will be waiting for you my friend."

"I hope so." He whispered before crawling toward the fire place to sleep. The females had all woken up by this stage and were wondering what had unfolded.

"That's Graham, he set out a few days ago to trade wares at the trade house." Beth said as she looked toward the broken table and the blonde woman dead on the floor.

"Why didn't you tell us there was another brother wandering around out there?" Natasha said as she narrowed her eyes towards Beth.

"You and your friends killed my kin in the fields. I have already thanked Joshua for your deeds. It was a tense situation. I thought you were going to kill all of us?" Beth said with a tone of brimming and righteous anger. Natasha shook her head.

"Shame on you all, I hope you all rot in hell!" She hissed before kneeling next to the corpse of Yolanda. "Shame on you all!" She whispered as she looked to Brae shuddering next to the fire hearth, mourning his lover. Joshua staggered into the living space, blood dribbling from his forehead.

"There's a..." He looked to his feet noticing the corpse with two bullet holes in his chest.

"I'm too late!" He moaned as he saw the bloodied corpse of Yolanda underneath the shattered wooden table. He looked at Brae and then to Natasha. He gave Beth an angry frown before he sat next to Natasha as she gently stroked the body of Yolanda.

Joshua and Brae took a while digging a deep grave for Yolanda, out in the wheat fields. They both were silent and Joshua wondered if Brae would carry on the quest to utopia. He would understand if he didn't. When they laid Yolanda to rest, wrapped up in blankets, Joshua opened the moth eaten book of the bright. Everybody gathered around the grave, but only Brae was weeping.

"Sleep tight my lover." Brae said wiping tears from his cheeks.

"As we lay this hero to rest, may the bright carry her soul to the warmth of the sun." Joshua said. He made an extra effort for his dead friend and read out many passages from the book of the bright. Brae was silent throughout the blessing, which was understandable. Natasha sprinkled earth onto the grave.

"I will miss her dearly. Yolanda was kind and affectionate toward me, she taught me how to field strip a rifle and to maintain my pistol. She was a good friend and always will be. My prayers to the bright will always include my good friend Yolanda." She bowed and kissed her own hand and then gestured toward the grave. However, she noticed Brae breathing deeply and pulling out his pistol.

"I'm sorry but Yolanda died because you failed to tell us about the other brother!" He had his pistol raised, aiming at Beth. His hands were shaking like a shitting dog. Beth started to flee, seeing the anger on his face.

"Yolanda died because of you!" Brae said as his finger locked on the trigger. The bullet hit Beth in her back, bowling her over into the dirt. Natasha tried to grab the gun as he aimed at Susie, but it was too late. The bullet hit Susie's forehead knocking her to the ground. He tried to aim at Mary but Natasha had pulled the pistol from his grasp and struck him hard against his head, knocking him to the ground. Mary stood breathing heavily but fixed to the ground, she was lucky, if Natasha hadn't grabbed the pistol in time, she would have been dead too. Brae started to sob again wrapped up in grief.

"She comes with us to utopia!" Natasha yelled. "She has had a shit life already and the promise lands await!" Natasha put her boot on Brae's back and shook her head in dismay.

"I'm sorry I don't know what to do!" Brae pleaded, his loss had taken a massive chunk out of his psyche.

"She is probably pregnant, have you thought of that?" She kicked Brae in his face, busting his nose. Brae recoiled from the impact and groaned.

"Never figured that!" He mumbled through staunching the blood flow from his broken nose.

The next morning the travellers set off. They armed the young girl with a double barrelled shotgun, with plenty of ammo. They didn't take much from the farmstead due to the radioactivity from the area. They did take the coffee tub along with other products that hadn't been farmed from the local area. The young girl, Mary didn't seem that bothered that her family had been wiped out. In fact she seemed quite cheerful. She kept her distance from Brae, but other that that she took a shine to the fellow travellers. Especially with the hope of the promised lands called utopia.

"We head north on this bearing." Brae announced to the group as he focused on the needle of his nautical compass. The landscape was hilly and dotted with stout pine trees. They camped down at night in available clearings and filled their canteens from clear running springs. They performed a quick trade at the outland trade house, mostly using the now deceased Yolanda's coin which she had in abundance. Brae didn't seem to mind using his dead lover's coin stash. Summer started to delve into winter, but it was unclear due to the evergreen trees. However, snow had started to fall on the high hills. The group of travellers had only passed by a small number of travelling folk. Brief trades but mostly they relied on hunting game. Brae bagged a few deer and the travellers used the cold climate to freeze dry the meat. They all hoped to get to utopia soon but it was still many miles to travel on foot. They had dropped down to a basin in the land and the land went from snow to hot sandy desert. Brae used his ranger training to find water holes. Sometimes his judgment was off slightly but eventually they found water to fill their canteens. There had been a lot of moaning and dehydration before he located a water hole.

"It can't be too far now?" Joshua said as he drank the last dribbles from his canteen.

"Not to far, now my friend!" Brae claimed as he pointed north to another oasis.
Joshua looked to Natasha and noticed her lips were cracked and her forehead red due to the unforgiving heat of the desert.

"Really?" Joshua said shaking his head. Everybody had taken off their armour and stowed it on their back packs. Joshua looked to Mary and could see she was seriously dehydrated.

"Mary is fucked, she can't take any more travel!" Joshua said. Brae doubled back and lifted the young girl to a piggy-back. She patted Brae on his shoulders.

"You okay?"

"Yes, now that I have a hero!" The young girl said as she leaned her head to him. They marched on through the sand dunes heading north toward utopia.
Hero! And to think I was gona murder the little bitch. He thought

CHAPTER 19

"I still can't believe how quick these bad boys run on the land." Jessica said smiling, hugging her arms around one of the legs of the mighty E.C.As. They had stopped to camp in a small clearing of trees to hide the tall mechanical war machines. Sandings had climbed up the back of his E.C.A and was sat on the right shoulder plate. Using the vantage he peered through his binoculars at the landscape past the trees.

"Hey guys, I can just make out Applewood in the distance." He said quietly.

"I've been thinking, we could bypass Applewood and stick with the plan. Or should we have a look and find out what the fuck happened there?" Edwards asked, she never really went against orders, but she wanted to know what happened to Captain Harris.

"So now that you're a drainer you think you can break command?" Angel, shot her an angry look.

"Edwards is right, I'm also curious to know. Maybe they are still alive but just have a busted radio set?" Sandings said from the top of his E.C.A. Jessica was still busy hugging her new toy to care about the conversation.

"What and I'm not curious?" Angel snapped towards Sandings.

"Nobody's saying that Angel."

"Look I'm in command, I'm gona let you all camp down and rest up for the night and while you cop some Zzzzs, I will scout out apple farm. It should only take four hours or so." Edwards said eyeing Angel.

"I'll come with you?" Jessica had decided to join the conversation.

"Naa, you will slow me down, stay here and protect each other." Edwards said and smiled at Jessica, it was nice to have some kind of backing, even from a bitch. While, they set up watch and ate supper, Edwards prepared a small kit and rushed off into the dusk.

"Who's next in command, if the drainer doesn't come back?" Jessica smiled, winking at Angel.

"That would be Sandings, he has rank. You're just a private Jess." Angel pointed at the newly drafted female ranger.

"I used to be a corporal when I first ran with the rangers, but that was long ago." Jessica said poking the small camp fire with a stick.

"Then in theory Jess, you outrank me too. Solo's don't carry much weight in the rank system. Because we can't order ourselves around. My rank is just all show, but I'm definitely no leader, nor do I want such a title." Angel said as she spooned hot beans fresh from the can into her mouth.

Edwards made good headway through the night toward Applewood. She was amazed how the new armour didn't slow her down, when she was setting off she did contemplate on leaving it, but now she was glad she kept the armour on. Another hour passed and she reached the foot of Applewood, she slowed her pace and started to use her night vision, to check for tracks. She found none, but that didn't mean anything, the soviets if they had compromised Applewood, could have taken a different bearing and it was unlikely they headed south. Heavy clouds had obscured the star light and the weather changed and started to drizzle. She picked her way up an embankment, still looking for tracks until she saw buildings and fortification ahead. She sniffed the night air and couldn't smell her kin on the light breeze but she could smell rotting flesh. She chambered a round in her carbine and skirted around a stockade. That's when she found the first ranger corpse, rotting and impaled on one of the stockades. *So they were attacked!* She thought. She put her back against an out building and skirted along its length peering around the corner of the wooden building. More corpses were scattered around and it was clear the rangers had been field stripped of ammo and weapons. The main building was peppered with bullets and damaged in many places from grenade explosions. Her keen eyes picked up a number of drainers, dead with advanced rot. They had been cut down by small arms fire, just outside the main farm building. In her mind eye she played out the fierce battle that took place here. *Harris must be here somewhere, one of the corpses probably*. She wondered as she entered the main building and shook her head seeing the corpses of farmhands, men, women and children scattered around the main living space. Rudimentary firearms still clutched in their rotting hands. It wasn't long before she found the decapitated form of Captain Harris. The head was missing but it was definitely Harris due to the medals attached to his armoured jacket. The soviets must have hit this place hard and then headed towards Main Bridge. She hoped Main-Bridge had broken the small soviet army? But chances are the soviets recruited infected folks here and filled out their ranks. She dismissed such thoughts and bolstered her mind like a ranger, in the hope the township had fucked the approaching army. Doubt still lingered and logic lifted in her mind. She puffed out her cheeks and shook her head.

"Stop trying to kid yourself. They are all dead!" She whispered to herself. In the corner of the room she spotted a radio set that looked to be intact. She balled her fist and tapped her foot, she didn't wish to tell Ash she had veered away from the mission, but it was only right to report what had happened here at Applewood.

"Fuck it!" She sighed and wandered over to the radio set. She switched it on and noticed the battery life was low, but still had enough power to communicate. She twirled the knob to set it at the ranger frequency and squeezed the handset button.

"This is ranger Edwards, I'm at Applewood. All are dead, including captain Harris." She felt the presence of Ash on the receiver.

"That was not part of the plan sergeant!" Ash barked from the safety of the new habitat, his voice was a mixture of anger and dismay.

"Sorry sir, I had to know." Edwards said. She could hear the click of another radio set coming on line. Angel, Sandings and Jessica had opened one of the E.C.As and were gathered in the confines of the mechanical armour.

"Ash was right, we should have pleaded with Harris to move everybody from Applewood!" Angel said through the radio communications.

"Angel stand down, I need to hear the sergeants report." Ash barked with a choke in his voice.

"Captain Harris..." Ash made a gesture to the bright and continued. "He should have sought my council, but now..."

"They put up quite a fight to the very last human life, including children, the bright take their souls." Edwards stated.

"We could have saved everybody!" Ash sobbed. His finger lingered on the speak button and the listeners could hear the torment in his tone.

"I'm returning to the mission!" Edwards said finally and tossed the radio equipment into the corner before smashing it to pieces.

"Ash! Are you still there?" Angel said as she elbowed the others to gain some space. Jessica and Sandings made some room to the point they were hanging out of the back of the E.C.A.

"I'm still here Angel, report?" His tone had switched back to the mission like he had somehow sobered up from the dire news.

"I won't tell you where we are, just in case this frequency has been compromised by the enemy. The solo stated, she had been accustomed to that all those years of being a solo operator.

"We will wait for our team leader to return and follow the plan!" Angel announced.

"May the bright guild your thoughts and god speed!" Ash said before clicking off the radio handset. The mission group followed protocol and on Jessica's watch Edwards returned.

"Jess?" Edwards whispered from the tree line. Jessica stood next to the camp fire with a battle-rifle in her arms.

"Is that you Edwards?" She stamped her foot to wake the others, just in case it was an enemy. Groans and moans came from the sleeping bags near the fire. She could see them kick themselves out of the bedding, standing up arming themselves and swaying around trying to fight sleep and rubbing their eyes.

"Yeah it's me." Edwards appeared near the camp fire with her arms in the air. She crouched near the camp fire and warmed her undead hands near the warmth of the fire.

"Such a sneaky little fucker, aren't you!" Jessica said trying not to chuckle, before shouldering her rifle.

"We move out at dawn as planned, everybody get some kip, I will be on watch now!" Edwards said as she approached Jessica.

"You said you used to be a corporal in the

rangers." Edwards smiled as she produced a silver corporal badge and began fastening the badge to Jessica's breast plate. Jessica looked down to the shiny badge and smiled.

"Thank you Sergeant..." Jessica said cocking her head to one side and peering into Edwards weird yellowish shining eyes.

"It's only right Jess, you earned this rank a long time ago."

"You took the badge from one of Harris's rangers didn't you?" Jessica frowned but still smiled proudly, as the sergeant finished off fixing the silver badge.

"Just remember Jessica, if I die, you and Sandings are next in command!" Edwards nodded and then pointed to the bed rolls near the fire.

"Now all of you get some sleep!"

The hulking mechanical armoured unit made a bee-line across the desert toward the destroyed ranger fort. The amount of ground the E.C.As could cover was phenomenal. It had only been a few hours before they could see the ruined fort in the distance across the desert. Each unit had headsets and communications on a private line between each E.C.A. Jessica thought it was amazing how the head sets drowned out the noise of the moving mechanical armour and the microphone near their mouth only picked up audible language and ignored the click, crunch and squeal of the ambient sounds inside an E.C.A.

"Is that the ruins of the fort ahead?" Jessica

asked.

"Yes, this is where it all started, the soviet attack from the ruins, the exodus, the attack in the desert that turned me into the..." Edwards said, she was still fighting between the memories of being alive and the new memories becoming a drainer.

"You are what you are, but you have proved yourself as a human sergeant!" Sandings commented over the communication line.

"We were lucky to get out of that fort alive, if it wasn't for you Edwards we would have all been dead or one of the undead!" Angel said, as she tried not to be prejudice against the sergeant.

"Angel, I would have laid down my life if my fellow rangers got killed or turned into the abomination that I'm now!" Edwards whispered over the communications.

"I didn't have a choice, I Just turned!" Edwards said sombrely.

"Draining bitch!" Jessica said as a joke and then laughed though the radio set.

"We are coming in hot! Everybody stagger your pace, the soviets could have R.P.Gs so each unit needs to fan out as we approach!" Edwards ignored the joke and got back to her team leader stance.

"Scanners aren't picking up much but we need to be careful!" Sandings said. The heavy armour units made the distance to the blasted and ruined fort.

"We are in firing range now, everybody bolster themselves!" Jessica yelled down the communications, as the armoured units climbed the last sand dune upto the ruined fortification.

"Weapons hot!" Edwards said, as she punched out some buttons in the suit, putting the E.C.A into battle mode. They all did as the sergeant stated and they could hear the left shoulder gun going a systematic auto-track mode. The left shoulder mounted weapon on the E.C.A was a twenty millimetre self-seeking automatic gun. Jessica clicked a switch inside the armoured suit which brought the missile launcher on-line. She looked to the ammo count and grinned at the full missile magazine of twelve, heat seeking missiles, ready to cause carnage.

"Missiles on-line!" Jessica stated while chuckling, she clearly wished to lose some of the major weapons from the E.C.A.

"Jess is now the heavy support, everybody, concentrate on movement in the fortress!" Edwards said as her unit entered the blasted fort. The mechanical units came to a standstill in the main courtyard of the ruined fortress.

"Is anybodies scanners picking up any kind of life-forms?" Edwards said as she looked at the pulsing scanner display inside her E.C.A.

"My suit is not reregistering shit!" Sandings agreed.

"We, erm... Maybe need to take a look around?" Edwards said through the communications, but her tone was cautious.

"Let's take a peek." Jessica finally announced.

The back flap of each armoured suit hissed open and each occupant leapt to the dusty floor armed with a variety of firearms. Each pilot of the suit clicked a hand held transponder which closed the back flap of the E.C.As. Sergeant Edwards looked to the others and nodded.

"You all ready?"

"Yeah!" came as unison. As the small armed group picked their way through the rubble towards what appeared to be a cave mouth of a collapsed concrete building. Jessica had stowed her battle rifle over her shoulder and pulled out both her pistols.

"I wouldn't be surprised if they have left a number of the drainers here, in ambush?" Edwards wasn't sure. But she wanted to warn her group to keep on guard. The group approached the broken doorway that she knew had a stairwell to the upper-floor. She had her carbine rifle to her chin as she entered the dark. She clicked on her gun flash light as Sandings and Angel did the same. As they entered, circles of light shined a path forward. Jessica had shifted her way forward and relied on the light coming from Edward's rifle. They ascended the dark stair and it wasn't long before they entered the old office of Captain Ash. The torch light from their weapons performed a sweep of the old office. It's when something stirred in the shadows. Jessica spotted the movement and open fired with both her pistols, missing the fast moving target making a bee-line towards Sergeant Edwards. The power of the pale armoured body bowled Edwards to the ground. It's thrashing claws a flurry as the squad backed off cursing. Jessica holstered her pistols and dived towards the melee with her boot bowie-knife, leading the way. She could feel the strength of the undead creature thrashing around below her as she tried to put her knife through the armoured foe.

"Get this fucker off me!" Edwards yelled as she tried to get a foot hold. Jessica's knife couldn't penetrate the steel armour the drainer wore.

"Shoot this fucker!" Jessica yelled as she combat rolled into the corner, still with knife in hand, she dropped her knife and went for her desert eagle putting two rounds in the side of the frantic foe. Angel and Sandings tired to get a proper shot with their carbines, but trying to aim at the creature thrashing around above Sergeant Edwards. The bullets ripped up the back of the drainer until it laid still, putting a dead weight on poor Edwards. She gasped for air and kicked the corpse away from herself. Angel grabbed hold of the sergeant and pulled her from under her gore ridden assailant as Sandings put another round in the drainer's head, just to make sure. Edwards climbed to her feet and punched the nearby wall, bursting concrete. She rounded on them all and spat at the floor.

"That was an elder Drainer, fuck knows how many more the soviets have if they can fuck over a few humans and a fledgling drainer like myself." Edwards braced herself against the concrete wall, her lungs breathing twice the normal human capacity.

"We need to step up our game..." Edwards hissed as she tied to slow her breathing.

"We are still strong Sergeant!" Sandings said.

"No! We fucking aren't, at all!" Edwards said between breaths, she rubbed the blood from her armour and curled her lip.

"What chance do we have against such a foe?" She shrieked.

"We have armour and a devastating weapon to deliver to those mother fuckers!" Jessica said as she grabbed hold of Edwards arm.

"We can do this now, but we need you onboard!" Jessica said as she locked eyes with Edwards. The drainer shook her head and nodded.

"You are a true Ranger Jess, all of you are!" Edwards said as she staunched the wound on her neck. Blood dribbled between her fingers. Sandings got out his field kit and started to bandage around her neck wound.

"I know your body will regenerate this, I'm assuming you require blood? The ranger said as she pulled up his sleeve.

"I can't..." Edwards gulped, as she slid down the wall. "I can't risk infection!"

"Fuck that!" Jessica stated as she grabbed hold of the field kit, pulling out the blood transfusion kit. She pushed the needle into her arm drawing blood around the needle head. She then found a nice vein on Sergeant Edwards and started to transfuse her blood into the drainer. Edwards grinned and relaxed, her eyes looked drugged as the fresh blood entered her body.

"Gee it looks as though you have just had a hit of morphine?" Sandings chuckled, watching Edwards rife around on the floor chuckling. Angel grabbed the drainers head to still her, she noticed the bleeding had stopped around her neck and the wound looked to be knitting together before her very eyes.

"I think you have had enough bitch." Jessica grinned and pulled out the needle from her arm.

"Oh come on just a few seconds more, it's wonderful." Edwards moaned. Everybody had started to laugh apart from Angel, all she saw was a junkie and a dangerous one at that if she got a taste for human blood. She had to walk away before she said something horrible to her commanding officer.

The travellers made a good sweep of the fortress, adding extra ammo to the stocks the E.C.As were burdening. Edwards had hidden stock piles of equipment they couldn't carry before the soviets arrived. They found some of the stashes but most were buried under a couple of feet of rubble.

"You certainly did a number on the fortress Edwards." Sandings said trying to remember what the fortress used to be like before they set all those explosive traps. "Jess, you should have seen the fucker go up when the filthy soviets entered the fort. It had to be the loudest explosion I have ever heard." He said winking at Jessica. Jessica grinned back and then stuck out her tongue and rolled her eyes at him. He took a little bit of offence to the gesture and looked away from her. If she continued to be nice to him it would only be a matter of time before he came on to her, so she thought it best to nip it in the bud earlier. She had grown tired of explaining to horny men what a lesbian is and they still don't secretly crave cock! Angel was busy strapping ammo-pouches and more water bottles to her E.C.A, when Jessica approached. She could feel tension in the air around Angel and had two minds to leave her be.

"What?" Angel huffed.

"Nothing, I just came over to see how you are? I'm fucking regretting it now though." She smiled trying to make it a joke, but Angel just ignored her and carried on securing equipment. After a few more seconds of silent treatment Jessica scowled at her and then began to wander away. Angel placed her palms on the cold metal of the walking armour and sighed.

"Jess we need to talk."

"Shit!" Jessica whispered, she knew what Angel was going to say, she had heard it many times before from other lovers. *I'm not ready for a relationship. I need some time to adjust. I'm not as keen as you are on pussy.* She ran through a few excuses in her mind.

"If you want..." Jessica began her speech to make it easier for Angel to break up with her.

"Eh? What? No!" Angel scowled. "The world does not revolve around you Jessica... What I needed to say..." Angel looked to Edwards chatting with Sandings over by the cave mouth, making sure they were not in ear-shot.

"The problem is Edwards being a drainer. I saw what happened and I know she is a ticking time bomb." Angel whispered. Jessica felt anger and rejection wash away from her mind.

"Go on?" Jessica prompted and walked towards Angel.

"It's a question of trust? Can we trust her to complete the mission, knowing we are about to exterminate her kin."

"She is a Ranger and she has already proved herself to be one of us." Jessica said attempting to dilute the doubt from Angels mind. Angel peered into Jessica's large green eyes and smiled.

"Maybe your right... I'm sorry." She smiled and rapped her arms around Jessica's shoulders and kissed her. Jessica relaxed in her embrace.

"I love you Jess and I don't want to break up with you, or whatever you might have been thinking in that fucked up mindset that you call a brain." Angel squeezed her again and then focused on securing the equipment to the E.C.A.

"Erm... Good." She nodded and left Angel to finish up.

The armoured column moved out, leaving the fortress behind them. Every step from the mighty walkers brought up sand and dust in their wake. In the confines of the E.C.A Jessica bit her lip thinking back to what Angel had said. Only a few of her past lovers had mentioned the L-word, but for some reason this felt like the truth.

"I love you too Angel" She whispered and then panicked and checked to see if the communications were still live. The red L.E.D pulsed on the communication setting. She thanked the bright the L.E.D wasn't green and live. She looked to the time setting on the heads up display and wished time would skip to night time quickly so she could bed down with such a fantastic woman. The communications hissed.

"We are about to head inside the ruined city. I will take lead, Angel on my six. Sandings and Jessica you watch the flanks. Set your bearing north east and the bright watch over us!" Edwards announced through the comms. The others did as commanded and manually set the bearing to north east. They all knew the ruins were going to be life threatening. Undead soviets were the least of their problems in the ruins. All manner of hideous creatures dwelled in radioactive ruined cities. The armoured units stomped into a small square where rusted cars laid flat on their chassis. The scanners had picked up movement and numerous targets from a high rise building to the south.

"Contact!" Sandings announced as a few bullets hit the E.C.A's.

"Cocky raiders I suspect, but I don't think they have the fire power to bring down our units." Edwards claimed. A few more bullets hit the group, mostly wildfire from the more adventurous or bored raiders. A small homemade rocket streamed from the upper floor of the building but it missed and exploded pathetically against a rusty old car, taking off a side door.

"We best give them a warning!" Edwards sighed as she shifted her walker to face the building. She clicked on the auto-gun which traced the movement in the building. She fired a number of twenty millimetre rounds from the mounted shoulder gun and witnessed a small mist of blood near a window. Audio-sensors picked up a scream followed by some guttered curses and then it all fell quiet.

"Move out! I think they have learnt a life lesson!" Edwards sneered, before taking back up the lead.

Angel had spent a long time in the ruined city and she knew of secret ways and shortcuts, but that was back when she was on foot and not in a hulking suit of mechanical armour. The party lost a number of hours navigating around blocked off streets and freshly collapsed buildings. She assumed the soviets had planted explosives, bringing down buildings to create a strategic maze. She was also thrown by some of the streets which had been cleared for tracked type heavy vehicles.

"We need to head south again to cross the bridge. We haven't tested the E.C.As to cross open water." Angel said referring to the many rivers that broke up the city. Everybody had noticed the built in giga-counter needle rising as they neared the main crater where numerous tactical warheads had landed. They were safe from the radiation in the E.C.As but their minds worried about mechanical failure. Jessica looked to her flank camera and could see the massive crater just past the skeletal buildings petering on the edge. It was a miracle those buildings still stood to this day. She could see it had rained recently and formed a potent looking lake with an almost mercury like film on the top of the shimmering water.

"Anyone fancy a swim?" Jessica chuckled over the comms.

"You first Jess." Sandings laughed.

"Knock that shit off!" Edwards barked. Something large surfaced in the lake and then ducked under the metallic looking water. Everybody gulped having witnessed the abomination or whatever the fuck it was?

"By the bright!" Sandings mumbled. "What in the fuck was that?"

"Stay on course, whatever it is? It's aquatic and dwells there." Edwards claimed with fear in her voice. They double timed it having seen the monstrosity and marched further inland away from the steady radioactive hiss of the missile made lake. The bridge was coming up on the forward camera. It seemed the soviets had been busy clearing a path for vehicles, pushing the ruined cars to each side of the bridge. The on-board scanners weren't picking up mines or traps so they ventured quickly across the bridge. With each heavy foot fall the bridge groaned and squealed on the old suspension ropes. Luckily the bridge wasn't too long. They had lost numerous hours navigating the ruins but the edge of the city wasn't too far. They could continue in the dark using the on-board night vision but decided to hole up at a wonky looking filling station called 'Billy's Gas Station'. The filling station had a faded 'BP' shield motif swinging in the light breeze. They figured they had reached an uncertain safety where the radiation had subsided and a good place to camp before the sun went down. Angel wished to carry on, but the E.C.As engine temperature had climbed into the red zone and required a cool off period. They parked up the E.C.As at the gas station and left them too cool off. They shouldered small backpacks and headed into the old filling station. After a quick sweep they prepared to camp down. Angel brought out a small battery powered camping stove. She warned them a camp fire would be bad so close to the main ruins. Edwards took up watch, she didn't require sleep so Sandings bedded down to get some Zs. Angel and Jessica climbed inside shared bedding and started to make out whispering to one another. Edwards turned a blind eye and ear to what was going on between the female lovers. Several times she walked the perimeter to get away from the sobs of sexual activity going on, which she took distaste to. Edwards looked upto the gibbous moon and took a deep breath, she cursed her extraordinary hearing and hummed a song to drown out the noises coming from the shared female bed. She thought of Ash, her captain, far away, alone. She knew her love for the man was cursed now that now she was undead. Her mind fluttered around all the wasted times when she was human and could have made a move on Ash. But reality set in and she grimaced. *Now that I'm an abomination Ash will never take me as his bride.* She thought.

"I'm destined to walk the ash-land... Alone..." She whispered into the night.

CHAPTER 20

With chapped lips the group approached the next water hole. Brae was staggering now, carrying the young girl in his arms. Mary had passed out hours ago and her breathing was shallow against the nape of his neck.

"Not far now baby... We will have water soon." He mumbled through tunnelled vision, he felt the weight he was carrying in his arms and his mind wondered if he would pass out now, even if the water hole was so close. He looked over his shoulders and could see Joshua in the distance arm in arm with Natasha. Both looked ready to drop. He placed Mary down into the sands and laboured to put his arm up.

"Water!" He tried to yell, but his throat just rasped with dehydration. He shook both of his fists and took another fiery hot desert breath.

"WATER!" He managed to point to the oasis before the tunnel of vision closed up into darkness. Time passed, it was a waking pass of time, drifting in and out of consciousness. His vision turned dark and in the distance he could see Yolanda, she was making her way toward him with a smile on her face and her arms open.

"Yolanda my love." He whispered. He felt water cascade over his face and felt his throat constrict as the dribble of liquid made him cough. He spluttered and tried to elbow himself up but the strength had left his body. Darkness fell again, but his mouth was no longer dry. A numb pulling registered on his mind, he felt his limbs stretched and a dull pain cascaded over him.

"Leave me!" He whispered through cracked lips, he was angry that Yolanda was no longer in his mind eye. A dull sound in his ears, a scraping on sand, darkness fell again but time must have passed and he felt a cool sensation of liquid on his face.

"You found water Brae!" He heard a voice he couldn't recollect. He tried to open his eyes but when he did bright light shone so he closed them quickly.

"Yolanda!" He moaned as more water trickled into his mouth. The darkness turned to light under his eyelids. He could feel his body, the pains of muscular activity. Every nerve ending hurt.

"Drink a little water Brae." A female voice? He felt the trickle of water in his mouth and again he coughed and spluttered but this time his vision focused. He was laid on the sand and saw angelic Natasha smiling back at him. Her face was sunburnt and her lips were cracked and sore looking.

"Natasha?" He mumbled.

"He is awake." Natasha announced as he saw Joshua face peer over with a beaming smile.

"We thought we lost you there, my son." He grinned. Brae could hear water sloshing in the back ground as his body started to come too.

"You saved Mary my friend. You are a hero."

Joshua smiled and put his forehead against his.

"I'm so sorry Joshua, my bearing was wrong."

"Your bearing was right my friend, you saved us all!" Joshua said as he placed a wet cloth against Braes forehead. Brae felt the cold compress on his head and started to weep again for the loss of Yolanda.

"Ssshhussh Now, my friend." Joshua patted his bare shoulder.

"My armour?" Brae wondered.

"Sorry sir but you are naked now. We took off your clothing and armour and swabbed water over your body to keep your temperature down." Joshua cocked his head and squeezed out the flannel on to Brae's head.

"Mary is okay then?" Brae asked with a frown.

"She is bathing in the oasis right now, she lives!"

"Is it okay if I pass out, I feel I need some sleep?" Brae claimed as he shut his eyes.

"Take some more water then sleep!" Joshua chastised. He reached for a cup of water and force fed Brae some water, before dragging him through the sand toward the shade of a palm tree.

"Sleep tight Hero!" Joshua said before starting to take off his armour and clothing.

It was dark when Brae woke up. His friends had wrapped him up in a tight fitting blanket. His body still felt he could drain an entire oasis of water. He kicked himself out of the blankets and noticed Natasha was on watch. She peered round and winked at him.

"Bet your thirsty buddy?"

"You wouldn't even believe how thirsty I am." He tried to laugh but his throat felt like a dried bone with the marrow sucked out. He crawled to the water hole and sunk his head in the cold water. He gulped a number of times, swallowing water and then crawled into the large pool. His body shivered as he made his way in too the oasis. He felt his body shudder, like waking up from a nightmare. The pool was shallow but he could feel with his feet that it got deeper. He cupped more water with his hands and smelt something nice cooking on the low burning fire behind him.

"Brae! Come back quick!" He heard Natasha's voice at a low whisper.

"By the bright why?" he moaned.

"Folk approach!" Joshua hissed as he heard fire arms being cranked and chambered.

"I'm coming!" He said but he felt so weak, but his survival protocols pounded his mind. He rushed out of the water and approached a pile of gear near the fire. As he pulled on his clothing he looked to the others who were on their feet, weapons hot. He reached down and grabbed up his carbine rifle.

"How many?" He hissed going into ranger mode, ignoring his weak body. Joshua had his shotgun in his hands.

"A group! Probably more than we can take down!" Joshua said alarmed and ready, backing up against Natasha holding a snub-nosed revolver. Brae squinted into the night and put his carbine scope to his eye. In the distance he could see a small group moving against the bearing of the light of the camp fire. He decided to do what Jessica would do and out flank them.

"Let them come to camp I will be out in the field!" He whispered before breaking off north-west.

They had kicked Mary to her feet and placed a double barrelled shotgun in her hands. Joshua and Natasha had their guns out and their left legs were braced as Yolanda had taught them. Firearms ready and aiming at the shadows, in the darkness of the night. The feral looking group approached the camp fire, each person armed with a firearm or a vicious looking melee weapon. When the group got more than twenty feet toward the camp fire, the leader grinned, the fire light reflecting the fire light on his rotting teeth.

"We heard that Rangers have come to our province! This is our land and Rangers have no jurisdiction here!" The scared middle aged leader claimed with the working end of an old army issue M16 rifle pointing toward them. Joshua noted that his minions were not as well armed with surplice pre-war firearms.

"I suggest you leave us be! If you attack us now then we will all die this day!" He said before cranking the hammers of his shotgun to punctuate his words.

"That's not going to happen my friend, you see as far as I see you and your folks lied at the river crossing! You claimed Rangers were coming this way. But it seems that was all Bull..." Before the leader finished his words a bullet ripped though his head. The leader hit the floor squirting blood from his skull. The others backed off with fear in their eyes but fear turned to anger quickly and they unloaded their firearms in the direction of the camp fire party. Joshua took a glancing shot to his left arm which he countered and unleashed both barrels of his shot gun into the mob, downing one of the scumbags. Each group exchanged more hot lead against each other but most of it was wild fire. Another bullet glanced Joshua, but had enough force to put his back on to the sand. He was winded but his body armour took the blow. The enemy realised they were out flanked and was taking bullets that they hadn't planned about. Several automatic bullets cut a line though the bandit ranks dropping more. But not before a stray bullet took a flap of flesh away from Natasha's shoulder. She went down to the sand screaming dropping her pistol, gasping for air due to the pain. Brae stormed in from the flank and emptied his carbine magazine into the assailants. They fell down like fleshy dominos. Half naked, wearing only meagre armour he rushed to the enemy yelling in pain and put them quickly out of their misery. When the dust settled he used the last of his vigour and pushed his fingers against Natasha's wound. She yelped as he compressed his finger to staunch the blood.

"Joshua! We need a field kit!" He yelled. Joshua rummaged through his back pack and quickly found a med kit. They both went to work and stabilised Natasha from bleeding out.

"You okay Natasha?" Brae asked as he inspected the bloodied bandaged wound. The sun was coming up and Natasha had been out cold most of the night due to the shock and the meds Joshua had given her. She opened one eye and smiled when she saw Joshua. She tried to move and pulled a face, pain jolted her and she settled back down to her bed roll.

"I'm okay Josh, but I don't think we are travelling any time soon." She said through chapped lips. Joshua bit back the thought of wasting several days of travel, but reality shook him back and his mind realised for the sake of Natasha's health they must stay at the oasis. Brae had started up the camp fire to cook breakfast, he was feeling a lot better now that his gut was full of water. He was still half naked but his rifle was slung over his back, just in case more dick heads came to the oasis. He was humming a tune, his mind on the task of cooking breakfast. And that's when he remembered, it was a tune Yolanda was fond of. He stopped humming and bit back anger and upset, he noticed his hands were shaking and he tried his best to think of something else.

"Brae. Have you got the dee-tee's?" Mary asked innocently, noticing his hands shaking. Brae looked at the young girl, he welcomed the distraction, but had no idea what she was talking about.

"What's dee-tee's?"

"Papa called the handshakes in the morning dee-tee's when him and the boys had been up all night drinking corn moonshine." Her face was blank, but her eyes shinned with knowing. Brae laughed and wiped a tear from his left eye.

"Naaa, not got dee-tees Mary, just a bit dehydrated that's all girl." His mind played over the day he was about to murder her. He was so glad Natasha had stopped him, even though in-bred, Mary seemed to have a spirit that most folks didn't have.

"Papa and the boys drank a lot, Mama used hide me in the barn when things got bad. She said the men would rape me if they found me. When then men gave up trying to find me they beat on the others or had sex with my sister." Her face showed fear with the recollection of hiding away hearing the shouting and screaming from the farmhouse.

"They were bad men Mary, they deserved the bullets we put in them." He stood from the campfire and hugged Mary close to him, his hand brushing her soft hair. "I will never allow that to happen no more, you are safe with us now." He felt anger brewing inside him, he cursed the Ashland and the badness it harvested from mankind. Joshua had wandered over to the camp fire and stirred the breakfast pot to stop it boiling over.

"Thanks Brae, I think we would have been killed last night if it wasn't for your quick action against those bastards." Joshua smiled and winked at Brae. "I think you have found a good friend." He gestured towards Mary in Braes protective arms.

"How's Natasha doing?" Brae asked.

"I think she will be okay, I just hope infection doesn't settle in."

"That's good. I think we should stay here at the oasis until Natasha is fit to travel." Brae said as he looked to Natasha sleeping in the bed roll.

"Yes, we stay until Natasha is better. But in the meantime we need to plan the trail ahead. And this time we need to make sure we can find the next water hole before things get bad again."

"Agreed." Brae chuckled. He removed his arms from Mary but Mary still hugged close to him for protection.

A few days passed by at the oasis and Natasha was now on her feet tending the morning fire. Joshua was again restless and wished to travel on, but Brae had dug his feet into the sand and refused to travel until he was sure Natasha could make the distance. Luckily infection hadn't settled in and the wound was healing up good. The bullet had passed right through the flesh so they didn't need to perform field surgery. Joshua had rationed out the supplies, but they still had enough to journey on. Brae had found some edible tubers at the oasis so they hadn't really needed to deplete much of their supplies. The tubers tasted like shit and they were stringy, but nourishing. None of them knew what the edible plants were called and if it wasn't for Brae's ranger training they wouldn't have known if they were edible. Later that day a merchant wagon had come to the oasis. They seemed friendly enough and Joshua had traded a number of items for coin. The merchant group was small, more a little family unit rather than the merchants in the south that travelled with mercenaries to protect shipments.

"Where are you folks heading?" Tony the master of the merchants asked. He was clearly the father of the family unit, in his late fifties sporting a bushy, salt and pepper beard.

"Heading up north." Joshua claimed not revealing very much.

"Well, you will hit grass land as a bee-line north. I'd say two days travel and you will be free of the desert." Tony said as he sipped a large cup of weak herbal tea.

"If you continue north over the hills you will reach the rock region. Its dry as hell so make sure your canteens are full. I've only been up north a few times and not really ventured far into the rock lands. But there is a tribe of folks up there. Beware though, the tribal folks in the rock lands can be friendly one day and evil the next. They are up and down like a bride's nightgown, if you get my meaning." Tony said chuckling.

"Thanks for the warning Tony." Joshua said as he clinked his mug of tea against his. The bushy bearded man peered at the heat trails off the desert to the north and shook his head.

"Its gona be another hot day. If it's okay with you folks, we are gona camp here until dusk before heading down south." Tony said as he watched his family members watering the drag-animals. The odd looking heavy set pack of dogs were being fed and watered by the merchant family. The dogs were friendly and obviously mutated in some form or another. Brae noticed they looked like regular yellow-dogs but these were more muscular and a lot bigger, standing about four and a half feet tall.

"Hey, you camp here as long as you wish, we don't own this place." Brae said as he patted one of the large yellowish hounds that had wandered over to greet Tony the master. He felt the strong muscles under the hairless fatty flesh and shuddered a little remembering encountering their kin during his ranger days. Yellow dogs travelled in large packs and would cut numbers from the ranger units if they attacked. Fast, agile and ruthless, he dreaded to think what these bigger dogs could do if they were un-domesticated. The main trade stuffs the merchants were peddling were sacks of salt taken from the salt flats to the east and dried salt meats from the ranch to the northern graze lands. Joshua had purchased quite a lot of the salt meat, enough to outfit the group for weeks. Mary had made friends with the younger of the merchant family and was hard at play kicking around a stuffed leather ball.

"It's nice to see the kids playing in such hard times, its rare to see such abandon and escape from the harsh reality of survival." Joshua said remembering the brief times on Sunday watching kids playing outside his church back in Redtown.

"Yes, we encourage play among the youngers, it brings such promise." Tony said agreeing.

"Is Mary your daughter?" He asked Joshua.

"No... She..." Joshua drifted off, he didn't really wish to tell the merchant how Mary had joined their group. Tony sensed the sore subject and quickly changed the topic of conversation.

"See that lonely tree out yonder." Tony pointed south to the lonesome tree. "Well, if we are lucky and it's about season, that tree might be bearing fruit." He picked himself up and gestured for Joshua to follow him. They wandered toward the tree and chatted a little about this and that. When they got to the foot of the bushy desert type tree Joshua smiled as he noticed in the thick spiny canopy it was indeed laden with small bluish berries. They spent some time gathering up the ripe squishy berries and chuckled to one another as they headed back to camp with fruit dye all over their hands.

"What is this fruit?" Joshua asked.

"We call it Jasper but I'm not really sure what its real name is?" When they got back to camp they shared the large quantity of berries among the campers. The youngers tucked into the sweet tasting fruit ravenously.

The sun had started to set casting red and purple hues across the sands. The merchants had readied themselves for travel, packing up camp and filling water sacks full to the brim. Joshua hugged Tony before they broke camp.

"I hope to see you folks in the future, it has been nice to find friendly folks in this harsh land."

"I hope that too Joshua." Tony made a religious bright gesture but Joshua noticed it wasn't correct but nodded at the thought the merchant was at least trying.

"Take care and travel well!" Tony said as he shouldered a pack and marched out into the dimness of the desert accompanied by his entourage. Brae had come to Joshua's side, waving to the merchants.

"Damned fine folks, I will miss them." He whispered. Joshua shoulder bumped Brae.

"By the bright keep them safe." Joshua finally stated. Natasha was hugging Mary who was sobbing seeing her new friends leaving.

"Maybe Mary would have been better off going with them?" Joshua wondered.

"Maybe... But I asked her if she wished to stay with us or go with the merchants. She declined and wished to stay with us." Brae said torn between the dangers of travelling north or the safety for the child being adopted by the merchants. Joshua patted him on the shoulder.

"She has a new father figure in her life, a father that won't beat on her or rape her innocence's from her. I think she choose well." Joshua said with comforting words which made Brae smile.

"I'm glad she stayed, but I worry about her safety during our travels, but hell we have got this far." In his bravado he forgot that he had lost the love of his life following the crazy preacher. Sadness washed over him snatching the smile from his face.

"I'm sorry Brae." Joshua said as though he had

read his friends mind.

"She is waiting in the bright's hands now, someday I will see her again." With that said Brae marched away to check on Natasha and Mary, leaving Joshua staring north across the lands. In his minds-eye he could see the promised lands of utopia.

Travel was hard across the desert, Natasha was lagging behind due to the injury but everyone seemed high in spirits. Mary stayed close to Brae, even mimicking his ranger like trot, which Brae found amusing. He had never realised he walked with a purpose like trot before watching Mary copying him. By the evening of the next day the desert started to change to brush land and then brush land into grass lands. They spotted a number of large bovine cattle like creatures roaming the grass lands, but hadn't crossed any paths with other folks. They had all heeded the warning not to shoot the cattle for food due to them being owned by the Mc'Avert clan who technically owned the graze lands. Not out of documental power, but the power of armed ranch hands. It was good of Tony to warn them, because otherwise they might have got into trouble if they had shot and eaten one of their herd animals. They camped down at the edge of the desert and watered themselves at a bubbling spring, which must be coming up from a deep underground lake. The water was warm and a tad smelly but it was clear and refreshing. Mary had already started on the camp fire and was learning quickly due to Brae teaching her survival tactics.

Natasha sung a few church songs as they prepared a rota for watch. Brae's ranger instincts told him his group would be safe here so they all relaxed for a while. During Brae's watch he spotted a mountain cat prowling around the graze lands. The large cat seemed not to be interested in the group of campers and was obviously stalking one of the younger cattle herd. The sleek black coat was more a blur in the moonlight, it seemed to rush quick and then pause, crawling across the grass then move quick again. It was beautiful to witness but he still kept his trigger finger ready on his rifle. He quickly scanned the desert and the small camp, a three-sixty kind of scan to make sure there wasn't any more dangers prowling in the night. His eyes fell on Mary tucked up in her bed roll, the double barrelled shotgun nearby. He nodded to the moon and made a mental decision. *Yes, Mary is my daughter, maybe not by bloodline, but I will adopt and teach her in the ways of the Ashland*. His thoughts cascaded as he planned her new up-bringing. When they finally reached Utopia he would travel back to Redtown, purchase a bar off the winnings of the contract and buy his daughter an education. He knew behind that childlike mind there was a glint of intelligence that sparkled from her crystal blue eyes. *Yes, a fine daughter she will be*!

Morning came quickly, they broke camp and headed north across the grass lands, by noon they encountered a long range ranch hand. He was riding a large animal which had a patch work of white, brown and red fine fur. The ranch hand approached the group holding a lever action carbine in one hand and the reins in his other hand keeping the beast focused.

"Greetings." Joshua said as the rider approached.

"You are a long way off the beaten track strangers, where are you heading?" The thin young man asked as he climbed down off the beast he was riding.

"We are heading north to the springs." Joshua claimed with a nervous smile seeing the armed man approaching. The man had a mixture of cotton like clothing and raw hide like armour. His rifle was cradled in his arms in more of a gesture for peace but Brae could see the glint of readiness in the mans, dark green oval eyes. The feller had seen too much sun and had fine tanned skin and had unruly brown hair and a reddish beard.

"Springs? Oh I see now, yes the springs to the north in the rock lands." The man said as he kept a watchful eye on the group.

"Yes that's right, in the rock lands. Is there a trade post nearby?"

"Not nearby sir. But if you travel east there is the township of Columbine. You can trade there for food, equipment and liquor?" The rancher claimed.

"Would the township welcome travellers?" Joshua asked, worrying about such outlandish towns.

"Yep, they welcome all travellers, but it's a good days march east if your upto that?" The rancher said as he looked over the group doubting they could make it. Before they built up the courage to reply, the man continued.

"Look you seem like good folks, why don't you accompany me north to the ranch, we have plenty of stocks to trade. Hell I'm done now having finished the night watch." Everybody agreed and followed the friendly man north, he even gave up his horse for Natasha and walked stride by stride with them.

"The names Samuel, I haven't seen outlanders such as yourselves for a good long while. You will be welcome in the ranch." The man looked Brae up and down and grinned. "Haven't seen a ranger this far north in a long time. Not since Ol' Steven, who is now one of the ranch hands. He has told me about the southern rangers keeping the peace and all that shit." Samuel laughed and nodded to Brae.

"I used to be a Ranger, but not no-more." Brae said with a little bit of embarrassment.

"Well that is a darned shame feller, Ol' Steven has told me many times through tale and song about the plight down south. Mutants and the likes. Up here the only menace are evil folks, tribal folk from the rock lands and mountain lions." Samuel said with a frown. "Mind you there aren't many ruined cities in these parts and the ruins that are in the local, we avoid them like the plague!"

"That's good to hear!" Joshua chuckled. Samuel lead them north across the graze lands and they saw many roaming beasts. After a good number of hours of travel they came upon a stout but sprawling farmstead, spilt up by fences and wooden gates. They passed an orange grove and a field full of cultivated grapes. Mary stopped to pick some of the fruit which she shared among the party. The bulbous fruit popped splendidly in the wearisome travellers mouths bringing a smile to every face. They were welcomed in by sun-tanned women from young to old. They were escorted into a fine dining area where they all tucked into a bowl of meat stew. With afters of orange flavoured sponge pudding. The elder of the house sat at the head of the table, he was maybe in his late sixties and liked to be called Papa.

"Be-careful up north, the rock lands are home to the cactus tribe! You may as well toss a coin to see which mood there in. We have little trouble from them but now and then they come down here and raid our livestock. To be fair we allow such small losses in the hope we don't upset them." The elder stated through mouthfuls of orange pudding.

"Heed his words travellers!" Samuel said as he elbowed Brae. The door to the living space opened and a weary looking ranch hand wandered in and filled a clay bowl with stew. He nodded to the newcomers and sat and ate. Brae looked at the old man and noticed he walked with a ranger type stride.

"So you be Ol'Steven an ex-ranger?" Brae announced cocking his head to one side. The man looked up from his bowl of stew and nodded, eyeing Brae.

"Yep, Indeed I'am!"
"You A.W.O.L then?"

"Nope... I am presumed dead. The ranger outfit all died. I wandered for weeks and headed north. I'm more M.I.A!" He barked and then continued eating.

"These good folks took me in and now I'm a ranch hand!" The old ranger said wearily.

"I meant no offence." Brae said putting his hands up in salute.

"No offence taken, eat your stew!" Ol'Steven said as he dunked another bread butt into his stew bowl, stuffing the moist bread into his mouth. The travellers spent the night under the kind hospitality of the Mc'Avert family ranch.

After performing a few trades using Yolanda's coin the travellers head out north. Samuel escorted them to the edge of the lands riding a muscular beast which he claimed to be a horse? They said their farewells and then ventured at Brae's compass bearing north. After a few days the landscape turned from grass land to baron rocks and rubble. Joshua being a scholar referred this land similar to the planet mars, but nobody could understand that there were other planets in the solar system. Reddish rocks flanked them as they made their way through the Rock lands. They stopped only now and then to fill canteens with water from bubbling springs. More days passed and the group were now hunting and foraging trying to make the provisions they had purchased last that little bit longer. Due to the merchant Tony, they harvested Jasper berries from lonesome trees. Keeping their vitamin C levels up. It was a welcome change of food stuffs from salted meat and grain to lush and sweet berries taken from the Jasper trees. Brae was now on full form educating Mary, he showed her how to cut cactus plants and rub the oil on exposed flesh to keep sun burn to a minimum. In the distance they could see the landscape climbing but it was still rocky and limited water springs to fill canteens. The rock tribe they had been warned about was still allusive. But Brae could sense there movements nearby and out of sight.

CHAPTER 21

Jessica watched Angel climbing up and into her E.C.A, she waved to her and shuddered recalling Angels fingers caressing her vagina the night before. She sighed and climbed up inside the mechanical monster. Once inside she pushed the button to close the hatch. The E.C.A came on line, bringing up a flickering heads-up-display on the outward camera. She relaxed and stretched before coupling herself to the machine.

"Move out on my mark!" Edwards stated as the comms hissed. From the outboard camera Jessica could see Edwards walker heading out towards the edge of the ruined city.

"Too your flank Sergeant!" Sanding's stated. As he manoeuvred the hulking machine to the left flank. Jessica took up the rear and watched her lovers machine move to the right flank.

"We will be out of the city soon. Digital maps say we are heading towards the suburbs!" Edwards claimed. The walking machines stomped their way towards the low buildings away from the enormous ruined buildings. By ten o clock the walking machines exited the ruined city into the outskirts. When they were passing some low office buildings, strange creatures slivered out of the ruins and started to clamber up the mechanical armour. From the cameras mounted on the side of the mechanical armour they looked like octopus kind of creatures, but land based instead of aquatic.

"What the fuck are they?" Jessica shouted though the comms, feeling all itchy all of a sudden. "They are climbing all over my E.C.A!"

"I don't think they can get through the armour, but it is worrying, there are a lot of niches and crannies between the armoured segments. I hope they don't slither inside and then attack us when we get out of the suits." Sandings said with a bit of panic in his tone.

"Odd? They aren't on my suit?" Edwards claimed.

"That's because your dead you bitch!" Jessica started laughing, but stopped as one octopus covered her forward camera. "Well that's me fucked!" She pulled the E.C.A to a stop. Edwards was still biting her lip, trying not to retaliate against Jessica's mean words.

"Me too!" They have covered my camera's too. Gona stop here!" Angel announced.

"And me, the bastards are mating with my camera's too." Sandings seemed frustrated and defeated already. Edwards manoeuvred her suit to face the others and they were indeed correct, the octopus creatures had covered the camera's as others waited on other armour segments. She just happen to glance in her flank camera and she could see white specks on segments of shattered glass.

"Stay tight, I'm gona check something out!" Edwards said over the comms as the others complained. She popped the hatch and leapt down to the ash ridden asphalt. As she wandered towards the nearby buildings she noticed more of the octopus like creatures. They seemed to either not see her or wasn't interested in her. On several fragments of glass were sticky white coloured eggs, clinging to the glassy surfaces.

"Shit! They are laying eggs on the glass for some reason?" She looked over her shoulder and laughed as she watched the creatures pulsating up and down over the camera lenses. She clicked her local communicator and switched it to the E.C.A frequency.

"They are harmless, they are just laying eggs on the glass lenses. Fuck knows why but I dare say they will be finished soon and then you can clean off the eggs."

"If that was so, then why didn't they attack your camera's?" Angel pointed out using her innate paranoia.

"Hmmm, I'm not sure." Edwards wondered for a while and decided to test out a theory. She wandered over to Sandings E.C.A which was the nearest. As the drainer got close the octopus started to scamper away and back toward the shadows of the building. She climbed up the armour and wiped away the eggs from the front lenses.

"That's better, whatever you did I can see forward again."

"Look, just march off ahead for a while then stop and wait for us." Edwards said to Sandings. She repeated this technique with each E.C.A until she was alone climbing up and into her own suit of armour.

It didn't take long for Edwards to catch up with

the others who were waiting at some pre-war bus-terminal. Rusted buses had rusted into the ground and half the sheltered terminal had collapsed under its own weight. She imagined it must have been very busy place before the war because she estimated the area to have at least fifty bus zones. The others were busy cleaning the rear and flank cameras when Edwards arrived. They all took this opportunity to have a rest, Jessica had a wander around the terminal to look for ammo or supplies. She climbed the stairs of a bus, kicking up bones and ash under her feet. She knew it wasn't wise to explore alone but she was in one of those 'Jessica I don't give a shit moods.' She opened up a small lunch box and giggled as she pulled out a bottle of 'Heart attack!' She knew this particular can couldn't be drank due to the radiation, but she had found other cans before in shacks deep out in the country. The sickly sweet beverage must have been some kind of pre-war 'pick me up.' She remembered getting quite a buzz off drinking a can of it years back, she felt like she had drank a full pot of coffee. She dropped the can as gun shots rang out close by. She instantly ducked into cover and peered through the shattered window of the bus. She could see her team mates had been pinned down and were using the legs of the armoured units as cover. The enemy fire was coming from the north, from what looked to be an old super market. Jessica cursed because she had only brought her pistols and was well out of range. She looked to her distant E.C.A parked up near the others. She peered down to the new armour she was wearing and grimaced. *That fucking robot better be right about the armours protective capabilities.* She took a deep breath and exited the bus and ran as fast as she could towards her E.C.A. cursing all the way. Luckily the enemy fire was being concentrated on her team mates, the enemy had yet to spot the stray human running in the back ground of the fire fight. She felt vulnerable because stupidly she hadn't brought her helm. A stray enemy bullet winged her right arm as she made the distance. She could see soviet drainers coming out of the building firing automatic weapons closing in on her team mates as she climbed up the back of her E.C.A. She bolted inside and closed the hatch, dimming the sounds of the outside battle. She hooked herself up to the suit and switched it on.

"Fucking hurry up!" She barked as the E.C.A warmed up. She noticed the suit could now move but the weapon systems were not yet on line.

"Fuck this shit!" She banged the controls with her fist and set the mechanised suit on a full on charge towards the enemy unit. The enemy were now concentrating all their fire against the nemesis coming their way quickly. The enemy even though fearless still had life preservation in mind as they tried to leap out of the way of the mechanised monster. She felt the armoured unit bump as it crushed several soviet drainers under its heavy metal feet. She had a quick glimpse in her rear camera monitor and could see her team mates climbing up inside their E.C.As. The weapons came on line and she went all hell with her forward facing cannon. The fleeing enemy unit tried desperately to get back into the ruined super market, but were cut down by the shoulder mounted machine gun. Now and then more enemy fire still came from the confines of the ruined building, but Jessica's charge had given her team mates enough time to start firing their heavy weapons too. A Rocket screamed from Edward's machine into the front of the supermarket building bringing down a large section of the building. Some of the others sent more rockets into the ruin until a massive shudder brought down most of the building on top of the enemy. Smoke and fire drifted for a while as the four mechanised units made a firing line ready for survivors. They waited patiently but it seemed none of the enemy had survived.

It had been a scramble but they headed north east quickly to flee the scene, just in case more soviets were in the area. They didn't even stop to field strip the enemy for ammo and weapons. The time approached 5pm and they had to stop, the E.C.As were climbing upto the overheating section on the needle. They parked up and made a small camp nearby a wooded area. They were now far from the city and their nerves were now calming down. Jessica stood in front of her mechanised unit and frowned at the bullet fire that had hit the front of the machine. It was still working fine but its armoured sections were pock-marked and charred almost black.

"By the bright they knew how to make shit back then!" She said referring to the pre-war folks. She did worry about the damage but was comforted by Edwards words.

"It's only the paint job and the dints just give it character."

"Do you wana swap then?" Jessica asked cheekily.

"Do I fuck like!" Edwards said with a grin. Angel had made a quick sweep of the area and returned to the camp.

"I can't find any boot tracks, the soviets must have another trail to the ruins. I did bag a few bunnies though." Angel claimed as she held up a brace of bloodied rabbits. They cooked the rabbits and shared the meat as Edwards stayed on watch. They laughed and sung old camp fire songs and tried to forget the danger they were marching towards. Jessica thought it was like old times between contracts, the calm before the storm when everybody's thoughts could just escape for a few hours. Angel cradled a small bottle of brandy that she had liberated from the army depot. She was giggly and a little bit wasted, smiling and looking beautiful again. Jessica was also a little tipsy but she stuck to cans of ale which she had also liberated. Sandings had brought a small mandolin and was busy strumming and singing songs to ease his fellow travellers. Jessica and Angel took turns taking the piss out of him because he wasn't very good on the mandolin. But it was all a welcome change in events and Sandings had a good sense of humour and didn't mind being ribbed now and then. *A true ranger!* Jessica thought. The sun had gone down and the camp fire burnt low, Sandings had the two females one on each side leaning their tired heads against his shoulders. He was now whispering his songs and trying to keep a low strum on his mandolin. He stopped his song when he felt the weight of Angel on his flank and the purr of a low snore. Jessica did a 'fire-mans lift' and carried Angel to her bed roll, tucked her in and kissed her forehead. She then returned to the camp fire and sat nearby Sandings.

"Don't stop playing." She offered him the last of the brandy which he took.

"Thanks Jess. I feel safe with you." His eyes were a little blood shot because he had also liberated a bottle of spirit liquor. "And thanks for saving our asses!" He drunkenly shoulder bumped her. Jessica laughed.

"When I was a ranger, I had a lot of shoulder bumps around the camp fire. But thanks its nice to be appreciated from time to time." She grinned and cracked open another beer.

"No really! I thought we were finished when those bastards attacked, if it wasn't for you doing that suicide run I think our mission would be over!" He smiled and wavered a little under the intoxicating flow of hard liquor.

"I've been in worse kind of situations when we didn't have those machines to protect us." She giggled and raised her can of old ale.

"I don't doubt that Jessica my friend." He clinked

the last dregs of the bottle against her can and saluted. "Here's to staying alive!"

"Yes, a cheer to surviving!" She took a good gulp of beer and was in two minds to climb in bed with Angel but she could hear her snoring so she decided to stay up.

Edwards had stayed on watch. She had patrolled the perimeter far too many times and decided this place was a safe location to hole up. She climbed up inside her E.C.A and closed the hatch behind her. She clicked the communications to the secure ranger channel and depressed the call sign six times in code.

"Report!" Ash said from far-far way.

"We got attacked today but we are strong, no casualties." Edwards claimed.

"Good to hear. Our robot friend has aligned the missiles, as soon as you get a target with that laser guidance system. We will rain down holy hell on the soviets."

"The mission is good sir and we are close. Not far now."

"Good... Any problems?" He asked.

"Not at all, captain! In fact Jessica saved our skins today."

"She had a habit of doing that back in the day... But be careful, remember she also ran with bandits. So keep a watchful eye on her!" Ash warned.

"She is steadfast... Steadfast... For now." Edwards sighed.

"I should be with you my friend, but I'm needed here to organise and..."

"No apologies sir, we will be back to base in no time and we will see each other again." Edwards balled her fist wishing she hadn't said that, she felt like she had showed her cards to the captain.

"I wish for that day sergeant..." She could hear the choke in his voice and before she could say any more... The radio hissed. She let the anger inside her drainer body subside. Her eyes opened wide and she felt primordial anger building up inside her tainted body. She bit back the thoughts of smashing the insides of the E.C.A up. But then she felt the last residue of humanity rising again in her belly.

"Why! Why! WHY!" She hated the day she turned into the undead, even if it made her so much stronger, faster, more agile... She felt doomed, she would be ever immortal. She feared watching Captain Ash grow old and she would still be. And he would never love her like he once did! She un-hatched the E.C.A and leapt in a massive jump into the tree line. She rushed through the wild wood, she could hear insects crawling along the branches. She heard wild animals bolting from the noise of her passing. She ran and ran through the woodland, agile and swift. The smell of blossoms, the tree sap, the moist earth, she brought up with every footfall of her boots. She finally stopped and fell to her knees and put out her arms, her fists balled.

"WHY!" She screamed into the woodland. She collapsed into the moist earth and rived around in a fit of anger, before settling down. Her heart beat was still a steady one beat a second. A normal human heart beat would have been twice that if she was human. She tried to cry but no tears shed, instead she settled down in the earth in a foetal position, hugging her legs for comfort. "Why?" she whispered. She lay there for a while listening to the ambient sounds of the woodland. All the while she hated what she had become.

Edwards retuned to camp, her face and armour was covered in mud. She eyed the others with jealousy. *They still lived and I do not!* She thought. Jessica and Sandings had heard her cry deep in the wood, but decided to leave her to her own torment. The team were busy checking the E.C.As when she returned.

"We move out in twenty minutes!" She whispered as she passed them, before climbing inside her E.C.A.

"Is she okay?" Sandings asked.

"I think she is fighting against her own demons!" Jessica suggested, she shrugged as though she didn't really care. Jessica looked to Angel who looked green from the brandy she had consumed the night before. She grabbed a bunch of her hair as Angel threw up her breakfast near the camp fire. When Angel started to come around and stopped spitting out gut bile.

"I will be okay! I'm never ever drinking brandy ever again!" Angel claimed with a pale face.

"Yeah I've said that a number of times, but I still go back during any kind of down time." Jessica said chuckling, remembering boozy times during missions.

"Not me... I'm done with booze!" Angel spat. Jessica aided Angel upto her E.C.A and closed the hatch before heading off to her own armoured, mechanised suit. The small unit headed out in unison through the woodland area. Edwards made a path through the woodland by smashing down trees using the mechanised powerful fists. They all followed the leader, who was forming a path. Due to the incline some of the armoured units stumbled over and took a while getting back on their feet, ripping up ferns and small trees in their wake. By night fall they had come to a swampy area, luckily this area was far from the cities and wasn't a high reading on the internal giga counters of the E.C.As. However it was hard going and they lost several days using tow lines to pull out submerged mechanised units. By the third day in the swamps everybody in the team had hit rock bottom. Moral was so low that you could cut it in the air.

"It can't be too much longer in the swamps!" Edwards said far too many times that they cared to remember. They had camped in some submerged ruins of a building. The bright only knew what the buildings used to be? Angel suspected this was once a pre-war university area. It was a definite place of study because they had found many libraries of mouldy books, inside the buildings they had camped in.

"We are shattered!" Sandings moaned. "We can't go on, not without rest!" Everybody agreed because travel had been cut in half due to the armoured units over heating trying to navigate the swamps. Edwards had climbed a lonely dead swamp tree and claimed she could see hills ahead.

"Captain Ash is full of shit!" Sandings barked as he put his head down. Edwards could see what was happening. The mission folks were ready to turn back. She needed to do something or else everything would be in vain!

"Gather your strength, we must push on. I can see hills ahead!" Edwards claimed but she looked to the pale worn out fatigued faces among her team members. She used her binoculars and could see a ruined building which was also submerged in the swamp to the east.

"We head east, maybe an hour. I can see a church. We get there and we can all have some rest!" The pale faces nodded but she could see they were broken. They pushed on, using tow lines and nearly burning out the on-board batteries but they finally made it to the sanctuary that Edwards had outlined.

They parked their E.C.As above the water level and went out on foot, wading through murky swamp water. Sandings checked the area using his giga-counter and shrugged.

"It's a little bit above background radiation. I'm sure we will be okay." He lied worrying about testicular cancer wading through filthy, radioactive swamp water. They all waded out towards the submerged church, in full kit. Nobody was taking any chances this time. Rifles, pistols and full armour. As they made half the distance towards the submerged church Sandings gave an alarm.

"Alligators, zeroing on our position!"

"Everybody rush to the church to get higher ground!" Edwards barked, her eye focusing on her reflex scope of her carbine rifle. She made up pace and the others followed worrying about being attacked under the waterline.

"Contact!" Jessica cried as she opened up with both her pistols, shooting into the murky water.

"On my bearing!" Edwards yelled firing a volley from her assault rifle into the water where she witnessed something stirring. She felt the mud under her boots rising towards the church building and fired another volley of automatic rounds into the filthy water. Angel had unleashed her combat knife as the ripples of the water lapped against her waist. Something grabbed hold of her and pulled her under. Jessica picked up pace towards her lover and watched as Angel disappeared under the water. The last thing she saw was her knife hand stabbing down.

"Noooo!" Jessica yelled as she thrashed away the surface of the dark water. Blood surfaced on the top of the water as bubbles surfaced. When all seemed lost and Jessica was about to dive down... Angel surfaced and spluttered her combat knife bloodied. She waded towards Jessica breathing heavily.

"Got the mother fucker!" Angel yelled, between spitting out dirty water. Jessica felt panic wash away. She grabbed hold of Angel and pulled her to higher ground on the mud flat.

"By the bright I thought I lost you!" Jessica said as she sheaved her knife, pulling on her girlfriend. As she dragged Angel away she saw a large bloodied alligator rising up in the swampy water behind her. They all rushed to the sanctuary of the church through two foot of water and mud. The stone building ahead was on the piss. The swamp water had obviously compromised the foundations of the building and the spire looked like those funny clay models of the leaning tower in that strange land called Italy. They entered the submerged church and headed up the spiral staircase to the upper floor of the spire. They all collapsed in a heap breathing heavily, hugging each other and patting down for wounds. When everybody got their breath back Edwards tried to settle her team mates down.

"We sleep here tonight on the upper floor, in the morning our E.C.As will have cooled down. From what I saw from the hill I could see we are nearly out of the swamp. The team were so fatigued by the last few days in the swamp that they fell asleep in their bed rolls, leaving Edwards on watch as usual.

"Fucking typical!" She said bitterly. *At least they are all too tired to fuck so I don't have to endure that tonight*! She thought as she found a seat to sit down. Her assault rifle resting on her knees like a long lost baby.

During the night Edwards got restless and went to check out the building on the lower floors. She didn't need her flash light because she could see quite clearly in the darkness. Luckily the moon shone through the shattered windows of the church which aided her vision. She approached the alter and spotted something odd. Usually old buildings were thick with dust and generally unruly with mould, and rotting furnishings, but the alter area looked like it had been swept clean. The alter itself had a black cloth over the top of its surface and several trinkets had been placed, flanked by numerous candles. Some of the candles had burnt down to the nub while others look fresh from the box. A sinking feeling raced down her spine as she heard voices approaching the church doors. She dived behind the ornate alter and chambered a round in her carbine. The doors opened and flash lights and lanterns shone the way for a group of humans.

"Silas better not be late tonight!" One of them warned but seemed to be ready to laugh.

"That bastard won't know what's coming!" Another one claimed. The torch light shined around the church hall for a while. "Pftt, typical, the bastard is late as usual!" The small group approached the front pews and sat themselves down facing the alter. Some of them placed lanterns on stands making the light sources more efficient. From behind the alter Angel peered around and counted twelve people, mostly male but some of them female. She could sense this through scent alone. They all wore the same white hooded gown, which cast their faces in shadow. The group sat in silence which felt like an eternity for Edwards hiding behind the stone alter. At last one of them broke the silence.

"Are we sure? I mean are we certain, this is going to be the night?" A female voice this time, quite compassionate, doubtful almost, a little fear in her tone.

"We all agreed and we are damned sure!" This voice sounded like the appointed leader. His voice was harsh, menacing and seemed to cut the air like a knife slicing through a main artery. Edwards snatched a peek again and couldn't tell if they were armed or not. One thing was certain; they must have donned the robes just outside the church, because the hems were not wet or muddy. She needed to contain the situation down here and away from her companions sleeping in the spire. She was certain something was going down and she could sense violence was looming. She didn't get the time to dream up tactics because the doors of the church opened. A man wearing red robes entered flanked by two rough looking body guards wearing a mishmash of armour. The patrons of the church all stood in unison and faced the man walking towards them.

"Silas! You're late as always!" The would-be leader moaned.

"Children of the deep ones, I bring news..." The red robed man claimed as he threw out his arms as though ready to embrace an old friend.

"We come to embrace the deep ones teachings. We do not come here to wait for you're pathetic time keeping Silas!"

"And so you all shall..." Silas seemed a bit hurt by

the-mans words. "Is there something the matter Logan?" Silas asked bitterly. Logan peered from left to right appraising the people gathered.

"Yes there is Silas!" Logan said angrily. Gunfire issued. Edward's eyes bulged as she witnessed a full scale fire fight. It was mostly shotgun type firearms coming from the group and rifle and small arms coming back from Silas and his two bodyguards which had fanned out and used the church pews as cover.

"Gunfire!" Sandings bolted up out of his bedroll and grabbed his carbine. He watched as Jessica and Angel going for their weapons with surprised and pale faces. Jessica looked around the spire room, illuminated by a single candle.

"Where the fuck is the drainer, wasn't she supposed to be on watch?" She growled. The others shrugged and listened to the gun shots that sounded from below the spire.

"Edwards is in trouble!" Sandings said as he gestured for the two rangers to follow. They got to the foot of the spiral stairs and listened again, as more gun fire, screams and shouting echoed up the spire.

"Fuck!" Jessica cursed. "Have the soviets tracked us down to this church?" Sandings ignored her question and was already rushing down the stairs towards the gunfire.

The main group of worshipers had dug in behind the church pews and were reloading shotguns.

"You're fucking finished Silas!" Logan yelled as he staunched a wound on his arm. He was bleeding heavily and sweating a lot. Meanwhile Edwards made a tactical decision and decided to aid the flock against the outnumbered but combat ready Silas and his two body guards. She used the alter to steady her carbine and waited for the next volley of firearms to hide her own shot.

"You are a traitor to the deep ones Logan!" Silas hissed from his hiding place. Edwards could tell he had been winged or injured due to the tone of his voice. The next exchange of gunfire started and she singled out one of the body guards, putting one in his head. A mist of blood exploded and one of the body guards slumped to the ground. She noticed that some of the flock were either dead or injured, because they laid-out near the pews.

"Barry? Oh by the deep ones Barry!" Silas wailed as he saw the almost headless corpse of his body guard lying surrounded by a pool of blood. "You will pay for that Logan!" Silas yelled as he emptied a submachine gun into the flock hiding behind the pews. Edwards waited and heard everybody reloading firearms, when more gun fire came from the spire door. Sandings was out first, going full auto on the other body guard. Jessica was next out and made her way to the wounded red robed feller holding his arm and trying in vain to reload his Uzi. Edwards came from out of hiding and aimed her gun at the wounded folks on her side of the church.

"We are rangers, everybody stand down or you

will be shot." Edwards warned. "How you doing back there?" She was referring to her fellow rangers.

"Got some dude dressed in a Red dress covered!" Jessica said as she booted the Uzi from his grip. Angel appeared from the spire door and spotted Edwards.

"You okay Sergeant?"

"Yep, but get your ass over here and cover this lot."

The rangers disarmed the folks and gathered the survivors up near the ornate alter. They tied up the survivors and gave medical assistance to the wounded or unconscious. The rangers tied Silas and Logan together back-to-back and secured the area for stragglers. Six dead, two badly wounded and unconscious but the others seemed okay. Jessica secured their mouths with duct tape, so that the rangers could have a discussion and respite to what had just gone down.

"This is not our beef!" Jessica said as she reloaded her pistols.

"We are still rangers!" Edwards chastised. Angel and Sandings agreed, but Jessica was still fighting between her disciplines.

"Time is wasting away, we need to get on track!" Jessica said but she could see the stern looks she was getting from the other rangers. She threw up her arms in defeat and wandered over to the alter.

"I overheard they revere something called the deep ones?" Edwards claimed as she marched up and down making sure the prisoners were secure. Jessica picked up a leather bound book and read the spine. 'H.P Lovecraft.'

"Maybe it's some kind of cult or religion?" She wondered as she held up the book to Edwards who scanned the spine and front cover of the book. She bagged the book wondering if Joshua would like the book for his collection.

"Whatever it is? We, as rangers need to settle this grudge now." Edwards leant over Logan and pulled the duct tape off his mouth.

"Speak?"

"That bastard Silas claims he talks to the deep ones, but his sermons contradict what the deep ones have told me!" Logan said between spitting up pink blood. His arm was bleeding and he had also been winged on the side of his rib cage. Sandings took a look at the wound and grimaced. He knew he would probably die by infection, especially in these hideous swamps.

"His, ribs are shattered on the right side and is probably cutting into his lung." Sandings shook his head to the others. "He might not make it." He then wandered towards the unconscious folks. Jessica replaced the duct tape and looked to Silas.

"Let's see what this fucker has to say?" She ripped the duct tape off Silas in a mean and painful way.

"Shit!" Silas yowled like a heel hound as though it had been kicked.

"You're up!" Jessica said with a grin, as Silas bit

back the pain.

"We are peaceful folks who worship the swamp gods, we mean you're people no harm. This situation was just a disagreement of leadership that is all. And I forgive Logan." Silas pleaded, but Jessica noticed he elbowed Logan, to keep him quiet. Logan mumbled something through the bondage of the duct tape and it was clear he hated Silas. Jessica thought this was all quite entertaining, she was tempted to allow Logan to speak but she thought it might escalate into an argument, which she couldn't give a shit about. Edwards crouched in front of Silas and met his eyes.

"Are you going to play nice if we let you go?"

"Yes, I'm sure we will come to some kind of agreement." Silas charmed with a smile.

"Good..." Edwards looked at the church windows and could see the dawn of the sun rising. It had been a long night and she felt tired even though her drainer body was alert and ever so ready.

"We will leave your weapons outside, we march now and I hope you can settle your differences and agree on hope, for mankind." She said finally and gestured to the other rangers to gather up weapons and stash them outside the church. She feared if these humans walked un-armed in the swamps then they would surely perish. The rangers kept there pact and secured the folks firearms outside the church. Angel, Jessica and Sandings headed off toward the E.C.As, leaving Edwards to cut the folks from bondage. She walked calmly to the church doors and as she shut the doors behind them, she could hear the mob descending on poor outnumbered Silas. There was a lot of screaming…

CHAPTER 22

It was the second morning when they first encountered the rock tribes. Joshua was just kicking sand over the camp fire when he spotted a small group of tattooed folks wielding bows with arrows notched. Brae and Joshua had seen the small group late afternoon the other day. They did the right thing and waved at them in greeting before the tribal folk scampered off into the rocky landscape. Mary had left an offering of Jasper berries and a small collection of shiny quartz stones. She wondered if they had found them when they moved on. She hoped they did because they seemed like nice folks. She thought in her innocent ways. Brae kind of liked her humanitarian ways and congratulated her for leaving an offering for the passing through the tribal lands. By mid-day Brae had spotted two groups now, they were flanking the traveller's position which he didn't particularly like, but he respected them because rangers would do the same thing when strangers came to their lands. Joshua seemed fascinated by these primitive folks and often stopped and shone his mirror catching the sun in their direction and blessed their passage under the bright god.

"I thought you had abandoned that bullshit?" Brae huffed.

"I have, but they don't know that!" Joshua said as he put away his mirror. Natasha grimaced at Joshua and shook her head.

"The bright is still with you Joshua! I fear you have lost your way to the true path." Natasha said hand on hip shaking her head in dismay. He smiled and put his arm around her wasp like waist and hugged her close.

"The sun will always shine our path my love." He claimed. Natasha smiled and snuggled close to him in forgiveness.

"Water hole ahead!" Brae announced while looking at his pre-war map and his nautical compass. The small group found solace in his words and picked up pace towards the next water hole.

They arrived at the edge of a small water pool which was constantly being fed from the mountains and then draining underground. They filled canteens and bathed for a while in the crystal clean water. Everybody was astounded by the fresh, cool, sweet tasting water that drained off the mountains ahead. Around the pool many types of plants grew, some plants were crop like so they harvested the grain, nuts and fruit. It had been a while since they tasted such juicy oranges and large fat nuts. They feasted for a while and forgot the toils and troubles they had been punished with every stride north. They camped down and it wasn't long before the local tribes sent a diplomat. The female approached the camp and she was dressed in raw hide armour and was armed with many bone, flint and other primitive type weapons. She stood at the edge of camp and cocked her head waiting for a greeting.

"You are welcome, please come and eat with us?" Joshua said as he prised open a tin of pineapple fruit in fruit juice. The woman paced around at the border of the camp for a while before cautiously making her way to the camp fire and sitting down. She looked at the tin of fruit as though it was the fruit bore of Satan.

"It's okay!" Joshua spooned a few mouthfuls of fruit form the can and offered it to the woman. Her deep brown eyes scanned the others as though they were predators, but after a while she tasted the fruit offered by Joshua by a single spoon. She mouthed the fruit and pulled a sour face and then laughed.

"Sour?" She played with the word and didn't think they understood.

"Yes, sour. Pineapple is sour." Joshua laughed and gave her the tin of fruit.

"You people eat can?" The tribal woman seemed to know a basic pigeon English.

"No, not only canned food, but many foods." Joshua said smiling. The tribal girl laughed as she understood the words. She broke out into her own language, it was fast but Joshua understood some of the words. After all he had been a scholar and read many books, some of which were the red Indian language. He knew he could only pick up some words but after a while he could communicate using her language. Brae felt like a fifth wheel but he allowed Joshua to lead the way.

"This is jerky." Joshua claimed using a language that Brae had never learnt.

"Dried meat." The woman said with a smile in English. They all nodded as Brae tried to get in with the conversation which he had no idea about.

"Your friends? Bring them to camp and let us talk?" He said In plain English. Joshua smiled and used his base knowledge of language to translate. The woman smiled and raised up her fist. Within minutes many more tribal folks gathered around the camp fire. Joshua tried his best to translate her words.

"This man is 'Walks through high grass.' This woman is the 'Bearer of mountain lions.'" He pointed and introduced folks on both sides. Joshua claimed that Mary was Brae's daughter which brought a smile to Brae's face and Natasha his wife.

As the night went on and food and water was brought from both sides, Joshua was happy being the translator. The tribal folk brought fresh meat in the form of rabbits and snakes. The camp were now twenty folks strong, everybody seemed to get along and relied on Joshua translating. It was fun and there was no hostility, in fact with the sharing of food it seemed to bolster the partnership.

"We are heading to the Utopia in the north, just past your lands." Joshua used his educated language to outline their way across the tribal lands. Often drawing pictures in the sand to aid communication.

"You are... Welcome... My words are slow..." The

male leader claimed. The female shrugged and said "You welcome, friends, we take you Utopia!" Joshua grinned and rummaged in his back pack and produced two bottles of brandy that he had been saving.

"Let us drink to that!" He passed two bottles counter clock wise and clockwise around the camp.

"You are all welcome in Utopia!" He said after a good glug of brandy from the bottle. "I want you all to come!" Joshua said as the brandy hit his bloodstream. Later on the tribal folk brought out bone pipes and started to smoke, sharing the pipes with the new comers. The smoke smelt sweet, an almost pine kind of smell, but burnt the back of your throat. The tribal folks laughed when the new comers coughed and spluttered.

"You ever been to the utopia place I mentioned?" He directed his question to the woman 'bearer of mountain lions' but by now that had been reduced to just 'lions'.

"No, we not go that far north. Caves and woods between. Terrible spirit wood and caves." Lions tried to explain.

"Is there a way around this terrible place?"

"Yes, mountain path, but path start near ruins of old man." Her eyes grew wide in fear. "Many braves go, few return!"

"Will you come with us?" He asked, hoping for a yes.

"Yes, me and Grass come with you. Find utopia then return with all people." Joshua had also shortened 'Walks through high grass' to just Grass.

"Thank you." He reached out and grabbed her hand shaking it up and down. She joined in for a bit but didn't really understand the gesture. Joshua looked over to Natasha who was playing a game with Mary, flipping coins into a camping cup. He smiled. *Finally we have something good going on*. He felt a kin to these people, they were simple and un-educated but they had a foundation of goodness. He could mould these people into civilized, folks, god fearing folks. Even though technically he no longer believed, but religion was a good tool to use. He had so many plans racing through his head and it seemed like every outcome was a happy life.

Dawn came quickly because they had been up most of the night talking and getting to know each other's cultures. Joshua couldn't believe that these rock folks had such a terrible reputation, but then he knew the power of words and how they can be twisted. He assumed the farmsteads in the south didn't want to be inbreeding with the savages and probably made up a load of lies and shit to bolster that unwritten law of mingling. Brae was still having a hard time communicating with the rock people, but he had started to get along by drawing crude pictures using a pencil and an old jotter pad. The travelling party set off around eight-o-clock a.m. Most of the rock folks disbanded leaving only Lions and Grass. Brae eyed the primitive weapons they carried and wondered if they would be of any use to them at all, but it seemed Joshua was smitten with the new people so he backed his play. Brae also eyed up Lions, but he couldn't tell if Grass was her lover or not? They looked similar so he wondered if they were brother and sister? Then his thoughts took a downturn and he remembered Yolanda. He quickly took point and tried not to shed a tear. They decided to take the mountain path which would take them near the ruined city. He wasn't very happy about this and would have preferred to head north through the woods which the rock folk refused to take. In the distance he could see the ruined city and fear crawled up his spine. They stopped to rest by mid-day and he wandered over to Joshua who was in deep conversation with the two new comers.

"Are you sure we are taking the mountain path Josh? That city could be seriously radioactive. Even from here you can see the city took a real beating from missile attacks. The skeletal buildings loomed on the horizon and he dreaded to think what would dwell there. *Trouble probably*! He thought.

"They know this land Brae and I trust the words they speak." Joshua countered.

"It's on you then Josh, if we run into trouble then don't come crying to me." He was about to wander off again but Joshua held his arm fast.

"They know what they are doing Brae, have a little trust."

The group set off towards the city and then veered off north-east following Grass who had taken up the lead. By late afternoon Brae pulled out his giga-counter and took a reading. The needle had started to rise with every mile as they neared the city.

"Josh, we need to head north!" Brae showed him the instrument and Joshua grimaced at the fluctuating needle. Joshua called for a stop.

"We need to head north my new friends, we can't go any closer to the ruins because of the radiation." His words fell on blank stares from the two rock people.

"Rad.." Grass, tried to mouth the word but gave up and looked at Lions shrugging. Joshua sat them down for a while and tried to explain the hidden, unseen danger of radiation, but Grass and Lions just laughed at him.

"They don't understand, do they?" Brae finally said. Joshua looked up to his eyes and shook his head.

"No I am afraid they don't know what radiation is and we don't have any spare rad-capes." Brae had given Yolanda's rad-cape to Mary.

"Look Josh, we will be okay with our respirators and rad-capes, but I fear we will poison the rock people. I know you are in a hurry to reach utopia, but you must make a decision about their welfare." Brae stated with his hands on his hips. Joshua put his head down for a while in thought.

"We will have to convince them to follow us through the woodland, we have no choice now. And you are right, these people are tomorrows people at utopia, we can't risk this and the next generation suffering radiation sickness and cancers." Joshua finally said. Natasha agreed, she didn't wish to poison the new folk either.

"Then it is settled we take the woodland route. Give me a moment while I explain the dangers again to Grass and Lions. They camped down while Joshua used all his priestly doctrines and charisma to persuade the primitive folk to follow them through the place they feared more than the ruined city. Hours passed and the conversation droned on. Brae could see the fear in Grass and Lions faces about the prospect of going through the fearful woodland. It got that late that day light hours had diminished and it was only wise to camp down for the night. The woodland was only a mile north and the rock folk had an unsteady sleep, due to the proximity of the terrible place.

By morning the primitive folks had come to agreement, it was touch and go and they were in half minds to set off back to the village where they lived and abandon the party. However, Joshua had done good and the promise of utopia for their people out-weighed the danger that they assumed they would face by crossing the scary place.

"We go with you Joshua. You lead and we follow." Lions said as the sun started to rise. Grass feigned a brave face but Brae could see he was shitting himself. But he then assumed he didn't wish to lose face in front of the females among the group.

"Stick close to me and I will lead the way." Brae said as Joshua translated. They all ate a light breakfast and then headed off north towards the woodland. Brae assumed the wood was all superstition tribal shit, but he worried about the phrase 'where there is smoke there is fire'. *These tribal folk are scared over something*. He thought. It was as if Joshua had read Brae's thoughts.

"We all need to bunch up and be ready for anything. Keep Mary close to you Brae and I will do the same for Natasha." Joshua said as he slapped Brae's back. The woodland seemed normal and it was a steady rise. The pine trees were broken up by jutted rock formations making small clearings in the compact woodland. Grass and Lions had arrows notched in their bows and they scanned the woodland like true hunter gather's looking out for prey and danger, with every stride. As the party journeyed north they passed several cave mouths, which were littered with animal bones. Brae assumed bears or other predators were using the caves as lairs, he kept his rifle off-safety. At times they had to follow animal tracks to navigate around steep slopes and rock formations but they still kept there guard. Brae thought it was outstanding how Grass and Lions spotted deer and other wildlife before his ranger eyes spotted them. With every minute that passed his respect for the earth folk was growing. *They are far better hunters than the southern folks*. He thought. He came out of his bravado and respect for the two hunters when they loosed two arrows, both arrows hitting a tree to his right flank. He was about to mention they had missed but then he spotted a large bear loping off east obviously startled or warned off by the arrows. He smiled and saluted to them as they went to retrieve the arrows. They hadn't missed at all, they warned the bear off which could have been dire to the party. His respect was growing even more for these people, whom he thought was primitive. He was even thinking maybe a bow is better in these situations, because gun fire might bring on more predators. Joshua was giggling, he had seen the awe on Brae's face.

"Not so primitive now are they my friend."

"You said it Josh, damn that bear could have ripped me all up." Brae joined in the laughter.

"Never judge a book by its cover." Joshua chided. Brae was never a man of books and only half understood what the priest meant by his words.

"My eyes are definitely open now Josh and I'm sorry for ever doubting these people and their ways and weird weapons." Brae wiped the sweat off his forehead and then replaced his hat.

After the steep climb they had come to a flat plateau, where the pine trees were broken up by small clearings of lush wild blades of green grass. Small blue flowers had bloomed between the ferns which made the small glades a wondrous sight to behold. Mary stopped to pick a blue flower and ran to Brae to offer the flower as a gift. Brae bent down and tucked the flower in her blonde hair. He kissed his fingers and placed them on her pale face, which brought a smile to her face.

"You will always be my daughter Mary, no matter what your lineage." He said as he pushed her long sun bleached blonde hair over her ears. She smiled and hugged him around his waist.

"Papa." She whispered. The word echoed in his mind and he bit back the urge to get too emotional. Natasha had come to his side and kissed him on his cheek.

"You will make a fine father to this child, Brae. Keep her safe."

"I will!" He said, as the reality of his words hit home. "I will!" He whispered. The sun had climbed and if it wasn't for the snatches of cover from the trees, it would be an unbearable heat. As they wandered through the patch work of ferns and lush long bladed grasses all thoughts of fear washed away under the steady haze of the beautiful woodland. This time it was Brae that spotted the coming threat. Tall, scrawny, naked humanoids started to race across the glade towards the party. The humanoids hissed with withered skull like faces and their arms were elongated and edged with sharp looking claws.

"Gather up!" Brae cried as he fired a few volleys of bullets into the coming ranks of twisted up humanoids. "Natasha! Keep Mary safe!" He yelled as he ran towards Joshua who expended both barrels of his shotgun against one of the fast moving assailants. Brae noticed two had been dropped by arrows and Grass and Lions had pulled out melee weapons. Joshua was bowled over by one of the vicious looking creatures and was yelling for aid, under the onslaught of raking claws. It had all happened far too quickly. Brae dropped to his knees and aimed at the other enemies shifting close. Spent casings ejected from his assault rifle scattering onto the grass like floor. He went full auto as Grass and Lions were engaged in melee combat. Curses and screams flourished all around the glade. He stopped to reload as another quick moving sinister mother fucker flanked him. He combat rolled to his flank and emptied half a magazine into the fucked up mutant that tried to ambush him. He just managed to get to his feet and look to Natasha and Mary who were both firing shotguns and pistols against the mob of devils coming their way.

"No!" Brae cried as he shot down more of the filthy creatures heading towards Joshua who was clearly having trouble with the raking claws upon him.

"Get this mother fucker off me!" Joshua cried as he reached for his boot knife. Brae was quick. He pulled out his side arm, aimed and shot the enemy on Joshua. Satisfied he would be okay he switched guns and fired at the stragglers that were making their way towards them. Grass and Lions had taken down a small mob using only primitive knives and spears. They were back to back and seemed to fight as one unit. Like the old tales of old Grecian warriors fighting against an out numbered foe. He quickly justified his next move. He raced to Joshua and grabbed him up off the grassy floor.

"You okay Josh?"

"Yeah!" Joshua claimed as he reloaded his

shotgun. By now the entire party had gathered up and was firing and launching arrows at the last number of enemies rushing to attack. Natasha and Mary were fast reloading but only a few enemies remained. It was Mary that dropped the last enemy by blasting off its head pulling both barrels of the shotgun. The dust settled and everybody reloaded and waited in the silence that often descended after conflict. Joshua was seriously injured, he tried to make out he was okay but the tunnel vision got to him and he slumped over into a bunch of ferns. Natasha screamed and rushed to his side.

"Brae, you gota do something!"

"I know!" He pushed Natasha away and inspected Joshua's wounds.

"Keep watch!" He whispered and then started to perform first-aid like he had been taught when he ran with the rangers. He noticed Joshua was bleeding but he would be okay, no organ damage or arteries sliced. Grass and Lions wandered over, both were covered in blood and from the outlook it wasn't there blood.

Joshua came too. Brae had bandaged and staunched his wounds.

"Tough little fucker aren't you Josh!" Brae smiled and dribbled water from his canteen over his forehead.

"Am I dead, is this utopia?" Joshua whispered and then suddenly realised what had just surpassed. He felt a little bit silly.

"You fought well my friend!" Brae grinned.

"You okay my darling?" Natasha asked with a

worried frown. Natasha smoothed back his hair and gave him a loving smile.

"I think so. By the bright I'm so thirsty."

"You have lost a bit of blood my friend." Brae said as he spilled a trickle of water into his mouth. Joshua gulped back the water and coughed a little. Lions offered her water-skin and trickled more water into Joshua's mouth. Brae looked to Mary who still cradled her shotgun.

"My daughter did good?" Brae asked Natasha. Who smiled and nodded.

"She did well." But Natasha was more worried about her husband.

"Can you walk Josh?" Brae asked as he trickled more water into his mouth from Lions waterskin.

"Yeah I think so." He gingerly got to his feet as a show of strength for the new comers. He wobbled around on jelly like knees but quickly countered the pain in his body.

"Let's move out!" Joshua stated through a master like tone. His body cried to rest but he ignored the pain.

The travellers moved out and Brae kept close to Joshua. He knew he was wounded and in pain but they needed to get away from this place. If they camped up here he assumed there could be more of those wretched things. Lions marched at the side of them eyeing Joshua for any kind of weakness. Brae wondered if the tribe had some kind of euthanasia rule built into their tribal ways? But when he questioned them it seemed they looked after the elders and revered them as a source of wisdom.

"What does your tribe call the things we encountered? In the south we call them 'Wretched folk' and sometimes the rangers call them 'Ghouls'?

"Evil Spirits!" Lions only half understood what Brae asked, but she was pretty sure they were on the same wave length.

"Okay, from now on we will call them Evil Spirits!" Brae agreed and smiled at the good looking sun-tanned woman. She smiled too and shoulder bumped him and laughed.

"Your accent, funny, sometimes I understand words. Sometimes I not understand words. Accent changes words." She said giggling. You learn some words that we speak. We meet half way, like Joshua?" She cocked her head and gazed into his deep blue eyes smiling. Brae stopped and patted her on her shoulder using his big hand.

"You will have to teach me." He said with a wink. She stopped and pulled a frown and locked eyes, with his. He noticed that she had large almond shaped hazel/red eyes. The kind of eyes, which a man, could easily fall into the abyss.

"I have a feeling we are going to get on like a house on fire!" He grinned. She frowned and clearly she didn't understand what he was saying, but she smiled back.

"House on fire?" She mimicked and frowned and tried to pick her words carefully.

"Are we the same?" She said puzzled by her own words, attempting to battle through the language block.

"Yes..." Brae said chuckling. "Yes, if you feel that way then I do?"

"Then yes, we are the same..." She took a pause, but she thought she had said the correct words. He hugged her and then eyed Grass who was grinning and cocking his head to the side.

"Grass is not your husband?"

"What is husband?" She asked, suddenly abashed.

"Life partner?" He said quickly trying to keep her interested. Joshua had overheard the conversation and quickly translated. While Joshua translated her smile grew bigger. She understood what the mighty warrior was trying to say.

"Then yes... Brae my friend." She took a deep breath and held his hand and put his hand to her armour plate over her heart.

"Be my husband." She was beaming. Joshua stepped forward still clutching his chest wound.

"As soon as we get to utopia I will marry you both under the law of the bright god!" He claimed, staunching pain to his arms and chest.

"Then so be it!" Brae said as he put his arm around the young Mary, in a show of his affection to his adopted daughter to this marriage. Joshua pulled a face and then explained to Lions that Brae had baggage. She seemed to be okay with that.

"Our daughter. Our union." Lions said as she got down on her knees. Grass approached and knelt down too. But Brae assumed that it was out of brotherly love for his sister. And he hoped he wasn't trying to marry both of them. He was relieved when he stood up and patted Brae on the shoulder before wandering off to sit with Joshua and Natasha.

The party had moved out and had to move out slow due to the wounded man they had to carry from time to time. By now they had moved off higher ground and were descending through the other side of the woodland. As the sun started to go down, they realised they needed to camp up somewhere on the descent. However, Joshua pushed them on in the night. The woodland broke up into more rocky ground and by an extensive travel they got to the foot of a sandy desert. They had left the woodland pines far behind them. They wandered out into the desert sands again but they all knew that utopia was not far now. They camped down next to a small spring that brought beauty to the desert in the form of palms and small fauna. They all laughed and sung songs next to the camp fire. Utopia was so near they could smell it and drink it all up. The hunters in the party went out into the desert for a while and then after a number of hours they brought back snakes, desert fox and a number of lizards to roast on the camp fire. Natasha and Mary had gathered up cactus blossoms and jasper berries from local desert trees. It wasn't a feast but they all dug into the food that was on the plate. They had their fill on what was on offer, including some root vegetables which Mary found near the spring. Natasha and Mary made a nice root vegetable stew, fortified by meat that the hunters had brought back. Joshua even opened a large can of vegetable stew which he purchased back in civilisation. It was an amazing time of food and it seemed nobody in the party held back due to the idea of utopia was so very close.

"We are so very close now I can smell it over the desert wind!" Joshua said as he stood up and raised his fist to the air. Everybody seemed excited by the concept that utopia was so very close.

"This utopia, can my people live, with no conflict?" Lions asked.

"Yes, there will be an abundance of food crops as far as the eye can see!" Joshua claimed.

"Tomorrow we will get to the foot of utopia and all our prayers will be answered!" Joshua had stood up nearby the camp fire and was convinced that all salvation will be promised.

"As, long as you are sure, my friend!" Brae nodded.

"Of course I'm sure. We are so fucking near!" Joshua looked towards Mary the youngling and apologised for his language.

"We are with you!" Brae said as he cleaned his rifle.

"We with you!" Grass and Lions stated.

"I with you, Joshua my husband!" Natasha claimed as she held fast to the young girl Mary.

"In the morning I will point out paradise!" Joshua

claimed with a fist pump in the air.

CHAPTER 23

They had left the swamp behind and were making good head away across the land using the E.C.As. They had travelled for two more days, resting in between. By noon Edwards had called a halt. They all gathered at the foot of her E.C.A and waited for her to speak. Jessica noticed she looked paler than usual and her cheeks were sallow emphasizing her high sharp cheek bones. Edwards was about to speak but Jessica spoke first.

"You're a mess sergeant, you need to hole up and hunt for rats or whatever you undead scum drink from, other than humans of course." Her hurtful words were deliberate.

"Yes, I know, I saw my reflection in a pool a day back and you might be right, I think I do need to feed." She looked to the floor and sighed. "This is why I called a stop. In the case I don't make it, I need to show you guys how to operate the laser pointer, otherwise the mission dies with me."

"We were all there when you was being taught you daft cow!" Jessica groaned, she fucking hated learning stuff. Edwards suddenly looked feral and even flashed her teeth for a few seconds before the ranger calm washed back over her.

"I need to be positive that you all know. I seem to recall you lot was just looking on while the robot showed me how to operate the device."

"Sarg, is right, I zoned out a little and too be honest I think I know how to turn it on, but other than that, I just assumed the sergeant would sort it out come the time." Sandings admitted. Angel nodded too.

"Yeah I kind of zoned out a bit too, I think its best we all learn."

"Sweet fuck!" Jessica spat on the floor and gave Sandings an evil look. Edwards unwrapped a large water proof sling bag and pulled out a heavy looking piece of kit. It appeared like an extended LAW rocket and a similar size, but it had fancy boxes attached to it and what looked like a sniper scope.

"Right then, let's get down to learning..." Edwards spent half the afternoon drilling the team in the use of the missile laser targeter. She explained that once targeted the tactical nuclear missile would launch and home in on the target. It would obviously have to be far away or otherwise it would be a suicide mission. Edwards had pointed out to all of them that if push came to shove, she would get as close as need be and sacrifice herself for the greater good. The team believed her. Jessica glared at Angel and gave her the look as though if you do something that stupid then big trouble! Not that she could punish her because she would have been vaporised. Angel gave her a punishing glare back and looked determined that for the sake of humanity on the brink she would sacrifice herself. At that point for one of the first times in her life that she wasn't looking out for number one, she would have to take care of the woman she had fallen in love with. When the tutorial was over they all climbed back into the robotic walkers and headed north east towards the bearing.

The sun had started to head down and they camped in an old ruined house in the suburbs. The city loomed in the far distance and moral had taken a real dive. This shit was now real, the mission tomorrow was ever closer and Jessica feared for the lives of her team mates and her own. She ate her soup sombrely and noticed her hands were shaking a little. It had been years since she felt the looming terror and anxiety crawling up her spine. Her team mates were all busy checking and double checking ammo, rifles and pieces of equipment. Jessica peered at her rifle leaning up against the wall near her bed roll. She looked at it as though that was the object of hate, but looking past the rifle in her minds eye she blinked at phantom enemies. Quick moving incredibly strong mother-fuckers, that could easily tear a human being a sunder. She settled on the hatred towards the drainers, which had turned her life upside-down. *How did I get in this mess?* She wondered, she had no inclination to ask god because that would be silly, but she felt she needed to ask somebody, anybody! Edwards broke the silence.

"Can you smell the salt in the air?"

"What?" Sandings asked as though confused.

"Salt air, it means we are not far from the sea." Edwards answered.

"I've heard of the sea and oceans and read about them in books but never seen such vast bodies of water." Angel claimed.

"I once was in a bar talking to a drifter and he claimed he had reached the sea to the east. He said it was such a beautiful sight to behold. I doubted his words but you never know he could have been describing his own memories and not just recalling what he had read from a book." Jessica claimed. "I've seen pictures of beaches and the sea from old magazines. I dare say we all have?" Everybody agreed and chuckled. Jessica couldn't believe that so few had ever witnessed the sea through their own eyes, but now the subject was in the air she craved for the idea of actually visiting the coast.

"If we all survive this, maybe we should all head south down the coast and go see this ocean called Atlantic?"

"Is that what the sea is called?" Sandings said with curiosity.

"I think so... I seem to recall seeing it on old maps." Jessica replied remembering a moth eaten old map of North America in an old ruined police station, years ago.

"Then that's what we will do. When the enemy is destroyed we will take some time off to go and see an ocean." Angel said with hope in her eyes. That night Angel and Jessica cuddled in their bedrolls, sex and toe curling orgasms were far from their minds. They both hoped for the chance to stand hand in hand overlooking the rolling waves of the sea. Once the enemy, had been vanquished.

They stormed through the suburbs and entered the main city, radiation seemed strong among the battered shells of the buildings, the onboard sensors depicted a climbing radiation meter. The city seemed oddly quiet and they hadn't seen much movement at all apart from the odd mutant cowering in the ruins as the armoured walkers thundered past their hiding places. They tried to go as a bee-line to the docks, but the main street was compromised by fallen buildings. They doubled back a number of times and found side streets which had been cleared. Obviously cleared by the soviet forces, possibly to move heavy vehicles around the city. They rounded a corner into a main square where a large statue of a man holding a book in the air had survived the nuclear attack. They had stupidly walked right into an ambush. A large armoured vehicle with tracked like wheels pulled out of a side street and let loose an explosive shell. Jessica screamed as her adrenalin levels peaked and everything seemed in slow motion. The explosive shell hit Sandings E.C.A blasting the top torso section from its mechanical legs. During the chaos the soviet forces opened fire with heavy-machine guns as ground troops closed in on their flanks. Edwards quickly organised a back to back formation and then unleashed the full fire power of the E.C.As. The team used the onboard rockets, machine guns and the shoulder mounted high calibre auto-cannons. Inside the E.C.As was a din of small arms fire dinging off the armoured plates. Jessica watched as Angel leapt from her armoured unit just before another shell hit. Jessica couldn't see where Angel had landed due to the smoke and the explosion. She grabbed hold of the controls and stormed towards the enemy tank. She kicked out right at the last minute which crushed the tank turret. They must have fired and the shell exploded inside the bent barrel. The tank exploded sending the heavy weight into the air and then back to the rubble upside down, burning its victims inside. She must have damaged the E.C.A performing the kick because the controls went all funny. She limped her E.C.A to a nearby building and punched through into the inside. Her E.C.A was now fucked and she had to near as damn it lever her way out of the armoured unit. She leapt to the floor and chambered a round in her rifle. During the battle she had lost where Edwards was and Angel if she was still alive? Life preservation took over and she raced into the shadows of the building, up the stairs to gain higher ground. She could only hear gunshots now and then, so she assumed they had fucked the ambush over. She got to the second floor and was quick to see two drainers rushing at her, howling and braying for her blood. She went full auto in a panic and dropped them both in a bloody display. Her breath came quick and her heart beat felt like a techno drum. She reloaded her battle rifle and rushed to a window to overlook the carnage. Smoke had mostly obscured the square, she could see the two smouldering wrecks of E.C.As and Edward's armoured unit still intact but the hatch at the back was open. She figured she ran out of ammo and headed off on foot.

"Where are you bitch?" She whispered as her eyes darted around looking for movement. She unclipped the bi-pod on her battle rifle and rested it on the sill of the window. She peered down the scope and spotted two drainers in full battle armour. They were rummaging around near one of the burning wrecks. She took a deep breath and aimed true. She fired and quickly shifted the rifle and fired again. Taking out both.

"Is that you Jess?" She heard Edwards voice across the street followed by an almost drunken giggle. Jessica knew better than revealing her position but something in her team mates tone alarmed her.

"Yeah that was me!" She yelled and silently cursed her stupidity.

"We won..."

"Where are you?"

"I'm here behind the rusty car, next to the tobacco shop." Edwards said, but her voice was choked and sounded like popping bubbles. "I'm pretty dinged up though." Jessica cursed and folded the bipod away. She took another sweep checking there were no more drainers about. She noticed there were a lot of dead drainers though. She made her way back down to the street below, her rifle leading the way.

Jessica picked her way through the numerous black armoured soviet warriors, all of them bust up good from heavy-machine gun fire or explosions. She got around the rusted car near the tobacconist store and her eyes fell on Edwards. She didn't know what to say, for the first time in her life she didn't have something spiteful, cocky or damned right evil to say. Edwards was hugging around the laser targeting device. But it was only her top half. A bloodied trail from her E.C.A ended here. Edwards coughed up blood and she was clearly fighting for the last of her life. Jessica rushed to her side and grabbed her hand.

"Fuck..." Jessica whispered as she tried to work out where the rest of Edwards was? "I'm sorry my friend..."

"I know, I'm fucked..." Edwards eyes started to roll backwards but she summoned more vigour. "Its upto you now bitch!" Edwards grinned and then her eyes glazed over. Jessica shuddered, she never really liked her and hated her for being a drainer, but now that she looked at the half of torso which crawled here to secure the device, Jessica saluted to her dead sergeant. She felt a little bit choked and then doom fell on her. She was the only survivor! She felt so alone. Jessica unravelled the sergeant's arms and shouldered the heavy bag.

"It was nice knowing you Edwards. But this was your job, not mine!" She hissed as she pictured Angel in her minds eye. She grimaced and howled to the sky.

"Angel!" she screamed into the ruins. The echo bounced around for a while but she heard no call back. Her hatred towards the soviet enemy raced through her body, every nerve ending, every bone in her body cried for revenge. She had lost everything and they would pay dearly! She knew the noise would have alerted other patrols but she risked it and climbed up inside Edwards E.C.A. The power was running low and only a few systems were on line. She clicked the long range radio and waited.

"Edwards, is the mission still good?" Captain Ash asked with worry in his tone.

"All dead captain, all dead, just me left." Jessica whispered.

"Jessica! Thank the gods. I'm sorry to hear your team mates are dead."

"I'm heading on, but on foot, all the armoured units are crippled."

"Jess… Jessica, you need to focus, humanity rides on your back now. The missile is prepped and ready, just give us the word."

"Under normal circumstances I would have aborted, but those mother fuckers and going to pay!"

"Good to hear Jessica. You are now the sergeant of the mission!"

"Fuck you Ash!" Jessica yelled down the receiver and powered down the E.C.A, cutting off any reply. Jessica exited the E.C.A and headed off to her smashed armoured unit to gather up provisions and extra ammo clips. Before she left the scene of the battle she took Edwards personal communicator from what was left of her. As she moved out a small patrol of soviets entered the city square. They did not find and kill Jessica, she was but a ghost in the ruins.

Jessica travelled across the ruined city, evading more patrols and road blocks guarded by the dark armoured soldiers. She noticed some of the armoured enemy were of all races. Not just the pale looking east European types, but oriental, African American and original indigenous Americans. It seemed the drainers had been busy recruiting by force. She also noticed bandit tattoos on their arms and faces. She figured the drainers had no racism when it came to recruited and turning folks into drainers. At the end of the day, creed or colour had no decree when it came to expanding their numbers. She passed ruined buildings where smithies had been set up where numerous lesser drainers worked the forge to make metal armour to outfit the ever expanding number of soldiers. The sun was going down and she found a high rise that was still in tact. She murdered a number of the enemy by stealth and knife, allowing her to camp down in the dark to ride out the night. Usually the radioactive cities were a breeding ground for abominations, wretched survivors and other mutants. But it was clear the soviet forces had cleared most of them out keeping only the animal and large insect life as a source of blood. The apartment she found must have been habited by a nest of drainers at one time or another due to the amount of animal bones scattered around the living space and the stench of fetid blood, which she associated with Edward's tainted smell. Sleep was hard to find being alone and on guard, she took a number of power naps, which she remembered doing when she was a solo in the rangers. She fought off sorrow for her dead lover and tried to concentrate her thoughts on hatred towards the enemy. However, in the early hours of the morning she wept violently and as silently as she could. Tears further bolstering her revenge. She must have nodded off just before sun rise as a boot pressed against the battle rifle she was cradling. Jessica woke with a start and realised she was fixed under pressure, a shadow looming above her. She reached for her side arm and tried to pull it from the holster.

"Shhhhh.!" In her panic she didn't recognise the voice.

"Damn it Jess, it's me!"

"Get the fuck off me!" Jessica sobbed, as she tried her best to raise her pistol. Its then she recognised Angels voice. Her pistol hand wavered for a few seconds before she dropped the pistol to her lap.

"Sorry Jessica, I tried not to alarm you. You know who I' am?" Angel asked as she pulled her boot away from her battle rifle. Jessica scrambled to her feet and hugged Angel, nearly squeezing her life from her.

"I'm here Jess." Angel said as she tried to wriggle from her lovers tight arms.

"I thought you died!" Jessica shuddered, her body weak with emotion.

"You're a hard lass to find, it took me half a day to pick up your trail." Angel threw her arms around Jessica and kissed her passionately.

"I'm not going anywhere Jess!" Angel kissed her

cheek and clawed at Jessica's bum, even though the armoured plates staunched the touch.

"Don't ever do that again!" Jessica spluttered through tears and love for Angel.

"I won't and I never will again!" She whispered into Jessica's ear. Angel climbed into the bedroll and hugged around Jessica, in an act of keeping her safe. They kissed and whispered to one and the other until dawn broke, it was a very emotional time for both of the rangers. Jessica told Angel of Sandings and Edwards, but Angel had scouted around and knew of their fate.

"It's just down to us now Jessica!" She whispered facing Jessica's beautiful face.

The next morning as the sun raised, they headed off to the dock area where the soviets had set up a network of buildings as a base of operations. They couldn't get too close but they found a tall building which was still intact. They managed to climb to the roof of the building and luckily they didn't encounter any resistance. They assumed this was due to the massive battle they had a while ago. Jessica took out her binoculars which over looked the dock area. From there she could see an ancient looking submarine which had soviet colours running down the side of the aquatic boat. They had no clue what the boat was called because most of the letters were backwards?

"Do you think they tried to confuse the pre-war Americans by putting alphabet letters backwards, as though they could only be read normally by the use of a mirror?" Jessica asked Angel.

"Not sure but I like your theory." She smiled and shoulder bumped.

"I zoned out again when Edwards tutored in the use of the laser targeting. If we secured the device and set a timer, assuming it has some kind of fuse like dynamite?" Jessica asked. Angel chuckled and nodded.

"It has a timer but we don't know how long the battery of the device will work, it is pre-war stuff so I'm not sure?" Angel shrugged. Jessica grinned and took off her belt and wrapped it around a drain pipe and tethered the device to it, nice and secure.

"It took us about twenty minutes to get to the roof of this building, so it's going to be close especially with flight time of the missile which must be at least ten minutes." Jessica concluded.

"First of all let's get this puppy targeted and then we will worry about timers and flight time of the missile." Angel stated.

"Agreed!" Jessica nodded. They set the device up so it was pointing at the buildings near the dock area. They kissed each other as though it was there last kiss and then tripped the failsafe. They both looked at the red button under the failsafe and joined hands to push the red button together.

"You sure about this? I mean can we get to cover, we are pretty open where we are and nuclear missiles even if tactical will take no prisoners?" Jessica said as they hovered their index fingers above the go button.

"If we die then so be it, we have allowed

civilization to live in the Ashland!"

"A mighty strike against the enemy!" They both said in unison as though they had read each other's thoughts. They giggled and then depressed the trigger. They got to their feet and ran like the wind, down concrete staircases, across rubble strewn rooms, until they reached the streets. They both sprinted like their lives depended on it, down rubble strew streets, passed burnt out pre-war vehicles. Across city squares where artists had erected sculptures and statues of folk who were famous but now dust and ash. They didn't stop running until the missile screamed across the sky above them, carving a path in the clouds. They stopped for a few seconds to look over their shoulders until a rumble came. A thunderous noise, louder than any gun they had witnessed. The ground started to shake as a white light washed over the ruins behind them. They ran to their flank and leapt into a ruined building while Shai'tan took what he needed to hell. They rushed into the nearby building and headed down to the basement labelled car park. An almighty boom erupted shaking the very foundations of the building the sought shelter within. Dust and rubble showered from above as the two lovers hugged each other tight. They felt the ambient temperature rise as the tactical nuclear missile raged above ground. Fire walls cascaded across the city. They witnessed fire lapping around the exit to the above ground. Tremendous heat and the power of the atom chain reacting. Nothing would survive the nuclear blanket that descended on the city again. For what seemed an age the buildings stopped swaying and the land stopped quaking. White smoke and dust made its way down into the bowels of the building which the two rangers sought sanctuary within. They still hugged each other close but had a coating of dust over there armour. The heat subsided and they journeyed to the streets. They stood and looked to one another and both of them smiled.

"We need to go now!" Angel claimed as she grabbed hold of Jessica's arm. She pulled her through the white smoke not knowing what was ahead, but she knew anything above ground would have been vaporised.

Jessica and Angel headed south, they knew the armour and helmets they wore would staunch off the most of the radiation. They got to the outskirts of the city but travelled on during the night. Behind them they could still see fires burning in the city. By the time the sun started to rise again they had exited the main city and were in the suburbs on the outskirts. Between them they had about two day's food and water. They followed Jessica's compass and headed South-East, towards the ocean. They pushed on and were seriously weary by now, due to the lack of sleep. They could smell the scent of the sea air in the ambience. They followed their nose to a lonely beach house where corn, tomatoes and other crops were grown in a large garden. Pigs and chickens were kept in out houses. As they approached, a stranger armed with a shot gun warned them of their passing. But once he saw they were two beautiful females he allowed them inside his house.

"I'm Alfred, I'm sorry I'm always weary about new comers!" The old man narrowed his eyes, sporting a grey beard and a receding bald head.

"We seek shelter and company, if that is okay? Otherwise we just want to head to the beach." Jessica pleaded. She was so tired and needed a friendly face.

"Well I have pork stew on the hearth and as long as you are friendly then my fire is always warm for strangers." The old man claimed. He lowered his shot gun and welcomed the females inside. Jessica shouldered her battle rifle but kept her side arm ready. They got inside the old house and Alfred started to prepare the dinner table, outfitting it out with clay bowls and wooden hand crafted spoons.

"Don't usually get folks passing by, especially folks who want to goto the beach." He chuckled as he opened a large bell jar of moonshine and poured some tumblers up.

"My wife died two winters ago and my son and daughter headed off west to find their life!" He sighed and then laughed. "It's not so bad being alone, hell I just look after myself out here." He took a breath and then continued. "What the hell was that earthquake about? I mean now and then the land shakes a while but damn... That was a quake!" He laughed not knowing the truth.

"No idea my friend." Jessica said winking to Angel. "But we felt it too." She sniggered. The old man looked to then and grinned.

"Foods not ready so you can go to the beach if you want? Old Alfred will still be here when you get back."

"Thanks Alfred, we will do just that." Jessica said before grabbing hold of Angels hand and escorting her off to the beach. They climbed the bluff and stood looking out to the ocean. Down below was a sparse sandy beach, cluttered by drift wood and flotsam. They picked their way down and were tempted to take off their armour, but the nuke would have advanced the background radiation so they thought better of it. They found a nice beach rock and sat down arm in arm. The sea was even better than the pictures they had seen in books. It wasn't exactly the same colour but still blue/green, topped by white froth. The sea was steadily washing in and out, lapping and caressing the sands.

"It's a far cry from the desert." Jessica whispered.

"It's wonderful, truly wonderful." Angel said as she leant her head against Jessica's shoulder. They must have been a while down on the beach because a distant yell brought them back to reality. Alfred stood on the bluff waving and shouting.

"Foods up!" They had a few more minutes staring at the ocean and then wandered back to the cabin. They wandered up the stairs and through the open door, steaming stew filled bowls had been laid on the table but Alfred was sat in the corner looking wide eyed. Jessica's smile dropped as she sensed danger. As she reached for her desert eagle something incredibly strong and powerful struck Angel around the back of her head, tearing off her head in a vicious sweep. Jessica watched in almost slow motion as her lovers head cascaded through the air leaving a trail of thick blood. She spun around firing at a large shadow that dodged to its flank as Angels headless body slumped to her knees squirting blood into the air like some kind of fucked up, macabre fountain. In the brief milliseconds that followed, Jessica's mind raced through, wanting to scream, probably resulting in the enemy taking advantage and killing her. She wanted to rush to Angel's side, hold her hand, very likely resulting in the enemy taking advantage and killing her. Or pull herself together and kill that mother fucker! She had already worked out it was a drainer which had survived and followed them here. But there was something about this blood sucker. This one was big, a true brute of the drainer kind. Jessica managed to get two good shots off that hit around the chest area. The heavy calibre bullets easily penetrated the metal breast plate the drainer wore. It even staggered it for a few seconds, allowing her a third shot which she put through its neck. Clearly the beast of a drainer was seriously pissed off by now and launched an all-out attack, crushing the dinner table between itself and Jessica. Jess thanked the heavens she wore that amazing armour and hadn't take it off at the beach. The drainer had pinned her to the cabin wall raking at the splintered wooden table to get to its prize. She still held her pistol but it was lodged behind a jut of wood. *This is it! This is how I check out!*

Her mind raced. A loud retort came from the back of the cabin, the drainers feet left the floor and sent its body cascading through the air landing in a heap at the door way. Jessica looked around and saw Alfred quickly reloading his double barrelled shotgun. As the drainer tried to scramble to its feet Jessica aimed her pistol true and emptied the magazine against its head, splintering the metal helmet the drainer wore. It thrashed around for a few seconds as Jessica reloaded and emptied another clip into it randomly until the bastard stopped moving. Her heart was beating so fast that she thought she would pass out but she maintained consciousness. Alfred unloaded both barrels again into the creature to make sure it wasn't going to get back up. Jessica stood for a while over the corpse of the drainer, willing it to move so she could go all hell again, but it didn't.

"You okay lass? Are you wounded?" Alfred was patting her down looking for wounds and found none. Jessica was still focusing on the dead beast. He noticed she was in shock and pulled up a chair and got her to sit down.

"I'm sorry, I panicked, I should have yelled out before you and the other girl entered. I should have warned you." Alfred's eyes were filled with tears, cursing himself for being a coward. He poured himself a drink and chugged it back wiping the tears away using the cuff of his shirt. It took a while before Jessica could find words.

"It wasn't your fault old man. Any person would shit themselves in a situation like this." She said this while still staring at the dead drainer, refusing to notice her headless lover.

"But thank you. You saved my life and acted quickly. My number would have been up and I dare say you would have been next." Jessica whispered with narrow eyes focused on the filthy creature, bleeding a sunder in the doorway. Her eyes fell on Angel and she felt her body shudder. She bit back the tears but it made her feel worse, her hands had started to shake and she felt sick to the bone. She ripped her helmet off and threw up on to the bare boards of the cabin.

"We need to bury her." Alfred said as he placed a comforting hand on her shoulder.

"Yes, we need to do that now."

Jessica gave Angels armour and rifle to Alfred. He took the equipment out of respect but thought he had no need for such stuff in his autumn years. They wrapped Angel up in her bedroll and both dug a grave on the beach. Jessica didn't have the words so Alfred read a few passages from his bright bible. All through the sermon, she realised she was alone yet again. Loveless, comfortless and abandoned... She shed a few tears but knew she would shed more in the future. They then dragged what was left of the drainer to the bluff and set fire to it. Later on back at the cabin, they ate and drank as Jessica spoke of the mission, of the folk that sacrificed themselves for a greater cause. It was late and Alfred had never heard such a tale and was in two minds to believe her words. But things did add up, especially the ground shaking and how the two surviving women were so well equipped. Alfred tucked Jessica up in his bed and stayed watch throughout the night just in case they were attacked again. Morning came swiftly and Alfred had made scrambled eggs. She noticed Alfred had cleaned up during her deep sleep. The bloody mess was but a dark stain on the bare boards.

"What now Jessica?" Alfred asked as he poured another couple of tumblers of moonshine.

"Well the rangers can go fuck themselves for a start. Word will get back to them at the base, word of our victory against the soviets. I think I will head back to Red Town, pick up where I left off." Jessica said as she swilled the clear liquid around in the tumbler.

"Are you sure you don't want to head back to your friend Ash, I suspect you need friends around you now."

"Nope, I need a saloon, hard liquor and a bunch of whores. But it's going to take months to get back, so something might crop up on the way." She chuckled, the buzz of the alcohol keeping grief at bay.

"Well I hope you find what you seek and god speed to you Jessica." He winked and shook her hand before she headed out. She thanked him for the hospitality and apologised for bringing a stone cold killer to his doorstep. He shrugged it off but was generally worried for her sanity. He offered her free lodgings, a break from it all and he also pointed out he would enjoy the company. She offered him coin, but he laughed and pointed out what he would spend it on? The nearest trade post was miles away and he was pretty self-sufficient where he was. She shouldered her gear, wrapped Angel's dog tags around the butt of her battle rifle and set off as a bee-line south west.

Jessica knew she would be heading through territory that she hadn't encountered before but she didn't care less. She knew there would be pockets of civilization and trade posts she hadn't ever been to before. It would be new scenery for a while until she got back to the heartlands and the desert. Apart from the grief rising in her gut, she did feel like she had been part of something great. And that was more than anybody could wish for. Jessica the saviour, Jessica the protector of human kind, Jessica the destroyer... She wandered for weeks, now and then staying and trading at townships which had their own troubles. Sometimes she stayed and did some gun for hire work but other times she just passed on through leaving the township troubles for other gun hands and hero's. Sometimes she tagged along trade routes being hired by merchants to protect the shipments, but all the while she was focused on Red town. She hoped she would get back to Red town and meet back up with Brae, Yolanda, Joshua and Natasha. She kept the hope in her heart as the weeks and months went on by. She travelled by river boat south having accumulated more coin than she could spend and relaxed for a while and took a brief holiday. She then joined up with more merchants and headed west, crossing deserts and rocky country until she heard whispers in the townships and farmsteads about the ancient enemy being vanquished far to the north. She chuckled and made out that it was new news and journeyed on knowing Captain Ash would be gearing up for the next ranger revival, which she didn't want any part of. Technically she was either A.W.O.L or M.I.A among the rangers but she didn't give a shit. After more weeks of travel she stood alone on a high rock looking down upon Red town, a bright smile fast on her face.

"Home sweet home!" She whispered and shouldered her pack to head down to the place she called home...

CHAPTER 24

The sun was burning hot above which made the desert sands shimmer. In the distance they could see juts of high rock but there was a break in the rock like a pass of some kind. Joshua pointed to the rupture in the high rocks and staggered forward to the head of the party.

"Through that pass is utopia, we need to be prepared." He was leaning into the desert wind and looked paled by the pain he was enduring. But it seemed the proximity of his quest was alleviating the pain that plagued his body.

"We need to be prepared, this is utopia so we need to look our best for the people who live there." He said as though giving a Sunday sermon. Everybody nodded and basked in his words. They must look their best, who knows who they will accept into the paradise land. The travellers dusted themselves off and made themselves look presentable as though angels guarded the gates. They headed off at an excited trot towards the pass. Everybody was eager and full of glee. They trusted Joshua's words and even dressed up Mary in her Sunday best outfit. They got to the foot of the pass and the high jutted rocks loomed on both flanks. The way ahead was a dusty road and clearly hadn't been trodden in some time. Brae felt the pang of doubt but kept it to himself. *Why would the path to utopia be so broken and unused*? He cleared his thoughts and came to the conclusion that folks who dwell in utopia have everything they require and had no need to come out into the desert. They marched up through the pass and took solace from the narrow pass obscuring most of the desert sun. A good half an hour passed by as they made their way through the shadowed pass, but in the distance they could see bright sun shine.

"We are at the foot of utopia, by the bright your guiding hand has lead your flock here!" Joshua yelled to the heavens, having somehow found god again.

"Amen!" Natasha bowed to his words. Mary followed suit and fell to her knees and started to pray. Grass and Lions both shrugged and chuckled seeing the spectacle of the civilized folks revering the bright god. Brae just grinned and gestured them to move on. It wasn't long before they came to a metal like double door gate which was at a jar. Auto-sentry guns covered in sand and dust did not come on line. Brae had spotted the sentry guns and feared very little due to their disuse.

"Joshua, wait!" Brae yelled as a warning. Joshua called a halt to the company.

"Is there something wrong my brother?" Joshua said with wide religious eyes.

"I just think we should be careful that is all. There might be more robotic guns that maybe still on line?"

"Nonsense this is utopia! They won't kill the chosen folk which I believe we are!" Joshua frowned and was giving Brae a look as though he was an infidel!

"I didn't mean it like that Josh, I'm just saying we need to be cautious!" Brae cautioned.

"Come my children let us bask in the light of utopia!" Joshua countered and set off staggering through the gates. They all followed but Grass and Lions heeded Brae's doubt and notched arrows, before proceeding past the gate. They all went into what Brae thought to be a murder chamber, he spotted many more auto-guns set in the rocks above but none seemed on line. They were weather beaten either out of power or out of ammo? The massive double metallic doors set in an arch way were also set at a jar. The travelling company pushed and prised one of the heavy set metal doors open and shimmied through. A dark tunnel lead the way, but there was light at the end. They marched quickly and entered a wide open sun illuminated space beyond. The space was massive, they could see high rocks surrounding the crop lands but a plastic or glass matrix made up a massive dome covering the extensive place, creating a hot and humid green house of sorts. Most of the crops had gone to seed but they could see wheat, corn, fruit orchards, herb gardens, vegetable patches and springs of water jetting from below ground constantly sprinkling the plants. However everybody could see this habitat hadn't been cultured in a long time. Grasses and weeds had taken quite a hold over the years. It was still lush but food stuff had been fighting the weeds and grass plants that had blown in as seed from the desert. Brae appraised the place and could see humans had not set foot here for decades. Brae raised his rifle when he spotted a number of robotic cultivators moving around the extensive fields. They were sluggish and were obviously fighting a battle against the weeds that had settled here. He looked up to the dome above and spotted numerous wind mills, probably powering pumps for water wells and recharging the cultivation robots.

"So far your quest has been true. There are crops and food here but I don't see any people?" Brae questioned Joshua.

"Maybe they are inside the complex, maybe these robots sustain them?" Even when Joshua said those words he started to have dire doubts.

"We can make a habitat here Joshua, but this is not the utopia that you spoke of!" Brae said angrily.

"The people must be near, let us venture on, surely this is not it!" Joshua said but even his words betrayed his own doubt. Joshua brought out a set of binoculars and scanned the way ahead.

"There in the distance I can see a door in the cliff side!" His voice was calm, obviously attempting to calm everybody down and not to seed a failed mission.

"I see it Joshua, but I have a nagging feeling that this place has not been habituated by humans in a long time!" Brae countered.

"Nonsense they are all holed up there, look at the robots cultivating the fields, humans must be maintaining them!" He was back using the charm of his sermons even though everybody had made up their mind. They wandered across the extensive fields of crops mixed up by desert weeds. Until they came to another double metal door set at a jar.

"I'm sorry Joshua but I need to take over lead here. There could be anything dwelling inside the habitat and I'm sure it will be un-friendly robots or maybe a few bandit's reaping what the robots sew?"

"Again I doubt your words but feel free to lead the way, I'm sure all you will find are friendly humans so please keep your firearm down!" Joshua pleaded, but followed Brae's lead.

They entered the metallic stronghold but even Joshua could see it the metal tunnels and corridors were in disrepair and rusted by the condensation from the desert air. They went from rusty room to rusty corridor finding nothing. Desert dust and sand had settled on every work space and wall.

"Maybe you are correct, my friend Brae?" Joshua was now seeing his hope shattered. After many hours and searching, even in the bowls of the extensive underground habitat, they found no man, no female and no child... Power still worked obviously by the many windmills above the complex set of the high rock. So the habitat still had illumination. They all gave up hope and headed back upto the surface when Joshua noticed one of the terminals still on line.

"This must be it, this must be the utopians terminal he has left me a message!" Joshua said with vigour. He pulled up a chair and tapped in the code which he had learnt from the journals he had found. The terminal was a green screen monitor and as soon as Joshua entered the code the terminal sprung to life with an audio log.

"We finally reached the base. Plenty of food and an abundance of water! But I can't keep folk here, human kind has the innate ability to seek out other things. Humans are curious, even after our mission to cross the lands to here, many folks died. But still humans wish to explore. At first I posted guards to stop stragglers heading out. But then I realised I had very few guards left to patrol, because the guards headed off into the land with what I call the agitated ones!" RADIO HISS.

"My son left this morning, he didn't leave me a message or why he left but I respect his wishes, after all I would have done the same thing. See the world!" The voice, chuckles. RADIO HISS.

"I have give up trying to work out the date, but I suspect my son is following in my footsteps. He is trained well but I wish I could be there for him!" RADIO HISS.

"I can no longer keep folk here at the new base, people wish to find ancestors and make a new life in the Ashland's. God have mercy on their souls!" RADIO HISS.

"I'm venturing out myself! I'm the last of the Exodus. By Jesus, please watch over me and keep me safe!" RADIO HISS.

"They, all left the sanctuary?" Joshua nearly cried.

He realised that the humans that once dwelled here are no longer and the robots are trying to keep the habitat alive.

"Why would they leave?" Joshua yelled at the top of his voice which made Mary hide behind a bank of dusty terminals. Natasha quickly rushed to console her with a hug. The rage and betrayal that Joshua felt was phenomenal.

"All that fucking money! All the lives lost and strife it has taken to get here!" He raged, he bit back the urge to smash the terminal just in case it stored more information. He slumped into a chair and cradled his head in his hands.

"Joshua, its not that bad, we can still make this place work, especially with our new found friends." Brae winked at Lions and Grass.

"But it is not utopia, the utopian man lied to us, leading us on a trail of despair."

"Pull yourself together Joshua, utopia is a dream. If you wish for utopia then step up and make one here!" Brae said in a pissed off tone.

"Maybe you are right Brae my friend. Maybe with a lot of hard work we can repair this place to its former glory." He said almost frothing at the mouth.

"We are all tired and wish to rest, let us start to rebuild tomorrow. Maybe Grass and Lions will go get the others and we can start to make a home here." Natasha said with spirit in her voice. Grass and Lions both nodded. "Our village is but a camp. This place much better. More food here and access to desert to get wild food."

"Then we are all in agreement, let us rest and camp down here and tomorrow we will make a new start." Brae grinned.

In the next number of days the tribal folks started coming to utopia, at first it was small families, but as the days bore on crowds of folks started to arrive. Natasha busied herself by organising lodgings in the habitat trying to make it fair for everybody depending on number of family members etc. Joshua began to do his morning sermons reading from the book of the bright. And Brae got down to security and organised hunting parties. As the weeks went by the tribal folks started to sew seed and plant new harvestable plants. Water was plentiful and before long green shoots started to sprout. The facility also had an abundance of fertilizer and some kind of water treatment facility which harvested human shit and turned it in to a kind of brown sugar rich in phosphates. By the next month Joshua had started to believe that this place was actually utopia and Brae had been correct. A little hard work but this place had started to come together and the people were so family organised that they didn't need for militia or police. Joshua sat with Brae watching the tribal folk busy themselves in the gardens. They drank strong coffee and chatted for a while.

"You have done it Josh, look at what you have created."

"I have haven't I? He grinned. "I've put the base

stones down on the path to building utopia." Joshua said with a beaming self-righteous smile. Brae had noticed that Joshua had started to get an even bigger head than he normally had, in fact his very presence was very fucking annoying.

"I'm leaving soon Josh." Brae announced. Joshua nearly fell off his seat.

"You're what? Why?"

"Much as this is a nice place to live, but I need to get my daughter Mary an education." Brae stated.

"Mary isn't your daughter and she belongs with us at utopia!" Joshua hissed, suddenly turning angry. "I can educate her from the terminals of knowledge in the habitat. You have no reason to leave us!"

"Mary is my daughter maybe not by bloodline, but she deserves a good start in life and I don't think this is the place. If we stayed here she would become weak and I want her to become worldly wise, you never know what is around that corner!" Brae said trying not to get angry by Joshua's harsh words.

"It makes no sense at all, you belong here! This is a new start in your life. I see no threat coming nor bad things happening in the future of utopia."

"I hope so too Josh and I hope your utopia lives on. But this place is not for me, I'm a ranger at heart and a hired gun. This is your utopia not mine!" Brae said with a curled lip of distaste.

"I forbid you to leave, you are my friend and companion, you have every right to live out your life in peace. Why sacrifice all this to go back to the shit that we once lived." Joshua was beside himself with rage and confusion.

"Its already done Josh, Mary is packed and we leave tomorrow!" Brae said as he stood up and started toward the habitat. Joshua kicked his chair away and started to thrash his fists around in a fit.

"As lord of utopia I forbid it! I forbid you abandoning us!"

"And Josh you still owe me coin for getting you and your wife here alive. I will collect from you tomorrow morning." Brae said as he wandered away.

"I forbid it!" Joshua screamed!

The next morning Brae and Mary packed up. He had collected his money owed from Joshua who had calmed down by then. With all the coin he carried now he calculated that he could purchase a bar in Red town. It would be what Yolanda wished and he thought it best to carry out her wishes even though she was in heaven. Joshua and Natasha came to see them off.

"I'm sorry about my outburst yesterday's my friend. I just wished for you to stay but having thought about it you are correct. Maybe this place is not fit for a gun fighter living on the edge day by day. I hope in a number of years you head back up here. You will be always welcome." Joshua said with a warm heart.

"I might just do that Joshua my friend. I will miss you both, take care of Natasha and thank you for being my friend." Brae said fighting back the urge to shed a tear. They all hugged and Natasha fixed Mary's hair with a desert blossom.

"You have enough food?" Natasha asked. Brae nodded and patted his back pack. He had raided the armoury that morning and outfitted Mary with a nice side arm with plenty of ammo. He grabbed his daughter hand and headed out toward the desert. South as a bearing on his compass. He knew it would be a long journey back to Red town but nothing was going to stop him now.

Days turned into weeks as the two travelled across the land, they traded for food at various stops on the way. They encountered a few undesirables and gave them a nice dirt nap. They avoided some of the places where Brae thought would be life threatening and so far it was good. During the travel he taught Mary in the ways of camping, foraging and set up targets for her to practice on. It seemed Mary took to the gun quite fast, obviously her brothers had trained her to shoot rabbits and small game. Mary was fast becoming a good shot almost like a younger Jessica. Brae missed Jess and often wondered how she was doing and if she still breathed the air in the land. He hoped she was still alive and now and then when the sun went down he stared for long into the camp fire and recalled good memories of his friend. In the second month they had camped down near a wooded area. Mary had gathered up quite a pile of wood for the fire and they cooked a brace of rabbits that she had bagged that day.

"I did the right thing by taking you from utopia?"

He asked Mary who was busy building the camp fire.

"Yes papa, I long to see Red town, you have told me so much about it." She looked up with a loving smile to her papa.

"Good. I fear we would become complacent and weak if we stayed at utopia. I need you to understand that the world is not a nice place to live and we must be always on guard. Even if your papa dies you know how to live and you are a keen learner my beautiful daughter." He whispered over the camp fire.

"Thank you papa, you have taught me well." She stated to hum a song which he recognised and filled in the words that he could remember. She stopped humming the song and cocked her head and stared across the fire into his eyes.

"You mention Jessica a lot and sometimes you whisper her name when you are sleeping. Is Jessica your wife?" She asked with innocent eyes.

"Nooooo! God no!" He laughed. Jessica is a..." He couldn't pick the words to describe her sexuality. "Jess, likes women, she doesn't like men, if that makes any sense?" He watched as she pondered his words and suddenly her eyes went wide.

"Ew Gross!" She spat and laughed. He kept on forgetting her horrible incestuous upbringing and felt sick with the fact she was familiar with sex.

"It's not gross Mary, it's my friends choice, she didn't choose to be a lesbian it's just how she is made up." He tried to explain and tutor her and realised he was fucking it all up. He laughed and Mary laughed with him, almost reading his thoughts.

"Anyway she is a good friend and let's keep it that way." He said. Mary fell quite for a while and nipped off a piece of flesh from the rabbits cooking.

"Rabbits are nearly done papa." She said mouthing a hot piece of juicy rabbit meat.

"Good I'm hungry like a wolf!" He watched her take down a spit deftly carving off the rabbit meat with her hunting knife and offering the meat to her papa.

"Did you fuck Jessica?" She said out of the blue. Brae coughed out a chunk of meat in surprise and gave her a frowning look.

"Mary wash your mouth out, please don't use that kind of language when you are around you papa!" He scolded. Mary sat back and put her head down in shame. He started to chuckle and remembered the number of nights he managed to seduce Jessica into his bed.

"We were young and we were running with the rangers. She was so beautiful and full of life. We did make love..." He paused remembering the night like it was the night before. "It was the best night of my life and I thought we would be lovers from then on." He sucked in a breath and shook his head. "But like I said she prefers women, so it wasn't to be." Brae sulked for a while remembering his heart breaking when Jessica told him that it was but a bit of fun to ride out a mission. Mary saw his face across the camp fire and frowned.

"Don't worry papa, when we reach Red town I will

find you a good wife." She said with innocent tones again. He laughed and reached across and patted her shoulder.

"Mary you are indeed a star, a bright one at that. But we get you an education first and I will set up a nice business for us to live a nice life." He cocked his head and smiled with a proud grin for his daughter.

Another week went by and they had a couple of scrapes with some nasty traders who attempted to rob them. They all had dirt naps and this time Mary bagged the most kills, using her berretta pistol. Brae got winged by a bullet in his thigh, the wound was inches away from his main artery and he was damned lucky to survive. Mary did a good job stitching and bandaging him up. She was truly becoming a warrior like her papa. One of the dead traders had a semi-automatic shot gun, a compact weapon which Brae assumed was used by pre-war police forces. Mary threw away her old double barrelled shot gun and took up the better firearm. She was learning at a phenomenal rate and he felt utterly proud of her. He made sure every time they left camp he would mark their position and bearing back to Red town. Just in case he perished.

"Remember if you loose your compass you can navigate by the north-star at night and by day find a tree and moss and lichens always grow on the north side." He said one night when they camped up.

"The north-star is that one, remember it's the brightest star in the night sky." He pointed it out and

Mary looked to the star laden heavens in awe.

"Papa, do you believe in the bright god?" Mary asked. The question caught him off guard.

"I believe in something, but maybe not the literature of man. Why do you ask?" He knew she still carried the moth eaten book of the bright. He frowned and looked to her back pack.

"Give me that book!" He said with under tones of hate. Mary did as she was told and rummaged through the back pack until she found the old book. She wavered for a few moments not really wanting to relinquish the holy book. Brae snatched it from her hand and threw it on the fire. Mary screamed and scrambled towards the book which caught fire faster than kindling. He grabbed her hand to stop her grabbing the burning book.

"Let it burn..." He waited until the book razed on the camp fire. "That book is full of lies. Lies made up by fanatical humans that wish to sedate and lord over human kind. Let the lies burn my child!" He let go of her hand and watched her staring at the blazing book.

"But..." Mary looked confused.

"But, nothing Mary! That book will fill your mind up with falsehood. It has been written by a deranged mind. I know this for sure. I never relied on the words of man. Life is real. That book of lies is not!" He said calmly.

"But, what of Joshua and Natasha? They believe in the bright the sun that shines." Mary claimed.

"They are weak of mind my child, this was one of the

other reasons why I had to take you away from utopia. I will not have my daughters mind filled with bullshit!" Brae said with vehemence.

"Okay papa, I think I understand. But I did gain solace from reading the good book when things went bad on the farm." She remembered the warmth of the words when she was hiding out away from her drunken brothers who had rape on their minds.

"That maybe so Mary, but best you forget about those lies you read in the book and the time you spent on the farm with your nasty family. This is a new chapter in your life. I will do my damnedest to make it good for your future!" He wished.

"We still should have kept the book to trade I'm sure there are folks out there who would find sanctuary in the words of the bright." She said with charity in her mind. He laughed and shook his head. He was overwhelmed by the wisdom in her words and of such a young age. He assumed Mary was the child of her older sister from incestuous inbreeding. But clearly bright and had a spark of intelligence. As every day passed he loved Mary as his own daughter more and more.

More weeks passed by as the father and daughter made there way back to Red town. They traded at outposts and passed through seedy town ships. They had got back down to the south heart lands and met up with a few rangers who told them about the victory against the soviet enemy. Brae asked about Jessica but the rangers could not say if she was alive or dead, but it was clear that Jessica had something to do with the victory. He hoped she was still alive but the stories and tales told of a nuclear strike. He assumed Jessica had perished in the nuclear blast. He wasn't a religious man but he did say a stupid prayer to his own idea of god. The ash land in the heartlands had started to become more policed by a staggered ranger presence. At one township they went to a stand which was enlisting new rangers.

"You sir, would you take up the rifle in a good cause, to protect mankind?" The skinny looking woman hawked at them and gave him a freshly printed flyer depicting a map location to join up with the rangers.

"I've already been a ranger." Brae mumbled as he read the flyer.

"Then sir we need veterans like yourself. Enlist in the rangers and never look back." The woman stated with religious fanatic like wide eyes. Brae noticed the empty bottles of whiskey near her stand and assumed the worst. It seemed the rangers were paying good coin to advertise.

"I'm sorry the life of a ranger is not for me, I'm a parent now so I have to think about my child." He said before wandering away. They took up lodgings above a saloon where whiskey was on tap and whores ready to fuck, both male and female. The township was kind of new and must have been set up in the recent months. Trade was strong here like a hub and he witnessed many well established merchants in the dust strewn streets. He remembered this place was just a mere camp site the last time he ventured these parts. He couldn't remember the name of the camp but the town that had built around the camp was now called Oak town due to the proximity of the woodland nearby where the populous were felling trees and manufacturing wooden planks to sell. Brae realised civilization was getting a hold back on the land. It seems the humans had been busy little bees in such a short time.

"What are soviets?" Mary asked as they left Oak town.

"A pre-war menace which has been crushed it seems?" He wasn't very sure. "You know as much as me from the tales we have gathered."

They travelled on not looking back to the place where Joshua called utopia. Now that Brae had got so far away from utopia, he felt the silver string in his mind eye snap. *Good riddance to utopia,* he thought. He hoped it would be strong but otherwise he had no allegiance to the promised lands. They travelled on south and came to the foot of a trade post. Brae elbowed Mary and gave her a look to be on guard. It was a gesture that she had become attuned to. Always be on guard. Her papa had taught her well. She unholstered her pistol and slipped it under the folds of her skirt, ready for action. The trade post ahead was a typical store house and tap room. The wooden building had seen better days but Brae assumed if the trade post has been operating for so long then it must be safe.

They entered into the tap room where a stout potbellied man awoke from sleeping. He instantly took up his shotgun and appraised the customers.

"You here to trade?" The man said with a southern drawl.

"Damned right we here to trade." Brae mimicked the southern drawl.

"Haven't seen many folks around these parts for a while. What you needing partner?" The man asked.

"The usual, we need meat jerky and any ammo you can spare."

"Well I only have wolf meat if that's okay and as for ammo I am pretty well low stocked, I do have some five fifty six and some nine millimeter, in stock, if you wish to buy?"

"Jerky, nine mil and some of that fine five fifty ammo." Brae claimed. He watched as Mary sized up the man and wondered if she would pull her pistol. He hoped she wouldn't. The man rummaged around for a while and put bullets and wrapped meat on the bar.

"Its gonna cost ya though, it's my last ammo so reach into your pockets for coin." The man said as he put his hairy, sweating arm around the items on the bar.

"You trying to rip us off my friend, how much we talking?" Brae said with a frown.

"Well let's see, two coins for the jerky and ten for the ammo." The man grinned knowing he had stumped up the price.

"Well that's not a good deal at all, the ammo is only worth four coins at best!" Brae said angrily, he hated these situations and knew the merchant had the upper hand.

"Well that's the price fella!" The sweaty man stated. Before Brae had time to use his barter skills, Mary pulled her pistol and shot the man in the head. The man slumped behind the bar and rattled out his dying breath.

"By the bright what the fuck!" Brae screamed. Mary backed off with a worried face, but pointed to the door near the bar. She had her pistol primed and ready. Brae looked to the door hat his daughter was pointing at as a number of men came into the bar area firing shotguns. Brae combat rolled and pulled out his pistol as Mary unloaded on the targets. It had happened so fast and Mary stood with a worried face as the assailants fell to the floor a bullet in each of them. By the time Brae got to his feet it was over.

"Sorry papa, but I heard the bad men in the next room." Her pistol hand was shaking, but she was still focused and ready. Brae realised that his daughter had saved there lives. He rushed to hug her and hugged her close while she still aimed her pistol at the bar door.

"Shit! I didn't see that coming. You did well my daughter," He said as the adrenalin rushed through his veins. He hugged her so tight that he felt her rib cage contorting.

"Let go papa." She whispered. Brae let go and allowed her to breath again.

"We need to field strip this place and be quick about it!" He hissed. As he looked to the exit. They spent a few minutes gathering up provisions and ammo. Brae knew this was bad but if it wasn't for Mary he would have been taking a dirt nap. Having got what they needed including grabbing up coin, they rushed from the trade post and headed south.

They camped up miles to the south and made a camp fire. Brae had so much respect and love for his daughter that it hurt. The sun had gone down and the night was coming fast.

"I didn't hear anything? How did you know the trade post guy was gona rob us?" He asked. Mary looked up from the camp fire and shrugged.

"When you have spent your days hiding out in the woods or in the out buildings you get an acute ear for men hunting you down."

"That is definitely a life skill that I could never teach you." Brae nodded. He looked at Mary and shuddered at the thought of her hiding out, terrified and alone.

"I'm glad I've found you Mary, no harm will ever come to you while I draw breath." He stated.

They kicked earth over the low burning camp fire and set off at dawn. Brae knew they were near to Red town. He calculated that it was but another two weeks march. He could feel the pull of Red town and already started to organise the tutoring of Mary. He had the coin and enough to purchase a business. Like he had said before it would have been Yolanda's wish. He worried about dying and leaving Mary alone, it came so close in the last trade house. *So fucking close* he thought. They climbed the last bluff which overlooked Red town.

"That's Red town!" He said with an excited tone. "That is where you will be tutored. That is where we will start our new life!" Mary hugged him around his waist.

"I hope so papa, I do hope so!" She said hugging him tight.

"Come now daughter let me show you what I already know." Brae said as he pushed Mary forward. They descended the bluff and got to the gate house. Stern looking wooden gates barred the way into town. One of the guards noticed Brae.

"Well I'd be damned is that Brae you son-of-a-bitch?" Clarence the guard lowered his Winchester rifle and waved.

"Open the gates, my friend Brae is here!" Clarence yelled. The gates opened and Brae and Mary walked in hand in hand.

"When your shift is over Clarence my mate, lets down some brews, I'm paying!" Brae hollered to the guard on duty.

"See you there gun-slinger!" As Brae walked up the main street of Red town he noticed that the place had changed for the better. Sewerage still washed down the narrow gully in the middle of the street but business seemed to be thriving. New shops and market stalls had been established. Brae and Mary headed off to the lodging house where he would start his new business...

CHAPTER 25

Jessica had made enough coin to purchase any establishment in Red Town. She made a bee-line to Roody's whore house she once frequented and wandered in. Roody looked up from the bottle of whiskey he cradled in his arms.

"Well I'd be damned, is that Jessica I can see?"

"It be!" Jessica pulled up a stool near the bar. The owner was already pouring a good double shot of whiskey.

"Long time no see Jessica." He paused in his drunken stupor and shook his head to get a moment of clarity. "I hear you are some kind of ranger hero?" He said through a potent whiskey infused breath.

"Maybe? But ones thing for certain I'm fucking rich now! So how can I purchase this whore house?"

"Well it depends on how rich you are lass?" Roody said staggering towards her and pulling up a stool behind the bar. She waited while the pissed up owner managed to get on the stool. He smiled drunkenly and then frowned when it dawned on him what she said could be straight up.

"You're not kidding?" His face was a combination of relaxed facial muscles and confusion.

"Naa, I ain't kidding, I really want to buy this place up." Jessica banged the bar with her fist to punctuate the truth.

"How much are we talking?" Suddenly very serious.

"Enough for you to crawl into a whiskey bottle for the rest of your life but looking at the way you hit the whiskey, I don't think you have very long." She said hurtfully.

"Fuck you Jessica." He got to his feet and bobbed back and forward. "I'm in my prime!" He grinned not even convincing himself.

"And I've also got a further deal! I keep you on as barman and pay you a basic bar wage." Jessica had been to the various stashes around town, friends that kept coin for her. She knew she had more than enough, but she was starting low.

"Six hundred!" Jessica blurted. Roody feigned a yawn.

"No chance, a thousand!"

"Six and a half hundred and I throw in the basement room free rent, unless you are sacked from the bar job." Jessica raised her eyebrow.

"Eight hundred!" He snarled, it was the figure he planned to close before it started.

"No way! If I give eight hundred then you don't get lodgings here, nor the bar job!" She hissed.

"Seven hundred I can't let it go for less." He pleaded as he slumped on the bar stool, a broken man. He had no intention of sleeping rough.

"Then it's a deal. I will get a law man over here tomorrow morning and we will draw up a contract."

Jessica grinned, pleased with herself. She knew she had shit loads more coin that she could have given him. But it was hard earned blood money and she would be fucked to part with it, especially to a hopeless alcoholic!

"Is my room free?" She asked. He squinted to the keys behind the bar and shook his head. "Sorry Jess, it's taken at the moment but it will be free tomorrow. I could discount the top room if you wish?"

"Discount you cheap bastard, I'm buying the fucking place tomorrow!" She raged. He had seen that look before and usually somebody got shot soon afterward. He put his hands up and tossed her the key.

"It's on the house Jess." He sighed and poured himself another whiskey while Jessica started to head upstairs. She stopped and stared at him for a few seconds and winked. He groaned and spat in the spittoon behind the bar.

"Look Minxy is free I will send her up in twenty minutes. Enjoy your night!" When she was out of ear shot he dared to whisper "Bitch!" But as soon as he said the word he nervously looked to the stair and hoped she wasn't coming back down to kill him.

The top room was one of the best rooms in the cat house. It actually had a built in bath tub, instead of the tin baths that the maids shifted from room to room. She sat on the edge of the bed and bounced up and down for a few seconds. The springs were shot and made a delicate ringing sound, but it seemed okay. She opened the door expecting the maid, who started up the fire and brought many jugs of water to warm to fill the bath tub. She was an older woman and she clearly had kids due to her body shape, she sort of recognised her.

"Haven't seen you in a while Jessica. Is it a flying visit as usual?"

"Well no, not this time, in fact tomorrow I will be your new boss." Jessica said sternly. The maid suddenly stood up and put her big fire-building, jug carrying hands on her hips. She was smirking.

"Well that's the damnedest thing I heard. Jessica the gunslinger settling down finally" The maid started to howl with laughter a proper gut wrenching laugh that made her double up. Jessica took a deep breath and lowered her anger levels. When the maid sobered up from her laughter she stood there in silence.

"I'm sorry I don't remember your name?"

"My... My name is Gretchen." She bumbled her words when she finally realised Jessica was being serious.

"Well Gretchen, I like your honesty." Jessica grinned. "How about the name Madam Gretchen, does that grab your attention?"

"It's a good as name as any other, but I'm not sure what you mean?"

"The way I see it, I need a strong woman like you to look after the running of this place, taking care of the whor..." Jessica shook her head. "Sorry Girls. I know being a woman you will take care of the girls that work here."

"You want me to be the madam?" Gretchen was stunned and didn't really know what to do next.

"I'm done with killing Gretchen, I'm retried and I'm going to turn this cat house from the shit hole that it is now, into a respectable gambling, stroke cat house." Jessica grinned again and waited for the words to settle with the new manager. Gretchen fell to her knees as though she would pray, she still looked dumbfounded.

"Oh thank you so very much Jessica." The older woman was shaking with excitement. Clearly nothing good had ever happened in her life of servitude.

"Stand up!" Jessica pulled out her time piece and a small bag of coins. She tossed the coins to Gretchen who snatched the pouch from the air.

"Goto the outfitters now and purchase a nice dress. You will need to look the part. When Gretchen unravelled the coin purse tied with twine she nearly fainted at the amount of coins inside.

"This is more money than I make in a half a year!" Gretchen's bottom lip started to tremor and Jessica could see tears forming in her eyes.

"Yes... Lady Jessica." Gretchen mumbled and picked herself up off the floor and headed off to the outfitters. It wasn't long before Minxy arrived at the room. The whore was in her mid-twenties and had bags under her eyes from lack of sleep. She had dirty blonde hair and was scantily clad in red and black underwear that had seen better days.

"Minxy, I presume?" Jessica pointed to the bed. "Get some sleep lass and I will wake you when the bath is ready." The tired looking woman nodded and climbed into bed, it wasn't long before the poor lass started to snore.

Later on that day, Gretchen returned to Jessica's room wearing a fine dark blue dress with a high collar. The outfitter had obviously spent some time widening the dress to fit the buxom middle aged woman.

"It's a little bit tight around the waist but it feels lovely on." Gretchen said as she brushed the fine cloth with her hand.

"You definitely look the part my friend." Jessica winked which made Gretchen blush. "Tomorrow you will begin a new life as the manager of 'Jessica's place'. I will have a new sign up within the week." Jessica paused and allowed the older woman to do a twirl in her new attire. Gretchen noticed Minxy was fast asleep in Jessica's bed and she also noticed that the jugs of water were bubbling away near the fire. Instinct made the ex-maid start toward the bubbling pots to fill a bath for Jessica.

"Stop! That is no longer your job. Your job is now the Madam of Jessica's Place, you organise the girls for the punters and make sure the punters are well looked after." Jessica had her twin 1911 pistol belt over her long johns.

"I need you to look after something. It was a gift which I no longer need. But keep it safe for me, just in case the future turns sour." Jessica said as she handed Gretchen a heavy Nichol plated pistol. "Hide it away from me until the day I need it again. Hopefully that day will never come."

"It's very heavy!" Gretchen chuckled as she felt the weight of the Nichol plated desert eagle.

"I will see you in the morning Madam Gretchen, goodnight!" Jessica finally said and pointed a thin finger to the door. When the older woman left the room, Jessica set about filling the bath tub with hot water for two. She refrained from waking up Minxy until the soapy bubbles covered the surface of the hot bath.

Morning came and Minxy kissed Jessica on her lips before exiting her chambers. Jessica pulled her clothing on and her pistol belt before venturing down to the tap room. Mr Gullwing waited in the tap room holding a portable ledger, ink and pen. Roody looked worse for wear but had made the effort to shave his stubble off.

"I will begin to draw up the contract of sale of said Roody's whore house into your legal hands." He bowed to Jessica as she sat at the small table. They waited as the law man filled in the hand written document which would finalise the deal of property exchange. When it came to Roody to sign his hand wavered over the dotted line but seeing the coin purses on the table he signed the document.

"Then it is all settled. Jessica you are now the owner of said property and every person under contract working in this establishment." Jessica signed the document and then waited patiently for Mr Gullwing to counter sign.

"All done!" The law man stated as he gathered up the documents and writs. "I will file these at the house of law." He stood and shook both party's hand.

"May you have good fortune Lady Jessica." He said and bowed before leaving. Roody greedily pulled the coin purses to his chest and then headed off to the depository to safe guard his money. Jessica felt a weight off her shoulder dissipate. She now had a business which would keep her flush and had no need to venture out into the ash land to collect bounties or assassinate some fucker that she had never met. Things seemed to be looking up for Jessica the ex-gunfighter, but she had so many plans to turn the establishment around. Part of the whore house had a dusty old back room which used to be a good old gambling den. She unlocked the old wing of the large building and wandered into the dusty old room. A rotten old bar, which still had empty bottles of whiskey upon it. Dusty old termite bitten tables and chairs laid in abandon. She grinned as she pictured in her mind eye a bustling gambling establishment which high rollers frequented and when they got bored they had the cat house to fall back on and fulfil their dreams.

A week went by and the new sign stated 'Jessica's Place'. They had started to renovate the old gambling den and made it look cleaner and more hospitable. Jessica hired a new maid and more bar staff to run the side room. It was slow at first but after a number of days 'Jessica's place' was filled to the rafters. Even after the coins she poured into the renovation of the establishment she still gleaned a profit. Jessica ran the gambling den and left Madam Gretchen to run the cat house. Jessica's notoriety as a mean gunslinger kept the peace. In fact she hadn't had the need to skin her pistols when things got a little bit out of hand. Instead she just beat the crap out of the folks that caused trouble. Several weeks went by and 'Jessica's place' was now the place to wind down and seek pleasure or gamble. Madam Gretchen was doing a fine job, even bringing in punters off the dusty streets to frequent the new establishment. By now Gretchen had three fine dresses which she rotated to keep them clean. It got to a point where Jessica hired a small staff of security so she could concentrate on reaping coin from the gamblers that wandered into her spider web. Even though the whores were run ragged, Jessica and Gretchen made sure they were getting their fair share of coin and more for the services that they provided. The girls who worked at the establishment were actually making more coin than they ever dreamed of. Two months in and Jessica hired a house physician to take care of rashes, dribbles and the likes. Dr Jenkins used to be more an animal doctor who serviced the livestock of animals in Red town. But he honed his skills and profits, taking care of the well paid women that worked at 'Jessica's place'. Red town was becoming an increasing hub of commerce which brought more folks wanting to spend hard earned cash at Red town. Be it gambling, trade or just getting their rocks off. With the threat of the soviets out of the way it seemed civilization was on the up, which spread all over the heartlands.

"House takes with a full house, kings and jacks." Jessica spread her cards on the table, much to the disgust of the ranger that had come to spend his coin. She recognised the ranger as one of Ash's men. But she couldn't recall his name, especially after all the whiskey she had drank. She eyed him for a while and properly racked her brain trying to remember his name. After a while she gave up.

"I recognise you? Aren't you one of the rangers that were at the new ranger base?" Jessica asked out of curiosity.

"Yes I'm Ranger Billings, I was one of the rangers that got dropped from the mission to deliver the bomb to the soviets." The ranger eyed Jessica but it was more out of awe for such a hero to the ranger cause.

"Ash, needs you back, as an experienced drill sergeant at the base. We have been getting an influx of new recruits and he hoped you will help out for the ranger cause... Again." Ranger Billings said with a hopeful smile.

"Tell, Ash he still owes me two hundred coin!" She frowned and dealt out a new game placing down three river cards face down.

"He knows that and said if you come with me, he will triple what he owes and set up a standard pay for you?" The ranger even though bitter that he wasn't chosen he still had great respect for ranger Jessica.

"Tell him to give me what he owes and I might think about it!" She lied. The gruff looking ranger laughed and put a coin purse on the river cards. "There is the two hundred Ash owes you. If you lose at the game then you come with me!" The cocky ranger claimed. Jessica looked at her cards, she had a double jack in her hand and could have more jacks or a full house in the river cards. She signed and she was a woman of her words but didn't wish to get mixed up with the rangers no more. She folded her cards and snatched up the coin bag.

"Ash owes me and I'm not willing to gamble on my future."

"That's a shame! We need a veteran and hero like you to fill our ranks." The ranger stood up and saluted to Jessica and wandered out of the bar.

"Keep what Ash owes. But remember the Ash land needs you!" The other patrons watched as the ranger left the bar and then all eyes fell back on Jessica, some of them in awe but some of them shook their head in disgust.

"Enough of this shit, who wants to challenge the mighty Jess at a game of Texas hold'em?" She barked, but clearly she looked angry and nobody wanted to challenge her, not even at cards.

The Mayor of Red town came to the establishment. Mayor Downey came to Jessica's gambling table.

"You up for twenty one dead mayor?" She knew it was his favourite gambling game. The mayor shrugged and went through the motions of placing down a coin on his two blind cards. The mayor was an old gunslinger like Jessica, but long in the tooth by now. His grey hair was scraped back over his balding head and his dark blue eyes were searching around like a wolf seeking prey.

"You know the rangers have set up an enlisting post?" He claimed.

"No I didn't?" Jessica replied, having heard this new news.

"Well, my fucking daughter Adelaide wishes to sign up, because of you! You being the hero of the Ashland. I wish she would reconsider. I've kept her house bound but I know she will sneak out and join up. Maybe, if you tell her of the dangers that come with being a ranger." The mayor pleaded, pushing a hefty amount of coin across the table. Jessica peered at the coin purse and her shoulders sagged.

"Send your daughter over tomorrow. I will teach her how to use firearms and do my best to keep her here. In return do not ask for taxes from my establishment." Jessica knew if the rangers had set up an enlisting post they would be pressing the town ship for tribute.

"Thank you Jessica and yes your establishment will go tax free for six months. After that we will review the tax. You and I know the rangers will push for tribute, but we have our own paid militia here." Downey claimed.

"Six months and then we review. And in six months I will help pay the ranger tribute as a business woman of Red town!" Jessica said bitterly.

"Thanks Jessica I knew you would understand." With that the Mayor left 'Jessica's place'.

Jessica did as she was asked to do, she took the mayors daughter under her wing and taught her how to use various firearms. Her daddy paid for the ammo expenditure. Adelaide seemed to be a good student. Many weeks passed quickly as the profit from Jessica's business racked up. She cursed the day for not doing this sooner, it wasn't as fun but the coin raked in. She hired Adelaide as one of the security staff which kept her busy due to the amount of merchants frequenting red town. After a while the young lass decided to stay due to the ever abundance coin that made up her wages. It was on a very strange day when business was low in town that a man with a young daughter entered town. Jessica got word from a runner that it could be a friend she once travelled with. She left a whore spread eagled and wet on her bed and quickly got dressed and went down to the bar area. She was just tucking her shirt into her pants when she looked up and spotted a weather beaten, sun-burnt man stood at the bar clutching his arm around a young blonde haired girl. It took her a while to recognise him...

"Brae!" She whispered at first until her mind recalled her friend face. "Brae!" She yelled as she rushed across the bar knocking over patrons getting up to purchase drinks. Playing cards and bottles of beer cascaded from tables causing a rumpus of smashed glass and many defunct hands of cards. Jessica wrapped her arms around the weather beaten man.

"Brae!" She whispered in his ear as she hugged him close. Brae being slightly taller than the woman hugging him didn't know what was going on until Jessica's green sparkling eyes met his. She could feel his body sag and shudder and his blue eyes started to fill with tears.

"Jessica! By all is which holy!" He cried, and hugged her close to his chest. He wouldn't let her go and continued to bear hug her. She didn't care, she gripped him tight and placed her cheek to his chin, feeling the warmth from his body.

"You are alive!" She pulled away so she could see his chiselled face and his bright eyes.

"Yes, Jess, I'm alive. I also have a daughter. Please meet Mary!" He pulled away from Jessica and pushed the young blonde haired girl towards Jessica's hug. Jessica hugged the little girl and then wondered about time lines and tried to think back if Brae had a daughter.

"Mary, is my daughter but not by blood line, I've adopted her. It's a long story" He said with an angelic smile.

It had taken many hours of chatting to catch up. Jessica was amazed at hearing about utopia and how Joshua and Natasha had set up an establishment very far to the north. Brae was over the moon about Jessica being the vanguard against the attack against the soviet enemy! The pre-war enemy, that had reaped out the Ashland. It was late and they were all whiskey ridden, the sun had gone down and Jessica's new establishment was full of punters, seeking all manner of things on offer.

"So you're the Hero of the Ashland!" Brae chuckled in a nice way.

"I was for a time but my lover died." Jessica claimed and filled in the gaps about Angel the ranger being killed by a powerful drainer, enlisted by the soviet menace.

"Well thank the heavens you are still alive!" Brae laughed remembering the many tales about the original nuclear strikes which crippled the world to its knees.

"It seems like you are doing well in Red town?" Brae asked as he noticed the abundance of coin being exchanged for pleasure, gambling and whiskey.

"Yes, it has taken many months but I think its finally working as a business!" Jessica grinned like a pussy cat, showing her white teeth.

"You still got the old house in the western quarter?"

"Yes, well I'm saying that. I hope it is still there!"

"Well my friend I need a security expert which might fill your need. I will pay you good coin for you to be head of security!" Jessica hoped.

"I've got to get my child an education first, but a weekly wage would aid me in such cause!" He said with a frown.

"How does, ten coins a week grab you to be head of security?" Jessica wondered?

"Sounds good! And with the coin I've accumulated maybe I can get Mary a good education?

"I will pay for your daughters education if you become my head of security?" Jessica claimed, knowing the numerous coins coming in she could quite easily pay that sum.

It was quickly established that Mary would have a good education, part funded by Brae and part funded be Jessica. Brae pushed for mathematics in the hope his daughter would seek a quiet life just building numbers. Jessica introduced Mary to the law man Mr Gullwing, who agreed to take Brae's daughter under the wing for a small price. Which Jessica and Brae coughed up the coin. After but just a week it seemed Mr Gullwing took to Mary as a prodigy. He buttoned down and made sure she accumulated the knowledge of law. Mary took to the books of law like a fish in water. After several months of research reading old moth eaten books and learning she took to the written law as fact! Brae took up security detail in Red town and organised security protecting business establishments making a good living, which paid for his daughters education. He made sure that his daughter stayed away from the temples and religious sites and in the back ground Jessica showed her the way of the gun.

Finally the Ashland was a safe place to live, even Brae nailed up his rifle in the tap room of 'Jessica's place'. In the hope he would never have to pull down that rifle ever again. The rangers moved into the township and enlisted many younglings. The township finally had a militia that they could trust and the roads were now guarded by patrolling rangers that all prompted for tribute. Many educated folks read moth eaten books and compared the protection of the rangers to old fashioned protection bullied by established gangsters. But the difference was the rangers kept danger from the door of a township instead of leaning on and bullying money from folks who were trying to make a living. Some rich merchants thought this was the same, but poor folks scratching a living on the Ashland thought it was a god send. Knowing if they were ever in trouble the rangers will come quickly to save the day!

The Ashland had begun to be safe place and it was the hero's that sacrificed their lives to make it so! All hail to the folks that laid down their lives to protect humanity. With the death of a hero comes a stronger populous. And each surviving member who witnesses the sun coming up, or tends the corn fields, each person in the Ashland remembers those who laid down their lives to make a better world! The list is many and the records are few.

R.I.P All hail to the hero's that died throughout time for human kind to live on! Let them all rest in peace, knowing that our way of life has been sculptured by their sacrifice....

Sickle Through The Sand

Printed in Poland
by Amazon Fulfillment
Poland Sp. z o.o., Wrocław